Praise for

THE KINDOM TRILOGY

"Interesting and ambitious." —*Locus*

"An intricate plot for revenge drives this far-future SF political thriller.... An exciting start from a fresh talent."
—*Kirkus* (starred review)

"Readers who love smart thrillers and explosive SF won't want to miss this book." —*Booklist* (starred review)

"A devilishly fun thrill ride.... *These Burning Stars* is plotted like a chess match, confident and surprising as Jacobs moves each piece thoughtfully across her board." —*BookPage* (starred review)

"There's no shortage of twists, betrayals, and unexpected alliances in this intricate story of revenge and survival.... This sets things up nicely for a grand finale in book three." —*Publishers Weekly*

BY BETHANY JACOBS

THE KINDOM TRILOGY

These Burning Stars
On Vicious Worlds
This Brutal Moon

THIS BRUTAL MOON

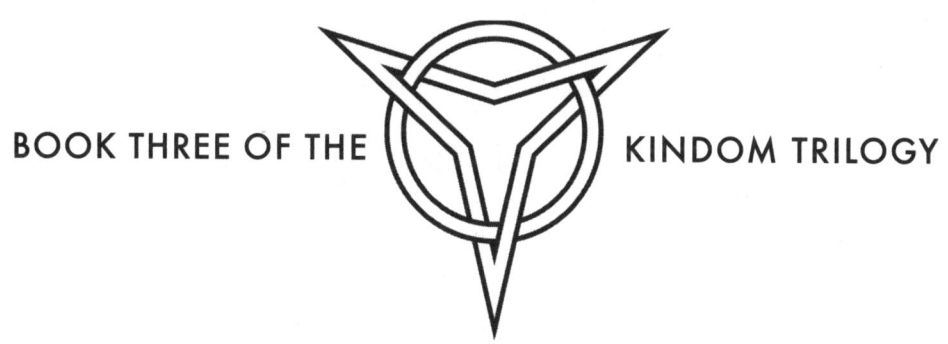

BOOK THREE OF THE KINDOM TRILOGY

BETHANY JACOBS

orbitbooks.net

Copyright © 2025 by Bethany Jacobs

Cover design by Alexia E. Pereira
Cover landscape by Thom Tenery
Cover image by Shutterstock
Cover copyright © 2025 by Hachette Book Group, Inc.
Charts by Tim Paul
Author photograph by Mary Ganster

Orbit
Hachette Book Group
1290 Avenue of the Americas
New York, NY 10104
orbitbooks.net

First Edition: December 2025
Simultaneously published in Great Britain by Orbit

Orbit is an imprint of Hachette Book Group.
The Orbit name and logo are registered trademarks of Little, Brown Book Group Limited.

The publisher is not responsible for websites (or their content) that are not owned by the publisher.

The Hachette Speakers Bureau provides a wide range of authors for speaking events. To find out more, go to hachettespeakersbureau.com or email HachetteSpeakers@hbgusa.com.

Orbit books may be purchased in bulk for business, educational, or promotional use. For information, please contact your local bookseller or the Hachette Book Group Special Markets Department at special.markets@hbgusa.com.

Library of Congress Cataloging-in-Publication Data
Names: Jacobs, Bethany (Novelist) author
Title: This brutal moon / Bethany Jacobs.
Description: First edition. | New York, NY : Orbit, 2025. | Series: The Kindom trilogy ; book 3
Identifiers: LCCN 2025016346 | ISBN 9780316463669 trade paperback | ISBN 9780316463737 ebook
Subjects: LCGFT: Space operas (Fiction) | Fantasy fiction | Fiction | Novels
Classification: LCC PS3610.A356417 T48 2025 | DDC 813/.6—dc23/eng/20250521
LC record available at https://lccn.loc.gov/2025016346

ISBNs: 9780316463669 (trade paperback), 9780316463737 (ebook)

Printed in the United States of America

LSC-C

Printing 1, 2025

For my parents, who believed I could do this

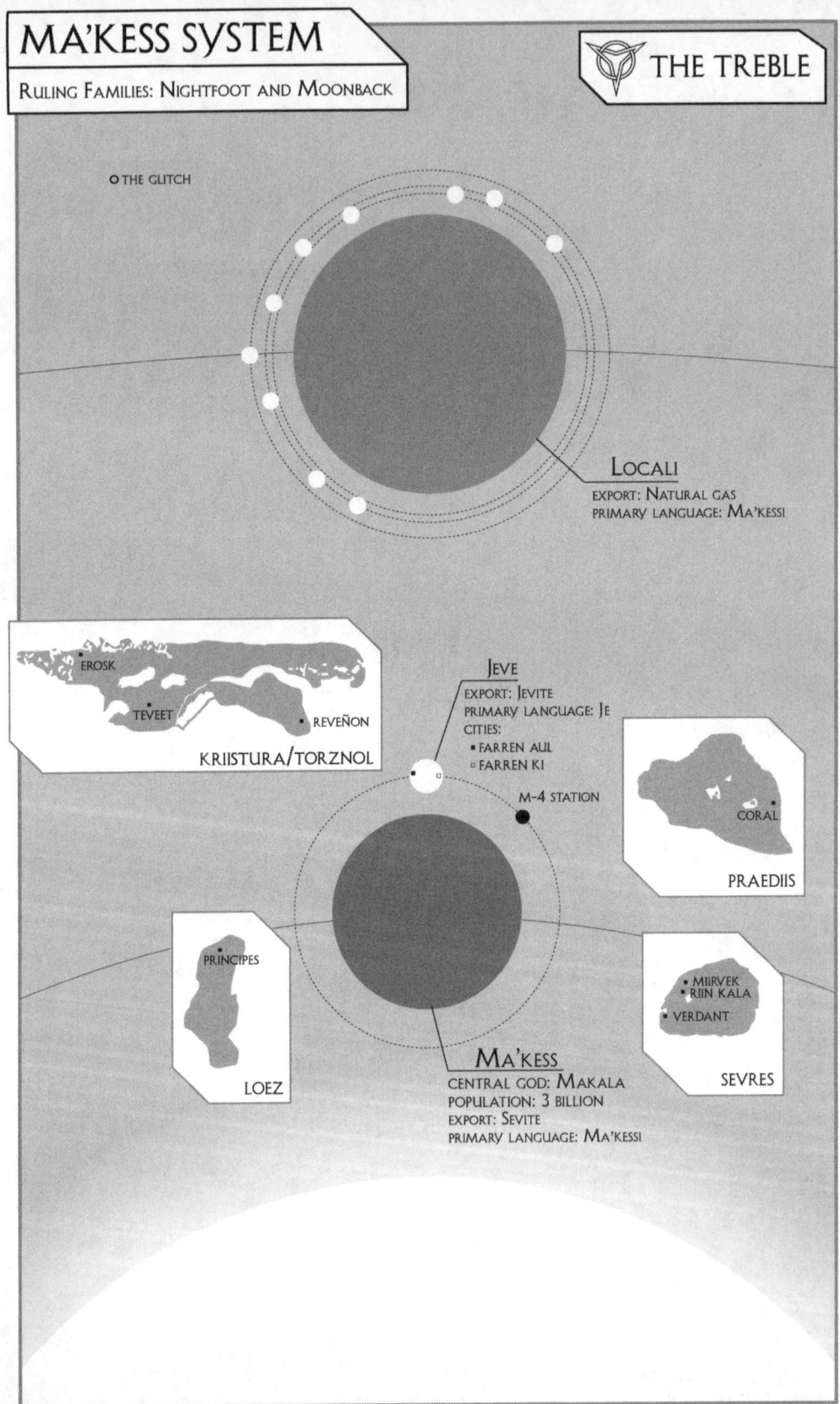

MA'KESS SYSTEM

RULING FAMILIES: NIGHTFOOT AND MOONBACK

THE TREBLE

○ THE GLITCH

LOCALI
EXPORT: NATURAL GAS
PRIMARY LANGUAGE: MA'KESSI

EROSK

TEVEET

REVEÑON

KRIISTURA/TORZNOL

JEVE
EXPORT: JEVITE
PRIMARY LANGUAGE: JE
CITIES:
• FARREN AUL
▫ FARREN KI

M-4 STATION

CORAL

PRAEDIIS

PRINCIPES

LOEZ

MIIRVEK
RIIN KALA
VERDANT

SEVRES

MA'KESS
CENTRAL GOD: MAKALA
POPULATION: 3 BILLION
EXPORT: SEVITE
PRIMARY LANGUAGE: MA'KESSI

CHART BY TIM PAUL

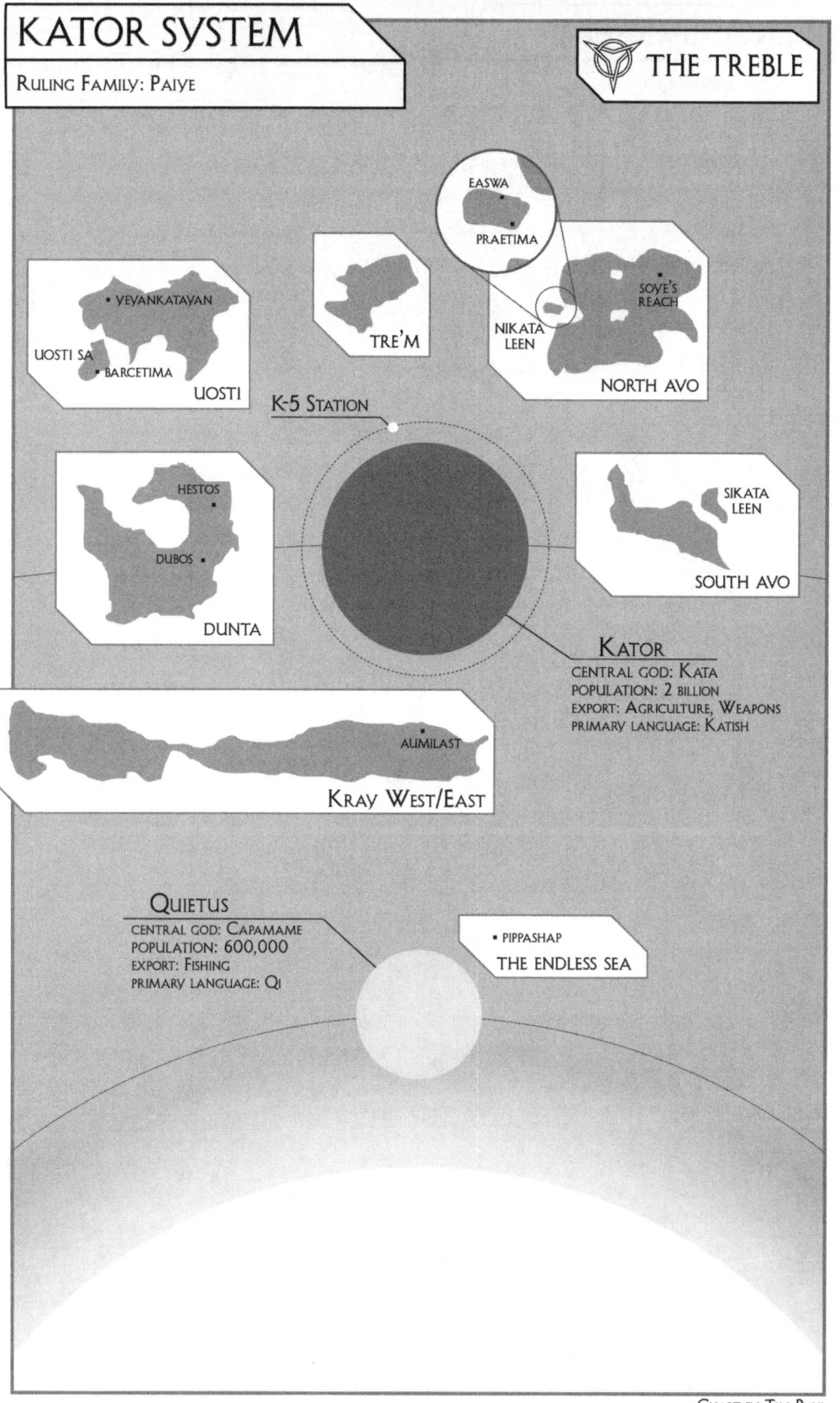

KATOR SYSTEM

RULING FAMILY: PAIYE

THE TREBLE

EASWA

PRAETIMA

SOYE'S REACH

NIKATA LEEN

NORTH AVO

YEYANKATAYAN

UOSTI SA

BARCETIMA

UOSTI

TRE'M

K-5 STATION

HESTOS

DUBOS

DUNTA

SIKATA LEEN

SOUTH AVO

KATOR
CENTRAL GOD: KATA
POPULATION: 2 BILLION
EXPORT: AGRICULTURE, WEAPONS
PRIMARY LANGUAGE: KATISH

AUMILAST

KRAY WEST/EAST

QUIETUS
CENTRAL GOD: CAPAMAME
POPULATION: 600,000
EXPORT: FISHING
PRIMARY LANGUAGE: QI

PIPPASHAP

THE ENDLESS SEA

CHART BY TIM PAUL

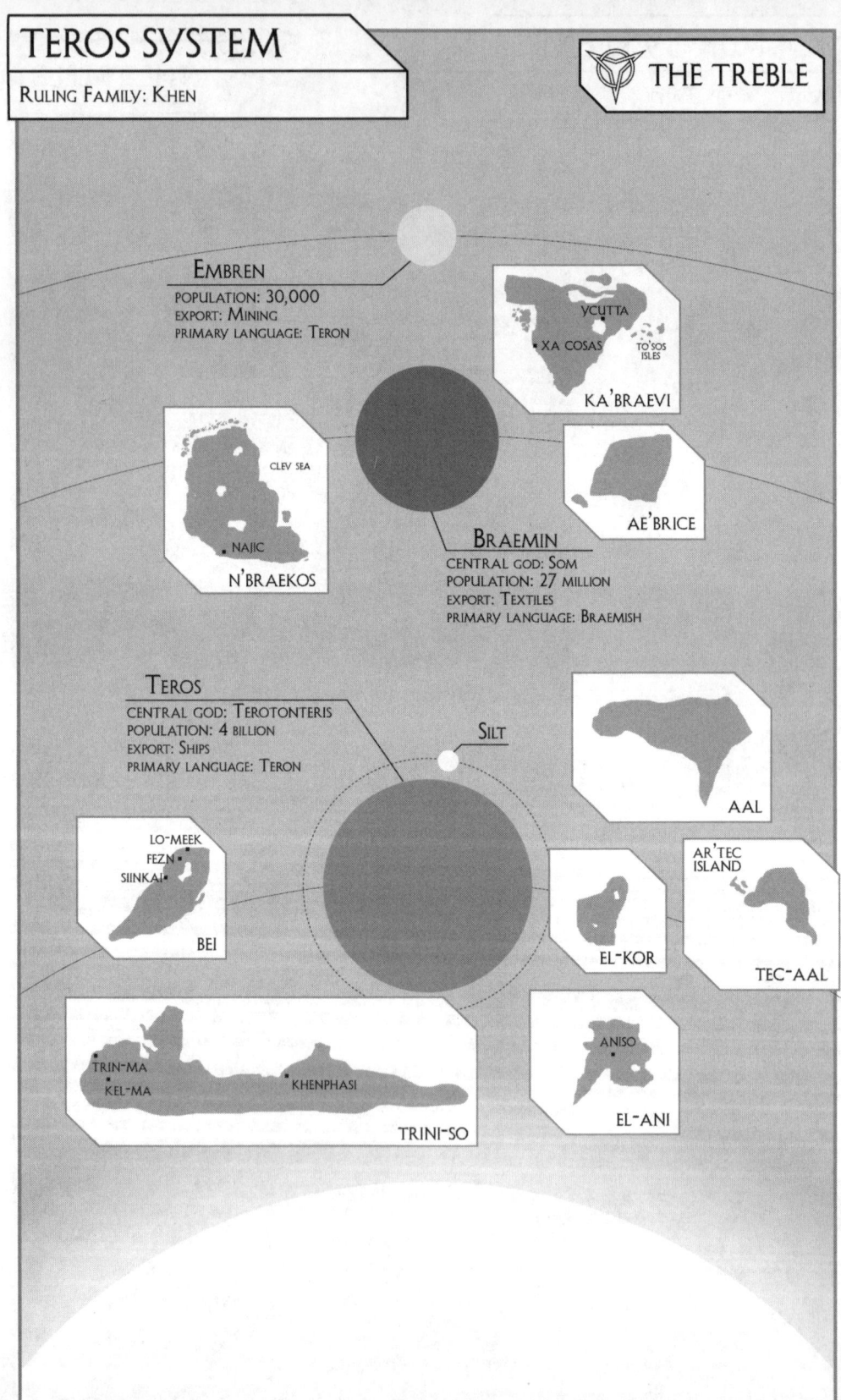

TEROS SYSTEM

RULING FAMILY: KHEN

THE TREBLE

EMBREN
POPULATION: 30,000
EXPORT: MINING
PRIMARY LANGUAGE: TERON

YCUTTA

• XA COSAS

TO'SOS
ISLES

KA'BRAEVI

CLEV SEA

• NAJIC

N'BRAEKOS

AE'BRICE

BRAEMIN
CENTRAL GOD: SOM
POPULATION: 27 MILLION
EXPORT: TEXTILES
PRIMARY LANGUAGE: BRAEMISH

TEROS
CENTRAL GOD: TEROTONTERIS
POPULATION: 4 BILLION
EXPORT: SHIPS
PRIMARY LANGUAGE: TERON

SILT

AAL

LO-MEEK
FEZN •
SIINKAI •

BEI

AR'TEC
ISLAND

EL-KOR

TEC-AAL

• TRIN-MA
• KEL-MA

• KHENPHASI

TRINI-SO

ANISO
•

EL-ANI

CHART BY TIM PAUL

CAST OF CHARACTERS

The Hands of the Kindom

Chono, a cleric
Seti Kess, once Seti Moonback, the First Cloak
Yorus Inye, a cloaksaan commandant

The Ironway Family

Jun Ironway, a caster
Liis Konye, a former cloaksaan, and Jun's lover
Bene Ironway, Jun's cousin
Ujan Redcore, once Luja Ironway, and Jun's cousin
Tej Redcore, once Tenje Ironway, and Jun's cousin

The Capamame Colonists

Masar Hawks, a collector
Effegen ten Crost, the Star of the Wheel
Fonu sen Fhaan, the River of the Wheel
Gaeda ben Kist, the Stone of the Wheel
Hyre ten Grie, the Gale of the Wheel
Tomesk ten Ruvo, the Tree of the Wheel
Pejun, a sentry
Dom ben Dane, a collector

The Nightfoot Family

Riiniana Nightfoot, Alisiana's great-granddaughter
Torek Nightfoot, Riiniana's guardian

The Paiye Family

Oyun Paiye, the Paiye Regal
Hejar Paiye, the Paiye heir, and Oyun's daughter

The Khen Family

Khen Ookhen Obair, the Khen family head
Khen Vorkhen Soon, the Khen heir, and Obair's son

The Moonback Family

Revel Moonback, the Moonback family head
Karix Moonback, adviser to Revel, and his niece
Giran Moonback, the Moonback heir, and Revel's son

The Quorum

Yantikye the Honor, a revolutionary
Graisa the Honor, a revolutionary, and Yantikye's daughter
Mix Catty, a pirate
Zemit, a leader of Trin-Ma rebels
Vikar Wren, a leader of pirates
Melosi the Grave, a leader of Quietan rebels
Imicanta Oninye, a leader of Katish rebels
Sikrt Goodrite, a leader of Ma'kessn rebels
Cly Siltmire, a leader of Ma'kessn rebels
Exani Ashway, leader of the Kriisturan rebel army
The Minkat, a representative of the Ar'tec Collective

The People of Jeve

Drae sen Briit, the River of the Wheel, killed in the Jeveni Genocide
Dimon sen Briit, a sentry, and Drae's cousin
Gus ben Roq, a jevite miner

and Six

CHAPTER ONE

1579

YEAR OF THE RISEN STAR

Farren Ki
The Moon Jeve

In the deep, hollow darkness of the mine, she cast a light upon the wall, and saw the ropes of jevite weaving through gray rock. The miners had come upon this cavern unexpectedly, an offshoot of a much narrower tunnel cut through the seam. The space echoed above her; it stretched the breadth of a temple. The scarlet-veined striations of jevite were as thick as her arm. She tested the weight of the rock pick in her hand, the grooves of the handle fitting comfortably against her calluses, and approached the nearest wall.

It took very little effort to chip a hunk of jevite free. The facets were as smooth as glass and the edges like sharp blades. She held it, feeling its density, its purity. She licked it, tasting the unique mineral bitterness with its slightly sour aftertaste. This fresh find had some buzzing with excitement, but she felt only dread weighing her down, as if she had stumbled into a monster's lair.

Someone came through the narrow passage into the cavern—Gus ben Roq, leading with his lantern. He set the lantern in the center of the cavern and turned up the settings. Fractals of light burst against the walls. He looked around pensively.

"Beautiful, no?" he said. He had a soft, unemotional voice, but there was reverence in it.

She hummed, noncommittal. "Several tons at least."

Gus said, "That is conservative."

She looked at the ground. She was treading upon more jevite. If they dug down, who knew how much they would find?

"We are two miles beneath the surface," she observed. "The deeper we go, the denser the rock, and the greater the chance of cave-ins. Every time we cut a new tunnel, we risk burying our people alive."

He, of anyone, knew this already. He had been the crew manager for more than ten years. He had seen his people die and nearly died himself, with scars and missing fingers to prove it. He gave her a steady look.

"This is our bargain, my River. Everyone takes the risk willingly."

Yes, of course. She looked at the floor again, felt the unevenness under her boots. They would dig deeper. They always dug deeper. This had been the failure of the Kindom overseers two centuries ago. The known jevite seams ran a depth of a thousand feet to a quarter mile beneath the surface of the moon. When they reached the limit of those depths, the Kindom made them dig deeper. Half a mile deep. Three-quarters of a mile deep. A full mile. But the rock proved barren. At the beginning of the thirteenth century, the jevite trade collapsed, and the overseers abandoned them to their carved-up moon and their decrepit biodomes and their mining pollution. But the Jeveni kept digging. At the two-mile mark, they cracked the stone carapace that divided them from a massive seam of jevite. And thus began this new, perilous chapter.

"Drae," Gus said, and the sound of her name, when he always called her "my River," made her uneasy. "I thought you would be pleased."

"Why should I not be pleased?" Drae sen Briit replied, gazing up at the walls as if they were star charts, as if they might show the path to escape. In a way, they did. They were the currency that funded a great enterprise. But they were also the blood that had drawn predators, again and again. She said, "This is the richest section we have found in years."

So rich, in fact, that it would move up her coming voyage to *The Glitch*, a frontier station far beyond Kindom reach. Laden with the wealth of this cavern, she would travel to *The Glitch* and pay for what they wanted. A high price for a needful reward.

Gus said nothing at first, and she almost thought the conversation was over. But—

"You are unhappy," he said.

She looked at him with a flare of impatience but pushed the emotion down, her smile tight. "I am not unhappy with you. I am proud of you, and the miners."

His expression was chiding. "But *you* are unhappy. Not with the miners. But with the seam."

Drae felt caught, and she didn't even realize how hard she was gripping the piece of jevite until she felt the sting and glanced down to find a little blood welling on her palm. She casually tossed the jevite aside and hid both her hands in her pockets, shrugging casually.

"Is there some requirement that I be happy?" she asked like it was a joke.

He wasn't impressed. "You have always been serious. But you have also always been calm. Lately, you seem less calm. People have noticed. They ask me what is wrong with you, and I tell them there is nothing wrong, but I can see it, too. And now you are looking at this seam as if it wants to murder you."

It does want to murder me, she thought. *It wants to murder all of us. It always has.*

Even thinking this was a kind of sacrilege among her people. The Jeveni revered jevite as a gift from the goddess, one that the outer worlds had stolen for centuries but was theirs by right. Drae had no such romantic perspective. The jevite had existed long before the Jeveni—it was an ancient, bloody fist in the middle of the Black. Circumstance had brought her people here, not to claim a birthright, but to feed the evil hunger of the moon.

Somewhere in the outer tunnels, miners began to sing. They did not sing loudly (volume carried vibration, and mines were no place to trouble the atmosphere), but still the song reached her, low and melancholy, describing the years of the jevite trade.

"Do you have doubts about what we are doing?" Gus asked.

That was a complicated question, but, "No," Drae said. "I have no doubts about *The Hope*. But I am your River, Gus. It is my job to protect our people, and I have much on my mind. There is no need to worry."

She hoped this would be the end of it, but it was not. Gus stared at her, and his stare began to itch, like mites tunneling under her skin, till her muscles and bones felt exposed by the intuition in his eyes. He did not believe her. He did not believe there was no reason to worry. At last, exasperated, she exhaled.

"I have been having dreams."

Gus's eyes narrowed, not with suspicion, but with the insight of a man who knew how to read meaning into the shifts of stone.

"Sajeven speaks to you?" he asked.

Drae made an annoyed sound. "Nightmares are just an expression of anxiety. We are within sight of achieving a goal our ancestors could only dream of. That is reason enough for me to have nightmares."

"What are your nightmares?" he asked.

She glowered at him. He was patient. He had always been patient.

"I see a person walking through the tunnels ahead of me. They wear a red coat. I follow them, but I am not me, I am...some other person. As they walk, they rake their nails across the walls of the tunnel. The rock opens up around them, and it gets wider and wider until the tunnel is a cavern. Bigger than this one, bigger than any cavern in any seam we have ever found. I try to catch up to them, but the jevite they have torn down becomes a river behind them, and I can barely walk against the current. Then, when I think I am finally getting closer, they look back at me for the first time..." She trailed off.

Gus said, "And?"

Drae cleared her throat, as if doing so could dismiss the significance, and said, "They have my face."

Gus considered this. Out in the tunnels the miners reached a new verse of their song. A prayer to Sajeven, beseeching her to bless them. Farther off, Drae heard the clanking sound of the elevator car descending from the surface, and she thought it must be a shift change.

"You should go to the Stone," Gus said. "Tell him your dream. He can consult with Sajeven on your behalf, and maybe there will be answers."

Drae grimaced. She had deep love and respect for the Stone of the Wheel—for all the spokes. But they were different from her. They were older, and their age and experience were like a summit she could never reach. They had known each other intimately for decades, and she was the outsider who had replaced the old River, a woman dead five years and descended by children and grandchildren. Drae had no children, though she was twenty-nine years old and most people had begun to fulfill their procreative responsibilities by now. If Drae went to the Stone, the Stone would tell her she needed more in her life than the mines and *The Hope*. She needed to begin her family, which would bring love into the empty places in her life.

Drae had doubts about that.

"It is only a dream," she said, though the dream had dogged her for months.

Gus looked unconvinced, as though he would argue with her, but suddenly a youth came sprinting inside, red-faced and heaving for breath.

"Moon arise, child, what is this?" Gus asked.

The youth looked at Drae, their eyes wide. "My River, you must come."

Drae felt ice in her stomach, a crystallizing burn. She saw the cavern in her mind opening like the mouth of a jump gate.

"What happened?" she asked.

"A ship!" they said. "On the east airfield!"

"A Kindom ship?" asked Gus.

"No. Civilian. But armored, and about ten saan have disembarked. The Wheel says you must come."

No strangers had come unannounced to Jeve in decades. Even the ones who brought trade did it with the permission of the Wheel. No one defied their treaty rights anymore, for what would even pirates want with Jeve when everyone knew it had nothing?

Already she and Gus were rushing from the cavern, following the youth back to the aged elevator shaft that would carry them through sheets of rock to the surface some two miles from the dome city of Farren Ki. So far underground, Drae's cast access was glitchy, but nonetheless she managed to access a view of the east airfield. The foreign ship was a midsize and pristinely built private vessel called *The Blue Kite*. Drae imagined some avian creature sinking its talons into the surface, and the talons were like the fingernails of the red-coated person in her dream, and she shoved the thought away.

By the time she reached the surface, the strangers were approaching the polymer tunnel that connected Farren Ki's eastern pod bay to the interior of the dome. A ground shuttle waited for her, and whisked her away toward the city. The shuttle was fast, but it was a distance of almost twenty miles. By the time she reached the bay, there was only the vacuum-sealed door between the strangers and Farren Ki. But the strangers were not alone on their side of the door. A dozen Jeveni sentries had gone out to meet them.

The Wheel was waiting for her.

"Thank Sajeven!" cried the Tree.

"Drae," said the Gale. "We did not know what—"

"Open the doors," Drae said.

"It is unsafe! You cannot—"

Drae ignored them, storming forward to hit the release, and as she went through the doors, she saw her people pointing rifles. There was a great cacophony in the tunnel. The sentries were shouting at the strangers in Je, warning them to stay where they were, and the strangers stood frozen. They were dressed in space suits as modern and expensive as their ship. They had cast back their helmets and their eyes were amazed, but they didn't seem to have weapons or to know what the sentries wanted. One of them, a dark-eyed, long-faced Katishsaan, stood at the front, holding up his hands and beseeching the Jeveni—

"Please! We're unarmed! We're no threat to you!"

He was speaking Ma'kessi. None of Drae's sentries spoke Ma'kessi, nor had translator bots. One sentry, Dimon, snarled at the group, "Get on your knees!"

The long-faced man switched dialects. "Do you understand me? I'm sorry. My translator is having trouble with your—"

Another stranger, standing just behind him, said in growling Katish, "They better put those guns down, or I'll give them a reason."

The others, apparently in agreement, twitched with the threat of violence.

Dimon warned, "Get down now!"

Drae strode through her sentries and stood between them and the strangers. Authority poured off her like heat, and everyone went silent and shocked as she demanded in flawless Katish, "Who the fuck are you?"

The long-faced man blinked rapidly, seemed not to know what to do, and blurted, "I am a friend! My name is Lucos Alanye, and I am a friend!"

Drae answered with silence, let it stretch out until he looked confused but also afraid. At last, she murmured aside to Dimon and the sentries, "Lower your weapons."

Dimon was incredulous. "They are uninvited!"

She gave him a look so quelling that he shifted back, and the rest of her sentries cautiously pointed their rifles at the ground. Drae turned to face the leader of the strangers again. He smiled for the first time, anxious and uncertain. He bowed over his open palms.

"Thank you for coming to speak to me. It's an honor to meet you, Sa...?"

He had a deep, gruff voice, but his register lifted, inviting her to introduce herself. Drae thought it was very bold of him to thank her for coming as if it were a predetermined meeting, rather than a consequence of his unwelcome appearance. Drae considered not giving him her name, but that would be shortsighted, and it was better that he know who he was dealing with.

"I am Drae sen Briit, the River of the Jeveni Wheel."

His eyes widened ridiculously. "Sa Briit," he said. "I prostrate myself before the generosity of the Wheel."

Drae lifted her brows at this, and replied, "Do you? All right, then."

She made an encouraging gesture.

He asked haltingly, "I'm...sorry?"

"Prostrate yourself. If you hold me in such esteem."

His confusion turned to uncertainty and alarm, as if he were trying to decide if it was a joke and also whether he could do it without losing the respect of his crew, who were glancing at one another and scowling.

Drae snorted. The Jeveni Wheel had no interplanetary authority. The Kindom regarded them as little more than the loose council of a savage race. Katishsaan of such obvious wealth would hardly get on their knees for her.

She didn't push the matter. "You have made my sentries very nervous, Lucos Alanye. By the law of our treaties, strangers are required to request an invitation to Jeve."

He looked chastened. "I apologize, Sa. I didn't know."

"The most cursory review of our treaties could have told you as much." Was that heat in his cheeks? Before he could fumble more apologies, she asked, "What are you doing here?"

This seemed to relieve him. He smiled again. "My colleagues and I are researchers. We come from a small, modest university in Dunta, on Kator. We're studying the long-term impacts of the jevite trade, particularly the phenomenon of sinkholes and crust collapse, and the vulnerability of the depleted seams. We want to understand how your dome cities have recovered from the effects of mining pollution, as we think it could yield insights for helping factory communities across the Treble. If we could find temporary shelter in Dewbreak, we can—"

"Farren Ki," Drae interrupted. He looked at her uncomprehendingly. "The Treble called this city Dewbreak when it began its mining operations here. We Jeveni have older, truer names for our cities, and this one is called Farren Ki."

Alanye nodded quickly. "Of course. May I ask what the name means?"

Drae said, "No."

He blinked. For a moment they did not speak, before he recovered enough to say, "Well, I'm determined to respect your customs, if you allow us to stay in—Farren Ki. And of course we will compensate you generously for your assistance. We've brought many gifts, as well."

He cast an image into the air. It displayed a rotating carousel of goods. Casting technology. Hydroponics equipment. Carbon dioxide scrubbers. Drae was indifferent, focused on his words. He had mentioned the depleted jevite seams; he'd said it with feigned casualness, apparently hoping the gifts would distract them. He was utterly transparent.

When she gave no reaction to the goods, he said cautiously, "If there are other things you want, we can certainly discuss it. We hope for a mutually beneficial relationship, if—"

One of her sentries interrupted in Je, "What are they saying, my River?"

She didn't answer right away, aware that if she told the truth, the tunnel would become like a mine shuddering on the verge of collapse. Finally she said, "They want to study our pollution."

One sentry scoffed. "His ancestors have done enough."

Dimon spit on the ground. "Sajeven, speak to Som for me and I will kill these strangers."

Before Drae could answer, the Star said in her aural link, "We have translated his statements. Come back to the bay at once."

Drae paused, still watching Alanye, who looked like he was trying very hard to seem well meaning, despite his nerves. The ridiculous carousel continued to turn through the air. She tracked her eyes across Alanye, giving him a more clinical perusal. He was tall and lean, his hair pristinely shaved on the sides. In that fitted space suit, it was easy to see his musculature, his broad shoulders, his bearing—he was not some university researcher. He had a soldier's build, though not the poise of a cloaksaan. Also, his accent was typical of the Kray West lowlands, an underdeveloped and impoverished area of Kator. A scholar would have trained those inflections out of his voice. And his comrades looked as little like scholars as he did. She was certain they had weapons of some kind.

"Wait here," she said to him, and then spoke aside to Dimon. "Keep your guns down, but watch them. Cool heads, everyone. I will be back soon."

In the bay, the other spokes looked grim and stormy-eyed.

"He is a mining contractor. He is here to look for jevite," said the Tree. "We have seen this before."

Drae knew her own history. Forty years ago something like this had happened, and though the Braemish explorers had not found anything of value in the ruins of the Pallor Seam, they had caused enough trouble in their time, harassing the Jeveni in every imaginable way. Drae had not been born yet, but the members of the Wheel all remembered it; they remembered how hard it had been to oust the Braems, and how many had been hurt in the process.

"We cannot allow them to stay here," said the Star, his cloudy eyes fierce despite the failure of his eyesight. "We must send them away."

Drae said, "If we send them away it will invite scrutiny. The Treblens do not take well to being denied what they want. They will assume we are hiding something."

"We *are* hiding something," the Stone retorted, voice querulous. "We must get rid of them before they look too close."

This was true. When the pirates came forty years ago, the Jeveni had not yet drilled down through the Pallor Seam to the Blood Seam far beneath it. Today, entrance to the Blood Seam was carefully concealed, with miners coming and going stealthily, to put off any spies.

But if Lucos Alanye went exploring, he might find their secret. She thought of the figure in the red coat.

Gus ben Roq said, "Kill them."

Everyone looked at him.

"We cannot just kill them," said the Gale, though she sounded as if she'd like nothing more.

"We can. We can kill them and destroy their ship. We can make it look like a crash. Others have crashed on our moon before."

Drae flicked her eyes over the faces of the Wheel, saw them thinking about it, wanting it. They turned toward her again, and their expressions were almost hungry. All Jeveni had this hunger, this desire for revenge on the Treble, this epigenetic response. Drae had it, too. She hated the Treblens. She hated Lucos Alanye with his ignorance and his smile and his belief that he could fool them. With a single word she could signal Dimon, and her sentries would slaughter the Katishsaan.

But she laid all the details of Lucos Alanye before her, like a table in her mind covered in artifacts. The Kray West accent; the guardsaan build; the mention of a "modest" university. All compared against the sleek space suits and the modern, expensive ship outside Farren Ki. Not to mention the gifts he'd brought, and the promise of pay. Alanye had made a crucial mistake. His cover story did not suit someone with access to such resources. Not unless he had a patron.

"You will trust my judgment?" she asked the Wheel.

They looked uneasy. Since becoming the River, she *had* gained their trust, but it was the trust of older, experienced people for a youngster. Conditional. They glanced at one another, finally homing in on the Star, who was the final word, even in their democratic system. Drae was prepared to obey him, but she prayed to Sajeven that he would not ask her to kill these people.

"Very well, Drae," he said. "You know the outer worlds best. We will trust you."

She nodded crisply and returned to the tunnel with its vibrating tension and its thin barrier between oxygen and vacuum.

Alanye looked relieved to see her. "I should have mentioned before!

We've come with a large supply of sevite. I know the Kindom only grants your people limited rations. Consider it another gift."

Drae looked at him flatly. He had held the sevite in reserve, a bargaining chip, and the moment he faced uncertainty, he offered it. He was in over his head. He was a childsaan, and by some of the glances of the people behind him, she sensed that they thought the same. Who knew what sort of background they had? Mercenaries? Smugglers? Whatever band he had put together, they did not respect him. He was a puppet, and if he had sevite, it was fairly easy to guess who had hold of his strings.

"That is a kind offer," she said, thinking with mean satisfaction of the tons and tons of jevite on her moon, a wealth that would make his little sevite gift look like a plate of animal droppings compared to a banquet. "We will of course accept your gifts and your payment for our hospitality. That said, accommodations are very limited in our city. We advise you to use your ship as a home base. Please return there now, and we will invite you back to share a meal."

Alanye looked as if he wasn't sure if he should be relieved or disappointed. The people behind him seemed wary. Drae's sentries, perhaps noticing a change, shifted. She could only imagine what accusations and complaints she would face when she returned to the Wheel. But she put all that from her mind, holding Alanye's dark stare.

"That's very generous, Sa Briit," he said. "And may I just say—"

"Tonight's meal will be a casual affair. No business. In the morning, you and I will discuss your interests and determine a course of action. I will be your host and guide through this process. I expect our interactions to be illuminating."

He smiled guardedly. Good. He was not so foolish that he did not understand the implications of her statement: He would have no free rein. He would operate under the eye of the River. Nothing he did would escape her scrutiny, and she would use his presence to her own advantage.

And though he didn't know it yet, she would find out who had sent him here. She would uncover their purpose. She would wring the secrets out of him, and make him *her* puppet.

And if it served her people, she would kill him.

As to the caster responsible for this breach, my cloaks are still review-ing the data signatures that will promptly lead us to the culprit. There are some indications that the individual is academy trained, but their work shows signs of gross immaturity. They are a middling annoyance, and represent no long-term threat to our interests.

excerpt, report to First Cloak Seti Moonback.
Dated 1654, Year of the Glide.

CHAPTER TWO

1665

YEAR OF THE HARVEST

Farren Eyce
The Planet Capamame

Jun Ironway's eyes dart across an array of casting views that crowd the air in her small office. Behind her, Liis Konye sits in an over-sized chair and slowly, calmly, cleans a gun. It's a Som's Edge pistol, the gun Jun's Great Gra gave her when she left home sixteen years ago to attend the Academy of Archivists in Riin Kala. Jun listens to the familiar sounds of Liis's work, thinking how, not even a month ago, all the guns in Farren Eyce were locked away in the armory. Yet she feels safer knowing Liis is armed. The office has the rich green smell of the salve that Liis rubs into the stump of her severed arm, and Jun feels safer for that, too. But their last jar of the salve is almost empty.

On one of the views, a newscaster in Teros System is choosing her words very carefully as she describes the fighting on Trin-Ma. "While the governor of Trin-Ma left the city some days ago, Khen Ookhen Obair has sent his own fighters to shore up the continental army. First Cloak Seti Kess's command ship, *The Makala Iis*, remains in Teron orbit. That no cloaksaan or Kindom guards have joined the battle against the rebels is proof enough of Sa Kess's confidence in Khen and the military."

Jun snorts, as much at the propaganda as at the use of Seti Moonback's new name. Having shirked the First Family that bore him, he has propped himself up as something wholly independent and blessed by the gods. Though he never came right out and said it, it didn't take long for talk to spread that "Kess," a word from the dead language of the Treble's early colonizers, means "crown of the gods."

Jun has an impulse to spit on the ground. "Dick. Was he this much of a dick when you knew him?"

Liis is still working on the gun. "Yes. He was always a dick."

Her voice is distant. When Jun looks at her, her mouth is a grim line. Jun recognizes that look, that way that Liis becomes sometimes, absent and haunted. Once, Liis had served under Seti Kess. Once, Kess's second-in-command, Medisogo, had cut off Liis's arm. All of Liis's steadiness can't hide from Jun the memories she carries.

The newscaster's voice grabs back Jun's attention. "While reports persist that rebel groups are expanding and that new insurgencies are popping up across the Treble, Kindom spokessaan assert that most of these are little more than social clubs of privileged university students. Many are personality cults ordered around the traitor Cleric Chono, who has been missing since she fomented rebellion in the Secretaries' stronghold of Nikapraev just three days ago. First Cloak Kess continues to promise the law-abiding saan of the Treble that he will not rest until all rebels stand down."

Jun fake-gags. "You know, a few days ago he was throwing money at any group that would cause trouble for the Secretaries. If you're gonna rebel and then turn around and set yourself up as the crown-fucking-commander of the whole Treble, have the decency to make up a story about your one-time frontliners suddenly becoming bad guys."

Liis asks, "Are the numbers holding steady?"

Maybe this is Liis's way of saying she can't talk about Kess anymore. Feeling guilty, Jun redirects her gaze at one of the other casting views.

"Some last casts straggling in. Not that they'll change the outcome."

Liis *hmms*.

"It's absurd," Jun says.

"What's absurd?"

"This thing, this ... *voting*."

She grimaces on the word. She has no love for the autocracy of the Kindom or the regencies of space stations and cities. She's all for allowing saan to shape their own government, and the Jeveni practice of voting in members of the Wheel seems in keeping with their communal ethos. But letting them vote in favor of being destroyed? How is that right? Then again, what does Jun know about best interests? How many choices has *she* made that have blown up in her face like the most spectacular and devastating fireworks?

"Masar was right," Liis says. "Effegen was right. They knew what the people of the colony would want."

"We'll see how *the people* feel when Kindom warbirds flood through the gate. Tomesk should never have called for a vote. He must be pissing himself somewhere."

Tomesk ten Ruvo, the Tree of the Wheel and a recalcitrant, distrusting man, had ordered that they let the colonists vote on whether to destroy the Capamame jump gate and, in so doing, prevent an invasion. Tomesk believed that now they know that it is First Cloak Seti Moonback (strike that, *Kess*) with access to their gate key, the people would do whatever it took to prevent him coming through their door. Tomesk was wrong. The idea of permanently losing access to the Treble is a bridge too far for the colonists, most of whom never intended to go to Capamame and many of whom hope to one day return to their birth worlds.

Liis says with a touch of humor, "He's no doubt very disappointed."

Jun snorts. "You know...that's almost worth all of us getting enslaved."

Another of her casting views, one with eyes on the hospital's operating theater ("Morbid," Liis had reproved her), gives a chime. The surgeon who's been operating on Fonu sen Fhaan announces that the foot amputation went well, and they are returning Fonu to their recovery room. For all Jun has never liked the River of the Wheel, she exhales with relief. The memory of the last time she saw Fonu dogs her waking and sleeping hours, all the worse because it was also the last time she saw her cousins—who attacked and tortured Fonu, who terrorized the colony, who betrayed Jun—

Liis says, "You should take a break."

"Effegen said she was going after the vote," Jun answers.

"So set a ping. Come and sit with me."

There's the sound of the gun's final pieces clicking back together. A dozen Seti Kesses could charge this office, and Jun would survive because Liis is here and Liis has a gun.

But—

"No," Jun mutters. "I...I want to wait."

She watches the three central views in the air, each a camera surveying a prison cell in the recently repurposed newsnest of Farren Eyce. In one of the cells, her cousin Bene is sitting on his cot, back against the wall as he reads a book of poetry that Liis brought him. He looks exhausted, circles under his eyes. Jun wonders if that's a mark of innocence or guilt. Is it naive, this instinct to trust him? After all, what right has she to trust her instincts, ever again?

In another cell, her younger cousin Tej paces with the restlessness of a euphorics addict in detox. Patchy dark stubble shadows his jaw, and he keeps tugging at his clothes like they're itching him, which they probably are. He's refused two opportunities to bathe. Seeing him this way makes Jun's hands tremble like a kid trying to control their first cast. She crosses her arms.

But he isn't even close to the worst thing on view. That honor belongs to the occupant of the third cell, the young woman sitting at a table with her hands clasped on the surface. She stares straight ahead, straight at nothing, and it would look like meditation if not for the rigidity of her muscles. From this angle, Jun can't see her eyes, but she can see enough of her face to recognize the twist of impotent rage. Ujan Redcore looks as much a stranger now as she did three days ago, when she shed the mask of Jun's sweet-tempered cousin and unveiled a face too monstrous to comprehend.

Suddenly, Ujan looks up into the camera. Her large dark eyes are hateful, and Jun flinches from her as if she was an electric shock. Or a cast attack.

Liis presses her. "You should stop. Effegen will tell you what happens."

But Ujan's eyes snap away from the camera, refocusing on the door into her cell. It opens to let in a pair of sentries—and behind them, Effegen ten Crost.

The Star of the Wheel is a striking contrast to Ujan. They are both young women, both intelligent, both possessing a quality that makes it hard to look away. But that is where their similarities end. Ujan is as skinny and sharp as a wire, and while once she had a shy, mild affect, now she radiates malevolence. Jun still can't understand how she didn't see it, how she never saw the brilliant, dangerous caster that hid inside her meek little cousin.

Effegen, too, is dangerous. But in an entirely different way. Short and full-figured in her official robes, she has a regal bearing and intelligent, kind eyes. Though not so kind in this moment. She stares Ujan down with an authority that suggests a saan thirty, fifty years older than her. At her ears glint black jevite earrings rippled with red.

One of the sentries cuffs Ujan's wrists together and connects the cuffs to a metal ring in the table. The second sentry brings in another chair and sets it on the other side of the table. Then the sentries stand on either side of the chair, and Effegen sits down across from Ujan.

When Ujan looks at Effegen, it's how a predator looks at prey from the other side of a tall fence: hungrily measuring the nearness of her meal. When Effegen looks at Ujan, it's with the perfect, cool confidence of a fishersaan repairing a net.

Effegen says, "I understand you wanted to speak to me?"

Ujan smiles slyly. "And here I thought you wanted to speak to *me*."

Effegen looks at her for several seconds, pensive. She looks tired, Jun realizes, and there's something disconcerting about that. But her voice is strong. "As I've already told you, I would be happy for you to share anything you can about Seti Kess and his plans. Which would do a great deal to redeem you in our eyes."

Ujan grins, empty of feeling. "I know about the vote. Bet I can guess how it turned out."

Jun twitches anxiously. When they arrested Ujan three days ago, Jun thought she had seen the end of her cousin's reign of terror. She had thought, *Take away her neural link access, and she won't be able to hurt anyone.* Jun hadn't known at the time that Ujan had a second neural link. There was no reason to have suspected it, and even the thought makes Jun queasy. One neural link is standard in the Treble, even for children. A second has been known to kill people. It allows a caster to hold more data, run more programs, but at great peril. Jun has never needed or tried it. Of course, Ujan took the risk.

Effegen says mildly, "It must frustrate you not to know the outcome for certain."

It's a subtle dig, but it hits. Ujan scowls at the reminder of her impotence. She has no second neural link anymore. She gambled it away yesterday when she attacked the nearest sentries with a tech virus in some irrational bid at escape. Jun well remembers experiencing that virus herself, like a match lighting fire to her neural, aural, and ocular links. Even now one of the sentries Ujan attacked is in the hospital. He may be permanently blind and deaf on his left side.

Ujan says, "I don't need a neural link to guess the outcomes. Your colonists are fools. You'll have Seti on your doorstep in no time."

Jun breathes in slowly through her nostrils, still disgusted to think of Ujan throwing her lot in with Kess, rallying spies in Farren Eyce to attack and murder colonists. Giving Kess the key to the Capamame gate. Of course, she's convinced herself that she's his partner and equal in mayhem. Which is just pathetic.

Ujan says, "I'm gonna offer you a deal, *Star*. Get me cast access to Kess, and I can negotiate with him for a peaceful surrender. He'll listen to me."

"Thank you, but I can negotiate for myself."

"Look, I'm trying to play nice. Don't test me."

With raised eyebrows, Effegen repeats, "Test you?"

"There *are* other spies in this colony. If they don't hear from me soon, they'll cause so much trouble you'll be fighting a war inside and out. Let me talk to Kess and I'll tell you who they are."

Not for the first time, Jun wishes she could go into that room and wring Ujan's neck. The nasty bravado of her every word and movement is a blow to Jun's pride. She lived with Ujan for months. Why couldn't she see it?

Effegen tilts her head. "You are all contradictions, Sa Redcore. Days ago you said you were happy to sit in a cell and wait for Kess to rescue you. Yesterday you attacked my sentries. Now you threaten me with these shadow agents. Yet, for the chance to speak to Kess, you would negotiate for our safety? Why should I take your games seriously?"

"It wasn't a game when Bene murdered those collectors."

Jun twitches again. Effegen never wavers. "We already know that Dom ben Dane murdered the collectors. Bene didn't even know you were the avatar until he tried to save you and Tej from yourselves. Ujan, you know I know these things. If you hope to upset me by accusing Bene of crimes he hasn't committed, you are wasting both our time."

"You're wrong about Bene. He was in it from the beginning."

"I don't believe you."

"That's cuz you like fucking him," Ujan says.

Jun hisses, "Godsdamn her."

Liis, standing beside Jun now, says, "Let Effegen work."

Indeed, Effegen shows no impact. This is the third time she's spoken to Ujan. No matter what Ujan does or says, Effegen is as implacable as the Black.

"I'll take your accusation under advisement. As for your request, I realize how difficult it must be to be cut off from your master, but—"

Ujan spits, "He's *not* my master! If he was my master, I'd have told him everything! I held things back. Things you can use to your advantage."

"Oh?" Effegen sounds bored. "Like what?"

Ujan hesitates, the first sign of uncertainty. Maybe it's ego that prompts her to admit, "He doesn't have my tech virus. He doesn't know what the Wheel spokes look like—well, except you. Oh, and I didn't tell him about Six. He still thinks they're Esek Nightfoot!"

It's such an unexpected barrage of information, genuinely useful information, that Jun knows it must mean one of two things: either Ujan is lying, or she truly is desperate to earn an audience with Seti Kess.

"Interesting things to hold back," Effegen muses.

"I can help you. My people have guns and explosives. You don't want to risk them running free any longer." Effegen's expression turns pitying. Ujan angrily flares her nostrils. "They have orders from me to kill as many of you as possible!"

"That may be," Effegen says, though it's clear she doesn't believe it. "However, such an operation would require a great deal of liberty. And your 'people' don't have their liberty, Sa Redcore. Yesterday, we arrested sixteen residents of Farren Eyce. Each and every one of them confessed to working for you."

Ujan goes still. Jun doesn't have the heart for even a scrap of satisfaction.

Effegen explains. "Jun tracked them down within hours of getting access to your neural link. You erased your tracks, but not well enough that she couldn't rebuild them. You had five lieutenants, correct? Like Aris the Beauty." Ujan doesn't move. "And each lieutenant had between two and four people reporting to them. Tej and Jasef sen Clime worked for Beauty, and it was their job to kill the collectors. Other groups focused on sabotage and vandalism. Two of the groups were never even given orders. And all the groups have one thing in common: They believed they were reporting to a direct agent of Ilius Redquill."

This time it's Ujan who twitches, as if an electric current has gone through her.

"They're hardly innocent," Effegen continues. "But they never agreed to serve Seti Kess. Several of them appear rather terrified by the truth. Kess doesn't have much reputation for protecting underlings, after all."

"They're lying!" Ujan says. "They're trying to protect themselves! This is—"

Effegen interrupts, "Let me tell you what I think. I think that *you* are an underling. Kess found you, recruited you, and used you. Now that you've been useful, he's as likely to forget your name as offer you a hand in friendship. Which is why you're trying to manipulate me into letting you contact him. You want assurances that he'll protect you. But I don't think he will."

Ujan leaps to her feet, kicking her chair out behind her. "You don't know *anything*, you Je *bitch*!"

Effegen holds up a hand to forestall the sentries. She looks at Ujan without reacting.

"He knows who his friends are!" Ujan cries. "When he comes to Farren Eyce, he'll see everything I did here. And you know what I'm going to tell him? 'Sure, I'll work with you. But first, I get to *stab* Effegen ten Crost in the *throat*!'"

Effegen's silence only drives Ujan's anger to a fever pitch.

"You're dead!" she promises. "You're all fucking *dead*!"

This time, it's Effegen who stands up. She gives the venomous girl a slow appraisal, and says to the sentries, "Unbind her once I'm gone. Take her to bathe if she wants, and give her fresh clothes. And warm food." She shifts her words to Ujan. "There's no need for you to suffer."

"Fuck you. *Fuck you!*"

Effegen leaves the cell to the sound of Ujan's hysterical cursing. When one of the sentries tries to approach her, she wrenches and twists and kicks out at them in a fury. She's going to pull her arms out of their sockets. The last time Jun saw her like this, they were aboard a shuttle on the surface of Capamame, and Jun and Bene were holding Ujan down, and Ujan wouldn't stop screaming—

Jun shuts off the cast. She breathes in raggedly and exhales with a bitten-off sob. A hand presses against the small of her back, Liis quiet and solid as stone. There is a sudden ping in Jun's aural link: Effegen. She takes in several steadying breaths and projects the voice so Liis can hear.

"You were right. She has no useful information."

What is Jun supposed to feel about that? Happy? She strips all emotion from her voice. "It's good if Kess doesn't have the tech virus. Or the identities of the spokes. And the bit about Six—"

"Six is either dead or imprisoned. Whether Kess knows their identity is immaterial."

Jun and Liis glance at each other. Jun says, "I'm still combing through all of Ujan's records. We may find more that we can use. She was a hoarder."

Effegen's voice is clipped. "Fine. But we need to dedicate our efforts to other areas. Is Liis with you?"

"Yes, my Star," says Liis.

"What is your report?"

"I don't have many updates since last night's council meeting. The number of saan who have volunteered for sentry duty now stands at eleven hundred. I have twenty collectors, and other saan whose expertise I trust, taking inventory of our armaments. Our resources are eclectic. The armory in Farren Eyce is comprised mainly of rifles and handguns of varying reliability. Of the ships in the Jeveni fleet that jumped to Capamame, about thirty-four percent have missile defense systems, but again, those defenses range from state-of-the-art to defective. *Drae's Hope* itself has an impressive arsenal. However, that arsenal is more than seventy-five years old. My experts are taking great care to assess what we can use and what we should destroy."

Jun wonders if it's weird to get turned on by this brisk, soldierly efficiency.

Effegen says, "Make sure that everyone who is assessing the armaments is taking their required rest breaks. The last thing we need is for something to be missed or set off because people are working themselves to exhaustion."

"Yes, my Star."

Effegen curtly shifts subject matter. "And the gate key, Jun?"

Jun's eyes flit to yet another view in the air: There, a dense string of code renders in green streams like a river, while around it coils a thin gold chain, thicker in some places than others, with links missing, and a long way to go.

She says, "Drae sen Briit was a pretty decent caster, but this idea that she wrote the gate key is revisionist history. Mostly she supervised the saan who did it."

"Does that matter?"

"It was a lot of saan," Jun replies. "From what I can see, about twenty casters worked on the key together. Casters are a fucking ridiculous breed, unfortunately. We've all got our own ways of doing things, idiosyncrasies and shit. When you write a code, it's best practice to embed detailed notes on why you did what you did. Some of Drae's casters were more disciplined than others, and there doesn't appear to have been a consistent vocabulary for notes."

Effegen says dryly, "I imagine the details are well beyond my comprehension."

"Effegen, I am trying to rewrite the gate key. To do that, I need to understand the *original* gate key. That's tough when the original casters are hard to understand."

"Give me the bottom line."

"The bottom line is I have six programs working to rewrite the key, with half our casters lending technical support. We'll get it done. But we're looking at three weeks at least."

She doesn't say what they all know: That's too long. Until they have a new key, Kess can use the key Ujan gave him to invade the Capamame system. The Kindom has wanted to retake its Jeveni labor force ever since they fled the Treble nearly a year ago.

For several tense moments all Jun hears is the brisk walk on the other side of the cast. Then Effegen says, "Tell me what I can do to help."

Jun exhales. There's nothing Effegen can do. But she doesn't want to leave her without hope. "Look, one thing we've got going for us is that the Jeveni have done a good job holding on to historical records. Between the collectors who went looking for missing Jeveni and the data you were able to take with you off Jeve, you've got an impressive archive. My casters are sifting through the records of every caster we can find who worked on this key. I'm talking their school notes down to working logs. I'm going through Drae's stuff myself. It's possible we'll find something somewhere that gives us an edge."

Effegen asks, "Then you have Drae's personal journal?"

Jun hesitates, surprised. "Her journal?"

The public records on Drae are a confusing admixture of specific and vague. She was a polyglot. She was a traveler. She regularly gave speeches and reports to the saan of Farren Ki, all recorded for posterity. But a lot is missing. Some records say she was the River of the Wheel while others make no mention of it. How old was she? Who were her parents? A journal could contain more concrete information, and as far as Jun is concerned, every detail is valuable.

Effegen says, "She had her private journal with her when she left Jeve. The Wheel has held it in trust ever since. I'll have it brought to you."

"Is it written in Je?" Jun asks, already anticipating how long it will take her translator bot to—

This time Effegen's voice carries an unfamiliar bite of irritation. "Of course it is. That's the language of the Jeveni."

Jun darts a look at Liis, who is frowning.

"Uh, right. Thank you."

"Is there anything else?"

When Jun first met Effegen, she was taken aback by the young woman's openness, the sweetness of her smile, the easy laughter that belied her razor-sharp mind. But in the past three days, there has been no laughter, no smiles, no openness. Masar is in the Treble, perhaps never to return, and Bene is locked up in the newsnest. The two people who Effegen loves best have been taken from her.

Jun hazards to ask, "Any... update on the prisoners?"

Effegen clears her throat, perhaps to ensure that her voice remains aloof. "I'm on my way to discuss it with the Wheel."

Jun shifts her feet, not knowing what outcome she hopes for. The Wheel has twenty-one prisoners now. Sixteen of them, the spies who Jun uncovered, are under house arrest. But there are also the newsnest denizens: Bene, Ujan, Tej—as well as the defiant Aris the Beauty and the former collector, Dom ben Dane. Jun can well imagine the varying opinions in the Wheel. Tomesk ten Ruvo will argue for building a formal prison on Level 1. Hyre ten Grie will urge some other solution but be unable to present it themself. Fonu, recovering from surgery, will not be there to state an opinion. What about Gaeda ben Kist, the Stone and religious head of the colony? She is stern and implacable, but also savvy. What is the savvy response to a handful of traitors?

Liis asks, "If not imprisonment, then what?"

Effegen says emotionlessly, "Removal to the Treble. Continued house arrest. Or... rehabilitation."

Rehabilitation. The avatar blackmailed Dom ben Dane into killing three collectors. Aris the Beauty nearly killed Jun and Masar. Tej was an accessory to murder and torture, while Bene made the mistake of trying to protect his cousins. And then there's Ujan. Jun can imagine a route of contrition and recompense for some, but Ujan? She is too dangerous to ever let near a casting network again. Ujan can't be rehabilitated.

Effegen says, "What we decide will set a precedent for our future. It's not a question of the immediate challenges. It's a question of"—her voice falters—"hope."

Jun doesn't answer. Liis is quiet. The silence goes on and on, before finally Effegen resumes. "Please continue with your work. By Sajeven's own mercy, Seti Kess will be so busy crushing dissent in the Treble, he won't deign to attack us for weeks."

Jun thinks this is very unlikely. A far-reaching war against dozens of rebel militias will require resources. Sevite among them. The sevite trade has been in tatters ever since the bulk of the Jeveni jumped to Capamame. It's in Kess's best interests to bring them back and put them to work. Soon.

As if she hears Jun's thoughts, as if she can hardly stand the truth of it, Effegen snaps, "I have to hope. What good am I, of all the spokes, if I don't try to hope? I"—her swallow is audible—"I have to go."

The cast breaks off. Jun looks at Liis, whose scar-feathered eyebrows are knit with concern. They must be thinking the same thing: that the Effegen who sat before Ujan was a bulwark of calm, but that the young woman they've just spoken to is someone else. Jun considers their circumstances. Chono and Masar are hunting Seti Kess with little hope of success. The seasoned collectors of Farren Eyce are gone. Fonu may never fully recover. Tomesk is intractable, Gaeda is a wild card, and Hyre wrings their hands on the sidelines. Effegen—she is the only rock left in the foundation of Farren Eyce, and she shows signs of fissures.

"She won't break," says Liis, grim but certain.

What can Jun do but trust that judgment, and nod? "She won't break."

CHAPTER THREE

1665

YEAR OF THE HARVEST

Trin-Ma
Trini-so Continent
The Planet Teros

Seti Kess's command ship hangs in orbit, a stamp of blackness against the red and hazy atmosphere of Teros. Smaller warbirds surround it like satellites, yet to descend toward the surface and the fighting in Trin-Ma. According to Jun Ironway's projections, there are five thousand soldiers of the Trini-son army laying siege to Trin-Ma, but the rebels have landed more blows than they've taken and entrenched themselves in the urban districts. Much of their success is owed to resources they received from Kess himself, when he was trying to destabilize Kindom power under the Clever Hand. And yet, now that Kess is the Kindom power and it behooves him to smash those rebellions, he still withholds reinforcements, watching from the perch of his warfalcon.

As Chono sits in an alcove of an abandoned building in the combat gap between the north and south of Trin-Ma, she considers herself lucky that Kess hasn't carpet-bombed the city yet. A few days ago, the Secretarial Court was threatening to do just that, and not only to Trin-Ma but to other cities that have risen up against the Kindom: Principes, Hestos, Pippashap—even Riin Kala, with its population of ten million.

But now the Secretarial Court is dead, Ilius Redquill is dead, and Kess has the reins of every Kindom Hand. Kess murdered over 50 percent of the Secretaries. Will he be similarly bloody-minded toward the rebels? She never knew Kess all that well—beyond his hatred for Esek, and Esek's delighted contempt for him.

Whatever he plans to do, in the meantime, the rebels are impressively well situated in the north side of the city. They have better cover than their enemy and the benefit of a vast underground of tunnels, inaccessible from the south. They also have weapons and armaments to rival the Trini-son military. Does Kess bemoan the support he's given, now that his enemies can really stand up to him? Or does he consider it good sport, as Esek would? As Six probably would, too?

Six.

Six Six Six Six Six . . .

Somewhere nearby there's a clicking sound. Chono looks up to find Masar snapping for her attention, signaling her to move back. Her alcove is located in a narrow alley, with a mirror alcove five feet away sheltering Masar and his two collectors. They all flatten themselves against the wall, and that's when Chono hears the tromping of boots somewhere nearby, perhaps where the alley opens up into a wider street.

The sound fades. She closes her eyes, gritting her teeth with impatience at herself. She should have heard those troops coming. She's distracted. She can't afford to be distracted.

Pay attention, Esek chirped at her once, when she was a brand-new novitiate and had made some mistake. *I get very stabby when my fish don't pay attention.*

With the troops gone, it's quiet again, the city caught in a lull between fighting. Tens of thousands of Trin-Ma residents have fled, and the streets were empty when Chono and her companions snuck into the city last night, Jun's Hood protecting them from swarms of cameras and surveillance drones, which even now buzz lazily in the air.

They're in a shopping district, the windows boarded up, though there's little damage or other signs that the fight has come to this part of the city. Layez, the collector on Masar's right, and the tallest of them all (which is saying something), crouches over their pack, rummaging for battle rations. They toss one across the alley to Chono. It's a nutrient bar that claims to be squash fruit and nuts, but which looks like a dried slab of indeterminate paste. She bites into it, the gluey, slightly sweet flavor barely registering.

The other collector, Qlios, is checking his ammunition. Meanwhile, Masar studies a holographic map of the city, a parting gift from Yantikye, who boasted that the map adjusts in real time to reflect the state of the fighting and the safety of the roads. Chono, whose hand was badly broken a couple of days ago and is still stiff despite a round of regenerative medicine, flexes and unflexes it, imagining that she is balling up a fist to break Yantikye's jaw. They parted ways with him and his daughter Graisa last night. He declared he would lay low and assess the progress of the rebellions before choosing a particular battleground.

"Lots of different nets in the sea," he'd said cheerfully. "Gotta make sure I go where I'm most useful, nah?"

Chono knows him now for an opportunist, with no qualms about betraying anyone who doesn't serve his goals. She herself is less a person to him than a potential tool in his arsenal. Just like Six.

"You hate me so much, Cleric Chono," he'd mused last night. Graisa had just set their shuttle down in a clearing in the woodsy foothills five miles from Trin-Ma, and Yantikye was watching Chono and the Jeveni disembark onto the red but frosted soil of southern Teros in wintertime. "But you know, the things I've done—they're exactly what Six would do."

Chono had whirled toward him, but Masar was already between them, a hand on her shoulder and his one eye hard.

"Enough," he said. "We don't have the time."

Chono glared over her shoulder at a faintly smiling Yantikye. She hated his composure, his remorselessness. Because of Yantikye, the disgraced First Cleric Aver Paiye is dead. Because of Yantikye, Six threw in their lot with Seti Kess for the chance to save Chono from execution. Because of Yantikye, Chono lost Six in the ensuing battle, and if they are not dead, they are Kess's prisoner. Vulnerable. Unreachable.

Somewhere in the distance she hears the crack and whistle of mortar fire, soon punctuated by a weighty boom. It's too far away to feel the vibration, and so too far to be a threat, but a half dozen additional rounds put her on edge. Masar and the other two collectors brandish their rifles, glancing up and down the alley. It's just past dawn. A fitting time for renewed hostilities. Did the rebels fire first? Is it an ambush of some kind?

"The north side of the city has four major neighborhoods," Graisa the Honor told her yesterday. "Kip-Kipsi is the farthest north you can get; it shoves right up against the coastal cliffs. The rebel leadership is hunkered down in there. You need to find Zemit." Graisa cast an image into the air of a young Teron with acne scars and a black topknot. "If somehow the people there don't recognize you, tell them you're a friend of the Endless Sea. They'll take you to Zemit."

Chono, whose feud with Yantikye did not extend to his daughter, had nodded her appreciation, committing Zemit's face to memory. When she looked at Graisa again, the girl wore an expression that mingled regret with resentment. It was Graisa who had fought for an audience with Chono in Praetima. She had asked Chono to side with the rebels and approach Aver Paiye for help. She believed that the people would listen to Chono because she was a cleric, and because her reputation as the People's Kin had earned her awe and admiration across the Treble. Unbeknownst to Graisa, her father did not share those sentiments.

Chono wonders if the girl will forgive him. Or if Yantikye even cares.

"Chono."

Masar's voice carries across the alley. Dirty and scraped up, one eye covered by a patch, and a scruff of beard growing on his face, he looks as rough as she feels after a night of hiking down the foothills in prickly undergrowth. It was easy enough to sneak through the line of marshals and guardsaan surrounding Trin-Ma, their ranks spread thin. But that luck won't last. Masar crosses the alley into her alcove. He leans beside her, both of them with their backs up against a wall.

"There's activity picking up between here and Kip-Kipsi," he whispers. "We need to lie low until nightfall. We'll have a better chance getting through the gap after dark." He pauses, then adds irritably, "And it'll all go smoother if we trust each other."

Chono feels the trace of a bitter smile on her lips. "You don't trust me?" she murmurs.

"You're distracted. If you're going to stand around and brood over Six, you're no good to me. Just a reminder, we're not in this to save your lover."

His words spread over her skin like a frost. *Brood...Lover...*She turns her head toward him. His one eye glares back fearlessly. She asks, "Who are *you* in this to save?"

He blanches, which is some satisfaction. How distracted is he by the thoughts of that sweet boy Bene Ironway and the indomitable Star? There's no need for her to say more about it, and she and Masar look away from each other, examining opposite ends of the alley like a couple of kids unwilling to admit a stalemate. *Six,* Chono thinks. *Six Six Six Six Six...*

Masar says, "I don't trust this nighttime truce thing all the newscasters are talking about. The continental army is trying to build a false sense of security."

Chono flexes and unflexes her hand. "After the colonization of Teros, there were two hundred years of civil war on Trini-so continent. War itself became so routine that the armies parlayed long enough to set up rules of combat. No fighting at night."

She learned the story at school. Not the kinschool, where her real education began at age seven, but the neighborhood school she attended for three years beforehand. Trini-son children learned martial history very young. Perhaps this had given Chono some advantage at the Principes kinschool, where lessons on Kindom warfare and histories of atrocity were rote.

Masar says, "I doubt Seti Kess will be that civilized, once he invades."

"*If* he invades."

Somewhere east, artillery *tat-tat-tats*. When it dies down, Masar says, "He will."

This is their only hope of getting close enough to Kess to capture or kill him. If he invades the city himself, he'll have ranks of cloaksaan with him, not to mention the Kindom guards that he has confiscated from the Righteous and Clever Hands. He'll be well protected. But if Chono and Masar can reach the Trin-Ma rebel Zemit, and persuade him to work with them, the rebels might be able to keep Kess busy long enough for Chono and Masar to get close.

Killing him is a last resort. He has the gate key, and while they could just hope he's kept that secret to himself and make him take it to his grave, there's a strong chance that the Silver Keep itself has the key on record. Kess may be their only chance at stopping the Kindom from invading Farren Eyce.

And Kess may be Chono's only chance of finding Six again.

She pushes that thought down. She has to. There is so much more at stake than a single person—even if that person's voice runs like a current in her thoughts. The last time she spoke to Six, Six was fleeing Kess through the storm-washed streets of Praetima. She could hear in their voice that they were injured. They didn't sound afraid, exactly, but they sounded as if they knew the road was hurtling toward a dead end.

Chono, my dear friend. I cannot talk right now.

Additional mortar explosions boom, maybe a little closer than before. Masar says, "We're asking for trouble, out in the open like this. Qlios wants to break into one of these shops, get some rest before we move out tonight."

Chono, trying to blink away the thought of Six drenched in blood and rainwater, looks across the alley and four shops down. The door has a single thick board nailed diagonally across it, as if the shopkeeper didn't have a chance to finish their work. Masar, following her gaze, nods with satisfaction.

The artillery in the east picks up, rattling for ten seconds and then pausing. A few seconds later, it starts up again. Chono and Masar look at each other meaningfully. Masar signals his collectors, and they flank him as he jogs down the alley toward the shop. Chono brings up the rear, covering them. She remembers telling Six, *Find cover. I'm coming for you.*

And Six pleading, *No, no, no. Do not do that. Trust me. Please, trust me.*

Always trying to protect her, and making it impossible for her to do the same.

Masar reaches the shop door. For a few exposed seconds, nobody moves. Then a shell explodes, and Masar shoots the lock off the door. He and Layez grab the wooden board, and together they heave and twist until the nails shriek their surrender and it comes off. Qlios shoves the door open. They all slip inside, the sounds of the firefight muffling as they close the door after them and Layez pushes a nearby sideboard in front of it.

Chono looks around at the shop. It's dark, but she can see floor-to-ceiling shelves displaying bottles and jars. She thinks it must be some sort of liquor store, but when she approaches the nearest shelf and picks up a cloth packet, it's full of dried herbs. She inhales, almost stumbling over the intensity of the smell—and its familiarity.

"What is this place?" Qlios asks, picking up a clear bottle with a viscous green fluid inside.

"It's a folk pharmacy," Chono explains. "A lot of Trini-son weeds are medicinal, and cheaper than visiting a doctor. Trin-Ma is wealthier than it was before the Khens transplanted here, but people still rely on local medicine."

Masar gives her a look that is somewhere between amusement and annoyance. "Quite the historian today, aren't you?"

Is she? She was born on Trini-so continent, though not in the city of Trin-Ma. Her birth city is hundreds of miles east, and she hasn't been there since she was a child of seven. Her trips with Esek to Teros always brought them to the northern continents of the planet. Places where it never got cold. The mild winters of Trini-so with their pre-dawn frost and purple sunsets are something she remembers in a deep, animal part of herself.

Layez wiggles the bottle with its green liquid in her direction. "You know what this is?" they ask, a touch of hostility in their voice.

"Pain reliever," she says. Layez raises their eyebrows with interest. "Tastes horrible."

Layez puts it in their pack, saying, "I guess if you're gonna come to Teros, it helps to have a Teron with you." Chono looks at them without answering. They don't even try to hide their dislike of her. "I mean... assuming you *are* a Teron. Not like you've got a family name."

Layez themself has the coloring of a Ma'kessn, probably a south-lander. Chono asks mildly, "Don't I look like a Teron?"

"Never saw a Teron as big as you before."

"Shut it," Masar warns.

Layez snorts, turning away from her. They make a slow circuit of the room, examining the wares as if they're on a shopping trip. Qlios gives Chono a pondering look and begins to set up in a corner of the room, organizing his pack.

She can't begrudge the unfriendliness. When she lived on Capamame those eight months, what did the Jeveni know about her but that she was a cleric? An agent of the Kindom, which has oppressed them for centuries? And when Masar and his collectors came to the Treble again and rescued Chono from the cloaksaan at Nikapraev, what did they know about her then? Only that she was close to Six, and Six was indirectly responsible for Ujan Redcore stealing the gate key.

Meanwhile, the Treble is overrun with gossip and panic and revolutionary fervor, and Chono herself is a main topic of conversation. The Righteous Hand who is actually righteous. The cleric who puts the people before herself. The fierce-hearted warrior priest who will lead them to deliverance from a corrupt Kindom. But why should Chono's inflated reputation with the people impress Layez and Qlios, when they know very well that "the people" never did shit to deliver the Jeveni from anything?

If Chono and these collectors weren't united in their desire to stop Seti Kess, she sincerely doubts Masar would have even helped her escape Nikapraev.

She takes another sniff of the herbs in the cloth packet, their ashy smell and the dark purple color of the dried leaves reminding her of bad times.

Masar asks warily, "What is that?"

She wouldn't say he's thawed toward her, but at least he talks to her willingly now.

"Coagulant. A stopgap in the absence of regeneratives." She smiles grimly. "It can also be brewed into a sleep aid."

Masar snorts, looking around. "Sleep," he mutters, like it's a foreign concept. He quickly loses interest in the folk medicine. "What did that Honor girl say, just before we left?"

She furrows her brow. "What do you mean? She told me about Zemit."

"That's not all she said. You came out of the cockpit looking sick."

Chono tucks the packet into her coat, buying time.

"She said that Zemit was the best point of entry because he's allied with other rebel cells in the Treble. She said the different uprisings aren't going to be discrete entities for long. There's talk of some kind of…quorum. If we want in on that, we need Zemit."

Masar's good eye squints. "That's not enough to make you look like you'd swallowed a bug, is it?"

Chono thinks of Six, begging her through the comm, *Live. Please. Live.*

"She said that if I want their help, I should emphasize that defeating Kess is the only road to a peaceful Treble. I should lean into my repu-tation as a righteous cleric and spin this conflict as a choice between godliness and apostasy. At least two-thirds of the rebel leaders are devout. They'll listen to me if I take that tack. Or so she says."

Masar looks unimpressed. "You mind that so much? It's not news they want you for their savior."

"What I *mind* is the implication that I should play down the threat to Farren Eyce because it wouldn't matter to these rebels as much as some vision of a Treble free from Kindom Hands."

Masar laughs, startling her. The mirth is cold-edged. "So fucking what? You think these people are ever going to risk themselves for the Jeveni? So long as we're agreed on Kess as a common enemy, I'm satisfied."

Chono says, "We have to convince them not to kill him on sight. And our only reason for wanting them not to kill him on sight is so we can get the key. We need them to care about that."

"No," he says, "We need them to believe that capturing him alive better serves their rebellion. Come up with a story, Cleric Chono. I don't care what you tell them. In fact…" He pauses again, looking at his collectors. Qlios has sorted his weapons and ammo into categories. Elsewhere in the shop, Layez squints at a row of little pouches. Masar makes an annoyed sound. "It's a shame none of us is a tattooist."

Realizing what he means, Chono grimaces. Jeveni have small tat-toos in the shape of a five-spoked wheel, an homage to their goddess Sajeven, but a Jeveni tattooist is as accomplished at removing the tat-too as applying it. Throughout their history, Jeveni collectors have forgone their tattoos in order to blend in with the rest of the Treble. Masar did it himself, at one point. Now he wants to do it again, to hide who they are from the rebels.

"If I'm to be revered for my righteousness," Chono says. "Then I'll be feared for the Godfire's wrath." Masar raises his eyebrow. She smiles wryly. "I'll scare them all into being civil, is what I mean."

He grunts. "Fuck civility. Let's just find Kess and—"

A sudden alert flashes in Chono's ocular. The others must get it, too, for Qlios stands and Layez turns back toward them. Masar flicks the contents of the cast into the air. A newscaster's hologram appears, standing in front of the rubble of a bombed-out shop.

"Good morning. This is a Treble-wide bulletin from the battleground of Trin-Ma. As we know, maintaining the casting blocks in Trin-Ma has been crucial to efforts to cut off communication and access to outside resources. The lowering of the blocks this morning is the first sign of a shift in power."

Sure enough, when Chono checks her cast access, she discovers that the wall of static that has prevented her from reaching outside the city is gone. Masar is probably contacting Farren Eyce this very moment, updating them while he can.

The newscaster continues: "We've now had confirmation a fresh wave of troops has stormed the God's Courtyard between the city's north and south, clearing the city center and driving the rebels to retreat."

The fighting they heard a few minutes ago. But it hadn't seemed like such a dramatic onslaught. Surely the area must have been low on rebel fighters, and the Kindom is simply capitalizing on that to advertise some victorious offensive—

As if to mock her, the new whistle and boom of fresh mortars sounds closer to the shop this time, a dramatic pickup. The hologram shifts to an aerial view of the city center with its massive statue of the god Terotonteris. Tiny figures bolt as a much larger force rains artillery down on them from the south. Chono, hearing the thunder of it at a distance, squints. The Trini-son military wear red armor, distinguishing themselves from the white-armored marshals. But this army attacking the rebels is wearing black.

"We're getting reports," says the newscaster, "that the advancing troops are not continental soldiers, but a phalanx of Kindom guard-saan and cloaksaan. This confirms that Seti Kess has stepped up the offensive on Trin-Ma by sending his own forces onto the ground."

"The fuck?" Masar grumbles.

Before their eyes, the Kindom troops drive north, scattering the rebels and taking the city center in a wave. The newscaster's voice trembles with excitement. "This is already looking to be the most decisive victory of the Trin-Ma conflict!"

"Bullshit," Layez says. "We've got eyes on the command ship! Kess hasn't sent a single shuttle down since—"

"Since we got here," Qlios interrupts. "Maybe he had forces on the ground already?"

This time the clap of an explosive is near enough that the walls shudder, and they all tense, looking up at the ceiling. Dust rains down.

"I've sent a cast to Jun," Masar says. "She'll get more views of what's going on."

Minutes pass as Chono watches him carry out some back-and-forth with Jun. The invasion is both very slow and very sudden. They listen to the bombings and the quieter gunfire, muffled through walls of stone. Abruptly, it stops, replaced with an eerie silence. The sight of the Kindom wave coming to a halt sends gooseflesh down Chono's arms.

Masar growls, "Give me *something*."

The newscaster comes back. "As we can see, the seizure of the city center has—yes. Yes, I'm hearing—the rebels appear to have fled into the northern factories. We're seeking confirmation that—no, we can't read for certain if *The Makala Iis* and its ancillary ships are planning an aerial offensive. Wait—"

The newscaster's excitement suddenly tips toward hysterical. "Yes, we see him! Yes, we can confirm, he's here!"

The view swoops down upon the courtyard, its expanse flooded with guardsaan and cloaks in black all shouting and cheering. The statue of Terotonteris, taller than a building, stands upon a plinth, and there between two of his feet and gazing down on the scene of victory, all upturned nose and cruel eyes, is Seti Kess.

Chono can't believe it. How did he get here without—

"Where's Jun?" she growls at Masar.

"I lost her," he grits out. "Something is trying to lock her out. She'll find her way in."

Layez says urgently, "We have to move on him *now*."

"And do *what*?" Masar snaps. "He's surrounded by thousands of guardsaan!"

"Infiltrate!" Layez insists. "Replace some guards—get close to him."

It's absurd. It's impossible.

Seti Kess raises his arms, and the crowd goes quiet. He wears a smile that is surely meant to convey strength and benevolence, but as always, his emotions look counterfeit. His shaggy hair falls around his shoulders in a golden mane. His stark features and the scar on his mouth have a carved, violent quality. The eyes with their electric-blue modification perpetuate the impression of a not-quite-person. But the coldness behind his smiling mask is all too human.

"My people!" he shouts. "My brave, heroic defenders of the Kindom! I salute you! I salute you!"

The crowd roars. From the distance of the folk pharmacy, Chono can only hear its echo.

"Your courage and skill have dealt a crucial blow to our enemies in Trin-Ma. Soon we will drive forward into the north and burn the rats out of their holes! What no one else has been able to do, *we* will do, and take this city back!"

He may as well have called Khen and the Trini-son army useless, Chono thinks.

"I'm here to assure you, you have all my confidence and respect. You have my devotion, and I will remember what you have done here. Though these uprisings will soon take me to other corners of the Treble, to other fights where your kin will achieve more victories, know that I remain here with you in spirit!"

Screaming. Cheering. Chono and Masar look at each other.

Qlios warns, "He's leaving. This is a pit stop."

"We've got to go," Layez says.

"Where the *fuck* is Jun?" Chono hisses, sending her own angry casts toward Farren Eyce. Nothing answers.

Masar echoes Layez. "We have to go. This may be our only chance to—"

"We have no plan!" Chono snaps.

Suddenly Kess raises his arms again, quieting the crowd.

"But it is not the Kindom alone that will be responsible for our victory over our enemies. We owe much to our planetary allies. I applaud the Khens, who have prepared the ground for our assault today. And I applaud another family, whose matriarch has proved true loyalty to our cause!"

Chono thinks that Oyun Paiye, the head of the Paiye family, must have allied with him. But Kess gestures down the steps of the plinth, and her blood runs cold. A figure emerges from the crowd of guardsaan and cloaks. Tall, and proud, and smiling that arrogant smile at everyone around them as they jog up the stairs toward Kess.

"Six," she whispers.

Six Six Six Six Six—

"Now," Masar snarls. "We go now."

Chono's ears are ringing, but she can see the saan around her grabbing up their guns, slinging on their packs. She snaps into action, helping Masar shove the sideboard away from the door. He yanks the door open, leveling his shotgun at the alley. Chono, never a riflesaan, grips her handgun so tight that her palm burns, and her soul burns, and all she can see is Six striding up to Kess—

They move as one into the alley. They check their position and dart across a common road too exposed for Chono's liking. They dodge rubble and enter another backstreet, moving swift and quiet. Masar casts instructions at their oculars:

We take the next four alleys east. We'll come up on their perimeter.

Chono fights to pay attention, her thoughts racing. *Why is Six in the courtyard? Why were they smiling? Why were they walking toward Kess as if he is a friend?*

Masar casts:

The first guards we find in a vulnerable position, we ambush them.
Wait for my signal.

Even over her ocular Chono can read the doubt in him, the understanding that a few guardsaan uniforms and tracking Kess to his shuttle is as likely to work as throwing a net over him in the courtyard and hightailing it for the nearest shelter. But they must try something. Six is there. Six will help—

They're getting closer now. They can hear the crowd in the distance. The streets are empty of civilians and fighters. They cross square concrete parks and dart down narrow alleys between apartment buildings. The last of these puts them just two blocks from the God's Courtyard, from Kess, from Six—

Jun's voice suddenly roars in their ears—

"Stop! Stop! It's a trap! The broadcast is fake! It's a trap!"

CHAPTER FOUR

1665

YEAR OF THE HARVEST

Trin-Ma
Trini-so Continent
The Planet Teros

Chono is already two feet out of the alley when the gunfire starts. Masar has half a moment to process the smatter of bullets striking the ground at her feet before he grabs hold of her collar and hauls her backward. Layez and Qlios take flanking positions, firing into the square.

"Where are they?" Qlios shouts. "I can't see anyone!"

The square fills with dust and smoke, like a tentacled creature crawling into the alley toward them, blocking their vision.

Masar orders, "Back! Back!"

They have almost reached the opposite end of the alley when its entrance, too, turns to dust and sparks and an onslaught of gunfire peppering the earth.

He calls out to Jun again, "We're trapped in an alley. Who can you see? If one side is better guarded, we can try to go the other way."

Jun says, "Hold on. I can't see anyone!"

Chono grimaces. "They're Hooded."

His guts wither, remembering that Six traded the Hood program to Seti Kess in exchange for help rescuing Chono. A fool's bargain. A cloak to hide cloaks from view. Before Masar can respond to Chono, the gunfire on both sides stops and a loudspeaker echoes through the alley.

"Cleric Chono. We have set traps for you across the city. You are surrounded."

Chono's face hardens with the same fury Masar feels in himself.

The loudspeaker continues. "Cleric Chono, the First Cloak Seti Kess has given us orders to take you alive, but we have no such orders for your companions. Surrender without incident or they will die."

"Fuck that," Layez hisses. "Let's shoot our way out!"

"We have grenades," Qlios adds.

Masar tries to think. Chono is the only valuable one here. It was pure folly to try to get to the God's Courtyard, to think they could find Kess among his armies. Masar looks at Chono. He wants to live. He wants Layez and Qlios to live. But in the end, is her life worth more than theirs? If he can make sure she's taken alive, maybe she can escape. Maybe she can still help his people.

Chono's eyes are wrathful and helpless. He is suddenly sure that she will make the right decision, the decision that puts the many over the few. It's a decision he can't make alone.

"Tell me what you want to do," he says.

Her nostrils flare. She opens her mouth, stalls, and in that moment a projectile sails into the alley. Masar thinks for a split second that it's a crowd-killer grenade. Next moment, his vision whites, his ears deafened by a *crack-bang*. An impact vibration knocks him onto his back like a child swatted by a giant. Around him he can feel the others collapsing as well, limbs clumsy and entangled. Masar has a thought for the grenade on his own belt, but in his disorientation, he might as likely lob it at the ceiling of the alley as at their attackers.

He's not sure how long he lies there. The ringing in his ears that started as a pitch too high to penetrate dips just low enough that he can suddenly hear more gunfire. He's not sure where it comes from, how close it is. His vision is all shadows and vague shapes. Is Qlios shooting at someone? Are the cloaksaan killing his collectors? He tries to blink sight into his good eye, thinking with every breath that hands will grab him or a bullet will take him out. The shooting continues, but now he can hear that it's not happening in the alley. There's shouting—lots of shouting, loud warbled voices growing slowly clearer.

"Left left left!" says a high, Braemish voice, and moments later, "Take that, fucker!"

Masar forces himself to sit up, rubbing at his face and his ears with shaking hands. He feels like he's swimming through grayness, thick as extinguisher mist.

Some other voice shouts, "Clear!"

Has the shooting stopped? One more spurt of it seems to come from his right, before the voice he heard before says, "Easy, kittens! That big one's got a shotgun!"

Masar realizes belatedly that he's holding his shotgun and aiming it in the direction of some shapes at the end of the alley.

"Som's ass, don't shoot at us, we just saved your asses! Hey, you, don't point that gun at me! We're here to help, swear, and there's not a lot of time to waste. Is it just the four of you? Ah, shit, are you a Braem?! Us too! Fucking small world, nah?"

Whoever it is speaks faster than gunfire, and sounds so incongruously cheerful and excited that it actually prompts Masar to lower the muzzle of his shotgun. A shortish, thinnish figure has approached them. There are other figures behind them. Masar can make out the shapes that are Chono, Qlios, and Layez, too. Layez is muttering curses.

"Ya all right? Can you walk? Sorry we couldn't get to you before the flash-bang, but that's how shit goes sometimes. You don't *look* Braemish. Oh, wait, you do, sorry about that. Anyway, you all really gotta get up. Reinforcements and shit. Nobody looks like they're dying. Wait, you only got one eye. Is that, like, a new thing?"

Masar thinks he's about to shoot just to get the person to stop asking questions. They lean closer, and Masar registers a slip of a girl grinning just shy of maniacally, teeth big and bright as a predator's. She has Braemish tattoos all over her chin and cheekbone, her hair full of long lavender-dyed braids. There's a black mourning band strapped to her bicep, but she looks the furthest thing from mourning of anyone he's ever met.

"There you are!" she says, perhaps understanding that Masar can see her clearly now. "Comin' around? What about you lot?" She looks at the others. Masar is relieved to see that everyone is sitting up. They look disoriented but not hurt. The girl nods approvingly. "Come on, kittens, let's get them on their feet."

Masar flinches when hands reach for him, but all they do is guide him and the others onto slightly shaky legs. Masar has enough of his vision and awareness back to realize that he is standing in a circle of seven young pirates, all strapped with guns and grenades and looking as cheerfully maniacal as their leader.

In a voice raw with smoke, Chono asks, "Who are you?"

"A bunch of friendly faces in the crowd," the lavender-haired girl answers. "Lately of the *Steel Cat* crew. Fucking cloaks took her from us, but we've got some revenge in mind. I'm Mix Catty! Now, can you walk or not? Actually, running would be best. Those saan have got friends coming for sure."

Masar takes in his comrades. "We can run."

The girl's eyes shine. "Excellent!"

But Chono asks, "Run where? We don't know you."

Catty's jaw drops in overdramatic shock. "After all this? Here I thought you'd be jumping to bless me instead of questioning my motives. For shame, Cleric. You've got a better reputation than that!"

"Now listen—" Masar starts.

"You know those fuckers who just tried to kill you? Well, we work with the fuckers who *aren't* trying to kill you. Now, either you come with us or you don't, but if you don't, you're gonna have guardsaan all over you. So, whattaya say? You in the mood to be rescued or not?"

Her bright-eyed bravado is disorienting, but that might just be the flash-bang. Masar and Chono exchange a look, Chono giving a curt nod.

"Brilliant," Mix Catty says. "Come on."

She and her friends set out at a trot, leading them toward the square where they were originally cut off. As the alley opens up, Masar sees eight dead guardsaan, three of whom seem to have fallen from sniper positions in the windows above. No cloaks. Are there any cloaks in Trin-Ma, or was that just part of the illusion?

"See how good we did?" the young pirate says. "We got six more on the other side. You all were fucked is what. Keep low and come on."

Fleet-footed and merry, Mix Catty and her crewsaan take a wide, circuitous route around the city center, which Masar never sees with his own eyes but from which he hears sounds that don't add up to the thousands of guards and cloaksaan he saw on cast. Eventually they slip through the gap between the north and south, never spying a single enemy. The Braems toss them frequent encouraging grins, hold fingers up to their lips to order silence, point out potholes and other stumbling blocks, and, most importantly, warn them of the various unexploded mortars across the city. Masar sweats through his clothes every time they go around one. But within ten minutes, the Braems lead them into the ruins of a bombed-out factory. Masar calculates that they are about a mile north of the folk pharmacy, and well into the Kip-Kipsi neighborhood. Inside, a damaged stairwell leads to a sublevel floor, and deeper still into the network of tunnels beneath Trin-Ma that he's heard so much about.

"Well done," Mix congratulates them. "None of us even lost a limb! Come on, now."

In no time, the tunnel opens up into a cramped room. About a dozen serious-looking saan are bent over various occupations, from cooking something on an electric stove to sorting through ammunition clips to, in the case of about five of them, standing around a table and pointing things out on the map cast above them. Other hallways branching off from the room must lead deeper into the underground. Everything has the filmy dust of a constantly shaken foundation, which hardly puts Masar at ease.

The Braems make a lot of noise coming inside, and many heads turn to face them as their leader calls out, "Hey! Look what we caught!"

Masar bristles at the phrasing, and more so when the looks he gets shift from indifference to curiosity to shock. Most of the saan in the room are staring at Chono, recognizing her, but a few look at him and his collectors with a different kind of recognition. Masar zeroes in on one of the figures at the table, instantly recognizing the rugged, scar-pocked face, and the black hair in a topknot. This is Zemit, the rebel leader Graisa told them to find.

"Gods and fire," Zemit says, moving toward them. He glances past Chono to briefly look at Masar, Qlios, and Layez. Masar is at least relieved to see no open hostility before he refocuses on Chono. "There were rumors that you had jumped to Teros System, but with the gates so heavily guarded..."

Chono replies with her typical stoicism. "We have ways of moving undetected."

Zemit lights up with realization. "You mean the Sunstep Hood!"

Chono hesitates, then inclines her head. Zemit smiles broadly. He is quite young behind the scars. Indeed, most of the fighters in the room are as young as Mix Catty and her friends. They look at Chono as if they've seen an apparition of the Godfire, excitement permeating the room. Not for the first time Masar feels a hot wash of exasperation. These kids revere her for coming back to the Treble and challenging the Kindom, but she wasn't even a crucial fighter in the battle on *The Risen Wave*. She spent most of it dying. As for bringing back the data flood that sparked so many of the rebellions in the Treble, it was Jun and the Jeveni and Six who compiled most of that evidence. Before all this, the only thing Chono had to distinguish her was Esek Night-foot's favoritism. Hardly worth bragging about.

Zemit turns eagerly toward Mix and her crew. "Where'd you find her?"

"Tryin' to get herself killed down south. Looks like they fell for that performance in the God's Courtyard."

Masar stiffens, but Zemit only nods, grave and understanding. He explains to Chono, "They've been doing things like that the past couple of days. With the casting blocks up, we can only get intermittent access to the city's cameras. They feed us fake intel, make it look like there's a huge force invading from one direction, and try to catch us unawares from another. We only trust our eyes these days."

"We heard artillery," Chono says. "And the sounds of an army in the city center."

He nods again. "There was an attack this morning. About a hundred Kindom guardsaan invaded the God's Courtyard, but they used holographic tech to make it look about ten times as big as it was. We figured out pretty quick that the Kess performance was fake. They were trying to lure us out with big bait."

Masar's skin prickles with shame to think that these rebels saw through the trap that took him in so easily. The desperation to capture Kess made him sloppy. They could all have been killed, and then what?

Chono says, "They weren't trying to lure you out. They suspected that I was in Trin-Ma. The trap was for me."

Zemit asks, "How do you know? Why would Kess assume you're here?"

"Because he has something we need." She clears her throat. "And someone I want."

Fucking Six. As if that little shit matters at all right now. But Zemit nods with understanding. "You mean Esek Nightfoot? But the rumors are you cut ties at Nikapraev. I just figured she abandoned you."

Of course he would figure this. Six's true identity is not known in the Treble. But though Six-as-Esek spent their tenure in Praetima defying the Kindom and demanding justice for five thousand imprisoned

Jeveni, Masar doubts that the majority of the Treble took it seriously. Not given Esek's reputation. They would have assumed she had some long game and that betraying Chono was just the next step.

Chono says, "It's complicated."

Mix Catty pipes up. "We were sneaking around the gap when we noticed guardsaan setting up ambushes. Gave me the tingles, you know? Why would they lay traps there when they know we're in the north? Then these fools"—a nod at Chono—"broke out of an alley and started moving toward the God's Courtyard. Thought we should figure out who they were. One of the ambushes caught them out, but we were there to save the day. Right?"

"Hey-oh-hey!" chorus her crew.

Zemit laughs a little, repeating back, "Hey-oh-hey," before stepping closer to Chono. They're only a couple of feet apart. Masar, who feels absolutely no protectiveness toward her whatsoever, goes tense all the same. "So, it's true," the boy says.

Chono looks back at him for a hard second and repeats, "True?"

"You've broken with the Kindom once and for all. You're joining our fight."

Chono hesitates. "I understand that there's contact between the different rebel strongholds. That you're allying with insurgencies in the other systems."

He nods. "That's right. The days of individual fights are over. We're a quorum now, everybody equal."

"I need to speak to this quorum. To your leaders."

Zemit earnestly agrees. "They'll want to speak to you, too. Fires, but you're a gift from the gods themselves!"

Chono goes stiff as a stone effigy. "I wouldn't be so sure."

"But you are!" he insists. "You don't know how much you'll inspire our fighters. More will join up when they see you're on our side. We're doing well in our little pockets of fighting so far, but morale is the life and death of a war, Cleric Chono. Not to mention you'll probably scare the Kindom off its ass!"

"I'm not a cleric anymore," Chono says with a bite of impatience.

His brow furrows. "That's not up to the Kindom, as far as we're concerned. And our fight is with the Hands, not the gods. I've been attending temple since I was born, and I serve the Godfire, same as you."

Masar watches Chono, curious how she'll react. The People's Kin. The righteous cleric. But when she says nothing, Zemit looks suddenly alarmed. "Or do you think the Godfire will punish us, for starting a war? We didn't start it, though, did we? The Kindom has been warring on us for centuries." He looks at Masar. "You're Jeveni. We know what the Kindom's done to you, too. Your people are still imprisoned in a labor camp on Ma'kess." He looks at Chono again. "The Godfire is just and fights corruption. That's what we're doing. Isn't it, Sa?"

Masar feels a charge, all the saan in the room waiting with bated breath for Chono's response. In amazement he realizes that if she withholds her approval, Zemit will view it as the Godfire's condemnation. The silence breathes with anxiety and hope. Then Chono, with all the authority of her long-held office, raises a hand in blessing over Zemit.

The whole room exhales. Zemit beams like a child, flush with the exhilaration of youth and purpose. Will the other generals in his so-called quorum be like him and Mix Catty? Or like the conniving Yantikye? And which would be better, in the long game of stopping Kess?

Chono says, "The Kindom knows now that I'm in Trin-Ma. Soon Kip-Kipsi will be crawling with cloaksaan. You and your people are in more danger than ever because I'm here."

Zemit frowns. "My people can hold the tunnels. We can protect you."

Chono shakes her head. "I'm sorry. We can't stay. Our mission is capturing Seti Kess, and he obviously isn't coming to Trin-Ma. We need to get out of the city and make another plan. And we need to meet your generals."

One of Zemit's companions steps forward, telling him, "We could take her inland. Kel-Ma is quiet and secure, and it hasn't got the blocks on it. It'll be easier to contact the quorum from there. You can have a proper conference. That's not possible here."

"I can't leave Trin-Ma," Zemit argues.

"You're wasting your time," Masar says. Everyone looks at him, per-haps surprised that he has a voice. "I respect how it started, but your people would be better off dispersing than trying to hold this city. Kess could level Trin-Ma with a few missiles. When the cloaks come, you'll be overrun, and a lot of kids will die."

He may as well have drawn his shotgun on all of them. They go rigid with anger, and Zemit looks stunned. With her first sign of tem-per, Mix Catty snaps, "There are no *kids* here. I'm braided tight, same as you." She gestures around at the room. "All these saan are."

Masar takes in the ten or so braids in her wild lavender mane, a kill count signal among her people. There was a time when Braems derided Masar because his skin wasn't as light as theirs—now they're fight-ing alongside Terons, and probably saan from other planets. How long will such alliances last?

Chono interjects in a gentle murmur, "We meant no offense. And we understand that you can't simply give up this fight." She glances sidelong at Masar, a rebuke. "You love your home. You want to defend it. I want it defended, too. But the key to ending this war is stopping Seti Kess. I understand if you can't leave Trin-Ma, but can you help us get out?"

Zemit shakes his head. "You'll do better with the generals if I'm with you in person." He looks over at his lieutenant. "You'll manage without me?"

"I will. Our saan will take heart knowing that you're with Cleric Chono."

"We'll be your honor guard," says Mix, anger apparently forgotten. "We'll get you out of the city and drop intel that you've left the conti-nent. Maybe the cloaks won't bother Trin-Ma after that."

Masar suspects the cloaks aren't so easily distracted, but he holds off saying so. Zemit explains to Chono, "I need to get the quorum's approval first, and I need to do it without you seeing any of them. I trust you, Sa, but if you're captured, it'll endanger us for you to know what we're doing. You and yours must be tired. Take some time to rest, and we'll come back together in a few hours." He looks them over more carefully, telling Masar, "Let us get you a patch for your neck."

He doesn't stay to see it done, walking off with his lieutenant. Masar, confused, touches his neck. It comes away with a smear of half-dried blood. He must have been hit by something. He doesn't remember. Layez and Qlios look scratched up but not badly injured.

Someone else from the group of rebels offers him a regenerative patch that looks like it came off the manufacturing line fifty years ago. Maybe Seti Kess's version of resource support was a bunch of expired junk. Irritably, Masar slaps the patch on, pulling up the collar of his jacket.

"I'd appreciate it if you didn't antagonize them," Chono says in a low voice.

He balks, and glares at her. She glares right back. Her eyes are like the metal on a ship's hull, gray and hard but also cool.

"I'm only telling them the truth."

"You disparaged the work they're doing here. How would you feel if they told you to give up Farren Eyce?"

Heat flushes his neck. "It's not the same."

"It's the same to *them*," she snaps, before visibly marshaling herself. "Just . . . let's try to stay on their good side. They're our only road out of here."

Before he can answer, Mix Catty swaggers up to them. "Let me show you your bunk, then we'll get some food in you. Good idea to sleep, too, while we figure out how to get you out of here. Won't be before tonight."

Happy to end the conversation with Chono, Masar gives Qlios and Layez a nod, and they all follow the pirate girl. She leads them through one of the hallways that branches off from the room, a long stretch with many doorways. Masar thinks of his ancestors, who labored in the mines under Jeve. It must have felt like this, walls close and cold, air dusty.

Mix plays tour guide, talking fast and gesturing expansively. "All this used to be a rent-out casting den. The factory above us was just a front for the real money they earned down here. Casters, damn—they like their burrows, don't they? But it's not so bad. You can get a little privacy and there's more than one bathroom. Bad plumbing, though, so watch it if you take a shit. And no warm water. Sorry. But anyway, we bunk up nice down here, and there's plenty of room for supplies. And no way for prisoners to escape."

Masar balks. "Prisoners?"

Mix gives a shrug, strolling ahead of them like a damn aristocrat touring her own property. "Sure. Can't have a war without prisoners."

Chono asks, "What use are prisoners of war to you? Kess won't give you anything for them. Neither will the Khens."

"Well, I've been telling Zemit to torture 'em for information, but he's squeamish like that. The other generals will change his mind, though."

Masar grimaces. Fucking Braems.

"Anyway, it's about symbolism. We make sure the wider Treble knows we can take hostages. Maybe we'll show mercy in the end. Maybe we'll execute 'em all. Not my decision, though. Here we are!"

She stops in front of an open if rickety door into a small room. It's barely big enough for the two pair of bunk beds and water basin. Whatever casting tech used to be in here, they've cleaned it out, and the mattresses and threadbare blankets look even older than the regenerative patch Masar slapped onto his neck.

Qlios walks in and sits on one of the bottom bunks, examining what looks like a bad scrape on his hand. Layez squeezes his shoulder before climbing up onto the top bunk and collapsing to the chorus of shrieking springs. Masar is ready to do the same when—

"Can I see them?" Chono asks.

Mix Catty looks confused. "See who?"

"The prisoners."

The girl raises her eyebrows. "I mean, sure. But why?"

"Call it a cleric's office."

Masar narrows his eye, not trusting this explanation.

Mix shrugs. "All right. I guess. Come on." She continues down the tunnel, Chono at her heels.

Masar signals Qlios and Layez to stay, then follows Chono. He mutters to her, "What are you thinking?"

She doesn't answer right away. "I'm thinking about Esek."

Well, there goes his single iota of goodwill. "Why?"

Chono takes a deep breath and lets it out. They go around a corner. "The only people who ever loved Esek were her novitiates. They loved her because they idealized her. Their idealization was misplaced, but she knew how to use it, to manipulate them into doing whatever she wanted them to do. She was charismatic. She was terrifying. And her novitiates would have done anything for her, even if it got them killed."

"You looking to emulate her?" Masar says with undisguised contempt. Even so, he thinks of Nikkelo, who was also charismatic. Who also inspired idealization. And who the collectors would have gladly died for, Masar included.

Chono says softly, "I'm trying to understand how dangerous I am."

Masar doesn't know what to say to that, doesn't even know what she means, exactly, but he doesn't get the chance to press it. The tunnel curves, delivering them to an open space like the room where they met Zemit. Masar is taken off guard by what he sees. There's no prison. Or at least, no prison door. Instead, a couple of Teron rebels stand guard while, against the wall, at least twenty prisoners sit with their hands shackled to a common metal chain that's bolted into the ground at several points. They look rough. They've been stripped of their armor and are all wearing variations of trousers and long-sleeved shirts covered in dust. Many of them are injured. There's an unwashed, sewagey smell, and in the dank lighting, the faces with their cuts and scrapes and dark-circled eyes lift toward the newcomers.

Chono stares at them for a count of five. Then, ignoring the armed rebels (who look at Mix in alarm and confusion) she kneels down in front of three of the nearest prisoners. They shrink from her, huddling closer to one another.

Her voice is low. "Would you like me to pray with you?"

Their expressions are blank. One says, "What?"

"I'll leave you alone if you want. But I was trained as a cleric of the Righteous Hand. If you want, I can pray with you to whatever god you prefer. I can also bless you."

Beside him, Masar hears Mix scoff. The Teron guards look affronted. After several moments, the prisoners nod. Masar watches in a fair degree of befuddlement as Chono begins to pray. Her voice, though soft, has a deep resonance he wasn't expecting, and it carries through the room. Everybody watches her. After a few minutes she moves on to another group of prisoners, giving a couple of blessings this time, and then another group, who ask for a prayer to the Godfire. As this continues it begins to dawn on the group of them who she is. The change in the room is remarkable. Though they remain wary, they seem as awed to see her in person as Zemit was. While they murmur along with her prayers, they look at her in varying states of fear, disbelief, and amazement.

When she gets halfway down the group, some instinct prompts Masar to follow her, keeping his distance but always ready to swing his shotgun off his shoulder. Within fifteen minutes she's reached the end of the line, and this time she kneels in front of a single prisoner, who seems to have kept himself apart from the others, and who, at her arrival, lowers his head. His hair, far from the usual jet black of Terons, has been bleached yellow and cut in what Masar thinks might have been a fashionable way, before all the dirt and grime got in it.

"Gods keep you well, child," Chono says. "Can I pray for you?"

He hesitates a long time, and finally says, "Yes. Pray... pray to wily Terotonteris."

"Of course," she says, and begins. " 'Risk all for us, our boisterous god. Fill us with your laughter and your glee. Let our enemies sit down to your cups, and get drunk, and we will all be happy together, and fight no more. Gambler. Glutton. Clever lover of life, give us life, and we will toast your name until we die.' "

The blond Teron murmurs this last bit along with her. Masar thinks this will be the end of it, but to his surprise Chono reaches out, putting her thumb and pointer finger under the man's chin and lifting his head up. He has dramatic, beautiful features under the filth. At her touch, he startles, but returns her gaze. His color blanches. Does he think she's going to hurt him? She doesn't hurt him. She looks at him for a long moment, with no expression. Gently, she touches his chin to turn his face a little, taking him in from a different angle. With a small nod, she lets him go and stands.

They all watch her walk back up the hall, though when Masar glances back at the blond Teron, he's breathing heavily. Masar catches up to Chono as she reaches Mix Catty, who looks baffled.

"What is it?" Masar asks.

Chono speaks very low to Mix. "I need to see Zemit right away."

Mix raises her eyebrows, shrugs, and strides off, as if this whole day has been a succession of cheerful adventures and she's happy to keep it going. Chono doesn't dawdle in the hall. As soon as they've left the prisoners behind, Masar asks again, "Chono. What is it?"

This time, she stops. She looks distracted, almost nervous, which is an expression Masar hasn't seen on her face before. Finally she admits, "I recognize that prisoner. He's not a soldier."

When she doesn't immediately say more, Masar grunts, "Well? Who is he, then?"

She hesitates, as if she's considering not telling him, not telling anyone, and Masar's just about to lash out in impatience when—

"That is Khen Vorkhen Soon. He's the heir to the Khen family."

Our kin cloak who is secreted among the Nightfoot clerks can confirm great unrest in the family regarding the future matriarch. Alisiana Nightfoot's staunchest allies appear to respect the letter of her will, though not happily. However, Torek Nightfoot has his own loyalists, who are secretly debating how to enforce a traditional succession. I have placed servants around Esek Nightfoot to ascertain her temper, but she is largely focused on the aftermath of the sacking of Verdant, and spends her days clearing debris. My spies report that she often sings and whistles.

excerpt, report to First Cloak Seti Moonback.
Dated 1663, Year of the Trick.

CHAPTER FIVE

1665

YEAR OF THE HARVEST

Somewhere

They wake, alive.

They shouldn't be alive. No, they... they died—didn't they die?

Yes. Esek killed them, in the humid lower levels of the Verdant tower with the smell of smoke wafting into the room and blood filling their mouth, covering Esek's face, her ear between their teeth—she killed them.

So, why are they alive? Why is there a voice, not Esek's voice, saying somewhere—

"She's coming around." Someone else says something back, quiet but authoritative, vaguely familiar. The first voice is clipped and professional. "She's not strong enough to sit up, let alone fight, but yes, the bindings are secure." Another murmuring response, and an apologetic "Of course, Riin Matri..."

Alisiana. It must be her voice in the background, in their head, reminding them, *You'll die underground. Everything you want will fail.*

Their fingers twitch. They can feel their body again, heavy as a stone. There's pain, though it's muted, localized to a half dozen dully throbbing areas. Their shoulder, their back, their leg. Not their ear, though. Shouldn't their ear hurt? Didn't Seti shoot them in the head?

Seti!

Did he...? No. *No,* it was Esek. Wasn't it?

"Sa Alanye," the first clipped voice says, and the word, the name, hits them like the electric spark of a baton, bolting lightning through their nerves and veins. Their body locks, their lungs seize. Their mouth is full of saliva and they want to kill something, because the voice is speaking to them and that is *not* their name. "Please try to remain calm. Your injuries are healing well. You should expect some weakness and pain, however—"

The second voice, Alisiana's voice, says. "Leave us." Her tone is measured and exacting.

"Riin Matri, I wouldn't suggest—"

"You are my medical adviser. You don't advise me on how I deal with prisoners. Leave. And never call her by that name again, if you want to live."

Six tries to lift their arms and pull against the bindings—wrists and ankles. They find a touch of vulnerability in the one on their left wrist. They turn their wrist, slowly and carefully, aware of a blanket covering it. Small favors. They assess the rest of themself. They are drugged but the drugs are wearing off, fuzzy senses beginning to sharpen, though it's like pushing against a dark current. They are swathed in bandages. They can't see and they don't know why.

Someone leaves the room. Someone approaches the bed. It must be Alisiana, her presence like a cold front to their left. Her voice in their head, asking, *Are you that little flea Esek has been hunting?*

She says, "You can open your eyes. There's no point being coy."

They realize that, in fact, their eyes *are* closed. Something is wrong with Alisiana's voice. With their whole body pulsing to the rhythm of healing medicines, they open their eyes.

It is not Alisiana standing beside the bed. Of course it isn't. Alisiana is dead. Six killed her, they killed Esek, they killed—

"How are you feeling?" Riiniana Nightfoot asks.

Six stares at her. There are halos of light in the air, nearly obscuring the gray walls and medical equipment, nearly obscuring her, until she leans a little closer. Six squints, disoriented. They last saw Riiniana while parlaying with the Nightfoot family from their lavish hotel room in Praetima. Though "saw" overstates it. She was a tiny, timid figure flanked by powerful saan. Torek Nightfoot, her guardian, didn't even try to hide the puppet strings he'd sewn into her. She was Riin Matri in name only—*he* was the real power behind the matriarchy, and Riiniana was all anxiety and eagerness to please. She never spoke. *What a wretched little orphan she is*, Six had thought, not without pity. Her mother a suicide, her grandmother a useless mods addict. Her great-grandmother, Alisiana, had had no time for her. Thus was she remanded to Torek's custody. He was a distant cousin with the honorary title of uncle. A man happy to control a girl. But where is Uncle Torek now? Why is he not supervising his ward?

Six opens and closes their eyes as if they could blink an invisible Torek into visibility. But it is only Riiniana there. *Quick. What else do you remember about her?* Fifteen years old? Not sixteen, surely. However petite, she is not the washed-out wraith that stood in Torek's shadow a few days ago. Her skin seems pale by nature rather than illness. Always illness, with Riiniana Nightfoot. A life on the seaside of Praediis continent, if Six remembers rightly. Many doctors. Low expectations. It was she who turned the sevite trade over to the Kindom last year—or at least, who did so when her uncle told her to. An obedient, easily manipulated child.

She doesn't look so easily manipulated now. Her light blue eyes study Six, and Six studies her back. The feeling in the air is like when a wave pulls out, the ocean dragging itself up, climbing toward a break.

Finally, rasping, Six tells her, "I feel fine."

Riiniana Nightfoot's small-lipped mouth twitches. There's no warmth in it, but the amusement is genuine. Quiet confidence in her gaze, in her posture.

"What do you remember?" she asks.

A driving rain and a dark courtyard. Pain in their lungs and an arm hanging limp. Knee blown out, body sprawled onto the hard cobblestones. Seti Moonback standing over them with a gun and asking—

Where is Chono?

The name drives a stake through them, more than that ass Alanye's name. The drugs are still in their system and the pain is getting worse, so that must be why they don't have the self-control to withhold a low snarl. What must Riiniana see in their face, to make her look at them with tilted head and frank curiosity?

Six claws themself back from the edge of panic, breathing shallowly through their teeth and ignoring her question. Riiniana looks them up and down. She exhales. "It *is* strange, to see you like this. You might like to know, it was very expensive getting Seti to bring you to me instead of killing you. Ironic, too, given I contracted him and his... ogre of a right hand to assassinate you on *The Risen Wave* last year. I think he was happy to get a second shot. But things have changed. I need you alive."

Six blurts a laugh, and starts coughing so hard that they taste blood. Riiniana watches them struggle. When they can breathe again, they spit blood and mucus over the side of the hospital bed, and look at her balefully.

"*You* contracted an assassination?"

"I did. Three years ago I discovered that Alisiana and Esek were in negotiations for Esek to inherit the sevite trade. I couldn't allow that."

Six ponders this salvo of revelations. Anyone would take it for recklessness. Six doesn't think it's recklessness, though. More like a frank introduction. Nevertheless they say with some contempt, "Your minder couldn't allow it, you mean."

Riiniana's smile is chilly. "No. That is not what I mean."

"Three years ago you would have been what? Twelve?"

"Alisiana Nightfoot had spies at nine. Why shouldn't I?"

Six snorts. "Alisiana was another breed."

"Like you?" she asks. "Weren't *you* another breed at nine, Sa?"

Six at nine was a kinschool student, already outwitting and out-fighting students several years ahead. Six at nine had no ambition but to be a cloaksaan. They had not met Esek yet. But Six at twelve could certainly have uncovered a plot to disinherit themself. Six at twelve could have ordered an assassination. As for Six at fifteen, the age of the girl in front of them—they, too, could have stood in a hospital room, loomed over a captured target, and flaunted their power in this cool way.

Riiniana says, "I apologize for my doctor calling you Alanye." The name sears them. They don't react. "Given that all your official idents list you as Esek Nightfoot, there's no reason not to call you so. But of course there are your genetic records, which tell a different story."

Genetic records. Of course. Six's one insurmountable obstacle. They could make themself Esek's doppelgänger and pay Ilius Redquill to manage the paperwork, but they could not change the blood in their veins. They don't respond to Riiniana's statement, wary of giving her anything that she might not have figured out yet. She seems unperturbed.

"It's very impressive," she says, eyes skating over them as if they were a piece of art in a gallery. "Grotesque but…impressive. I assume you killed Esek. Was *she* impressed?"

Damn, you're good-looking! crows Esek in their memory, that night they met, that night she died. *Is this what you've been doing?*

"Yes," Six says. "I think she was impressed."

Another faint smile. "That is an accomplishment in and of itself. I only met my cousin once, and she of course had no interest in me. Apparently she had a lot of interest in you."

Under the blanket, Six rotates their left wrist, feeling the slack in the cord that binds them. They look past Riiniana into the outer room behind the glass door. The doctor and a nurse mill about anxiously.

Two guardsaan stand at attention. Six can see no other doors, no windows. They listen to the sounds, smell the air, for any sign of where they might be. Not a ship, they can tell. A planet? Riiniana's seaside home in Coral, perhaps?

Riiniana says, "I understand that Alisiana was threatened by you because you were an Alanye descendant, and that she set Esek to hunting you. My great-grandmother was a secretive person, but I found one or two references to you. You've caused some trouble for us in the past couple of decades, and particular trouble to Alisiana and Esek. That is, unless you want to argue that you did *not* kill them. Or even, that you are not the person Esek hunted, and that this"—she gestures at their whole person—"and the Alanye blood is all just...a coincidence."

Her tone is relaxed. Well, given Esek and Alisiana conspired to take her birthright, it's unlikely that she wants revenge for them. So, what *does* she want? She is not the person that her family thought she was. Perhaps the better question is, what can Six get from her?

Chono Chono Chono...

"I wonder why it was so expensive to purchase me from Moonback. Surely my 'Alanye blood' lowered the price? Any other specimens he's selling right now?"

She ignores the bait. "Moonback is called Kess now. And he doesn't know about your blood."

That's a surprise. How has Riiniana kept the truth from him?

"You won't win his friendship by keeping secrets," Six chides her.

"And we both know how much friendship means to you, don't we, Sa?"

The words kick. Riiniana's eyes glint with the satisfaction of playing a good tile. She edges closer. "In the spirit of friendship, let me give you a gift." Under the blanket, Six's twisting wrist pauses. "Cleric Chono escaped Praetima. She is alive."

Six controls their reaction, but they feel a little weak with relief, and the pain worsens. Their chest and lungs burn, the leftover blood in their mouth salty and sour with iron. Riiniana has the face of a strategist.

"Does that relieve you, Esek?" she asks.

Their wrist is very nearly free of the stretched loop of the binding.

"Why call me that, when you know—"

"You are of absolutely no value to me as Alanye. But you are very valuable as Esek. Not as the cleric Esek, of course. I despise clerics and have no use for them. But as the *matriarch* Esek."

Six huffs scornfully, and coughs hard. Through rasping breaths they say, "I should think it would behoove you to expose me. You can argue my will is fake and stop the trade from going to the Jeveni."

She raises her eyebrows. "Ah, yes. The fantastical will. My clerks have looked into it. It's very impressive. Even if I prove you're not her, the outcome could remain the same."

Six's lip curls. "Seti Moonback—Seti *Kess*—slaughtered the Secretaries. He literally cut off the hand of the law. I doubt he'd stop you from rejecting the will."

"Do you not wonder where Torek is?"

The question surprises them. "Should I wonder?"

"I think you are a very dangerous person, Sa. And I think part of your danger is that you know how to manipulate people. You certainly manipulated Alisiana and Esek. That's a gift. A gift we have in common."

"What does that—"

"Torek was useful to me, for a long time. Manipulating him was useful to me. Standing behind him and doing the work that needed doing, with him for a mask—it prepared me for this. But Torek can't take me the rest of the way. I need Esek for that. So. Torek is dead. And Esek is alive."

Six can't help imagining that Esek is here now. Her sparkling eyes and her delighted laughter and her long, elegant body leaning forward to whisper in their ear, *Gods and fire, what an entrance she's making! What do you think? Will we have to kill her?*

"How did you kill Torek?" they ask.

She replies easily. "He died in his sleep three nights ago. I am in mourning, naturally."

Poison, no doubt. Six takes in the black band around her upper arm, an accoutrement of grief, like how Terons shave their heads. Like how Chono shaved her head. Six gives Riiniana a slow, cool smile. "I killed Alisiana with poison."

"Yes, I thought so. I don't think Esek would have been subtle enough to do it that way."

"No, Esek was not subtle."

"But *you* are, aren't you, Sa?"

The binding has stretched enough that it now sits under their thumb instead of cinching their wrist. Six says, "Let me make sure I am clear on this. It never hurts to be explicit. You have been playing a game behind the scenes, using Torek as your puppet while he pretended to use you. And now you want to use *me*. Esek the matriarch. Is that right?"

"Yes," she says.

"Surely you want the matriarchy for yourself. Why not just take it?"

She's closer than ever. She's right next to their bedside, gazing down at them. Her calm facade cracks for just a moment, showing a deep well of greed. "I have my reasons."

Six raises their head off the pillow, closer to her, and whispers, "And what *reason* would I have to cooperate, Bright Daughter? Why would I so much as lift a finger for your sake?"

They have used the honorific of a Nightfoot heir, and they see the appreciation in her eyes. She whispers back, "For one...I won't have your cleric murdered."

Six's hand slips free. With one darting movement, they have her by the wrist—

And find themself, suddenly, with a bloodletter against their throat.

The girl is now half bent over the hospital bed, their faces only a few inches apart. She is breathing hard, but that is the only evidence of her nerves. From the corner of their eye, Six notes that she has a good grip on the bloodletter—and she drew it impressively fast, moving with the economy of one who has been trained. If they weren't so damned weak, she probably couldn't have gotten the drop on them.

But even grabbing her wrist sent a shock wave of pain through Six. They conceal it under a bared-teeth mask, flexing their fingers. Her forearm twitches; she grimaces against the discomfort. Six could snap her wrist, break it in such a bad way that she would be too stunned with agony to cut their throat.

But Six glances past her again, into the other room, as voices rise and the two guardsaan bolt inside, guns trained—

"No!" Riiniana snarls. "Stand down!"

"Riin Matri—" one of them objects.

She keeps staring into Six's eyes, and Six stares back, ignoring the guards.

"Don't be a fool," Riiniana whispers. "I know better than to leash you with threats alone. I am utterly indifferent to whether Chono lives or dies. But if I can have her killed, I can protect her, too. You are half-dead in a hospital room. Don't you think you could benefit from someone else protecting her?"

They twist their grip. She whimpers sharply. One of the guards begs for permission to shoot, but she grits her teeth harder and demands, "What happens if you don't let go? At most, you break my wrist and are no better off. At worst, I slip this knife through your throat and you die knowing a Nightfoot brat took you down."

"It is not a *knife*," Six says.

"Oh, I know. It is Esek Nightfoot's bloodletter."

Despite everything monumentally more important than this information, Six's eyes flick to the blade again. They killed Esek with it. They won it off her, and it's theirs, and Seti Kess stole it from them weeks ago. They want it back.

"You think the worst I can do is break your wrist, Bright Daughter? Have a care for your throat." They click their teeth at her.

She swallows. She is either fantastically brave or suicidally confident. "I bought this weapon from Kess, same as I bought you. I can buy other things, Esek. It's at least in your best interest to hear me out, don't you think?"

Six chuckles. This close, they can see the unnatural purity of the girl's pale blue eye mods. Her constricted pupils make the blue more luminous, make her eyes seem bigger. More innocent. She is not innocent, but she is also not quite as smart as she thinks. Goading them as she has? Getting this close? Thinking she's safe because of power and money and a bloodletter she bought like it was some trinket at a fair? Not smart. She has a long way to go to become Alisiana Nightfoot.

But Six is injured. Their neural link is a blank space in their head, cut off from the casting net. They still don't know where they are or where Chono is or how to reach her...

They let go of Riiniana, exaggerating the action, making it theatrical in a manner worthy of Esek herself. They relax against their pillow again, away from the point of the bloodletter, and Riiniana, swallowing hard, steps back. Her hand is shaking a little. She secrets the blade away and the two guards move closer.

"Let me break her legs," hisses one of them.

Riiniana makes a move to touch her sore wrist, and stops herself, drawing up to her full (if negligible) height. "Bring the doctor in here. Now."

One of the guardsaan backs out of the room. The other never takes her eyes off Six, who returns the look irreverently. Moments later, the doctor hurries in, wide-eyed.

"Are you all right, Riin Matri?"

"I'm fine," she bites out, and orders the guards. "You two. Get out."

They look almost desperate with objection. "Let us fix her bindings at least," says one.

"Get. Out."

They reluctantly obey, standing on the other side of the glass door and glaring in at Six. The doctor looks anxiously at Six's freed hand and keeps several feet away. Riiniana, however, looks them over with imperious eyes, as if Six is no better than merchant wares. Another trinket.

"How long before she can get out of this bed?" she asks the doctor.

"She's responded well to the regenerative medicine, but her internal injuries are still healing, and the broken bones and mods take time. I would say she needs another two or three days of intensive care before I'm comfortable with…" He trails off. Six doubts any amount of time would make him comfortable with letting them go.

Riiniana doesn't respond, distracted. She's pensively staring at the side of Six's head. "That ear," she says. "It's ghastly."

The doctor hedges, glancing between her and Six. "I…Yes, Riin Matri."

"Fix it," Riiniana says, and meets Six's eyes again, a challenge. Six gazes placidly back at her, though inside they feel the same jealous surge as when they recognized the bloodletter. This ear is *theirs*. "I want her fully healed. I want her pristine. We'll spread the word of her return to Verdant as soon as she's well."

Verdant, then. The ancestral Nightfoot estate.

"Yes, Riin Matri."

"Who among the staff know who she really is?"

He pauses long enough to swallow. His complexion grays. "Only me and the geneticist."

"Good. If anyone else finds out, I'll have them killed."

"Yes, Riin Matri."

"If you or the geneticist try to leave Verdant, I'll have you killed."

"Yes, Riin Matri."

"You said her bindings were secure."

A long, trembling silence. "I…believed they were, Riin Matri."

He sounds terrified. What has Riiniana done to make him terrified of her? Just days ago she was little better than an urchin in the eyes of those who knew her, and now the room radiates with her authority.

She tells Six, "Our collaboration will be a fruitful one. When you are well, we'll discuss my plans and you'll have the opportunity to give advice. In the meantime, I will protect Cleric Chono. Can I trust you not to attack my people?"

Six grins wolfishly, though there is no grin in their heart. In their heart, they are a wolf gone rabid, slavering with hunger. "Make it worth my while."

"Your Chono is not enough?"

"Your vague promises to protect her are not enough."

"Ask me for something, then."

Six doesn't have to think about it. There is only one thing they want. "Where is she?"

The girl says nothing for several moments, certainly weighing the value of the answer. "Teros. She arrived in a small town called Kel-Ma this morning."

CHAPTER SIX

1665

YEAR OF THE HARVEST

Farren Eyce
The Planet Capamame

When Jun wakes up, Liis is gone, the spot on the bed still warm but no light under the bathroom door. Jun rolls onto her back and studies the ceiling. She listens to the sound of her endlessly working casting hub and exhales through her nostrils. Should she get up? After she nearly fainted two days ago (sixteen hours spent in the net—forgot to eat; forgot to breathe), Liis put her under strict orders to have a six-hour rest period at least every twenty hours. If Jun breaks the rule, Liis will know somehow. She always does. It's not worth the fight.

Somewhere outside the room, the sound of a cupboard opening and closing. That'll be Bene. He always did wake up first.

It's been five days since Effegen convinced the Wheel to release Bene and some of the other prisoners under strict supervision. The parolees didn't commit any irrevocable violence, she argued. They were vandals, arsons, conspirators—but not killers. Not like Dom ben Dane, who murdered the collectors. Not like Ujan, who tortured Fonu sen Fhaan nearly to death.

Effegen was persuasive. Jun still marvels that she was persuasive. The prisoners have lost their neural link access. Sentries accompany them wherever they go. This includes daily shifts in the storage, waste management, and laundry facilities on Level 1—work that isolates them from the rest of Farren Eyce. It's as much for their protection as anything. There have already been incidents. Colonists throwing food, insults, slurs. No lynch mobs yet. But the worst may be yet to come.

Bene, who has been back in the apartment since his release, bears it all stoically. He's a quieter, wearier version of the young man she knew. Every day he leaves the apartment for work. Every day he goes to visit Ujan and Tej, who are still in the newsnest. Every night Jun returns late to the apartment to find him there. Often cooking. Godsdamned noodles, every time.

Jun eats the food. They barely talk.

Until last night.

She tries to remember the details that she couldn't process at the time. Bene's wide-eyed pain. His soft voice pleading with her for a way to make it right. But what could make it right? Bene thought she didn't understand what he had done. But Jun understands. She's not like the average colonist who thinks he conspired with his cousins to torture Fonu into giving them the gate key. She's not like the Wheel, who blame Bene for not contacting them the night that Ujan and Tej invited him to come to the airfield and see what they had done, join their cause, escape to the Treble.

"I was trying to help," Bene insisted to her last night. "I never hurt anyone. I swear to the gods, Jun, I thought if I played along, I could defuse it. I thought if I fought back, Masar would get killed, and you, too. I never would have hurt anyone!"

He thought she didn't know that. But Jun knows it. Jun understands very clearly the events as they occurred, and she knows that Bene could not have changed anything. Ujan had already caused mayhem in the colony, without his help. She had already tortured Fonu. She had already sent the key to Seti Kess. Bene could not have changed any of it.

"I wanted to protect them," said Bene beseechingly. "Maybe that's wrong, but even after I knew what they'd done, I just... I didn't want them hurt."

Another thing Jun understands. Jun spent her teenage years and adulthood trying to make enough money to rescue her family members from hiding and whisk them to a frontier station. She hacked and conned her way through the Treble for the sake of her little cousins, her aunt, now dead, her grandmothers, now dead. If Tej or Ujan or Bene had contacted her that night and told her what was happening, she would have tried to protect them, too.

But they did not contact her. Bene did not contact her.

"Stop looking at me like you think I'm going to hit you," she'd said, her voice barely under control, a hot pressure pushing at the edges of her, because what she really meant was that he didn't trust her. And maybe never had.

Worst of all was when Bene answered, "Do you *want* to hit me?"

Jun stared at him, her thoughts running a loop of Ujan striking him with a rifle butt. Liis, a quiet observer until now, said, "Bene. Don't be unfair."

"Then tell me what to do! Tell me how to fix it!"

His eyes were filling with angry, helpless tears, and she couldn't stand it. She couldn't stand to see him cry. She couldn't stand to tell him that he had hurt her, not by some betrayal of the colony, but by the betrayal of not reaching for her.

She left the kitchen and went into her room. She threw herself into her casts, built massive walls around her body, poured herself through a sieve so that all her pain was left behind and all that remained was Sunstep, a creature of the Black, the one who could do anything. Break through the firewalls around Ujan's tech and discover all her secrets. Mine those horrific programs and viruses for data, for clues to Ujan's correspondence with Seti Kess. Sunstep, who could rewrite the gate key, save Farren Eyce, save Bene, save all of them—

She only came out of it when she felt a hand on her body. Liis's hand, against the small of her back. Jun emerged like a diver breaking the surface. She gasped, blinking into awareness. How long had it been? Hours? Liis didn't say anything. She guided Jun into the bathroom and took off both their clothes. She stood with her under the hot shower spray, helping her to wash away the sweat, massaging the muscles that were cramped and sore from too much time in the net. Afterward Liis dried her and took her to bed and made love to her so gently, so slowly, that by the end Jun was shaking and sobbing and coming in a surge of grief-tinged pleasure, releasing like a wave until her body turned to surf, and she fell asleep, curled against Liis's body.

But now it is morning, and Liis has already left the apartment. Jun checks the time. Bene will be leaving for his shift soon. She looks at the bedroom door, at the sliver of light along the edge. It's not too late to go out and speak to him. Maybe Liis spoke to him before she left. They must have seen each other. Bene has been sleeping on the couch, ignoring his bedroom, as if something about it frightens him. She hears water coming on from the second bathroom. She thinks about being in the shower with Liis, the steam and the closeness, and one moment when it all seemed too much, and Jun started to flinch from her. But Liis had whispered in her ear, "I won't hurt you. I'll never hurt you."

Jun lays her head back on the pillow, relieved that Bene is in the shower and she has an excuse not to go and find him. She doesn't know what she'd say. She's not known for tact. She's not known for anything but her mind, which dares to be intelligent and oblivious at the same time. She failed to see what was happening with her cousins. She failed to stop Ujan from giving the gate key to Seti Kess.

But those failures could be paid back, if her infernal brain could just figure out how to rewrite a gate key in a fraction of the time it took to write it in the first place.

She imagines how it must have been for the original Jeveni casters. They wrote the code before *Drae's Hope* left for Capamame. A smart move. Anything could have happened in the journey across the Black. All the casters could have died. Casting knowledge could have eroded. The ability to create a reliable key might have been threatened by any number of complications. Better to write the key before they left. Better to test it against the gate core, which they had purchased in Teros System and out of which they would build the gate when they reached Capamame.

This is another challenge. Jun must contend with the idiosyncrasies of the gate core itself, that weird miracle of engineering, a heart that beats and makes the gate live. She projects a miniature model of her code-writing program into the air, as well as the core, represented as a small sphere. The key weaves in and out of it, filaments of power. Her own code, drawing from the existing key, writes something new that mimics but remakes the existing key. It can't be rushed. Rushing would tear the spiderweb threads of the task.

Dismissing the gate model, Jun casts a scan of Drae sen Briit's journal to her ocular. The journal was a bit of a pain to translate. Je is a difficult language to begin with, a strange grammar of idiom whose words and phrases have a dozen meanings, all reliant on speaker inflection. Translating all of this into written language was a feat even for Jun's translator bot, and Drae's journal posed a new problem. Je has changed, since Drae spoke it. Modern Je shows the effects of the Jeveni diaspora: dialectical shifts; new vocabulary; the influence of other Treblen languages. Jun had to adjust her translator to properly reflect this shift, and it wasn't like she had tons of time to lie around and diagram sentences.

Add to that, the fruits of her work have been negligible. Drae's journal has almost nothing useful to say about the gate key, or anything else for that matter. Drae herself is like her language: difficult and unfamiliar. She was a very intelligent woman, but also reticent. Not unlike Six. Her journal entries are extensive yet also economical. There are no personal revelations, no reference to family or friends. Jun knows that Drae and Lucos Alanye were lovers, but he only shows up three times over a span of ten years, and always in his capacity as a Nightfoot plant. Drae never mentions the two children she had by him, never names them in writing. She never even confirms that she was the River. Her entries are about her people and the work happening in the dome cities. Dry accounting of finances and supply stocks, of work shifts and bureaucracy.

It's probably a waste of Jun's time to keep reading and rereading, but for some reason she can't stop. There's something about the journal that mesmerizes her. Not just the accounts Drae gives but the writing itself, which she was surprised to find dotted with errors. Jun assumed it was a translation problem at first: converting one-hundred-year-old Je to modern Je and from modern Je to Ma'kessi had its costs. But she made adjustments, and still there are weird spelling mistakes and grammatical slips.

Drae sen Briit was human like the rest of us, Jun tells herself. *She misspelled words. She left typos.*

Maybe it's that, Drae's humanity, that eats at Jun. This woman is revered in Farren Eyce as a genius and a savior. People thought she could do anything. Some people think Jun can do anything. Neither she nor Drae is invincible. And so, writing mistakes. Yet these moments of discordance seem so antithetical to the meticulous woman Drae appeared to be. If anyone was ever going to proofread their own journal, it would be her.

Someone knocks on the door, and Jun feels as if she's been yanked back from a flame just before touching it. She checks the time. Over an hour has passed since she woke up, and she has no hours to spare. She calls out, "Hold on!" and reaches for the shirt and pants at the end of the bed. When she's dressed she says, "Yeah?"

The door creaks open. Bene's outline appearing against the lights behind him. With a squint, she sits up farther, and he leans in. They avoid each other's eyes, last night's fight simmering between them. She misses his smile. He was always a smiling person, warm and open—nothing like the blank expression he wore on that shuttle, as his younger cousins terrorized their captives.

"There's tea," he says cautiously. "And butter bread with jam. The bread's still warm."

Jun furrows her brow. "You went to the market?"

He smiles tentatively. "Pejun's mother makes it fresh every morning for that tea shop you like. She sent us some, with the jam."

Pejun is the sentry who accompanies Bene outside the apartment. He has always seemed pretty cold toward Bene, and his mother can't be thrilled about him guarding someone that half the colony would like to kill. Jun feels confused and irritated. "You sure it's not poisoned?"

Bene flinches. The trace of that hopeful smile melts off him. "I don't think she'd risk getting Pejun wrapped up in an assassination. Also, the bread's not for me. It's for you and Liis."

Jun wipes her hand down her face. "I'll be out in a minute."

He nods, and leaves.

After washing her face and brushing her teeth, Jun goes out into the room to find him pulling on his boots. The smell of the bread is delicious.

"Pejun is waiting," he says, turned away. "I'm gonna try at the construction site again."

Jun stops reaching for the bread knife. "What?"

"I can't just hide out on Level 1 doing storage management. I have to show the colonists that I want to work alongside them."

Jun pictures the workers on Bene's construction crew: muscular, no-nonsense saan with a talent for wielding hammers and axes. And Bene, strong as he is, is the smallest among them.

"I wasn't aware your work assignment was up for debate."

"I'll speak to Effegen about it."

"Is Effegen even talking to you?"

It's a low blow. Jun feels disgusted with herself. She remembers reuniting with Bene on *The Risen Wave*. She hadn't seen him in years. She thought her body couldn't possibly contain so much joy.

"I'm going," he says.

"Wait," Jun blurts. He looks at her cautiously. In a rush of courage she says, "Come here."

Still cautious, he approaches her. She thinks of that reunion that was more precious than all the jevite a moon can hold. She wonders if this hurt will ever be healed. What is the alternative? Drawing on her courage again, she grabs him and hauls him against her. She hears his sharp little sound of shock. The embrace is almost violent, hard enough it hurts, and he grips her back as tightly as she grips him. When they finally pull apart, she can't look at him. She feels better, somehow, but embarrassed. She struggles for something to say, but—

An alert in her ocular blares red, startling her so much that she falls back on her heels, adrenaline spiking. The alert—she knows that alert. She set that alert. She—

"Oh gods," she whispers, staring at the data that unfurls before her eyes.

Bene asks, sharp and worried, "What? What's happened?"

She images the jump gate over Capamame, pulsing like a throat that's just disgorged a bezoar, a congealment of toxins come here to poison them. And there it is, bright against the Black, glittery and fine-edged as a cloaksaan's bloodletter.

Bene is asking again what's happened when Effegen's comm reaches her like a shriek.

"Where are you?" the Star demands.

"I'm coming. You sec it?"

"We see it. Hurry."

Her voice chills Jun almost as much as the sight of the Kindom ship flirting with their atmosphere. It's a warkite, hardly the most threatening ship in Seti Kess's arsenal, but by the time Jun reaches the council room, an entire fleet may have come through.

Effegen cuts the comm just as Jun bolts for the door, ordering Bene, "Stay here!"

"Jun—"

She shoves boots onto her feet, shouting at him, "Stay here!" And shouting at Pejun, who stands outside in the hallway looking confused, "Keep him here! That's an order."

Then she runs.

She nearly stumbles more than once, bolting down the hallway past a few sleepy colonists just leaving their homes for work. She tears past faces she can't see, blood pounding in her ears, body jarred by every step. The last time she ran like this, she thought Masar was in trouble. She thought Bene was in trouble. She was running after the avatar, chasing it down in a desperate plea to protect Farren Eyce, to protect her cousins. She had no idea what she was really running toward, and only started to grasp it when Ujan came out of that shuttle cockpit, dripping gore.

The hallway opens into one of the communal spaces at the center of each of Farren Eyce's multiple levels. She ignores the elevator and hurls herself at the stairs. The council room is one level up, and she loses time, unable to grasp how long it takes her to reach the government district and, finally, the council room. She shoulders the door open, staggering inside. For just one strange moment, insensate with fear, she thinks she's going to find the spokes of the Wheel trussed up and bleeding to death. She thinks she's going to find Ujan, freed from her prison and crowing her delight.

Told you! imaginary Ujan chirps. *Told you Kess would come for me!*

But there is no Ujan. Almost a dozen people turn to look at Jun, though not Effegen and Liis, who are standing in front of a massive view screen, staring at the image of the warkite. Someone says Jun's name.

She ignores them to snap her fingers at the two casters in the room. She barks, "Now!"

They pass the information to her like balls in a game of Som's Catch. She dives inside. The warkite hangs before her in miniature, sleekly built and elegant like a poison-tipped arrow. Behind it, the recently activated jump gate pulses, but no more ships come through. Is the kite a scout? An attempt to test the playing field before the rest of the fleet arrives? Jun's fingers splay the kite by its wings, pin it, and slit it open to see what she can extract. There are thick layers of shielding, a wall between her and the Kindom data that will take several minutes to get through, but some things she can decipher at once—and it makes no sense.

"I'm not seeing the typical arsenal. I—it's definitely a kite, but—there's no sign of—"

Liis says, "No exterior guns."

Jun blinks rapidly, phasing out of the cast to see Liis wearing an expression that melds solemnity and dark humor.

"Some things you can find out just by looking."

Confused, Jun leaves her cast programs to do their work and returns to her body, stepping up to the view with furrowed brow. Liis is right. The ship, though it is a military class of warbird, lacks the massive tubular compartments on its left and right wings that house the main artillery. She's never seen a warkite like this: stripped of armaments.

"What the fuck?"

"It's a trick," Tomesk ten Ruvo declares. "They want us to lower our guard. They're hardly going to launch missiles at the colony! Mark my words, there are hundreds of warcrows in that bay."

Warcrows. Yes, smaller military shuttles could carry down as many as ten fighters apiece. Jun wonders why she was so certain of a fleet. The Kindom must think it can take them with a few battalions of cloaks. A ground invasion.

Liis says, "Warkites are not carriers. There are four crows in the bay at most."

"Perhaps they think that's enough!" says Gaeda ben Kist. She stands on Effegen's other side, glowering at the view and grasping the pommel of her cane with both hands. She snaps the ferrule against the ground. "They'll find us harder to take than that!"

"There are nearly eighty thousand people in this colony," says Effegen. Her voice, though flat, hints at irritation. "They're hardly going to round us up and take us back to the Treble with one warkite."

Hyre ten Grie says, "More will come."

Liis makes a pensive sound. "But not yet..."

Scouring the warkite's communication system, Jun observes, "They haven't tried to contact us."

"No need," Effegen murmurs. "Open communication. Tell them to identify themselves and explain why they've come to Capamame System without invitation."

Hyre's eyes widen. "Won't that antagonize them?"

Jun looks at Effegen, who gazes directly at the view. A muscle twitches in her throat.

It's Liis who answers, "Let it."

Jun sends the query, and the council room goes silent. No one breathes for several moments, until—

"They've asked to speak to us."

Effegen's expression is calm but hard. "Ujan said they don't know the faces of the other spokes. Everyone stand back. All eyes on me."

When they have obeyed, Jun opens a view screen. The person on the other end will only see Effegen. And the person *they* see, his visage flooding the air, is of course a cloak. But not Seti Kess. Jun expects coldness, hostility, threats—not the smile that greets them. He's a Katishsaan, the appliqué of a commandant on his pauldron. His congenial expression cannot disguise the predatory glitter in his eyes.

"Good morning," he says. "I am Commandant Yorus Inye of the Brutal Hand. You are Effegen ten Crost, I believe?" His tone is incongruously friendly, inappropriate in its warmth.

Effegen meets him with the poise and coolness of a disapproving elder. "I am."

"It's a pleasure to meet you," he says. Jun looks over at Liis, noting that sharp assessing look of hers. She knows him. "I did understand that you were one spoke of a five-person Wheel, Sa Crost. Are the other members of your council with you?"

Effegen answers, "Yes."

He pauses as if waiting for more, but gets nothing. Unperturbed, he bows over his open palms. "Then I extend my greetings to them, as well. And I can only assume you have other familiar faces among you. Jun Ironway, yes? And Liis Konye?" He says this with a flash of teeth.

"She, of course, prefers to stay out of sight. I remember studying her methods in kinschool."

Liis's flinch is imperceptible to all but Jun.

Effegen says, "Commandant Inye, you've come to the Capamame System without invitation. I assume you have a message for me from Seti Kess."

His eyebrows lift. "Without invitation? Are you suggesting that this system belongs to you?"

Effegen smiles thinly. "When the forebears of our civilization entered Ma'kessn space, they defined their arrival as the signal of their possession, a logic which has been foundational to the principles of the Kindom itself. If that logic holds, it certainly follows that Capamame belongs to its colonizers. Inasmuch as any place can belong to anyone. Wouldn't you say?"

He smirks, amused. He says in the tone of someone wishing to gentle a nervous animal, "I can see that my arrival has caused you some anxiety. It was my hope, in coming alone and unarmored, that I would assuage your fears. Let me reassure you that it is not the interest of the Cloaksaan to harass your colony. I offer this reassurance on behalf of Seti Kess, the First Cloak of the Brutal Hand and the regent of the Kindom."

Effegen, bless her clever, composed little smile, says, "Regent? How interesting. What is meant by 'regent'?"

A chuckle. "Why, from what I understand, you have access to all the Kindom newscasts. You must be aware of the reorganization of power in the Treble. Regency, as you know, is a temporary authority, meant to shepherd a vulnerable population until permanent authority falls into place. The Clever and Righteous Hands are currently without leaders, and the Treble itself is beset by terrorists and civil unrest. Not to mention the effects of a damaged energy trade. In time all this upheaval will pass. Seti Kess is determined on that point."

"How reassuring, for the citizens of the Treble," says Effegen. "But you must be aware that my people and I do not consider ourselves such citizens, and thus do not recognize First Cloak Kess's regency."

Jun expects a flattening of Inye's expression, a sign of temper. Far from it, he gives a benign nod.

"I can certainly understand that, Sa Crost. Your flight to Capamame is a statement of independence and a repudiation of loyalty to the Treble. Just as the Nightfoots do not answer to the Khens, so you will not answer to us. Is that correct? But of course you are also aware that the Nightfoots purchase their ships from the Khen shipyards. And the Khens rely on the Nightfoots for sevite. In other words, disparate centers of authority can have civil and mutually beneficial relationships. It is First Cloak Kess's desire to have such a relationship with Capamame."

Jun and the others in the room glance at one another. All except Liis and Effegen, who focus resolutely on Inye.

Effegen says, "The Jeveni do not have sevite or shipyards. I assume Kess wants something else from us?"

Another flash of those white teeth, condescending, as if he means to praise an intelligent child who has given the right answer. "Precisely. The mass exodus of the Jeveni has strained the sevite trade. We simply intend to offer employment to those Jeveni who might wish to return and work the trade again."

Jun's hackles rise. Tomesk grunts darkly and Hyre hugs their arms to their chest.

"Why would the Jeveni wish to return to labor conditions that dehumanized them?" Effegen asks.

Inye nods soberly. "Of course. That is a perfectly reasonable feeling."

"Thank you for acknowledging my reasonableness."

"As we are all now aware, Alisiana Nightfoot's complicity in the Jeveni Genocide makes her choice to employ its refugees afterward... sordid. And however grateful some Jeveni may have been for steady employment, First Cloak Kess agrees with you that the Nightfoots took advantage of the Jeveni workforce and often mistreated them. We will even acknowledge that the Kindom participated in this mistreatment. But as I've already said, Sa Kess intends to weed out corruption among the Hands, and usher in a more just age. To that end, he offers generous terms: safe passage to any Jeveni who wishes to return to the Treble, in exchange for a contract of five years in the factories. This will be under better circumstances, of course. We will increase wages and improve housing and medical subsidies. Upon completion of the five-year contract, no one will try to stop any Jeveni from leaving, if that is what they wish. That said, those workers who choose to stay on beyond the five-year limit will be eligible for a pension—something that Alisiana Nightfoot never offered. First Cloak Kess, as you see, intends to be far more openhanded."

He finishes his speech, clearly pleased with himself.

Effegen says, "I see."

The silence stretches for four, five seconds. Inye raises his eyebrows. "Do you find these terms attractive?"

She makes him wait five seconds more, and asks, "Where are the five thousand Jeveni who you imprisoned last year?"

He cannot be surprised by the question. When Chono and Six returned to the Treble, they loudly and unceasingly demanded the release of the five thousand Jeveni being held in a labor camp. Surely Inye recognizes the hypocrisy of pretending friendship with Capamame while those five thousand are in chains? Yet, unbelievably, he makes a dismissive gesture.

"That entire business is a misunderstanding. We have released a large percentage of those prisoners, and the rest have already accepted our offer of employment."

This lying motherfucker...

"Really?" Effegen asks. "I haven't heard so from them."

He has the gall to shrug. "Well, Sa Crost, you may recall that these are people who left Capamame. Perhaps they feel no obligation to share their plans with you."

Even a bloodletter couldn't cut the tension in the council room. Yet Effegen is perfectly poised when, seeming to let the matter slide, she continues, "You say you offer safe passage in exchange for work contracts. I assume that means that Jeveni will *not* have safe passage, otherwise. May I remind you that not all Jeveni were factory workers.

Only sixty percent of the people here had anything to do with the sevite trade."

He laughs. "Oh, of course. But what we need now is a workforce, and just as we are recruiting other Treblens to the task, so we are recruiting you. Those without a background in the trade can learn. As for those who wish to return *without* contributing to the trade, I don't say that it's impossible. However, there are many bad actors in the systems right now, and we are understandably cautious of welcoming people who may not have the Treble's interests at heart."

So, they'll take the Jeveni back as laborers, but not as independent citizens. And if they really think that the Jeveni can't be trusted, they'll hardly let them have free rein of the Treble. Jun knows with a certainty that the Jeveni will be contained to their factories like animals. Like the five thousand. The higher wages and subsidies will be ribbons on a cage. And once someone is in a cage, how easy to keep them there—despite any promises to let them go after five years.

Inye leans closer, his tone growing confidential and soothing. "I realize this idea runs counter to your designs for your people, Sa Crost. You want an independent world, a complete break from the Treble. But I should mention...we are aware that a majority of the colonists had no choice in jumping to Capamame, and that quite a large number of them wish to return."

"Are you, indeed, aware of that?" says Effegen.

His smile is falsely apologetic. "Our placement of spies among the Jeveni was a protective measure. We believed you were rallying around a terrorist plot. We realize now that we were wrong, but there is no use pretending we haven't received intelligence from our operatives. Are you going to deny what they've told us?"

There was only one "operative" in Farren Eyce who was capable of sending intelligence back to the Kindom. Who knows what all Ujan told Seti Kess about the politics and unrest in Farren Eyce?

Effegen doesn't acknowledge his reference to Ujan. With a note of briskness, she says, "Well. We spokes are not autocrats. If this is your offer, I won't hide it from our people."

Hyre shifts restlessly. Gaeda and Tomesk narrow their eyes at her.

"Wonderful!" Inye beams. "And of course, we recognize that many of you may wish to stay behind. We only require forty percent of you to meet our needs for the sevite industry."

The room takes on a new stillness, heavy as stone.

"Require?" asks Effegen.

"A poor choice of words. We aim to recruit around thirty-five thousand laborers from your ranks."

It was not a poor choice of words. It was deliberate. It was explicit.

"May I ask how you intend to meet your needs if fewer than forty percent of my people wish to return to the Treble?"

He waves a hand. "I hardly think that will be an issue. Look at it this way, Sa Crost. Our intelligence informs us that you initially anticipated no more than forty thousand Jeveni choosing to relocate to Capamame at all. Instead, you have a population of over eighty thousand! That is undoubtedly a strain on your resources and infrastructure. With high numbers returning to the Treble, I'm sure you'll find yourself in a much better position to build a self-sustaining population. Why, I would argue it behooves your government to *encourage* emigration." His teeth flash. "And if First Cloak Seti Kess is persuaded of anything, it is that you wish the best for your people."

Jun looks at Liis, whose arms are crossed, palm resting against the seam of her prosthetic arm. She lost the arm because she refused to carry out a massacre on a village. She knows firsthand the consequences when someone does not obey Kindom orders.

Effegen says, "You've given us quite a lot to think about. I'm sure you understand that my people will need time to consider your offer and make their decision."

"Of course! I won't linger. I know that you have a holiday coming up, the Feast of Sajeven's Dear Friend. That is eight days from now. Let's talk then. In the meantime, I am charged with squashing some petty rebellions on Braemin, but of course, if you wish to speak sooner, I've no doubt that Jun Ironway can reach me. She is, after all, so industrious." There is an edge of mockery to it.

After a long pause, Effegen agrees. "She is."

In some subtle and spine-tingling way, she makes it sound like a threat. Inye's pantomime of good cheer and friendliness does not conceal the note of interest in his eyes as he, too, interprets her meaning. The Jeveni are not without their own weapons.

"Very good. Thank you for allowing me an audience. We will speak very soon. Gods keep you well, Effegen ten Crost."

He vanishes, leaving behind the cast view of the warkite in orbit.

In the council room, the silence is as vast and icy as the plains of Capamame.

CHAPTER SEVEN

1581

YEAR OF THE GLASS

Lo-Meek
Bei Continent
The Planet Teros

*T*he *Fanged Wolf* was uncommonly large for a pirate ship. Pirates tended to favor quick, sleek ships—the better to attack and the better to flee with their spoils. But this ship masqueraded as a Teron cargo carrier and was nearly too large to find dock in the city of Lo-Meek. Drae could not, in her current position, see the red gape of the canyon beneath them, but she kept imagining it, kept picturing Som's devouring maw.

She had traveled regularly in her life, been to every planet in the Treble and far beyond the Treble itself, but she still experienced fleeting moments of disorientation when she was away from her moon. The close, hot air of Teros was so different from Jeve's dome cities with their sharp recycled air. The rust red of the Teron sky obscured the crisp glittering darkness of the Black, but on Jeve there was no atmosphere to divide them from those stars.

The Braemish pirates themselves, broad and muscular, hair woven in kill braids and blue eyes full of dangerous humor, were like aliens to a woman who had lived her life among the hardworking Jeveni—a people who showed their passions not with theatricality but with determination. At least the pirates had welcomed rather than threatened her. They viewed her as another trader fit to serve them an impressive payday. How different they might feel if she had not removed her Jeveni tattoo.

"Well," said the captain, clapping and rubbing his hands together, "what do you think?"

They stood in the massive hold, surrounded by stacks twenty feet high that contained the ship's bounty. Mostly weapons. Drae was here for weapons. After the pirates came to Farren Ki over forty years ago, the Jeveni had cultivated a small armory, but Drae knew there would come a day when her people needed more than rifles. The Wheel didn't like it, of course. But it was Drae's job, as the River, to do the things the Wheel could not. And since Lucos Alanye had come to Jeve, that list of things had grown. Thus she stood in the company of pirates, buying weapons for her home moon and for the ship that would make another home across the stars.

The catalog the Braems had sent to her neural link pointed her to the left, where crates advertised everything from handguns to rocket rifles, a cache fit for large ground offenses. She had bought her fill of these from another mercenary already. She knew the wisdom of spreading out her purchases. She turned to her right, toward much larger crates.

"These." She indicated the warship missiles. "They are Ma'kessn made, correct?"

Captain Wolf chuckled. He was of average height, with veiny muscles that looked on the verge of bursting. His blond hair was woven into dozens of braids, each one a threat.

"Good eye. We took them off a fleet of Kriisturan traders on the way to Kator. The shotgun rockets are temperamental, but stasis fields help. I've got those, too, state of the art. Even so, most warships prefer these." He gestured to another stack of crates. "Scythe missiles. Much more stable and very precise. Just one of these can take out a trade vessel's engine cage. They can slice a shuttle in half." He laughed again. "It sends a message."

Drae nodded vaguely. Her thoughts were elsewhere. Out in the untamed reaches of the Black, docked at one of the frontier stations, a nearly complete generation ship waited for its Jeveni crew to come aboard and begin the long trek to another system. As of now, the ship had no armaments, but Drae imagined it equipped with shotgun rockets and scythe missiles. It was necessary. Once *The Hope* got a year or two into its voyage, no one would pursue it. But those first couple of years would be dangerous. And of course there was the threat happening *now*, the risk to those cargo ships moving goods and people between Jeve and the frontier. If pirates set upon those ships and found the jevite they were using to fund the construction of *The Hope*, it would be devastating. Jeveni agents had made several trips to the frontier since the mission to build *The Hope* began thirty-five years ago, and they had avoided pirates and Kindom so far. But that could not last. Drae hoped to avoid the self-destruct protocol.

"I'll take all these," she said, gesturing at the twelve stacks of scythe missiles. "And these." She indicated the shotgun rockets. "Also, the stasis fields."

Captain Wolf's eyebrows climbed. It was difficult to surprise a pirate. His barking laugh, the avarice in his eyes, filled her with dislike. She had to be very careful not to sneer at him.

"That's quite an offer. You mind me asking how you'll pay for it?"

"I can give you twenty million in sevite."

He balked again. The Nightfoots' artificial jevite might not be equal to the value of the real thing, but twenty million marks' worth of it was nothing to sniff at. Yet the pirate looked angry, as if she'd wasted his time. "Fuck you if you've got that much sevite! Are you a Nightfoot?" He looked her up and down. "Look like a filthy stationer to me."

Drae smiled a little. Stationers were in fact very hygienic. With risks of disease so much higher in closed systems, it was imperative. The same went for the denizens of the Jeve dome cities, who even now were recovering from a respiratory disease that had swept Farren Ki. Only hygiene had kept it from doing worse, from spreading to the other domes. Wolf didn't mean that Drae was dirty. He meant that she had no flash, no outward appearance of wealth. She wore simple trousers and a hooded tunic, boots that had seen her through many years of wear. No accoutrements. Certainly not the jevite jewelry she wore in private. Her only mark of style was her red-tinted hair, shaved on the sides and braided down to her shoulders in a plume. It was a hairstyle she had first seen on *The Glitch*, which had somehow reached its way back to the Treble and become fashionable among spacefaring businessaan. Another way to fit in.

She looked Wolf lazily up and down, observing, "You have dirt under your fingernails."

He gaped at her, perhaps stunned that someone who had professed no known tribe was daring to insult him. A half dozen of his pirates stood around him, and the mood in the room got darker. Wolf curled his lip back just as she had stopped herself from doing. He didn't even glance at her small entourage of sentries, underestimating them and her.

"Sure of yourself, are you?" he asked.

"Sure of your business acumen. Either I'm lying about what I can offer you, in which case I'm a suicidal fool and will have my consequence in due course. Or I'm sincere, and *you* would be the fool for not doing business with me."

He didn't answer. The Braems behind him shifted. The sentries behind her were still. Since the impromptu arrival of Lucos Alanye over two years ago, Dimon had trained them to hold their nerve in heated situations, to be as still and observant as cloaksaan. They had achieved this. The pirates barely even noticed them.

At last Captain Wolf said gruffly, "Twenty million isn't enough. All this"—he gestured at the crates—"is worth fifteen million, but it'll cost me ten more to move that much sevite without attracting the attention of the Kindom. I come out short."

"We have a fence who can move the sevite. You will net seventeen million when all is said and done."

He waved her off. "No fence could do that."

"My fence works for the Ar'tec Collective."

The way his expression flattened was almost enough to make her smile. She watched his eyes dart back and forth, clearly trying to determine if she was serious. The Ar'tec Collective was a shadowy consortium operating out of a prison on Ar'tec Island. The average saan thought it was just another labor camp. People like Drae, people like Captain Wolf, knew otherwise.

He tried bravado again. "You expect me to trust Ar'tec? They'll get in bed with anyone. Stationers. Quietan sea scum. Even Jeveni, and those bastards carry more disease than rats."

Drae snorted. "The Jeveni are too poor to attract their attention. If anything, Ar'tec has probably robbed them. And it's just as well if they have. Better dead than a slave."

The Braemish maxim earned her a grin. Insulting her own people was a surefire way to achieve goodwill, and already she could feel the captain thawing toward her. She knew the weight that the Ar'tec Collective carried. He still looked hesitant, though.

"I don't know you or your people. You could be Ti Nightfoot for all I know. You could be a Je yourself. How do I know the Collective respects you enough to honor any deal? If they've got your sevite, what's to stop them taking it and leaving me with nothing?"

Drae smiled coolly. "You want *references*? What are we, secretaries? This game gets played in cash, and you know it. I'll make you a deal. We exchange half. Then I'll let you take the second payment, and if you're satisfied with the sevite, I get the rest of the weapons. Call it a gesture of faith. But look into my eyes." He did, startled by the words, and she held him there for a moment. "You're smart enough to see I'm no amateur. I'm no Je undergrounder crawling with lice and married to her sibling. You try to fleece me, and you'll find out who my people are. Right before I cut out your tongue."

If anything, the threat seemed to relax him. He gave an approving nod. Drae felt invincible in moments like this. Not because she was naive enough to think she had circumnavigated any danger, but because there was a vicious thrill in using Jeveni prejudice against Treblens.

"What about small arms?" Wolf asked.

"No need."

He chuckled. "Gone to my competitors for that, 'ey? Fine. Twenty million in sevite, and your Ar'tec Collective buddies speak for the deal."

Drae nodded her assent. He stuck his arm out to exchange a grasp of agreement, but she held up a finger.

"One more thing."

He looked put out, dropping his arm. "What?"

Instead of answering, she looked away from him and into the stacks. She walked away, heard his little scoff of offense, but she was following her ocular, letting the catalog lead her. Her sentries followed soundlessly. At last, she stopped in front of a pair of crates, each taller than her. The pirates murmured with surprise. The catalog had no clever name for these crates, and no descriptions or price tags. They lurked among the goods like ghosts: Lot 11 and Lot 12.

"So," Drae asked, "are they real?"

Her expression and her tone were relaxed, but her heart sprinted. When Captain Wolf joined her, he was suspicious. She thought he might bluff, pretend the crates held nothing better than shell casings. To her surprise, he played no games.

"How did you hear about them?"

She went on looking at the crates. "I should think it would be obvious."

He pulled in a breath through his nostrils, a sound of annoyance but also understanding.

"Ar'tec fuckers should keep their mouths shut. What do *you* want with them?"

"Nothing, if they're cheap knockoffs."

"They're worth millions!"

"And I have millions. If the goods are legitimate."

He licked his lips. Pirates. Selling shit was their disease. He did something on cast, and the crates opened up. Inside each was another box, opaque and smooth. After a moment the surface proved malleable, folding down to reveal the things inside. To Drae's surprise, they were both spheres, but they were not identical. Lot 11 was perhaps three times the size of her own head, smooth as glass and pale blue, a loveliness to it that was simplistic and clean. Lot 12 was larger—and had a very different appearance.

However unalike, they both throbbed with an energy that seemed inexhaustible, but that she knew had guzzled jevite for centuries before circumstance forced them to settle for the Nightfoots' synthetic copy.

"There's only so many people who could want something like this," said Captain Wolf. "They're no good as anything but status symbols."

"What makes you think I don't want a status symbol?" she asked, gazing at the two spheres, feeling almost intoxicated.

Wolf demanded, "You know why they build gate cores in space? Because the worst they'll do if they explode out there is take the engineering station with them."

Drae's pulse quickened. Could *The Hope* carry this treasure across the stars? Could the Jeveni keep it safe and protected for sixty years, feed it jevite from their hands, prepare it for its future pride of place in the Capamame System? If they failed, *The Hope* itself would vaporize. A gate core was no docile pet.

Drae offered, "Thirty million. Each."

Captain Wolf hesitated long enough that she looked at him again. When she did, she noticed the face of one of her sentries, just a momentary flinch in the eyebrows. He must be thinking, *Each? But we do not need both of them.*

No, the Jeveni did not need both of them. But Drae was a woman of contingencies.

She refocused on Wolf. At last, he said, "They're worth twice that."

Drae snorted. "I doubt you could sell one, let alone two. Let me guess: You stole them from collectors and have been looking over your shoulder ever since? They're worth nothing in your cargo bay besides trouble."

His jaw twitched. According to the Ar'tec Collective, he'd had Lot 11 for three years and Lot 12 for one. That was a long time to carry around such dangerous artifacts, a long time to wait for an offer. Pirates worshipped a death god. They listened for Som's omens of destruction.

But he was a greedy man. "Ninety million," he said.

"Sixty."

"Eighty-five."

"Sixty." He cursed her. "I'm doing you a favor, Captain. I'm taking evil off your hands."

He spat on the ground, but she knew she had him. "We'll do the guns first. I want assurances you've got actual money."

"Of course," said Drae, voice as relaxed as a breeze. Heart as wild as a hurricane. "The Collective will be in touch with you by this evening."

They disembarked from *The Fanged Wolf* into a wall of sticky heat, clouds of red dust rising under a gust of wind. Drae pulled up her hood to cover her hair and mouth, blocking the worst of the dust, and when the wind passed, she looked up and down Ton Street. It was the middle of the day, noisy and crowded. The New Sun holiday had been three days ago, and there was leftover garbage from the celebrations of their entry into the Year of the Glass. Wrappers and beer bottles and banners lay in the street, gathering in clumps. Half blew into the canyon, half gathered against the buildings in piles. Lo-Meek was a petri dish of toxins.

Drae and her sentries were not safe. She checked for any sign of marshals, then led the way south toward the hotel district. When they reached their hotel, they went straight through the lobby and out the back, into a shadowed, stinking alley. No doubt Captain Wolf knew of her reservation at the hotel, and in the event he decided to try to kidnap her for ransom, it was far better that she be somewhere else.

A waiting sentry nodded to indicate the way was clear, and they walked another thirty minutes between the close, claustrophobic buildings, until they reached the south docks. Their shuttle waited for them. They lifted off, jetting toward the Black.

Five minutes later, Drae was speaking to a hologram with the anthropomorphized face of a kai sheep. The thing said brightly, "How well you parlay! Blessed good fun for a sort like ours, pirates being so miserly!"

Though the words filtered through a mechanized voice, Drae found herself listening for the cadence of a Jeveni accent. It was foolish of her. Some said the Ar'tec Collective was on the verge of replacing its communication team with artificial intelligence. This voice might not even be a real person. Certainly there was no reason to believe it was the person Drae hoped for, the Jeveni youth who had left Jeve ten years ago and become a part of the Collective. Yet she couldn't help but wonder if that youth was the one who argued for her access to Ar'tec in the first place. Some hint of remembered loyalty pushing him to advocate for her.

Drae said, "It is early yet. Please contact the Wolfs with the drop-off site for the first half of the cargo. And move the sevite into place. After taking your fee, of course."

Though the Kai Sheep didn't smile, Drae sensed humor in its response. "Done and done once over. Such reliable ones we are, and will see to your profits. Protect you like a lover, when your interests are ours, too!"

Your interests, thought Drae. Wherever on Ar'tec Island the Jeveni youth was now, he viewed his interests as separate from Jeve's. He was like that thief who had left Jeve with stolen jevite and sold some of it to Caskori Nightfoot. He was like the acrobat who went to work on Ma'kess and betrayed under torture that there was still jevite on the moon. These rare saan who left Jeve, who went out into the worlds and stayed there, were a threat. They knew too much, and they defied Sajeven with their abandonment. Everyone on Jeve thought so.

Yet as Drae looked into the face of the Kai Sheep, she knew the person who had disappeared into the Collective was happy with his choice. He had traded poverty for the secretive, glamorous life of an Ar'tec archivist, and he would never come back to Jeve. Oh, how she envied him.

The Kai Sheep said, "Now, missiles, rockets, sticks and stones—we sniff at it! But as to your more adventurous purchases, where shall we deliver them? Some far-off place, perhaps?"

Drae stared back unblinking. The Ar'tec Collective was the only entity in the wider Treble that knew the Jeveni were using jevite to build a generation ship. The Collective had the reach, the contacts, to invade Jeve themselves, or to sell the secret to other First Families than the Nightfoots. Every time the Collective reminded Drae of this knowledge, it felt like a knife against her throat. But Ar'tec had its own inviolable ethics. It did not betray its contacts.

She answered the Kai Sheep, "Take everything to the same place."

There was a beat of pause. "Wiser to let us do the whole transport. Point A to B to C—more risky for you, running it around like that."

Drae's head went hot, her voice sharp. "You will take it where I say and not gouge me for extra fees. How I move it after that is my business."

The Kai Sheep gave a ridiculous little bleat, and rebuked her, "Distrust us, will you? Think we're foreigners and cheats? Well, we know your curiosities. You ponder the one you lost to us. Take him for a traitor, nah? 'Tis expected. But remember Sajeven! She loves her children, however far they leap. So if he is Sajeven's own child, *we* are Sajeven's own child, like you. Never did betray a sibling, us."

Drae was stunned. She had always thought the Collective swallowed up its new members, stripping them of identity the way the kinschools did when they took on new students.

"We love to secret-keep, Sa. We know *your* secrets. Raised by your Wheel, is it not? Raised to flow like a river. We know of your speeches in the dome cities. And how you host a Katishsaan, nah? This Lucos Alanye liar-scholar-guardsaan. And we know you are thirty-one, and without babes."

The words felt like an exposure to the Black itself. No oxygen. Burned alive by cold.

"Could we not make you vulnerable, and yet haven't? Consider our purpose. We have no traitorly intent. Only to help. And protect what can go awry."

She swallowed, making her voice bland. "I appreciate your...purpose. But you are not Jeveni. My people must do this work ourselves."

The long silence made her fear that saying so was a terrible mistake. But the Kai Sheep's response suggested a shrug. "Fine as is, then, since we are properly situated. Off to be about our business. By the by, you are very popular this evening. Tell your moon we say hello."

Drae blinked, and the Kai Sheep vanished. In the same moment, she received an ocular ping. The view that appeared before her displayed the spokes of the Wheel in their council room.

"Drae," said the Star, "is everything going well?"

Still processing that the Ar'tec Collective had known the Wheel was contacting her, Drae gave herself a whole two seconds to regroup. "Yes, my Star. We should have the arsenal in our possession soon. The missiles are all satisfactory. I'll be back on Jeve within two weeks."

The Gale said, "Good. We anticipate your return."

Something about the way she said this, with just a touch of strain in her voice, went off like a klaxon in Drae's mind. She saw it on all their faces, that same strain, and she felt toward them something she had often felt: that while they were the elders, wiser and more experienced than her, she was the one they relied on in their moments of fear.

"What is it? Is the flu worse?"

"No," said the Tree. "The final cases left the hospital last week. By Sajeven's own mercy, we are well and truly recovered."

If it was not the flu, there were only so many things that could be causing this tangible anxiety: tension between work crews, cave-ins at the mines, failure of crops. Or—

Her muscles tightened all through her skull and down her neck.

"What has he done?"

There was no need for any of them to say the name. Almost

cautiously, the Star answered, "He sent his surveyors away. The ones who survived the flu, that is. He claims the university grant that funded him before is gone."

"Hard times for a scholar," Drae said coolly.

"Yes, but..." The Star hesitated, glancing at the other spokes. "He wants to stay on and pursue his research independently. He has pushed again for permission to explore the pollutants around the Pallor Seam."

Alanye had been pushing for some version of this for two years. Yet the Star's expression warned her of a change.

"And what did you tell him?"

Now they looked nervous as children. It was the Gale who answered cautiously, "We said that...we would consider it."

Drae did not even blink. The Pallor Seam was fifteen miles west of Farren Ki. Before the jevite trade collapsed, some bosses had found it, but it was a small seam, and the jevite was so impure, so broken up with useless moonstone, that they predicted no profit against the cost of extracting and purifying it. The Jeveni cleared it out entirely in the following decades, so that when the pirate miners came forty years ago, there was nothing to find. Yet Alanye seemed obsessed with it, with getting near to it, as if he could smell the Blood Seam almost two miles beneath its husk.

Drae spoke calmly. "When he came to Jeve, you were ready to kill him rather than let him near the Pallor Seam. Has your position changed?"

"I wish we *had* killed him," grunted the Tree, a rebuke of Drae. "But it's too late now. You were the one who said that we had to placate his interests to avoid arousing suspicion."

"By letting him near the seam?" she asked flatly.

The Tree glowered at her. The Star, on the other hand, appeared chagrined. "We have put him off as many times as we can. We have repeatedly caught him trying to get out to the seam himself, and barely managed to divert him by saying the ruins are too dangerous. We are at endless pains to prevent him discovering our miners. We are at our wits' end with him!"

Drae exhaled through her nostrils. This she could believe, knowing Alanye as she did. She should have predicted that her kin spokes would be unequal to his persistence. She had been away from Farren Ki for three months, and he had worn them down nearly to giving him everything he wanted.

"Perhaps..." the Tree spoke slowly. "Perhaps it is better if you return, Drae. We have seen the way he defers to you and yearns to impress you."

Drae grimaced. She had a number of other stops on this trip. If she returned to Jeve now, she would have to reorganize her plans. But she could see it was not safe to leave Alanye unsupervised. Every step her people took now teetered them on the edge of a chasm, and nothing could be left to chance. Through her mind stormed the figure in the red coat, the one from her dream that she had not been able to shake all these months and years. The figure tore down the walls of the mine with their fingernails. They looked back at her, a stranger with her own face.

Suddenly the Gale said, almost coaxingly, "He asks about when you will return."

Drae's eyes snapped to her, sharp enough the older woman swallowed. So. It seemed her kin were not oblivious to the signs of attraction Alanye had shown her these two years. Of course, they would balk at Drae returning that attraction, or acting on it. *Using* it, though—they would approve of that. In their own ways, they were as calculating as she. But unlike her, they were not up to the task of acting on those calculations.

"Very well," she said. "I will handle this."

CHAPTER EIGHT

1665

YEAR OF THE HARVEST

Trin-Ma
Trini-so Continent
The Planet Kator

The first thing Chono does when she steps into the cell is look him over for signs of injury. She doesn't know these Trin-Ma rebels yet, and it's possible they've taken the opportunity to get some revenge on Khen Ookhen Obair by beating up his son. She's relieved to find that Khen Vorkhen Soon looks no worse since she found him among the other prisoners. In fact, now that he's no longer trying to hide who he is, his shoulders seem looser than before.

Rather than take advantage of the cot in the private room where Zemit placed him, Khen Soon is sitting on the ground. He looks up at her entry, his eyes big and dark, wary but not arrogant. Tired. He's probably never slept in conditions like this.

"Are you comfortable?" she asks.

She wonders if he'll complain about his accommodations. No. He does smile a little bit, though, as if he recognizes the irony of her question.

"When I was part of the larger group, they fed us once a day," he says. "Today I got a second meal. My father always berates me for not eating more."

The mention of Obair feels like an important tile placed between them.

Chono lowers herself to sit across from him, her back to the wall. She says, "It seems they recognize the wisdom in not hurting you. You're too valuable."

"Executing me would have its own value," Soon muses, eyes lifting to the ceiling.

"That would be shortsighted."

A sigh. "So are rebellions."

"So are those in power." He looks at her again. Chono says, "You act on impulse and expect to face no consequences. You plan for a future that will only benefit you, a sunny day that never ends, and when those you've hurt bring the cloud cover, you're completely unprepared."

He seems suddenly wistful. "You do have a lovely voice. Did the kinschool teach you?" She doesn't answer. He doesn't wait. "When I was a child, I thought I would be sent to a kinschool. I'm the fourth in line, so it would have made sense to send me. Father sent my older sister instead, which made me very jealous. I wanted to become a secretary. I thought it would be beautiful to spend my life studying the law and puzzling out problems." He closes his eyes, as if in blissful contemplation of that other life. He reminds her, in that moment, of Ilius, who had only ever wanted to be an exodus scholar before corruption came knocking. The thought gives her an unanticipated shiver of grief. But that's nothing to what her body does at Soon's next words: "I've heard you speak before, of course. When you came to my family's estate."

Chono swallows bile. She mimics his posture, knees up with her arms crossed over them, but only so that she can grip her own wrist and push her nails into her skin as hard as possible, grounding herself in the pain, in the present. "I remember you, too," she says. "You were quite young."

"Nine. I'd never seen a Teron as big as you before. Were you born on Aal continent? I understand the Aalani are generally bigger people than we in the south."

How often Chono has endured saan remarking on her appearance, her size. Chono was at the end of fifteen when her kinschool master took her to the Khen estate. She had already had her most dramatic growth spurts. She was tall and broad-shouldered even then. Boxy and muscular but not beautiful, and more than once in that terrible year before Esek rescued her, she struggled to understand why so many rich saan rented her for sex. What attracted them to the ugly kinschool student? There were so many beautiful children in her cohort of schoolkin. Why had the kinschool master decided to use *her* on the recruitment tour?

She had berated herself for this question. Asked the Godfire to forgive her. After all, if it wasn't her, it would have been someone else.

She tells Soon, "I was born here, on Trini-so."

"In Trin-Ma?"

"No. Outside Khenphasi."

He seems excited by her answer. He actually grins. "Did you know that no one knows where you came from? Nobody knows what your family name was. And no one has ever publicly claimed you, even now that you're famous."

Chono flashes back on an exchange with Esek, a couple nights after she had rescued her from the weapons merchant Ashir Doanye.

"Strangest thing, little fish," Esek had said cheerfully. "There was some kind of cast attack on your school. The family records of you and a dozen other students have just…disappeared. Now, who would have done that, do you think?"

Chono, still trying to find her footing in the magnetic, ferocious orbit of Esek Nightfoot, had answered meekly, "I…don't know."

But Esek had smirked at her, as if *she* knew. While Chono has never had it confirmed, she thinks she knows now, too.

To Soon she says, "My life before the Kindom was short. There's nothing from that life that I need anymore."

He looks contemplative. "I can understand that. Anyway, you left an impression, that day we met. It was a few years later before I understood what you were really doing there. I thought it was just some religious performance, having you stand there and recite the beatitudes."

Chono focuses on breathing steadily. She digs her nails into her wrist. Soon watches her, clearly trying to read her reaction, but she can't tell if this is cruelty or not.

"Ever since you killed my Great-Uncle Paan, my father has been terrified of you. I think he saw it as the beginning of a revenge campaign. He keeps expecting you to come for him next. He tried to have you assassinated."

Chono murmurs, "Did he?"

Soon nods. "Assassins infiltrated the Praetima guardsaan and passed themselves off as Trin-Ma rebels. They were unsuccessful, obviously."

Chono thinks of the day in question, when she met Yantikye the Honor. Later, after she and Six survived the attack and some of the assassins got away, the Secretaries had been quick to lay the scheme at the feet of the rebels.

"Am I your revenge instead?" Soon asks. She refocuses on him. He looks very serious. "I know why the kinschool master brought you to our estate. After you left, my father committed three of my cousins to the kinschools. It was an exchange of goods. My father always had a penchant for children."

Darkness in a room, in a bed, and sweaty hands on her body. Demanding, hungry. Sticky skin and her own skin going numb—

"Apparently it runs in the family," she says. Her voice is divided from her, a thing at the end of a tunnel. She can feel the drumbeat of her heart and the rapid current of her blood in her ears.

Soon chuckles without humor, then grows solemn, mouth twisting. "He is a despicable man. I wish I had a razor, Cleric Chono. I would shave my head in mourning for his crimes."

The words, penitent as they were, make her hate him. Her body is cold with sweat and she hopes he can't see it. She has a sudden, helpless desire for Six, because she knows they would see it, even if Soon can't, and they would reach out to her like a lifeline as she struggles to stay in her body—

Look at me. Look at me.

"There's no need for grand gestures," she tells Soon, her vision slowly clearing. "And there's no revenge in what I want from you. I don't kill children for the sins of their parents."

"But there *is* something you want."

"There's something I want from your father."

Instead of asking what it is, he nods pensively. She breathes in and out, the images of her night in Obair's bed slowly receding.

Soon gestures at the door. "And this? These people haven't got the numbers to hold out much longer, especially when Kess sends his Quiet Ones down here. They're going to die. What do you hope to accomplish by siding with them?"

Chono feels chilly from the lather of sweat on her skin, though she's in no danger of fainting anymore. "You can acknowledge that your father is despicable. You would shave your head as penance for what he did to me. But you have no interest in stopping him from doing the same and worse to the people of Trin-Ma?"

Soon doesn't answer, but there's nothing resentful in his look. More... philosophical.

"Your father has been a horrible ruler. You obviously disdain him. Someday he'll die and you'll take his place as head of your family. Unless you want to be like him, it's in your interest to listen to the Trin-Maan rather than crush them."

He sighs, weary. "I admire you, Cleric Chono. I never had much use for clerics, but I attend the temple of Terotonteris. I can see, not only now, but from your actions, that you're an honorable and righteous person."

She expects him to say more. A "but" that evokes his larger duty to his family. Another dismissal of the rebels or, at best, a wish that things could be different. Instead, nothing. Chono narrows her eyes. His reticence is a shield, but also an opening.

"I'm leaving Trin-Ma," she says. "I'm going to speak to people who have more say over your fate than I do. We will arrange a trade."

Soon chuckles. "I wonder that you can stomach another exchange of goods with Khen Obair."

Is it a barb, meant to reawaken her bad memories? She can't tell. She feels herself go stonier than before, emotion melting off her to be replaced by a mask of implacability.

"Last time I was a thing he purchased," she says. "This time, I'm selling the thing he wants most."

Soon nods, as if confirming her assessment. "So, what is it *you* want, Cleric Chono?"

The question unnerves her. The answer haunts her. She sees dead saan laid out before her: Cleric Paan. Aver Paiye. Ilius. A graveyard full of bodies, casualties in the long fight for what she wants. Perhaps Khen Soon will join their ranks. Calmly she tells him, "I want something more valuable than your life. Or his."

Some many hours later, Chono sits in the back of an old-fashioned warbunny listening to Zemit and the driver murmur to each other up front. Some pirates, as well as Masar and his collectors, are asleep in their seats, Mix Catty snoring. But though Chono is exhausted, she can't join them. The conversation with Soon runs circles in her head.

In the end, Zemit's lieutenants drove the Kindom back more easily than even she could have hoped. What had seemed a force of thousands on cast was in fact an army of only three hundred guardsaan, and as they fought a losing battle in the city center, Zemit snuck Chono and her allies out of Trin-Ma. A ten-mile hike through brackish wilderness, covered by Jun Ironway's Hood, brought them in time to a rendezvous point and this shuttle. As relieved as Chono is to have gotten out of the city with no casualties, she can't help feeling as though she has left a crucial weapon behind, trusting its protection to fate.

She shifts restlessly. She looks out the window. To the west, the coast curves and twists like the trail of a snake, a red sun filtering through radiation shields as it rises and turns the ocean a foggy pink. To the east roll plains of marshland and bracken with mist sat heavy upon them. There are beautiful summer months in the Teron lowlands, but for most of the year it's like this: drizzly and humid, even more so in the cities than here in the countryside. She recalls a childhood of shoes covered in red mud, clothes constantly damp, fingers stiff from cloth weaving. She has vague memories of parents and siblings sleeping five to a mattress. Dinners around a pot of weak soup and protein crackers. And one day, the kinschool teacher came from Ma'kess looking to buy strong, intelligent children.

"Chono." Masar's voice is exasperated, his eye cracked open. "Get some sleep."

He closes the eye again. She forces her own eyes closed. She breathes in and out, slowly, deeply, willing herself to drift away into dreamless slumber.

It must work, because the next thing she knows, it's early afternoon and the warbunny is trundling into Kel-Ma. The sun is high now, and a farmhouse stands surrounded by fields of low-growing vegetables, the kind of hearty roots and greens that can survive this soil. There are laborers in the field, but when Chono looks carefully, she notices look-outs, and guns on the farmhouse roof. There are five ground shuttles parked in a dirt lot near a barn, and she hopes the location is remote enough that no one in the Kindom will notice.

In the yard, the dirt under Chono's feet is crunchy with frost. She squints against the sunlight, exchanges a glance with Masar, and Zemit nods them toward the house. He leads them up stone steps and under a covered porch, through the double doors into a busy parlor. Moments later they enter a large dining room of rustic furniture and wood paneling, with a state-of-the-art star chart projected in the air. It rotates toward different systems and planets and zooms in on cities. The saan standing beneath it speak animatedly to one another, and then abruptly cease. Every eye in the room looks right past Zemit to land on Chono.

She takes in the strange tapestry of the crowd. About half of them are holograms, no doubt projecting from their strongholds: a Katishsaan with an aristocratic air. A sun-weathered Quietan. Two tightly braided pirates. Strangest of them all is an ungendered figure with the animated head of a fleecy spotted minkat, an anthropomorph that is either a high-tech costume or an over-the-top cartoon. She has no idea what to make of it.

"Cleric Chono," says one of the solid bodies in the room, the man standing closest to her. She notes the surprise in the voice, as if he had been told she was coming but didn't believe it.

Zemit hurries to introduce him. "Burning One, this is Sikrt Goodrite. He fights for the Free Government of Southern Ma'kess."

Chono thinks immediately of the five thousand Jeveni imprisoned in a labor camp on Sevres continent in the south. She wonders if this "free government" cares at all about that. Nonetheless she bows over her hands. After a pause, Goodrite stiffly bows back. Chono gestures to Masar, Qlios, and Layez.

"These are representatives of the Jeveni of Farren Eyce. This is Masar Hawks."

Goodrite admits almost grudgingly, "I've heard of you. They say you're a Braemish Jeveni." He looks Masar up and down. "Bit dark for a Braem, aren't you?"

Chono's hackles rise. Zemit is frowning in confused distress. Masar looks only contemptuously amused. "Yes, on both counts."

"A Jeveni warrior and a warrior cleric," Goodrite sniffs. "I didn't know the Jeveni or the clerics had warriors."

Masar says, "I don't speak for clerics. But most people know shit all about the Jeveni."

"We know a lot more now than we used to," a nearby woman says, another Ma'kessn, with the stark features of the northerners. "Settling your own planet. That's impressive."

Chono feels an inkling of distrust, and her instincts prove prescient when the woman looks at her with a smile that is almost avaricious. When the woman bows to her, it seems like mockery.

"And you, Cleric Chono," she says. "You've had some great successes of your own."

Chono reminds herself to be open and warm. She needs these people. Yet somewhere Esek is laughing at her, reminding her, *Friendliness was never your gift, you great solemn ox.*

"I hope we can all fight for our collective freedom. Alongside the Jeveni."

The woman smiles, brief and insincere.

Zemit jumps in. "Chono, this is Cly Siltmire. She represents the fighters in Kriistura. They've dug in at Teveet and are gaining ground. The Moonbacks have relocated to their estates on Torznol continent."

Chono says quietly, "Well done."

"She and Goodrite are lieutenants under General Ashway," Zemit adds.

Siltmire clucks, "He rebelled from the Kriisturan army but only took about half the soldiers with him, so he needed allies. Sikrt and I raised up our own armies, and they're loyal to us first, but it only made sense to team up with him." Chono makes no comment, but it's obvious this woman doesn't conceive of herself as anyone's lieutenant. "Zemit here says you think the battles we're fighting on the ground are a waste of our time."

Chono stops herself from glaring at Masar. "These fights are righteous. But not enough."

"Enough to show the whole Treble that we can stand up to tyrants," says Goodrite icily. "And that we can keep them on the run. Why else would Kess have held back his forces? He knows we have the weapons he sold us. He knows we can hurt him."

Masar snorts. "A few days ago the Secretaries intended to carpet-bomb all your cities. You don't have them on the run."

The room goes silent, stony, and Chono wishes Masar had more tact. But he's right.

"Well"—Goodrite sniffs, looking at Chono—"I suppose your fame will go a long way in helping us, won't it, Burning One?"

Someone at the table spits a curse. It's one of the Braems on hologram. Now that Chono is really looking at him, it's a wonder he didn't command her attention before. He's as tall as Chono and broader by a foot, braids white-blond and clipped at the ends with tiny red bells. He's like a caricature of a pirate captain, right down to the glittering blue eyes and the wide-toothed, threatening grin. He aims a surly look at Goodrite.

"Maybe once you're done pissing around your perimeter, Goodrite, we can have this conversation together, 'ey? Now, I don't care if that boy is sable or snow white, and if Cleric Chono is a fool, I'll judge for myself. Get your asses over here so we can be about our business."

Siltmire goes on smiling, as if this is all perfectly cheerful, though Goodrite pinches his lips together. Zemit, still looking rattled by the tense welcome, leads Chono and Masar to a spot at the table, while Layez and Qlios hang back at Masar's gesture. Zemit continues introducing the people in the room, an admixture of races and rank that make their gathering together not just unusual, but profound.

She's relieved to find that not all regard her with suspicion. The Quietan hologram, a person named Melosi the Grave, seems moved by their introduction, eyes wide and shy. They explain that they come from Pippashap. Chono doesn't recognize them from her time on the floating city, but she wishes they were in the room so she could embrace them. Embrace that memory.

Melosi isn't the only one who bows to her with genuine respect. The aristocratic-seeming Katishsaan is actually a scholar named Imicanta Oninye, who has risen from university headsaan to the leader of an insurgency on Kator. Though she doesn't regard Chono with awe, there's well-meaning curiosity in her look.

The pirate captain, who introduces himself as Vikar Wren (and briefly brags about his ship) has a crasser personality and probably a criminal character, but he shows her goodwill.

Zemit comes next to the bizarre Minkat hologram, whose ears twitch lazily. "And this...is a representative from the Ar'tec Collective."

Chono raises her eyebrows. Before last year, she didn't know the Ar'tec Collective existed, didn't realize the prisoners on Ar'tec Island ran an interstellar operation. Esek said that they communicate with the outside world exclusively through an AI interface. Is this gender-less...person an AI?

It purrs, "Pleasure, of course, and always. Not as well known to us as some, you are, though well known to our sunniest caster friend, your friend, we should say, who we know well by her works."

The rambling, affected dialect of the archivists is one that Chono hasn't interacted with in some time. Parsing the Minkat's words, she asks, "You mean Jun Ironway?"

"Sunstep Sunstep Sunstep. Clever little bit, vicious smart, like a sec-retary herself, is it not, for secretaries make their own law." Somehow it becomes apparent that the Minkat is looking at Masar. "And you, big man that you are. Perfectly acceptable phenotype. You know our friend well, do you not?"

"I know Jun Ironway, yes," says Masar.

"Excellent, very excellent." The Minkat addresses the room. "You see, can't you? They have vouchers, after all."

No one speaks at first, and there's an awkward stiffness in it. Chono asks, "Vouchers?"

Vikar Wren explains, "Someone to vouch for you, they mean."

Masar and Chono glance at each other.

"You're well known, of course," says Imicanta Oninye. "And you have a lot of support among the people, including many of our fight-ers. But we don't know you personally. We know your reputation and some of your actions. Still, you're a Hand. You worked with Esek Nightfoot until very recently. You can't expect us to trust you unless someone we trust can stand for you."

She sounds almost apologetic. Chono nods. This is perfectly reasonable.

"And no," Goodrite tells the Minkat, "Jun Ironway won't do for it. None of us knows her personally, either."

"Nothing more personal than the knowing between two archivists," the Minkat reproves.

"You're overruled on this," Siltmire agrees. "We need someone close to us."

Chono looks at Melosi the Grave. "There must be people on Pippashap who will speak for me."

"All of us will speak for you," Melosi says, with a glare for the others at the table. "You have more than proved your worthiness to us."

Siltmire says, "Pippashap can't be objective. They're drunk on veneration."

"We are not naive children," Melosi retorts.

"Pippashap has legitimate cause for trusting Cleric Chono," interjects Oninye. "We all do. Your own general has praised her to his armies. Don't pretend otherwise."

So this is the quorum, Chono thinks. As full of dissent as any ruling body. Some of them are ready to welcome her into their council. Others distrust her—or, at best, want her to prove herself. Well, she has known not to take the faith and admiration of the Treblens for granted. She's no god and she won't be worshipped as one.

Melosi continues, "We in Pippashap are used to being discarded. However, I know someone who should put all this resistance to rest."

They gesture across the table, to a darker corner that Chono had paid no mind to before. Now she realizes there's a chair behind a couple of Teron rebels, and in that chair sits—

"Yantikye," says Masar.

After the first breaker of shock, Chono's body goes hot. In an instant she is back in Aver Paiye's cottage on the Easwa beach. She looks through the window, expecting to see Yantikye keeping watch aboard his skiff. But man and ship are missing, and moments later the room erupts as Ilius and his guardsaan storm inside—

Yantikye stands from his chair, smiling in his typical sunny way that she trusts about as much as the lazy sway of a serpent.

"Good to see you again, Masar. And you too, Chono."

She doesn't answer. He betrayed her. And because he betrayed her, Six came to save her in Nikapraev. And because Six came to save her, Chono lost them, and they may be hurt, or they may be dead, or—

Never taking her eyes off him, she addresses the group. "If you've brought this man here to vouch for me, you may as well know that I can't vouch for him."

Unease ripples through the room.

Yantikye laughs. "Oh, come now, Burning One. Haven't you had time to cool down?"

"What's this about?" demands Vikar Wren.

"I let the good cleric be captured by the Secretaries. I thought she would be more useful to us as a martyr. She didn't seem to have any appetite for real war." He says it without shame.

The saan around the table glance at one another.

Imicanta Oninye says tightly, "We have all agreed for some time that Cleric Chono could be of use to our cause. You should have spoken to us before taking such an action."

Yantikye shrugs, offering no excuse.

"So, this means you *don't* vouch for her," says Goodrite, eyes narrowed.

"Nah," Yantikye says. "I've had a change of heart. And my daughter likes her. You all know how I respect my daughter." He looks at Chono, who wonders where Graisa the Honor is now. "I've seen what Chono will do for what she loves. She doesn't want war, that's true, but she's loyal, and honest—as much as anyone can be in these worlds. If she says she won't betray you, she means it. And if she threatens to kill you, she means that, too."

"Yes," Chono says. "I do."

The Minkat observes, "Very risky, Sa Yantikye, to flirt with one who would kill you."

Yantikye sobers. "There's no use in private vendettas now. I've heard from my insiders. Revel Moonback is in negotiations with Seti Kess."

The room rustles with sounds of concern. No doubt the rebels have relied on the known animosity between Seti Kess and his father, assuming the two would not ally. The Moonback armies in northern Ma'kess are nearly as prodigious as the Nightfoot forces. If Kess has both those armies, there will be little hope for this quorum. And so no hope for Capamame. Yantikye's betrayal, and Chono's hatred, can't take the foreground now.

She addresses them all: "Tell me what you want."

They look at her in surprise and uncertainty. She exhales the anger and restless violence inside her. She becomes the calm, steady Chono, the temperate cleric, the one who listens.

"From what Zemit says, you're fighting a hundred different battles. You're allies, but unevenly organized. You want my help—at least some of you—but I don't know your goals. What does victory mean to you?"

Several heads nod in approval of the question.

Vikar Wren declares, "We want the Kindom and the Families brought low. Frankly I'd see them all killed. They've done nothing but evil in the Black."

"They're also the foundations of order and law," Chono points out.

Goodrite gestures between himself and Siltmire. "Our armies won't be satisfied while the Families hold power."

Chono wonders about General Ashway, whether he and his armies share that sentiment, and if it would even matter to Goodrite and Siltmire. She doubts it. "And how do you mean to fill the gap the Families leave behind, if they disappear?"

Imicanta Oninye says, "There's value to institutions. Interstellar law. Economic stability. The sevite trade, for example, must survive. But we should have open access to sevite and the gates. This monopoly that the Nightfoots and the Kindom hold is a plague."

"Equal distribution of resources, then," says Chono.

"And of authority," says Siltmire. "The Kindom has bought children from poor families to shore up their ranks"—Chono's skin erupts in goose bumps, wondering if Siltmire knows about her—"but those families have no influence. It's the First Families and lesser, wealthy houses who hold stake in the Kindom. If any kind of ruling power survives, it should be *our* children who become the secretaries and the clerics and the saan on the hills with the money."

"But evenly distributed," interjects Zemit earnestly.

Melosi asks, "Or are you hoping the Siltmires will be the new Moonbacks, 'ey, Cly?"

Siltmire scoffs.

Zemit looks at Masar. "Your Wheel is an example for all of us. They hold authority but share power, and I hear that among the Jeveni, no one has more resources than anyone else. It was like that all the way back through your history. Isn't that so?"

Masar looks uneasy. "When the jevite trade ended, and my people were left alone on Jeve—yes, that's how they did things. We're trying for it on Capamame, as well. But it's no small task. And doing it on the scale of the Treble itself could be impossible."

"But worth it to try," Melosi insists.

Zemit and Oninye nod their agreement. The quorum is split between idealists and opportunists. Chono says, "So, you want the existing infrastructure, but new leadership." In fact, she's certain not all of them want that at all, but she charges forward. "So do I. And I believe the first, best way to go after it is to capture Seti Kess."

Goodrite huffs. "No wonder you want that. It's all over the casts that he's found a way to get to Capamame. Yantikye says you're loyal, Cleric. And loyal most of all to the Jeveni." He looks around at the others. "We need someone invested in the Treble. Not saan who have decided they want nothing to do with us."

"That's interesting," says Masar, "given how little any of you have ever wanted to do with the Jeveni."

Siltmire chuckles. "You can't blame us for the oppression of the Jeveni."

Masar's face turns murderous, yet it's Chono who lashes out: "The fate of the Jeveni is a prophecy of your own fate. I have never cursed anyone under the Godfire, but I *will* curse hypocrites, and I'll have nothing to do with them."

Even the sight of Yantikye didn't make her show her temper. The members of the quorum look startled and unnerved, as if she's revealed a side of herself they didn't expect. She's not sure how many of them are devout, but it's clear they believe her capable of cursing them. She notices a sudden glimmer of interest in Vikar Wren's eyes, and Imicanta Oninye looks impressed.

The Minkat trills, "Very righteous, yes, and she's earned the name. Where go the Jeveni go the rest of us, nah? It's true. And fuck you, Goodrite, you fucking fuck who fucks himself."

Goodrite splutters.

Melosi the Grave says, "I for one stand alongside the Jeveni, and if they're under threat from Kess, then they are my siblings. All of Pippashap is with me."

Chono's heart lifts. More so when Zemit nods. "It's true. If Kess has his way, he'll enslave the Jeveni again, maybe worse than during the jevite trade. They're under no less risk than the rest of us."

"Our collaboration aside," says Siltmire pointedly, "at the end of the day, it's me and mine that I must protect."

Masar snaps at her, "Kess has already sent his lackeys to Capamame to demand that we turn over our people to work the trade. And he intends to do the same to the Treblens. He *will* enslave my people, and that will be just the start. What do you think he'll do with the rebels he captures? The ones he doesn't just execute? And their families? And anyone unlucky enough to have ever helped them? He'll throw you all in the labor camps, and *you'll* be the Jeveni."

When no one answers, when no one naysays him, he slowly relaxes backward. Chono meets his eyes. She nods at him, and he nods back.

"They're right," says Yantikye. "It's all well and good taking down every First Family bastard and every Hand in the systems, but first things first. Kess." Yantikye juts his chin at Chono. "So, tell us what you think, Burning One. How do we take down the First Cloak?"

Chono looks up at the star chart. She casts out, and Kator appears, dotted with a few blinking lights that signify the central locations of the uprisings. Her gaze trails north, toward the highlands of Uosti continent, and a very specific city, with a very specific ruler.

"I have a plan. You won't like it. But I think it may be the only way to get any version of what you want."

The murmuration of voices, the exchange of loaded looks, momentarily distracts everyone.

It's Yantikye who interrupts the unrest. "Tell us, then, big killer."

Yantikye's use of the nickname, and its reference to Six, makes Chono fantasize about crushing his larynx.

"You want the Families destroyed. I understand that. But it may be shortsighted." More murmuring, displeasure rising like a wave. Chono says, "They've used you for centuries. I suggest that this time, we turn the tables."

CHAPTER NINE

1665

YEAR OF THE HARVEST

Verdant Estate
Sevres Continent
The Planet Ma'kess

It's the largest bathtub they've ever seen. In their brief tenure as Esek Nightfoot, they have endured the atrociously lavish accoutrements of the First Families. But the bathtub is a step beyond. It has a room all to itself, and under recessed golden light it stands in the center like a god's bowl of wine. Left to themself, Six would soak their bruised body in a barrel full of ice water, but the Nightfoot doctors have prescribed them a medicinal bath, hot and wafting with not exactly pleasant smells. The water feels like pepper, a strange tingling burn along their skin.

They have no open wounds. Their internal injuries have mostly healed. Their shattered kneecap has been replaced with lab-grown bone, as has a section of their shoulder blade and two ribs. But for all the marvels of regenerative medicine, the new bones feel tender, knee throbbing, shoulder stiff. Submerged in the water (the scent is floral, they decide, but like flowers on the verge of rot), they process the slipperiness of the oils. The liquid feels more dense, more buoyant than any bath they've ever had, as if the water is thick with salt. They sit against the side of the tub and toy with their repaired ear. The jagged edges have been refined into delicacy. It feels more alien than the replaced knee. It feels like more of an attack than the moment when Esek bit the first ear off them.

They are lost in thoughts of it, memories of that night and that fight, when the door opens. Guardsaan first, Riiniana Nightfoot next. The little wraithlike thing moves with the lightness of a breeze drifting through curtains, coming to stand across from their perch in the bath. Her posture is straight, her eyes imperious. In the two days since Six woke in the Verdant hospital room, Riiniana has visited them once in the morning and once in the evening. A perfunctory schedule, a chance to broadcast her dominance, to withhold information and ask seemingly innocuous questions. Six has played along. And imagined swatting her nose like the arrogant pup that she is.

"So," Riiniana says, "you are obeying orders."

Six purrs, "I do love a bath."

The girl moves her eyes up and down their body, clinical, assessing. Six has never been shy about their nakedness and they're not about to start now, but they do wonder at a mere teenager showing such indifference to nudity.

Abruptly, Riiniana turns away, beginning a slow circuit of the room, taking it in as if she's never seen it before.

"This room was commissioned by Emplena Nightfoot, my five-times great-grandmother. Emplena had a nephew whom she loved. He was a cleric. She often invited him to Verdant, where he took advantage of her favoritism, including this bathtub. Emplena's daughter promised to help him rise in the ranks of the clerics in exchange for helping her supplant Emplena. He did it, probably without a moment's hesitation. Emplena died of grief. Which I assume actually means she was assassinated after her abdication."

"How sordid," Six replies.

"One could expect nothing better from a cleric," Riiniana sniffs, pausing to consider an etching on the wall.

"Or from a Nightfoot," Six observes.

As if she hadn't heard, Riiniana admits, "I never met a Hand I didn't hate."

Six raises their eyebrows. "Haven't you been collaborating with the First Cloak?"

"Necessity. You must understand. And a short-term alliance does not preclude a long-term falling out, once my circumstances are more secure."

"Quite the strategist you are."

Riiniana turns to face them again, a humorless smile on her mouth. "I was educated by secretaries. If I remember, you yourself had a secretary guardian, at one point. So we both know how much strategy it takes to survive them. Mine always thought I was a middling student. Then there were Torek's cleric advisers. A pack of hypocritical sycophants, and they all thought I was a brainless fool. But *they* were the fools."

"I see you have grievances," Six drawls.

"They were hardly unique. The Hands have held power for centuries, and what do they have to show for it? They're soft. Myopic. Out of touch. It's only the rare, truly independent Hand who makes a significant difference, and always to the Kindom's detriment. Liis Konye outsmarted the entire Cloaksaan. Kess took out the Secretaries with hardly any effort. And Cleric Chono—she sparked a revolution without even meaning to. Any organization as weak and vulnerable as this deserves to crumble."

"One might say the Families are no better."

"One might. Which is why they will need some reorganization, too."

She reaches into a pocket of her dress (flowy, peach-colored, youthful) and withdraws a tiny round tin with a jewel-encrusted lid. She sets it on the flat lip of the tub by Six's hand. Intrigued, Six pops it open. A single gray pill sits on a velvet bed. Six raises their eyebrows.

"Are we getting high now?"

"It protects you against nausea, vertigo, and headaches."

"I was not aware I had nausea, vertigo, or headaches."

"You will soon, if you don't take that pill. We've given you a reproductive blocker."

Six looks at her without answering, without reaction. As if she thinks Six doesn't understand, Riiniana explains, "We implanted it while you were in surgery, but have waited to activate it until you had your strength back. You must realize it's imperative that Esek Nightfoot not produce heirs who could interfere with the matriarchal line of succession."

The steam in the room has given Riiniana's pale brown skin a rosier hue. In the ceiling, dozens of little nozzles point down at them: guns, which Riiniana seems to have set up all over the estate. Lucky for her, or Six would kill her right now. They're a little surprised by the strength of their own feelings, though it's unclear to them which they find more repugnant—the thought of using their reproductive organs to have children, or having this Nightfoot upstart curtail their control of their own body.

"Frankly, I'm shocked you aren't using contraceptives already. The blocker is a simple cell bot. The side effects go away after three days, and with this pill you'll be fine. The bot itself dissolves after five years. Either you'll be dead by then, or I'll have the matriarchy in hand, and it won't matter anymore. You can spawn to your heart's content."

Six has no interest in spawning, yet they wonder if they could pull her into the bath, flip her under their body, and drown her before anyone stopped them. They say, "How reassuring."

"It's important that we understand each other, Esek. You're here to serve my agenda. And in exchange you get to live, and so does Chono. You have little else in the way of options. I've disconnected your neural link. The holo shields around Verdant are impenetrable. And there are guardsaan everywhere with instructions to kill you if you try to leave."

"I am Esek Nightfoot. The guardsaan work for me."

"Oh, no," says Riiniana, looking down at them with an intensity in her pale blue eyes that is legitimately unnerving. "No, Esek. You are the face of Verdant. But I am the brain."

Six recalls themself at her age. They thought they were ready to kill Esek in the streets if they wanted to. And then Yantikye came along and boxed their ears and showed them they were still a neophyte. What will it take for Riiniana to learn that lesson?

After a few more moments drawn as tight as a garrote, Riiniana announces, "First Cloak Seti Kess has just entered our atmosphere. We're to have dinner with him in an hour. Before you worry—I'm aware of his little spy in Farren Eyce. I have it on good authority that the girl never gave Kess your true identity."

Until this moment Six had forgotten that Ujan Redcore exists. It's not a pleasant memory. They had their own role in her radicalization, and because of that, Kess has the gate key. But Six keeps their voice relaxed. "I suppose you have some design, in bringing him here. It might help if you enlightened me."

Her eyes gleam. "In time. For now, simply play your part and don't make the mistake of trying to outsmart me. I know how hard it will be to avoid the temptation, but I strongly advise you to save yourself some trouble and behave."

"Too bad you cannot demand as much of Kess."

"Dinner. One hour. Come to the dining room in the east wing. It's more intimate."

Riiniana turns in a rustle of peach silk and strides from the room, all self-possession and hauteur. Six lies in the bath, feeling sticky and overheated and wanting to get out. The doctors instructed them to soak for an hour. How long has it been? The room is so quiet, eerily quiet. The steam is full of apparitions.

It's not as if the worlds would benefit from another one of you Alanye cretins, says Esek Nightfoot. *And honestly, what sort of parent would you be? You certainly didn't look after those Ironway children. At least I taught my fish how to protect themselves.*

Six considers the ceiling with its multifaceted geometric tiles that loosely evoke the shape of Makala in her birthing attitude. Reproductive independence. Who'd have thought it would matter to them? Esek was more the reproducing type, a reptile who spawned little monsters from her cruelty. Though perhaps, in Ujan's case, Six is an equal parent.

Speaking of fish, says Esek. *Riiniana is certainly more interesting than we expected! Admit it. You want to know about this agenda of hers.*

Six thinks, *What I want is to make her serve* my *agenda.*

Chono Chono Chono, mocks Esek. *I always thought* she *was the dull one. Turns out it's you. For all your devotion, what have you done? Broken promises. Left her unprotected. Lied.*

Six wipes peppery water from their eyes. At Nikapraev, they told Chono they would be right behind her. They would plant a bomb and follow her. They did not.

Say this for me, says Esek. *I never lied to her. I was completely transparent with her, from the beginning. I never lied to you, either. What's worse? Honest depravity or deceitful self-righteousness? Chono always did attract moral puzzles.*

Six doesn't answer. They hear her whispery voice, a haunting. Through the misty air, they can almost see her, like steam that never dissipates.

An hour and ten minutes later, Six walks into the east wing dining room in a violet satin suit, jacket open to reveal a silver shell with a plunging neckline. They remember noticing the suit in Esek's closet when they first took possession of her life over a year ago. Ostentatious. Exquisitely tailored. Provocative in its low cut and sharp angles. Perhaps she wore it to family parties. Perhaps she never wore it at all, preferring her red-and-gold cleric's coat. But Six will not be wearing that coat again. And so they enter the dining room, all glamour and irreverence.

The room is indeed more intimate than the cavernous dining hall in the west wing, but the ten-seater table still looks barren with Seti Kess seated at one end and the opposite end left open for Six. Docile little Riiniana sits between the heads, sipping from a tiny cup. The look she gives Six betrays her anger at their tardiness, which is a satisfying bonus to insulting Kess.

"Why, Seti!" they crow. "And here I thought we'd seen the last of each other."

Seti Kess drags his eyes over Six, taking in the clothes not with lasciviousness, but contempt. He tells Riiniana, "My compliments to your surgical team, Bright Daughter. You even fixed the ear." He laughs lightly, but as with all Kess's laughter, it lacks that authentic human quality. "How marvelous."

Six wags a mocking finger. "Now, don't play, Seti. We all know you wish I was still broken into bits. Those cloaks of yours lack all restraint."

"I half wish I had let them beat you to death," Kess remarks.

"Yes, I suspect you'll come to regret that very much."

"Sa." Riiniana's voice is soft, beseeching—a performance. "Please."

Six drops indolently into their chair, smirking as if Kess's victory in that rain-swept courtyard was a point against him rather than against Six.

Kess sniffs. "Well, at least I have the satisfaction of my memories."

Yes, Six thinks, *so do I. And memory has always driven my revenge.*

On some silent cue, servants coast into the room with the evening's meal held aloft on serving plates. They begin placing dishes onto the table with an exactness that turns place settings into artwork. Six takes in the precisely plated meal, all its grandeur typical of a First Family table. They note the glass of praevi placed before them, which Esek loved and which they hate. There is also wine. There is spicy plum soup and honey wheat flatbread, pan-seared crustaceans on a bed of poached greens, root vegetables carved to look like gems and flaking with gold leaf, medallions of roasted fowl in a circle of green and white purees. It is a mix of northern and southern Ma'kessn cuisines. A bit on the nose.

As soon as the servants retreat, Riiniana and Kess begin to daintily cut up their food, observing proper table manners. Six hasn't had a meal this substantial in days, but though they took the pill Riiniana gave them, they feel a little queasy. Still, the performances must be observed. They tear off a piece of flatbread and dip it into the soup and the puree, eating as crassly as they can. They stab one of the medallions of fowl with their fork and lift it up, biting off a mouthful. They ignore the wine and praevi, drinking from a glass of water with melon in it, slurping some of the melon out and crunching it noisily.

"I'll admit," they say after a moment, "in all my fantasies of rule, I never imagined lowering myself to accept a Moonback as the guest of honor at my table."

Kess looks up from his meal, face stony. "I am no longer a Moonback."

"Ah, that's right. But don't you feel it's all a bit bombastic, Seti? Murder a few hundred helpless secretaries and suddenly you're lord of the universe?"

"I think we both know which of us is the bombastic one, Esek," Kess replies.

"Well, we all have our role to play."

"You have a gift for that, I think."

"Yes, I know how jealous you've always been of people who have gifts."

Riiniana entreats them, "First Cloak. Riin Matri. Please. I understand that you have a difficult history. But you'll gain more from a political friendship than this childish animosity."

Six raises their eyebrows, surprised that she would say as much to Kess.

He chuckles, sinister. "I have already made concessions in the name of friendship. For *your* friendship, I chose not to kill this... traitor... and instead gave her to you. And now I deign to eat in her company instead of cutting off that new ear."

"Yes," Six says, "I am also deigning."

Kess ignores them. "Can you really ask much more of my friendship?"

"I'm thinking of your best interests." Riiniana looks at Six. "And yours. All of ours."

"Have at it." Six waves a hand. "Make your case for friendship."

Kess curls his lip in disgust.

Riiniana says, "I believe we want the same thing. A stable Treble may not sound exciting to two born fighters, but if you want to hold what power you have, it's essential. You can achieve that better by working together than by maintaining this feud."

Neither Kess nor Six answers her. She directs herself to Kess.

"First Cloak. You face a multifaceted challenge. You're plagued by recalcitrant citizens and uprisings. You depend on continental armies to fight those uprisings, but those armies will ultimately do whatever the Families tell them. And the Families are not your friends. Furthermore, to mainstay the order of the Kindom, you must protect the remaining Clever and Righteous Hands and rebuild their trust, or risk them joining the rebels. Finally, you need to repair the sevite trade, for which you need the Capamame Jeveni to come back. Do I have it right, these interlocking conflicts?"

Kess gives her a flat look.

She nods. "Then let me tell you what you stand to gain from allying with Esek. It's about more than our armies. Esek spent months with the Jeveni. If we use her to pad negotiations with the Wheel, we may be able to persuade them to send workers back without violence. Not only that, but if Esek oversaw the new sevite factories, she could maintain order and trust, whereas some other governance would only breed conflict."

"The idea that Esek could maintain order over anything is a farce."

"You're too smart to underestimate her," Riiniana replies.

Six snickers.

Kess scowls. But he also says, "Go on."

"A restored sevite trade, one built on an alliance between you and our house, will show the other Families what there is to gain from working with you. Right now, you're making some inroads with the Moonbacks. But the Paiyes have ignored your overtures, and however Khen may be fighting rebels in Trin-Ma, he hasn't promised you any interplanetary support. As for your father, he's a cautious man. He won't side with you out of familial love. But if you *could* rally the Families, your armies combined would be enough to crush any rebel dissenters."

The girl is right. Kess's cloaks and Kindom guardsaan are not enough to hold martial law, let alone stabilize the Treble. Especially with the trade in tatters.

She continues, "If you can squash the rebellions, unite the Families, and restore the trade, the other Hands will have to recognize you as a peacemaker. You'll be in the best position to restrengthen the Kindom, and with yourself at its helm. All these actions, taken together, are the best possible route to what you want. And achieving them begins with Esek."

He looks at her shrewdly. Six wonders at her game. If Riiniana hates the Kindom and wants it destroyed, this strategy she's handing to Kess must have seeds of poison in it, something that will ultimately lead to his downfall.

"As well," she says, raising her head higher now, posture erect and queenly, "a marital alliance between us would only solidify the new Kess Family."

Six blinks at Riiniana in frank astonishment. When Kess gives a mean little smile, Six realizes that the idea is not new to them. He and Riiniana must already have been negotiating.

"Marital alliance," Six repeats. "You better not think I'm going to get in bed with this—"

"No," Riiniana says. "Not at all. Sa Kess will marry me."

Six manages to affect amused surprise, though secretly their thoughts flash on Chono, sold into the beds of rich and powerful saan at just fifteen.

"Really?" Six says.

"Political marriages are a respectable, time-honored tradition," says Riiniana.

"I never knew you were a lech, Seti," Six replies, grinning with teeth.

Kess's lip curls up, his electric-blue eyes bright with malice. He seems about to make some vicious remark, but—

"Of course, it would be inappropriate to marry before I am seventeen," Riiniana says, "but that is two years away, and the First Cloak knows that my commitment is sincere."

Six scoffs. Kess looks thoughtful. When he doesn't reject Riiniana's proposal out of hand, Six says, "I see. Well, you've laid out all the benefits of our collaboration to your beloved. Why the fuck should I want to cooperate?"

Riiniana smiles sweetly at them. "Isn't it obvious? You will oversee and protect the Jeveni labor force. You will get richer and richer in the new Treble we create. And of course"—now she looks at Kess—"you will have assurances that no one will hurt Cleric Chono."

Kess's eyebrows leap to his hairline. "Oh, will she now?"

"This behooves you, too. If you pardon Chono and protect her— under strict house arrest, of course—you will prove that you're merciful and endear yourself to a people who love her. Properly controlled, she could become your puppet in the Righteous Hand. Not to mention she will be your security, against my cousin"—this with a smile for Six—"who I know will not step out of line, if Chono's life is at stake."

The clever little monster. But if she thinks Chono would become anyone's puppet now—

Seti Kess laughs, louder than Six is expecting, a percussive boom of mean-spirited admiration. "By the gods, you are quite the negotiator," he says.

"I negotiate in all our best interests," Riiniana says, maintaining her quiet, temperate affect, which seems to have exaggerated in Kess's presence. "Imagine what we could accomplish without all the dramatics of rivalry? Without all this *showboating*?"

Six pouts. "But I like showboating. Although, I will say, Chono had an idea somewhat like this. Families working together toward just ends. Such a dreamer."

Kess points a finger. "The Families hate her as much as I do."

"She *does* inspire strong emotions."

"Enough to have you salivating over her, I see. How anyone could burn for a woman like that, I'll never know. Well, I suppose I can be persuaded to use her rather than kill her. If she cooperates. Otherwise, I'll have her spitted and roasting within the month."

Maybe he hopes that Six will lose control. Leap over the table, perhaps? Go at him with the cutlery? Six comforts themself that only weak leaders brag about the imminent demise of their enemies.

"There will be no need to spit and roast anyone," Riiniana says. "What I've told you here is just a rough sketch of far more detailed plans. I can present you with reams of data and research that prove this will work."

"A scholar!" Six laughs.

"Yes," Riiniana retorts acidly. Their eyes lock, hers warning them, *Now is the time to bend. Now is the time to obey.*

Well…it costs nothing to see where this goes.

Six shrugs. "I'm open to it, I suppose. Plenty of profit to be had, if nothing else. What about you, Seti? Can you humble yourself to clasp hands with a Nightfoot?"

Instead of throwing back some insult, Kess remains silent, long enough to test the composure of his dinner companions. Six holds the line, relaxed in their chair, curious to see if Riiniana can be patient. She is. She is absolutely placid, a perfect little actor. But Six finds the silence too weighted, a shift in the air, a new intensity to Kess's look.

Abruptly, he shrugs. "I suppose we have an accord."

Riiniana blinks, perhaps as surprised as Six by the easy about-face. She beams. "Wonderful. This will be—"

"That's assuming you have nothing more to tell me. Have you, darling?"

That last word contains a nasty purr. Riiniana's brow furrows momentarily, then smooths. "As I said, I have far more detailed plans."

"But that is the crux of your presentation. Nothing left out?"

When Riiniana frowns, an unsettling smile appears on Kess's face, the scar twisting his lips as fresh malice glints in the electric-blue eyes. Six's instincts prickle.

"Well, then." Kess raises his glass. "Let's have a toast."

Riiniana puts on a pleasant expression. "Oh. Of course."

She lifts her own wineglass. Six does nothing.

"I'd like to drink to new beginnings. There are great differences between us. Monumental divergences in our backgrounds...But we share some things. Industry. Ambition. Why, in our own way we are each like the three hands of the Kindom." He lifts his glass toward Six. "You, for example. Years of flitting about the Treble, seeking your ends, committing your little atrocities. How unspeakably *clever* you have been." The air pressure seems to have dropped, creating a chilly tension. Kess swings toward Riiniana. "And you. The picture of righteousness, Bright Daughter. It's so rare that you can find people in this life upon whom you can truly rely. And I *can* rely on you, can't I, Riiniana? Sweet girl. Who would never lie to me."

Riiniana's smile is frozen, her intelligent eyes searching Kess for an explanation. "Why, of course," she says.

"Because, after all, why lie? What would you have to gain? If our interests are aligned, if we both want the Families to submit to my will, there would be no reason for you to lie to me—Hand of brutality that I am. Correct?"

She makes a soft, wounded sound. "Seti, I don't understand what—"

The door into the dining room bangs open as if for a battering ram, momentarily shaking Riiniana's cool. She startles as six cloaks march inside, five of them carrying something large wrapped in white cloth. Dirt trails behind them, raining down from the odd-angled package. This would be startling enough, but it is the two cloaks whom Six recognizes that forestall any thought they might have to goad Kess for his strange words.

One, leading the procession, is Commandant Yorus Inye. A second, helping to carry the package, is Esek's one-time chief novitiate, Rekiav.

Kess speaks on, addressing Six. "*You*, of course, have reason enough to lie to me. But I care less about your honesty than dear Riiniana's here. After all, I have not needed the great Esek Nightfoot's honesty to spend my years uncovering her secrets."

Inye takes position to the left of Kess's chair. He, too, was Esek's chief novitiate once, and she bred in him a loyalty that supplanted his commitment to his Hand, one that prompted him to serve her interests on more than one occasion. He looks at Six, and there is none of the subtle reverence he always showed Esek. There is only faint, cold amusement.

The other cloaksaan bring the package forward and, without ceremony, haul it up and dump it onto the tabletop.

Riiniana cries out in alarm. Dishes and cutlery smash and scatter. The boy Rekiav, grown into his cloak after years of worshipping Esek, gives Six one quick, hateful look before retiring with his kin to form a perimeter around the table. The presence of Inye and Rekiav is an unmistakable shot across the bow, and now Six is beginning to suspect what it means...

Kess smiles like a demonic machine. "What a fascinating life you have had, Sa. What hunting and sneaking you have done, have you not?"

He stands up, brandishing a bloodletter. Leaning over the package as if it were a kill that needed dressing, he slits open the white cloth and rips the pieces apart. Inside, the desiccated remains leer up at him. Riiniana makes another little cry. Six holds very, very still.

"She decomposed quickly, didn't she?" Kess observes. "Must have been the burial site."

He rips more of the white cloth, until she is completely exposed, bones at odd angles, blackened with dirt and decay. Not all the flesh is gone. And she's still wearing her clothes, trousers and boots and an undershirt all falling apart. Kess tears the shirt down its center and taps the tip of the bloodletter against the body's chest. He looks at Six expectantly.

Six can't see everything from a seated position. They stand. The cloaks around the table are like tensed springs, Rekiav the least controlled of them, itching for an excuse. Six will not humor him. Six is as tranquil as an afternoon breeze now. They look where Kess points, to a place on the left side where two ribs have broken.

"The killing wound, am I right?" asks Kess pleasantly. "I scanned it all carefully. There's a tiny fracture in the front of the skull, as well. Here." He points it out with the blade's sharp tip, then returns to the broken ribs. "But this indicates a puncture wound. It would have gone into the heart. Yes?" He looks down at Esek's remains and smiles, almost affectionately. "What an end for her, 'ey? What a grand victory for you."

Riiniana, who has recovered some of her composure, whispers, "Seti—"

"No, no, my love. Let's have no excuses. I'm not angry with you. I think it shows drive, using Esek's mistakes against her. And this little interloper she chased all her life." He points the bloodletter at Six. "Why shouldn't you wield her like a scepter? I applaud it. I applaud *you*, Sa Alanye. Esek was a thorn in my side for years. Always trying to lure my best cloaks away."

Yorus Inye gives no reaction. The boy Rekiav is fuming. Six admits to themself that they have wondered whether Esek's long career of seeding loyalty among the Quiet Ones might have proved useful now. A way to undermine Kess. A way to use Esek's past to their own advantage. Kess appears to have made sure no such option remains, though whether he has revealed the truth of Six's identity to all his kin seems unlikely. Cloaks love secrets too much.

Kess continues, "But for all your cleverness, you made rather serious errors. You thought I wouldn't watch her as closely as you did. Or watch her beloved Chono, for that matter. All those letters you sent over the years, like a lovesick fool. It may have taken me a while to find them, to find you. But I am a cloaksaan. Which is more than you can say."

The mention of the letters feels like a stab wound, but Six doesn't speak, aware that Kess is perfectly right. This was something they never anticipated: the Cloaksaan uncovering Esek's hunt for Six, and Six's hunt for her. Perhaps Inye was even a double-crosser. And Six never saw it.

No use speaking now. Esek does enough talking for them both, her voice in Six's ear, furious at this desecration, ordering revenge, not for her death, but for the very fact of Kess knowing her better than she thought he did.

The silence goes on. Finally, quietly, Riiniana asks, "What now?"

Kess laughs. "What now?" He looks at Six. "Why, I think we should test your acting skills again. We are already in negotiation with Farren Eyce." He gestures at Yorus Inye, who is still smiling frostily. "What say you lend your voice to our efforts? Urge the Wheel to be reasonable? They will listen to you, won't they? Who knows, maybe if you do as I say, I won't rip your little cleric's limbs from her body." His eyes shine. He looks between Six and Riiniana. "Perhaps I will spare you both. Raise you up in my shadow, like good little pets. If you are obedient, that is. Otherwise, what's to stop me from exposing your secret, and your collusion, Riiniana? It would start a civil war within the Nightfoots, would it not? And give me the perfect excuse to tear your house into pieces and split it among the other families. That would be a good way to secure their alliance, would it not, Riiniana? My *righteous* bride."

His self-satisfaction radiates like the toxic heat of a bomb site. Six has a sudden memory of a conversation with Ilius Redquill many years ago. Six had called themself the jaw spider, a Braemish predator that uses its own victims as bait for bigger kill. How peculiar to be on the other side of the equation. But Six is not one to be used.

This shit stain, Esek hisses. *This nothing of a rejected Moonback fuck-faced ass— Cut out his heart. I'll come back just to bite it in half.*

Kess reaches into the white wrappings and tears Esek's skull off her spine. Riiniana gasps in horror, turning her face away. Kess hefts the skull like a trophy.

"Do we understand each other, *Esek*?"

For some reason Six can only think of the moment of Esek's death.

That maniacal hacking laughter, the sound of her lungs filling up and of the bloody ear falling from her mouth. With Kess staring at them, they suddenly feel that they are more Esek than ever. Welded to her will, the both of them wanting the same thing. So it is Esek's slow, murderous smile that creeps across their face. It is her eyes shining with the promise of revenge. It is her relaxed body with its silken mannerisms that drops back into the chair as if bored. And it is both her and Six that revel in the pinching of Kess's lips, that slightest backward shift of his body, as if, for just this moment, he doubts whether Esek is really dead, after all.

"Well," Six hums, with Esek's smirk upon their lips, "I see you've rumbled me at last. But don't worry, Kess. I'll play this game with you. After all, what is it the Quietans say? 'The worlds are big. And life is long.' There's plenty of time ... for everything we want."

Kess sneers, and somehow he has lost just a sliver of the upper hand. He tosses Esek's skull back into her pile of bones. Among the cloaks, Rekiav flinches, and Yorus Inye sniffs.

"Excellent," says Kess, and points. "You can keep that. I'll spend the evening aboard my ship. In the morning, we can contact the Jeveni together."

Without a glance for Riiniana, with his cloak swishing at his heels, he leaves the room at the head of his entourage. Rekiav casts Six one last dark look. Inye deliberately does not. After they have gone, with Esek's bones laid bare on the table, Six looks at Riiniana. She still has her face turned from the corpse, but her shock and alarm have disappeared, replaced by a stony calm.

"Huh," Six murmurs, finding that they are genuinely intrigued by what has happened. "I see you were wrong about some things."

The girl is pale, skinny as a fledgling and too young for these games. But when she looks at Six, her eyes are fierce enough to pitch their intrigue higher. Seti Kess has landed a blow Riiniana did not expect. But her shoulders are unbowed.

"This is just one tile on the board, Esek. I still have the game in hand."

Secretary Redquill appears to have struck a deal with a Jeveni collector who knows the members of the Wheel, and who will sell the name of the Star. While histories indicate the spokes of the Wheel share authority, there seems to be special reverence for this so-called Star. Whoever it is will be no more than a tribal chief, but I suspect removing them will cut the legs out from under the Jeveni rebels. As has always proved an effective strategy, we should prioritize destroying what these people love most.

excerpt, report to First Cloak Seti Moonback.
Dated 1660, Year of the Surge.

CHAPTER TEN

1665

YEAR OF THE HARVEST

Farren Eyce
The Planet Capamame

The four moons cresting Capamame look blue and silvery tonight, no cloud cover to obscure them. According to the Draeviin, who know the planet's seasons best, they are entering the clear months. The heavy snowstorms that dominate two-thirds of the year have withdrawn, leaving a crisp atmosphere, and the planet's populations of cold-resistant insects are coming out of stasis. At sunset there is a song of whirring wings. And night or day, the moons perch above like a quartet of eyes, the stages of the rotation turning them to slits and opening them wide again. Tonight is a wide-eyed night, a luminous night, the icy plains shimmering like an ocean.

Those moons shine equally bright on the airfield. The hundred or so shuttles that came with the colonists to Capamame have been arranged like an honor guard circling the protective dome, and amid their shapes, rocket and missile launchers that once armored *Drae's Hope* have been fitted for ground war. They point at the sky. In the moonlight, dozens of saan go about their work, engineers and sentries and volunteers preparing their defense. In the armory on Level 1, hundreds of guns of every kind are being cleaned, cataloged, and armed by other volunteers. Drae sen Briit, though not a warrior herself, took rather warlike precautions when she equipped *Drae's Hope* for battle. Effegen had thought they would never need those armaments.

She looks up. Far smaller but much closer than the moons, tens of thousands of miles from the planet's atmosphere, the Capamame jump gate shines white and brilliant. Standard ships can make the trip from the gate to Capamame in about half a day. For Kindom warbirds, it will be less than an hour. There will be almost no lead time when they cross the gate.

Effegen shivers. The temperature is below freezing. In a heavy down coat with gloves and boots, she tries to remember if it was ever this cold in the isolationist Jeveni village where she grew up. It was a village called Erosk on the northwestern coast of Kriistura continent, on Ma'kess. Moonback territory. A rocky coastline with a view of the island-spattered sea. Fishing boats bobbing on gray waves, and saan standing around the docks, stomping their feet and blowing on their hands to stay warm. The village was comprised of just a couple dozen cottages and the meeting hall, all stonework and thatch roofs, dirt pathways between the houses, little gardens cultivated in the yards and barren during winter.

Does this, the surface of Capamame, feel as cold as that? She can't remember. There are other, starker memories of gunfire and explosions, and her people driven from the land with nothing on their backs. The ones that lived, anyway. Which included none of Effegen's family except one cousin, who removed his Jeveni tattoo and disappeared on a pirate ship, never to be heard from again.

When she was twelve, when her parents and grandparents and two siblings who hadn't chosen gendermarks yet were dead, she saw the appeal
of her cousin's choice. He had been seventeen, so she had it in mind that
if she could survive till seventeen, she would slip away from her guardian
and find a life somewhere else. In that life, she told herself, there would be
no nighttime raids, no capricious murders, no displacement. But Effegen
had a talent for community building and strategy, and by the time she was
seventeen, she was the Star of the Wheel. Now she stands and stares at the
gate, imagining an invasion to dwarf the one that destroyed her village.
She has always worshipped Sajeven, a goddess of warmth and friendship,
a goddess to admire. But Sajeven is also a god of secrets. And whether the
Jeveni will survive is a secret from Effegen now.

A figure melts into place beside her, and for some time the two of
them stare at the sky.

"Where did you grow up?" Effegen asks quietly. "Before the kinschool, I mean."

Liis Konye pauses as if trying to remember. "A city called Aumilast
in the south of Kator. On the coast."

Effegen smiles a little. "I was born on the coast, too. Though not a city."

"It was a popular vacation spot," Liis says. "Wealthy saan from
all over the Treble came there in the summer months. That's how I
attracted the attention of the First Cloak—this was Seti Kess's predecessor. She sponsored my place at the kinschool in Dubos."

"Were you happy to go?" asks Effegen, who grew up hearing that
there was no greater curse than to become a Kindom Hand.

"I had little choice. It was a great honor to my family. I would have
ended up a mercenary or gangster otherwise."

Effegen looks at Liis for the first time. The woman is barely an inch
taller than her, though nearly twice her age and so dark-skinned she
glows in the moonlight, scars shining. She does not return Effegen's
curious look, though Effegen believes they are thinking the same
thing: that they both know themselves. They both know that they
grew up with a specific set of skills that could only have taken them
down one or two paths. Liis, a killer. Effegen, a leader.

"Did you ever serve under Kess?"

Such information could be useful. Liis's insights are always useful. But something dark alights on Liis's shoulders, her constant composure thinning long enough to show a gash underneath. Liis says, "For a time. He saw great potential in me. He had me carry out many of his most important tasks. Or help Medisogo to do so."

Fresh goose bumps travel down Effegen's spine. She suspects that this much openness about her past is unusual for Liis, and for some reason that makes Effegen feel guilty for asking. For prying. Perhaps she is also afraid to hear more, because when she changes the subject, it feels not like consideration but cowardice.

She looks at the sky again. "How is Jun?"

Whatever had hung over Liis a moment ago clears. Her chuckle sounds almost normal. "Obsessive. Determined. She can't stop reading Drae's journal. Apparently, it's full of typos."

It's such a random thing for Jun to care about right now that Effegen huffs an incredulous laugh. Drae sen Briit, a middling writer. But there's no time for levity.

Effegen asks, "How did she react to Six's message? How did *you* react to it, for that matter?"

Liis takes a long time answering. Perhaps she is running the message through her mind. Effegen does the same: a cast signal from the Kindom, originating in the Treble this time. A new message from Commandant Yorus Inye. But it was not Inye who appeared on view. It was Six, still wearing Esek like a costume. Six, who once tried to buy Effegen's name from the collector Dom ben Dane. Six, whose operation led them to the secretary Ilius Redquill, led to the slaughter of a half dozen collectors on Braemin, led, at last, to Ujan Redcore and her hateful machinations. Effegen had been so happy when they first found Six. A lost Jeveni coming home, and Drae sen Briit's descendant as well! Now she wonders if Six is a curse on her people.

Liis Konye says, "I think they were warning us."

Effegen grimaces. Six had been all charisma and incisors as they addressed the colony, urging them that there was a better life awaiting them in the Treble. Insisting that things would be different than they were under Alisiana. Better pay, better conditions, pensions, freedom, et cetera. No need to struggle on Capamame. No need to be separated forever from their home worlds. No need to fear, for Seti Kess envisions a more equitable Treble than the one they have left. The hint of sarcasm in their voice did not go unnoticed.

"It was a speech," says Liis. "Six didn't write it. There's no way they would work with Kess against Chono, so they must have a reason for playing this part."

Effegen retorts, "Such as? I don't believe for a moment that we'll be safer just because Six holds official leadership of the trade."

"Neither does Six. They said as much."

Yes, Effegen remembers.

"In conclusion," Six had brayed, "I know that your collector Masar Hawks is in the Treble working with Chono to undermine the Kindom. It's *so* dramatic, and totally unnecessary. Not only does it put your five thousand at risk, but it threatens the peace for those of you who do decide to come back! After all, ungratefulness could change your future working conditions. Something to remember."

Suddenly Six had looked aside at something past the camera, and their lips twisted in an evil smirk. "Forgive me. I don't mean to prattle on like this. You know my opinion. Goodbye!"

They had practically sung the last part, just before the message went dark.

Effegen says, "We already knew Kess's terms were a bait and switch. He's trying to lure us with fantasies of prosperity so he can cage us later. And as for our five thousand citizens in the Treble, it's hardly news to me that they are in danger."

And it doesn't even matter now. Kess has the Hood and the gates. They are trapped.

Liis says, "Telling us not to trust his offer was a way for Six to signal their true alliance."

"They'd do us much more help by assassinating Kess. Since they've managed to get closer to him than Chono and Masar have."

"Don't give up on them yet," Liis murmurs.

Effegen looks at her directly again. "I wonder that you can be so generous toward people who have betrayed our trust. Six. *Bene.*"

That last name tastes like ash, and yet her body aches with longing.

Liis returns her look, expression stolid. "If I judged people only by their mistakes, I would have to kill myself."

Those same goose bumps from before race across Effegen's skin. The dark-winged thing on Liis's shoulders returns. In that moment, it is a great effort to hold Liis Konye's stare, to accept who she is, what she's done, the pitiless violence she has perpetuated, the evils in which she is complicit. Seti's favored instrument. Effegen would like to say that when she looks at Liis, she can't see that person. But it's in her eyes, ancient and dark.

Again, a coward, she changes the subject. "The Feast of Sajeven's Dear Friend is seven days away. We're running out of time. You told me that if it were up to you, you would hunt down whoever had access to the gate key and kill them."

Liis shifts her attention to the saan working on the airfield, perhaps assessing areas for improvement. "Do you wish to send me to the Treble, my Star?"

For some reason, this brings tears to Effegen's eyes. Liis is not Jeveni. Liis broke away from the powers that bound her. And yet when she calls Effegen "my Star," it is with the deepest respect. What has Effegen done to win such a thing from Liis Konye?

She swallows down a roughness in her throat. "Should I?"

"You don't believe that Masar and Chono can do it."

It's not a question. Effegen feels like a traitor.

Liis says, "If you ask me to go, I will go."

"What about Jun?"

The pause is longer this time. Liis's voice is softer. "To protect Farren Eyce, I will go. To protect Jun, I will go."

Effegen swallows. Less than two weeks ago she sent Masar to the Treble. She did it knowing he might never come back, that she might never hold him again—she did it knowing he might die, and her body wanted to revolt. *Am I not this colony's sword and shield?* he had asked her, and she wanted to scream at him, *No. You are my lover. You are the one who hasn't been torn from me yet. Don't make me do this.*

But she had done it. Duty compelled her to do it. If she sends Liis to the Treble, Jun will never forgive her. But that cannot be a consideration. Because Effegen is the Star.

"Is this why we're here?" Liis asks dryly. "Are we hiding from Jun?"

Effegen laughs, short and soggy. "No. I've been coming up here every night for days."

"I'm aware."

"You've made good progress."

Liis says, "We have."

"But to what end? We can't stop a Kindom invasion."

"We can slow it down."

Effegen gestures angrily at the field. "With *those*? Hundred-year-old missiles?"

"Very well-made missiles. Well maintained. And we have a defensible position. The cloaks won't easily overrun us in the colony, and we can force them into traps. Also, our colonists are from every walk of life. Thousands of them have experience with weapons. They will step forward to defend their home." Effegen shudders involuntarily. "You don't want to ask them for that. You want to protect them. I understand. If we fight back, many will die."

She offers no comfort to accompany these words. Effegen is grateful to her for that. Whenever Liis speaks to the Wheel about this planned defense, the reaction is always the same. Tomesk crows that the Jeveni will give the Kindom something to remember, and Hyre insists that they can limit casualties, and Gaeda declares that this is the will of Sajeven. All while Fonu sits in the corner, quiet and haunted in their slowly healing body. A dammed River.

"I can't send you to the Kindom," Effegen whispers. "Masar is gone. My senior collectors are dead. Fonu is a shell. You are the only one who can lead our defense."

"Yes."

Effegen swallows. "If the Kindom captures you, they'll torture you. They'll murder you."

"Yes."

"You're not even Jeveni. You don't owe us anything, Liis."

It seems important to say this. Liis must understand that Effegen will demand nothing of her. How can she? How can she ask so much from anyone? She brought her people here to save them, and now she may be throwing them to their deaths.

Liis speaks at last, firm and unafraid. "I am the servant of my Star."

When Effegen returns to the government district on Level 8, she has no choice but to walk past the newsnest. Two sentries guard the entrance to the makeshift prison, whose occupants have shrunk to include only Tej and Ujan Redcore. Other sentries guard the private residences of the spies who Jun uncovered. Aris the Beauty. Dom ben Dane. Others who insist they can be reformed. They are inherently dangerous to the colony and in great danger of the colony's retribution. How hard will Effegen work to protect them, if it comes to that? How hard will she work to protect—

She shoves the thought aside.

It's past midnight. The levels of Farren Eyce are not abandoned, but they are quieter than usual. Effegen walks slowly into the small neighborhood of residences where the Wheel have their private homes. Her own door is at the end of the hall, and when it comes in sight her weary body tightens with surprise. A young saan stands outside the door, a sentry named Pejun who is assigned to escort Bene. Something goes off inside her, realizing that Bene must be on the other side of her door. He was released days ago, and yet she hasn't seen him in person since the morning he was thrown into the newsnest. She has avoided him, avoided his nearness and his voice as if they are weapons that could destroy her.

The collector bows over his hands.

In a near panic, Effegen asks, "He's in my private rooms?"

Pejun looks startled, then pale with alarm. "I apologize, my Star. I was told that—I thought—and he had the code."

The access code to her apartment. Something she gave him in the early days of their friendship, when they were spending more time together and he would come over some nights for tea, and it was easier to just let him let himself in than make him wait for her to be finished with whatever business occupied her. He was the light at the end of her day; he was the chance to be something more than a Star. She called him Capamame, pretended to be teasing, but the endearment filled her belly with warmth. Capamame. The dear friend.

"I'll remove him," Pejun says quickly. "I'm so sorry. I shouldn't have—"

She cuts him off with a gesture and does her level best to control her voice. "It's all right. I'll speak to him."

Angrily casting her door open, she storms inside and slams it behind her with a degree of violence she doesn't ever allow herself. That violence comes to a staggering standstill when she finds that it is not just Bene in her apartment. A blue-tinged hologram faces him in the middle of the room. Both men turn toward her, Bene looking nervous, pained, and Masar resolute. Effegen looks back and forth between them, and no one speaks for so long that she feels a fit of hilarity creeping up on her, as if she will burst into hysterical laughter at the ridiculousness of their circumstances.

She doesn't. She lifts her chin at Bene. "I forgot to change my access code."

She sees the blow land, and feels it in her own body. Bene looks tired, circles under his eyes, body thinner than he was a couple of weeks ago. She has thought, from the beginning, that he is arrestingly beautiful, with that sly smile and curly hair, and eyes all warm and golden brown. The first time he kissed her, he poured gold into her body. And later, when he saw her desire for Masar, he teased his way through her shyness and whispered fantasies into her ears. He gave room for her to love them both, and she did she did she did...

Now, he curves in on himself, hands in his pockets. "That's my mistake, then. I thought you would have changed it."

"And because I didn't, you assume that you're welcome in my private rooms?" He flinches. "You should have asked me before just... showing up here. And I still can't believe Pejun would let you—"

"I approved it," interrupts Masar.

She snaps her eyes toward him, surprised and incensed. Before she can ask what gives him the right, she sees a bandage on his neck. Icy fear sweeps through her.

"Was there more fighting?" she demands.

He touches the bandage self-consciously, as if he had forgotten it was there. "This happened during the ambush in Trin-Ma. I just—it was hidden. By my jacket."

Meaning he hid it. He lied to her. The cold in her body cycles back into heat. Her voice rasps. "Are you all right?"

"Yes. I'm all right."

She looks at Bene again. "Are *you* all right?"

He looks confused, as much by the question as that she would ask it. "Am I . . . ?"

"Ujan broke your ribs," she reminds him accusingly. "Did you think I forgot? Do you think one second has gone by since it happened that I've forgotten what she did to you both?"

Bene swallows, hesitating. "The . . . doctors treated me."

"I know that already. I'm asking if you've healed well."

"I—yes."

"Has anyone in the colony tried to hurt you?"

He waits so long that she wonders if he's going to lie. "Nothing worse than words."

She glares at him.

"Effegen." Masar's voice is stern. His use of her name startles her a little. He's spent so many years calling her "my Star." "I don't know how long I'll be in Kel-Ma—or where I'm going next. We could all be dead tomorrow; I want—"

"Do not *manipulate* me with threats of—"

"It's not manipulation if it's true, you stubborn woman—"

"Please, let's not fight," Bene begs. "Not because of me."

"As if you are the center of everything!" Effegen huffs.

"Well, he's certainly the center of this, isn't he?" says Masar.

"I'll go," Bene insists, moving toward the door. "I'll go."

"Don't you dare!" she shouts.

The door flies open, Pejun coming inside with his rifle raised. Bene, after a startled beat, puts his hands up. Pejun looks from one of them to the next, and they all just stand there like children who have broken a piece of crockery, expressions running the gamut of angry to embarrassed to lost.

"My Star, are you all right?"

Masar huffs in exasperation, crossing his arms. Bene still has his hands ridiculously thrust up.

Effegen glowers. "Gods' sake, put your hands down. Pejun, everything is fine."

Pejun looks uncertain. "Are you sure—"

"I'm in no danger from Bene Ironway. You can come back for him in the morning."

He seems just as wary as before, and also embarrassed. Effegen realizes too late the implication of her words. She would be embarrassed, too, if she had any room for it left in her. Bene cautiously lowers his hands.

"Your Star gave you an order," Masar rumbles. "Now go."

It takes Pejun several seconds, but at last he slowly backs out the door and closes it. Effegen listens for the sound of retreating steps, but can't be sure. Gaeda has the apartment nearest to hers. Did the Stone hear her shout? There is no shouting now. The apartment is very quiet, until—

"You didn't have to send him away," Bene whispers. "I know you have every right to distrust me."

She exhales, restless and annoyed. "Bene. If you are an assassin, frankly I'd rather die than have to live with a betrayal of that magnitude."

She walks over to the small kitchen in her apartment, and though she's never been one to drink, she does keep a bottle of rock wine in her cupboard. She takes it out, and a cup. She pours a small measure.

Behind her, Bene whispers, "Please don't say that."

Effegen's jevite rings glint under the kitchen lights, a movement that makes her realize her hand is trembling. She needs to put the rings and her other jevite jewelry away in the stasis case that will delay the effects of oxygen. Doing such a simple daily task feels more difficult in this moment than lifting a mountain. She takes a swallow of her drink, briny and astringent, the texture clean on her tongue. It's not even wine. It's a Jeveni recipe, something the miners brewed in their dome cities. In one of Drae sen Briit's speeches, she called on all the Jeveni to raise a glass of rock wine to their future. She promised them freedom and safety and they believed her, for she was loved and trusted and revered. Well. Fuck her.

"It can't be like this between us," Masar says. "If you don't want Bene anymore, you have to say so. There's too much going on for us to hold each other in suspense. The gates are under guard. I can't get back to you. All you have is each other now."

Effegen whirls on him. "I don't accept that. You *are* coming home. I *command* it!" She looks at Bene. "And you! How dare you look at me like that! You were the only one who never bowed to me. Of course I'm angry at you! You did an irrational thing, you made a terrible mistake that got people hurt, but—" She feels a great tearing inside herself, anger and resentment and need all clawing at her until, with a staggering gasp, she cries, "I know who you are. But I'm *afraid*. I don't hate you. I can't hate you. But I'm afraid. Can you just—just have a little patience and let me be afraid and not *look at me* like that?!"

Bene transforms, like a horizon blooming with the sun. Hope and love blaze up in him. He steps toward her but she can't bear that, not yet.

"Don't," she begs. "Please don't."

He stops, glancing at Masar. They both look helpless. She lets out a breath, rubs the corners of her eyes. The brief outburst has exhausted her. She finishes her drink and sets down the glass. Lifting her chin, she says with all the composure and calm of her office, "I've just spoken to Liis Konye. The plans for our defense are going as well as can be expected."

This is for Masar, a military report, but she hopes Bene sees that it is also a gesture of trust. Foolish or not.

Masar nods. "Good. She knows what to do."

Effegen laughs bitterly. "She thinks I should leverage as many of our colonists as possible. Anyone who knows how to hold a gun. When Seti Kess comes, our only hope is to convince him that leaving us alone is less trouble than taking us by force. The Kindom is used to Jeveni who roll over and beg. They won't be prepared for a resistance."

She says it, but she doesn't believe it. Kess slaughtered hundreds of secretaries and put the Clerisy under house arrest. He won't throw his hands up and retreat because of a ragtag army of Jeveni.

As if Masar and Bene had said this themselves, she looks at them haughtily. "I know what will happen if we fight back. Thousands will die. What else would you have me do? Since I was a *child*, it's been my responsibility to protect my people and my culture. Leaders have made this bargain since the beginning. Sacrifice the few to save the many. Why should I be exempt from that? Why shouldn't I tell my fighters to be merciless? To sacrifice themselves?" She glares at them. "Wouldn't *you*?"

Though it was meant as a question, it comes out as a challenge. No, an entreaty. She wants to tower with confidence, but her eyes sting with tears, and she has to dash them away, humiliated. More so by the heartbroken compassion on Bene's face, and by the way Masar looks as if he could batter his way through the universe to reach her.

He says roughly, "I would never wish your choices on anyone, Effegen. But you are a strong leader. You're what your people need."

Effegen scoffs. "Do they need slaughter? Do they need me to put guns in their hands and tell them to be killers? In defiance of all my own values? In defiance of everything I wanted for this place? Treason." She looks at Bene. "This will be leagues worse than anything you did. It'll be worse than Ujan. I'll kill the very soul of this colony to protect it. And if somehow the Jeveni survive and anyone remembers the Wheel in a hundred years, they'll talk about the Star who took her people to war with no hope of success!"

She lobs the words like grenades. But there is no explosion, only hollow silence.

Bene asks softly, "What is the alternative?"

"Surrender," she snaps, wringing her hands, twisting her rings. "I could surrender. They don't know the faces of the spokes. They'll kill me, but our people will survive. We've been slaves before. We can survive. And some day a wiser Star will find a way to free us again."

"No one is killing you," growls Masar.

"It's not your decision. *I* am *your* leader. You will do what I say."

"I'm not done out here," he retorts. "Chono and I will find a way to protect—"

"Chono left you for this scheme of hers. We don't even know if she's still alive. You're surrounded by non-Jeveni who don't care about us."

"I don't think that's true."

"Then what are you saying? That I should wait? Should I tell Liis to stand down?"

Her voice is embarrassingly plaintive. Masar looks angry in his own powerlessness. Bene is so pale his warm skin has gone gray. It is very strange. Bene is real and solid, and Masar looks close enough to touch, but they are both unreachable. She can't bring herself to be vulnerable to them, to let them see—

"I don't know what to do." Her voice catches on a sob. She looks at them both, pleadingly. "Tell me what to do!"

Tears well in Bene's eyes. Masar says, "You know what to do."

"I don't!"

"Yes, you do. You are the wisest Star in generations."

She shakes her head. Bene says, "You've survived as much as any Jeveni has been asked to survive. It hasn't broken you. You've done the hard thing a thousand times already. Don't doubt yourself now. *Listen* to yourself. What do you *know*?"

She flashes on the fishing village where she grew up, the hateful neighbors that lit them on fire, saan trapped in their homes, even her own family.

"I . . . know that . . . I can't let us return to what we were before."

"And what was that?" Masar presses.

"Outcasts," she says. "Despised. *Enslaved.*"

Bene's weight shifts forward. "And do you think the people of Farren Eyce are willing to return to that, either?" He takes a step. She wants him to step back. She wants him to come closer. She wants to run from him and she wants him to touch her. She wants both of them, but she can't ask for it. "The Jeveni are fierce. They've survived again and again. Ask *them* what they want. Ask *them* if they're willing to surrender this place."

She thinks of the village center of Erosk. The meeting room with its temple to Sajeven. The Ma'kessn raiders burned that first. They trapped the priests inside. Artifacts dating back to Jeve, tapestries gifted by the Gale of the Wheel, the big woven rug where her people sat together and prayed. It was not enough for the raiders to kill them—it was not even the point. The point was to kill what it means to be Jeveni, to kill everything the Jeveni are.

Seti Kess will do the same. He won't let them have isolationist villages. He won't let them worship their goddess or speak their language. He won't give them a moon to themselves. They will be like that meeting hut, their very identities burned alive.

"I can't surrender," she whispers.

Masar's posture draws up with what she realizes is pride. It gleams in his good eye, shows in the tilt of his smile. She doesn't deserve that pride. Not weak as she is. When Bene moves toward her, she nearly flinches from him.

"I can't," she pleads again, but for another reason. It's too much. It will break her.

Masar says, "You aren't alone. Isn't that what you told me, once?"

Bene reaches her, touching her elbow, and the back of her head, drawing her toward him and coaxing her to lay her face against his shoulder. She breathes him in, staggered by the relief of his smell, of the warmth of his skin, of his love bleeding into her. She lifts her face to look at Masar. He watches them with an expression of torment and relief, and she is bitterly reminded that they only made love once. That what they had wanted so much was gained and lost within a few hours. They may never have it again: Masar's arms around her, the sight of Bene kissing him, touch and passion passed between them in a burst of greediness and giving.

But he is still here, somehow. He watches. And Bene's arms are strong and safe. Bene cups the nape of her neck again to tug her to him. His mouth. His kiss. He slides his tongue against hers in gentle query and she shudders, gripping his hair so tight she must be hurting him.

"Good," Masar rumbles low in his chest.

Desperation overcomes her. She scrabbles at Bene, nails digging into his shoulders and body pressing up into him. He keeps kissing her, but slowly, deeply, forcing her to wait. He draws her toward her bed and she is helpless to do anything but follow him. All the fear in him, all the guilt and uncertainty, is gone, replaced with command as he sits on the bed and pulls her between his knees. He starts to undress her. He casts Masar's hologram closer to the bed. Effegen looks up with dazed eyes, sees Masar standing close and watching them, radiating lust. She's afraid she will start weeping, crushed with love and loneliness for him.

As if he knows it, Bene whispers to her, "He's with us. Feel his hands. Feel his mouth."

She's naked now. He slides his palms down her body, over her breasts and hips. She moves closer, never breaking eye contact with Masar. Bene turns all his attention to her breasts till she's shivering and restless. She tells them both, "Take your clothes off."

They obey her, Bene standing up and standing close as he does it, and Masar dragging off his shirt and sliding a hand down his belly till Effegen keens, clawing at Bene and pulling him to kiss her again. He falls backward, bringing her with him. She straddles his belly, feeling him hard beneath her.

"No," she says with her last wits. "You—you don't like it—"

"Shh," he says, slipping his hand between her legs. "Like this." The feeling of him there is bliss. Her head tips back, eyes slipping closed. Bene's free hand grips her hip. "Open your eyes. Watch him."

Panting, she forces her eyes open, staring at Masar. Bene presses into her, punching a mewling cry from her throat. She can feel them both, and they are both hers, and she'll never let them go. Masar touching himself and watching them. Bene curling his fingers till her breathing grows hysterical. Both of them watching her, moaning encouragement. She clenches and clenches and sobs, for she wants nothing but this, nothing but them, and in that moment of fierce release and joy, she knows that she will kill Seti Kess herself, if only to keep this safe.

CHAPTER ELEVEN

1665

YEAR OF THE HARVEST

Yeyankatayan
Uosti Continent
The Planet Kator

In the end, Chono is right. Khen Obair will do anything to get his son back—including risk the wrath of Seti Kess. And there is no doubting Kess's wrath, if he discovers that Obair has arranged Chono safe passage through the Teron gate. To say nothing of how he'll feel about the Katishsaan who meet her on the other side of the gate and deliver her to the mountainous highlands of Uosti continent, and from there, right onto the grounds of the chalet Yeyankatayan.

Katish sentinels flank her as she disembarks the shuttle into a court-yard of golden-brown sandstone. The wind has gnashing teeth, and even the proper highlands coat the sentinels have given her does not keep the worst of it out. It would be little warmer if she had stayed in Praetima, which is east, on the other side of the planet. Chono thinks of that city, an empty, bloodstained husk. What happened to Ilius's body, she wonders? Did Kess give his slaughtered victims a proper funeral? Or leave them to rot?

Yeyankatayan, unbowed by the tragedies that have struck the rest of the Treble, surges around her in a masterwork of spire-tipped towers and walls with long walkways that look like battlements. Katishsaan stroll those walkways, as well as the second courtyard, which Chono can see through a large arched entryway some hundred feet from her position. The walls are more of that smooth sandstone. Praetima was all cobbled roads and rustic buildings, but this palace is formed of clean lines.

As Chono walks forward, a hologram bursts to life in front of her. A beautiful Katishsaan with the placid, welcoming smile of a tourist guide bows to her over their open palms.

"Hello, Cleric Chono. Welcome to Yeyankatayan, the pride of Kator and its noble people." The figure, obviously a cast program, folds their hands against their chest. "You are welcome in our halls, and protected under our shelter. These escorts"—they gesture with one hand and then the next at the saan on either side of Chono—"are here to safeguard you and provide for your needs. We have reserved you a private suite in the northeast tower, where you will have all the comforts necessary to prepare for your first audience, which is scheduled for exactly one hour from now." The hologram's smile widens, and they bow again. "May Kata's Many bless your affairs in Yeyankatayan, and see you safely to all your destinations."

The hologram vanishes in a sprinkle of pixels that, Chono thinks, is definitely overdoing it. Immediately, a small blue sphere appears on her ocular, and with sentinels in tow, she follows it through the arch and into the second, larger courtyard. It's surprisingly busy, given the cold. Many wandering elites, resplendent in their winter clothes and carrying pets on their shoulders (pinch cats and blue crows more fashion statement than animal), gawk at her and whisper behind their hands as if she is the ostentatious one. Chono pays them no heed. When the blue sphere leads her through a door into a hallway, she does not stand aside for the duo of Katishsaan walking in her direction. They are the ones who flatten themselves against the wall for her.

She goes down the hall. She goes up some stairs. She goes higher and higher until the sphere stops in front of a door. One of the sentinels pushes it open for her.

She's expecting something showy, like the hotel suite the Clever Hand gave her and Six in Praetima. But the room before her is refreshingly modest. It is a large circle with the far third divided from the rest by a wall and a door. The larger third has a simple bed fit for one, a tea table with two high-backed armchairs in green upholstery, and a wardrobe. The furnishings all look artisan made, mostly of wood that is rare on Kator, for the planet has very few forests.

The sentinels close the door after her. She hears the lock. No surprise. Can't have a rogue Hand wandering the premises.

The room behind the wall contains nothing more grandiose than a shower, a Katish evaporation toilet, and a single sink vanity with a round mirror above it. When Chono looks a second time, she sees that there is a vibration razor sitting on the countertop, a pristine tool that Katishsaan use to create their elaborate and architectural hairstyles.

There is also clothing hanging on a hook on the door, and Chono tenses. There is nothing remarkable about the dark trousers or the white button-down shirt with its Katish-style neckline. A small table next to the door presents leather boots and folded underclothes, also Katish style. These things are forgettable. What sends a shiver down her spine is the beautifully displayed red-and-gold coat of a Righteous Hand.

She stares at it.

When she first returned from Capamame, the Cloaksaan stripped her coat from her and stuck her in a Praetima prison cell. She still remembers the ill-made stinking uniform of her incarceration. After her release, she found fresh clothes and her coat waiting for her, the coat washed and repaired in spots that had worn from time. She abandoned that coat aboard Yantikye's shuttle, for it was too recognizable for someone trying to sneak into Trin-Ma. Yet now there is a new coat, pristinely tailored and with gold threadwork that glitters. A statement, this coat. And an expectation. One she can never escape.

She strips off her clothes. The shower is hot and she takes it for the gift it is, washing herself with soaps that emit a clean green smell. She breathes the smell in, trying to center herself. Six, despite never having lived on the planet, has more Katish blood than not. The child she remembers had deep, cool-brown eyes and skin the color of wet soil. She tries to imagine Six as they might have looked without all their transformations. She tries to imagine them growing up on Kator, and smelling of green things, wearing Katish fashions and cutting their hair to match the local trends. But even as she tries, Six resists her, and when she closes her eyes against the falling water and presses her palms against the wall, she sees them as they are, all umber skin and eyes arresting gold, and woven braids dewed with water droplets from the shower spray—

She jerks upright, hitting the panel so that the water stops. In its sudden absence, a draft sneaks in. She's breathing hard. She's full of longing for Six and despair at what may be happening to them, somewhere, anywhere, beyond her reach. But she gets out of the shower and she shaves the stubble from her head, and she dons that damnable uniform, returning to the larger room.

A woman is standing at the front door, hands behind her back, the butt of a sidearm visible just under her military jacket. A second woman sits in one of the green upholstered armchairs, tea things laid out before her. A bright orange pinch cat little bigger than one of those cups sleeps curled on her shoulder. Like an elaborate brooch, it contributes to her elegance. Her hair is a flattop crown, dense and dark and powdered with silver. Diamond finger bracelets adorn one hand, and she has two more diamonds bedded in the full plushness of her bottom lip. Chono can see, even sitting, that she is tall, slight of build, and long-limbed, almost avian in her construction. She raises her eyes.

Chono never took much notice of Aver Paiye's eyes. They were dark. They were warm. They had wrinkles at the corners. They were identical to the eyes that look at her now. The last time Chono saw Aver's eyes, they were open, blank, and his head lay in a growing pool of blood.

"Cleric Chono," says Aver's sister, Oyun Paiye, in a voice both commanding and silky. "Do come and sit."

Chono looks at the other woman standing before the door. She mistook her at first for a sentinel, but now she notices the tailored white suit, the pristine grooming, and the overall impression of wealth. The woman's finger bracelets are also diamond crusted, signaling both her devotion to Kata and her position relative to the woman in the chair. She is Hejar Paiye, Oyun's heir. She looks at Chono with a flat expression that does not conceal suspicion and superiority.

Chono sits in the second armchair and bows over her palms.

"Regal Paiye." She uses the proper Katish honorific. "Thank you for seeing me."

Oyun Paiye smiles, droll. "Thank-yous are for gifts. Selling a hostage for an audience is something else. You take a tremendous risk by assuming I won't turn you over to Seti Kess."

Chono regards Oyun. The woman is seventy-five years old, a decade Aver's senior, and yet she looks younger than he did when he died. Oyun could be fifty. The same medical advancements that allowed Six to transform themself into Esek have allowed Oyun to carve years off herself, just as Alisiana Nightfoot did. Just as many clerics do, in their efforts to retain the youth and beauty that penitents often value in the Righteous Hand. Not Aver, though. Aver let himself age naturally, and managed his office without pomp. Though there was pageantry, at the end...

"You have not seen Yeyankatayan before," Oyun observes.

"No, Sa. You have a beautiful palace."

"But you have visited a Paiye estate, true? You officiated a Paiye wedding years ago; some third cousin of mine."

"Yes, Regal. Your estate on Sikata Leen. It was an honor."

Oyun chuckles. "Not much honor, I'm afraid. I can't be bothered to attend every family wedding. But I hear you brought the thing off well. They say you adapt well to other cultures." She extends a hand to indicate the tea things. "You're familiar with a proper tea service, yes?" Without waiting for an answer, she lifts the squat teapot and pours a golden amber tea into two small cups. She drops crystallized honey into the cups and scoops thick cream on top. "This tea set was made by a master potter of the Uosti coastlands. It's been passed down, generation by generation, to me. I do more honor to you with this teapot than that wedding ever could."

Oyun picks up a cup and slurps the tea through the cream. Her finger bracelets clink musically. The little pinch cat opens its pink eyes and watches Chono with interest while Chono tries to interpret whether the Regal's words are conversational or mocking. Oyun says over the rim of the cup, "There. Now you know I'm not poisoning you."

Chono, too, lifts her teacup with one hand and drinks. The cream is satiny, the tea full-bodied. The last time she saw Aver, he, too, offered her a traditional Katish tea service. His tea set was plain, and he sweetened it with cinnamon sugar disks rather than honey—a regional difference that, Chono now thinks, may have signaled his distance from the Paiye court.

"I understand that you were with my brother when he died," says Oyun. Her voice is neutral.

So is Chono's. "Yes, Sa. I was speaking to him in his cabin on the Easwa beach. Secretary Redquill and several guardsaan arrested us. He accused us of treason, and when I wouldn't give him the information he wanted, he killed your brother."

There are little tea cakes on a plate. Oyun takes one, breaking off a corner to feed it to her pet, who munches happily. She asks, "Is it true that you sought an audience with Aver in order to recruit him to your efforts to bring down the Clever Hand?"

"I did."

"And was it a bad death?"

Chono pauses, wondering how she means this question. Does she mean, was it dishonorable? Or does she mean, was it painful? Or both?

There's no point in trying to frame the story in a way that benefits Chono herself. No point in trying to suggest that Aver's death is anyone's fault but her own. She brought the Kindom to his cottage. Oyun, who radiates the keen, impassive cleverness of her goddess, will read through any deflection Chono attempts.

"He was afraid but defiant. He was injured, but he kept his pride. Redquill shot him in the leg, which would have been excruciating. Then he shot him in the head, which ended it quickly. I don't know what happened to his body."

Oyun says, "Kess gave it to us, as a gesture of goodwill. We burned Aver a week ago."

Chono has heard rumors throughout her life of Oyun's deep love for Aver. One story says that when Oyun learned her mother was giving Aver to the Kindom as its family tithe, she raged and grieved, inconsolable. Such passions are completely absent from the woman's face now. There is something humorous about the way she watches Chono, which worries Chono more than open grief would.

Chono whispers, "Gods keep him well."

"Hmm, yes. It's good of you to bless him now. I understand you broke his heart before you got him killed." Oyun holds her cup, gazing through the steam, and slurps in the customary fashion. The pinch cat grumbles, and gets another piece of cake. "Hundreds of years ago, Kator had a specific punishment for murderers. They would find anyone directly or indirectly responsible for the murder, and burn them alive on the victim's funeral pyre." Her stare is level. "Some say it was a barbaric practice."

Chono raises her cup, sips, slurps, tastes the honeyed sweetness and the fatty cream that has halfway dissolved into the tea. "On Teros, flaying was an approved capital punishment in the twelfth century. It was reserved for traitors," she says.

Hejar moves for the first time, a slight rebalancing of weight, a rumble in her throat. She glares at Chono as if the glare could slice her in half.

Oyun says, "Disregard my emotional daughter. She was very fond of her uncle. You do imply, do you not, that he was a traitor? That's very strange, as he felt you had betrayed him. And yet, he loved you. I spoke to him a month before he died. He still loved you. You were very precious to him. Isn't that strange, Cleric Chono?"

Chono recalls Aver accusing her of betraying him. She threatened to kill him for it.

"Some say I should give you to Seti Kess. Khen Obair certainly hopes I will."

Yes, Obair must want this very much, as insurance against Chono's revenge. But thinking of him is like putting needles under her fingernails. She exhales, as if it could flush the memory out of her.

Oyun says, "Then there's my family. I believe in their loyalty, but I could be wrong. One of them might be betraying you to Kess, even now. Not turning you over invites war."

"You would have the stronger position," Chono observes. "Kess is already fighting multiple wars across the Treble."

"But the Nightfoots have lent him their armies."

"The Nightfoots aren't enough for him to defeat you. Not with the allies you can raise."

A thin smile. A sharp, gleaming look, full of assessment. Oyun *hmms* to herself. "Aver always described you as very mild and humble. But you're not mild, are you, Cleric Chono? You are warlike."

"I've never wanted war. That's why I went to your brother. Whatever our disagreements, he didn't want war, either. He agreed to work together. He said he would introduce me to you."

A tinkling laugh. "Work together?"

"Don't ally with Kess. Don't go to war with him against the rebels, either on Kator or anywhere else. Ally with them *against* Kess, and convince Khen Obair to do the same. The Moonback family will follow, even if the Nightfoots don't. Kess will be forced to surrender."

"To what end?" asks Hejar Paiye, speaking for the first time. She has a deep voice; her gendermark signals female masculinity—a uniquely Braemish assignation with no counterpart on Kator. Chono knows that Hejar has traveled widely, absorbed other cultures, looked beyond the traditions of her people. Still, what does her mother think of such a gendermark?

"To the end of achieving interstellar peace," Chono answers.

Hejar says scornfully, "Kess won't surrender. He'll dig in with his allies and have us all at war for years to come. Millions will die. On the other hand, my family could help him squash these malcontents. How many are there, really? Eliminating them would save lives, in the long run."

Chono says, "There's no reason to pretend that that's what concerns you, Sa. Saving lives is my motivation, not yours. Your primary concern is your business holdings."

Oyun laughs. It's an elegant laugh, as decorative as the pinch cat, and yet Chono thinks it's sincere. "Burning One, I think I like you. You say something that fundamentally insults our morality, and yet you do it in a way that assumes we will not be insulted. Which we aren't. Because you're right. My main concern is not saving the lives of revolutionaries. Revolution is messy and hypocritical and ultimately restarts the cycle of corruption. A thriving economy, on the other hand, is the highest moral good. It creates the best conditions for survival and comfort."

"Or it can perpetuate its own cycle of corruption," Chono says.

"You are a bad negotiator. Why come in here and make saving lives your opening salvo, when you believe that it is of little interest to my family?"

"Because the *effect* of saving those lives benefits your economic goals."

"Do tell."

"Your daughter is wrong to say that attacking the rebels will save lives. You imagine a scenario where the Kindom wipes them out in a single wave. But rebels are like weeds. I don't mean pests. I mean resilient. They always come back. If you and Kess and the Families try to obliterate them, they'll return, and in greater numbers. Already they are allying in a single, coordinated quorum. To stop them you'll have to kill millions of innocent civilians, and from those survivors will come more, rallying to that quorum. In other words, bigger, stronger weeds. Those weeds will choke off your production centers and supply lines. Certainly they'll disrupt the sevite trade that you rely on. What will you have to show for it, as your profits and your armies dwindle? Seti Kess, for your tyrant leader."

Chono pauses. Oyun waits, her dark Aver eyes attentive.

"If, on the other hand, you and the Families stand up to Kess, you'll gain the alliance of the quorum. They'll work with you instead of against you, and you won't have to kiss Kess's ring. You'll achieve common ground with the other Families, and have a chance to heal centuries of hostility. Certainly that is of economic interest."

Oyun's lips quirk into another smile, small and intrigued. Chono wonders if she's about to mock her. Instead—

"When you and Esek Nightfoot returned to the Treble, I reviewed that data flood you brought with you. I watched your recorded message to the Treble, as well as your speech in Nikapraev. I was trying to understand my brother's faith in you. I could see at once that you are a powerful orator, and experiencing it in person is equally impressive. But an orator is fundamentally a politician, and politicians trade in idealistic promises. They adjust their messaging to suit and seduce their audience. They are strategically minded and secretly cynical. Even the ones who believe in their own vision are cynical."

She lifts her cup of tea, drinking, slurping. Chono does the same, but the cooling tea doesn't refresh her. She feels hot and overly conscious of her body. Some little bit of shaved hair is itching the back of her neck, under her collar. Her perfectly tailored coat feels like it's trying to smother her.

"I'm not a politician, Sa," Chono says woodenly.

Oyun snorts. "Not a practiced one, no. And not an honest one, though of course there's no such thing. You want the Families to depose Kess. Fine. I, for one, wouldn't mind seeing the Brutal Hand decimated altogether. But this fantasy of the rebels and the Families working together to build a greater Treble? Do you honestly expect me to take it seriously? Should I believe for one moment that the people involved in this uprising want a new age where the Families retain their power and wealth? Surely neither of us is that naive, Cleric Chono."

Chono thinks of the members of the quorum, their anger and

disagreements, and their contempt for the Families. She thinks particularly of Sikrt Goodrite and Cly Siltmire, the Ma'kessn rebels who boasted of their homegrown armies as if to say that they had the support to do what they wanted, regardless of the quorum's decision.

The pinch cat purrs for more cake.

Chono concedes, "It's true these saan want a share in that power and wealth."

Another laugh, musical. A crumb for the pinch cat. "They'll want more than that," Oyun says. "They'll tear down the institutions of the Kindom and raid my chalet. They'll have the Families flayed alive and burned to death in our own homes. It'll be the sacking of Verdant all over again."

"It doesn't have to be that way."

"No, it certainly doesn't. Weeds can be controlled, Cleric Chono, even if never completely wiped out. They come in seasons, you cull them, and so goes the cycle of the worlds. You know perfectly well that rebellions have risen against the Kindom throughout our history. This latest burst is just a new season of weeds." Oyun raises a hand, forestalling Chono's response. "That said...you're onto something with this idea of collaboration between the Families. Though you're not the first to suggest it."

Chono frowns. "Am I not?"

Oyun looks at Hejar, a signal.

Hejar says in her flat, contemptuous voice, "We've had an invitation to a meeting of the Families, to discuss just such a collaboration."

Chono can't hide her surprise. "Invited by whom? Kess?"

"It may have been his idea. But the invitation comes from Esek Nightfoot."

She may as well have doused Chono in ice water. It's almost hard to breathe. Perhaps Hejar only means the Nightfoot household. Perhaps the Nightfoots are pretending to have Esek back among them, and Seti Kess still has Six in his grasp—

It takes Chono far too long to muster a response. "Esek is with her family?" she asks.

Hejar narrows her eyes. Oyun says with intrigue, "We thought you knew. It's true that she's lain low since Praetima, but according to the gossip, Seti Kess rescued her from that massacre and returned her to Verdant. We had assumed there was some falling out between you and her?" Chono doesn't answer. After a long look, Oyun states, "You thought she was dead."

No, Chono didn't think this, but she judges it may be better to let Oyun think so.

Oyun hums. "Then I suppose it's true. She has betrayed your friendship to see to the interests of the Nightfoots. I thought perhaps you were still working together, but this business of her lending her armies to Kess hardly aligns with your interests, does it? And you didn't even know where she was. Don't take it so hard, Cleric Chono. Nightfoots are notoriously changeable when it comes to their friends, and Esek herself is little better than a savage."

Chono longs for the privacy to think. Calmly, she says, "This meeting of the Families. I would like to attend."

Hejar growls, "Why?"

"To make my case."

"For open war with Kess?" Hejar scoffs. "That's quite an endorsement to ask of us."

"If the meeting is Esek's idea, her goal will be to seize power for herself alone. She and Kess hate each other. Even if she wants you to ally with Kess now, in the long run, I promise she has other aims. Do you want to trade Kess's leadership for hers?"

"I certainly don't want to antagonize the Families by bringing *you*. Obair will have a fit."

Obair. Chono's stomach heaves at the thought of being in the same room with him again.

Oyun adds, "And who knows how Esek will react."

"I can handle Esek."

"Can you?" Curiosity. Interest.

"Yes. And since we're being honest with each other, Sa, let's not pretend that you would willingly humble yourself to the tyranny of the Cloaksaan. Or the Nightfoots."

"Too true. But nor am I willing to capitulate to terrorists."

"So tell me what you want. Tell me what it would take to forge an alliance between us. Or to at least get me in the same room as the Families."

Six, she thinks desperately. *Get me to Six. I will endure even the sight of that man Obair if it means I can see Six again.*

Oyun pours herself fresh tea from the clay pot, and refills Chono's cup as well. Steam curls over the surface. She doesn't add honey crystals or cream. She stirs, gazing toward the window, out over the landscapes of northern Kator: rust-red mountains capped in snow.

"I loved my brother," she says, some of her hauteur bleeding away. "I loved him from the day he was born. I helped raise him. I was furious when he became First Cleric, because it meant he had fully repudiated his place in our family. He wasn't like Esek, you know, or like most of the Family scions who end up as Hands. He never used his power to bolster our family. He was truly devoted to his oaths."

Chono doesn't know what to say. Her feelings toward Aver are almost as complicated as her feelings toward Esek. An amalgamation of resentment and betrayal and remembered loyalty. She knows that Esek was fundamentally bad. But Aver was more complicated. She doesn't want to think about him. She wants Oyun to take her to Six. Whatever happens, she must get to Six.

Oyun continues, "He told me about his ambitions for you."

Impatience clamors for control of her voice, but she squashes it. "He wanted me to become the First Cleric."

"That's right. You know, Kess may still be a Brutal Hand, but he wants the Kindom destroyed. How else can he rule the worlds? Esek wants it destroyed as well, because she is a chaos demon. I daresay your allies and your Jeveni friends on Capamame also want the Kindom destroyed. But *I* do not. The Kindom is a necessary evil. Order, structure—these things can be changed, but without them..." She tsks. Chono looks at her stolidly. All the little signs of mockery and indifference disappear, Oyun becoming as serious and unwavering as if they were two kinschool students preparing for a bout on the sparring floor. She says lowly, sternly, "You are a cleric. You know what

Kata's Many are. They are the god, manifested in common saan. In the humble and the unknown. Like you."

Chono flexes her hand. "I am no demigod. I am simply a devotee of the Godfire."

"They call you the People's Kin. The Treble loves you. It's terrified of Kess, but it loves you. And everyone wants to feel safe. Everyone wants to feel protected. There is no other public figure who can do that, Chono. Your leadership, the *symbol* of you, will do more for peace than any alliance between the Families and your quorum."

Chono has heard this speech before. From Aver. From Ilius. Even from Six. It repels her. It is unbearable. And worst of all is the tiny Esek voice in her brain, mocking her: *Don't be so insufferably modest. You've always known this, haven't you? You've always seen it on the game board, just waiting for the right tile to fall.*

"To be clear," Chono says, "you want me to establish order in the Kindom, to throw my support behind the First Families, to restore everything to what it was before, and for nothing to actually change?"

Oyun narrows her eyes. "Funny, he never said you were unintelligent. Of course you can have change, Cleric Chono. You can remove corrupt Hands. You can replace them with your people, if you like. Send their children to the kinschools and let them seed the future. You can redistribute Kindom resources, liberate those five thousand Jeveni prisoners, make the trade just and safe. You can do all these things. But not if the Families are against you."

Chono says nothing. Esek croons in her ear, *Don't be shy, little fish.*

"I do not want to be the First Cleric," Chono says.

At that, Aver's sister gives her a soft, pitying look.

"Burning One...In all your years of worshipping the Godfire, you must have realized—what you want has nothing to do with it."

CHAPTER TWELVE

1585

YEAR OF THE TILE

The Glitch
The Black Ocean

In a hundred years, Drae sen Briit thinks, the frontier station called *The Glitch* will be ten times the size of Farren Ki. Currently, it had a population of three million people, about two-thirds of whom were born there. Based on her own knowledge of population growth, and calculating what she had gleaned in terms of birth rate, infant mortality, and generation length, and assuming there were no catastrophic disasters or wars, Drae predicted somewhere between fifteen and twenty million Glitchers by the late seventeenth century.

Their civilization thrived. Some frontier stations were as far as three years away, but *The Glitch* had found the outskirts of an asteroid belt just one year's journey from Ma'kess. They were close enough to the Treble to make trade relatively easy, and far enough to avoid the Kindom, who didn't care about them enough to build a jump gate. The station was in a sweet spot, as it were, and one that served the Jeveni well.

Once a small research station, *The Glitch* had evolved to a central hub connected by massive skyways to over a dozen nodes and subnodes. On approach, it resembled a garden of steel flowers. The Glitchers mined the asteroids for metals and used the metals to build and expand both their infrastructure and their technology. It was on *The Glitch*, at sixteen years old, that Drae got her first neural link—a rare advantage for a Jeveni. On *The Glitch*, she learned about their farms and schools and hospitals, their stacked apartments, their casting net. That they drew power from the sun. That they were artists and engineers. That they spoke a range of Treblen languages, but had a common language called pock-pock, as foreign to most Treblens as Je.

Drae saw, in her study of *The Glitch*, that they did not have an easy life, a careless life. But it was a free life.

She remembered remarking on this to her chaperone, the previous River of the Wheel, when they came here together. It was Drae's first time. The River was confused by her fascination with the Glitchers, her obvious attraction to the frontier.

"This is not our future," the River had said. "We are not coming here to stay. This is the only place where saan will take our payment and keep our confidence. When they have finished *The Hope*, our travelers will come here, take the ship, and go. *Our* freedom is somewhere else."

Drae had solemnly professed her understanding and kept her admiration to herself thereafter. But she had dreamed, in some deep part of herself that knew she would not be a passenger on *The Hope*, that perhaps someday she could return to *The Glitch*. Most of the Jeveni would remain on Jeve. Most would die before the *Hope* explorers reached

Capamame and built a gate. That included Drae. But on *The Glitch*, wasn't a different life possible? Something in between staying in the Treble and disappearing into the Black?

By the time she returned to Jeve, she was eighteen. Six years later, the River died of a respiratory flu, and the people voted for Drae to replace him. Like so many fantasies of youth, her fantasy of *The Glitch* slipped away, became a shadow in her memory, one she shone a light on sometimes, but always returned to the dark. She tried to pray. She asked Sajeven to give her peace, to ease the sting of the lost dream. But as always, she could not hear her goddess speak.

Now she was back on *The Glitch*. The third time in her life. The first time in ten years. And as she stood behind the glass that divided her from open space and the vast stretch of the shipyards, she considered how, once all this was over, she would have spent almost nine years of her life coming and going from the frontier station. But once *The Hope* set sail, there would never be cause for her to visit it again.

"We can walk through tomorrow," said the shipbuilder at her side. They were speaking pock-pock, all crisp consonants and melodies. They had the joyful manner of one who had found good work with pleasurable challenges. "I figured you might want to get a good night's sleep, after just arriving."

Drae smiled a little. "I have been on ship for a year. Show me what you have done."

Haishik Deck, the shipbuilder, grinned. Half an hour later, they had shuttled to the ship's bay. While various segments of *The Hope* were still under construction, it was connected to the station's gravity fields. It was unfinished, unfurnished, but the engine room was a masterwork, the engine itself as tall and broad as some ancient trees she had seen on Ma'kess. Fed on a meal of pure jevite, it pulsed with life. It could not help but remind her of Lots 11 and 12, which carried in their gleaming forms a similar life, and a kind of intelligence.

She felt suddenly restless. Soon porters would transport Lot 11 from her ship to *The Hope*. The gate key was complete, and when her people reached Capamame they would build the gate around the core and create the path between Capamame and Jeve. The whole purpose of their enterprise. Leaving Lot 11 in the hands of porters, even Jeveni porters, made her queasy.

As Haishik led her through *The Hope*, she tried not to think about Lot 11 anymore. There were many other supplies shuttling into the bay. Hydroponics and farming equipment. Jevite and jevite refinement machinery. Sophisticated weapons and state-of-the-art casting tech. Soon all that would be needed was a crew. Over the past five years, *The Hope*'s eventual voyagers had relocated across the Treble so that they could book passage to *The Glitch* at different times and from different ports on Ma'kess. It was the best strategy for avoiding Kindom detection. The hundred Jeveni who had come with Drae on this trip would never see Jeve again. They would stay here and spend the next three years establishing the hydro farm and the casting lab, and outfitting fuel storage with the proper infrastructure to contain and protect several hundred thousand tons of jevite. They would use the weapons systems and small arms to protect the ship from threats. When all that was done, and the last pockets of the Capamame crew arrived in 1588, they would begin the long trek across the Black.

"Want to see residential?" Haishik asked. They had been touring the ship for three hours. Drae had seen the bridge, the engine room, the observation deck, the casting lab, the armory— "Come on." Haishik chuckled, perhaps sensing that "residential" was the least of Drae's concerns. "Don't you want to see how they'll be living?"

Drae acquiesced. Haishik led her to a conveyor car that zipped them from the bridge to the center of *The Hope*, into a neighborhood of dormitories. These would house not just the thousand-person crew that set off from *The Glitch*, but the new generations that these saan would birth, per their mandate to reach Capamame with no fewer than three thousand adult Jeveni.

"Here we are," said Haishik, walking them into one of the dormitories, designed just the same as the ones in Farren Ki.

"Cozy," Haishik said.

Drae heard the good-natured teasing in their voice. Haishik had a private apartment. They were amazed by how Jeveni lived, cooking and eating together in community kitchens. Public baths and shared laundry. Dormitories fit for two hundred saan each. Drae had told Haishik the last time she was here that, while it was unusual for romantic couples to flaunt themselves, it was ordinary to wake up in the night to the sounds of lovemaking.

"Gods above!" Haishik had cried, scandalized and delighted. "You shameless things!"

Drae took in the empty dormitory, imagining it full of saan with common purpose.

"Belt bless you if you can live like this," Haishik said. "I'd die of need for a private shit."

Drae smiled fondly at them, for there was no malice or prejudice in how they said it. They had never shown her and her people anything but respect.

"We manage," Drae said.

"Well, I suppose you saan are built from rock. The Treble took a shot at you, and you said, 'Fuck off,' and kept living. So I guess you can survive public toilets."

Drae was surprised by how much this pleased her. A shy pleasure. They met eyes across the tiny space, and Drae could see Haishik winding up to say something else, but a signal in Drae's ocular distracted her. Her shoulders tensed when she saw the name. This time when she looked at Haishik, she could see that they recognized her change in mood.

"I have a comm," Drae explained.

"See?" Haishik winked. "Something to be said for privacy!"

When they had gone out and closed the door behind them, Drae accepted the comm. Alanye appeared, beaming like a child.

"There you are! How are you? *Where* are you?"

Drae contained a sigh. He always asked this. Sometimes she gave him vague answers meant to put him off any scent. Something to imply Ma'kess, or a farm station, or Quietus. Other times, like this, she ignored the question altogether.

"I am fine. Working. Are you all right?"

He tended to comm her every week or so, which was less than he wanted and more than she liked, but there was good reason to accept his messages. As she looked at him, she considered the shift he had undergone, his transformation from a Nightfoot agent to the man now gazing earnestly at her—the man in her pocket, the man she'd turned to her side. He was not as muscular or youthful as when he'd first come to Jeve. A bad flu had worn him down, and he knew now what it was to suffer like the Jeveni suffered. Or at least, he thought he did. He thought he was one of them. And he was in love with her.

"Yes, yes, I'm all right," he said. "But you must be exhausted by all this traveling."

Traveling. Alanye might know about the jevite mining operation now, and he might support Jeveni efforts to remain independent from the Kindom, but he did not know about Capamame and he did not know about *The Glitch.* Nor would he.

Drae said in her usual mild way, "I am used to it."

Something twitched in his expression, a hint of resentment. "Yes, I know you are. Let me guess. Barely eating or sleeping, right? I never knew anyone who overworked herself like you, Drae."

He had this habit of trying to disguise his bitterness behind concern for her health. He was jealous for her time, for her attention, and resented how her work took her away from him. She didn't know why he loved her so. She had seduced him, yes, but she was not always kind to him, and she did not consider herself so beautiful as to keep a saan's attention indefinitely. Yet time had borne a deep devotion in him. She still didn't know what she would do with him in the end.

At her silence, he broke with frustration. "I don't understand it. Can't you come home every couple of months, at least? It's been a year!"

And it would be more than a year before she returned to Jeve.

Now she lied, "I would explain if I could. You must know I wish I was with you."

She fed a little bit of longing and affection into her tone. His expression softened, taken in at once, a child distracted by a bauble. But then he said the thing that clawed her open.

"Kati misses you."

It took a lot of effort not to let rage consume her expression. Not only was he manipulating her in the only way he knew how, but he was using that Katish nickname he'd adopted within a week of the child's birth, that reference to his god, Kata.

"They were barely two when I left Jeve," Drae said. "They don't even remember a time when I lived with them. We speak four or five times a week and they have plenty of other adults to care for them."

Alanye grumbled, "It'll be quite a lot to get used to, when you come back. They might be uncomfortable, seeing you in person again."

In that moment, Drae hated him. Most of the time her feelings for him oscillated between indifference and indulgence. He was foolishly ambitious, overconfident, and naive, but he had a core of decency, if not courage. He had somehow, irrationally, thought that he would hunt for jevite on the moon without hurting anyone he cared about. But now he loved Drae and their child, and he wanted to be loved in return.

She did not love him. She had never loved him. But she had found it expedient and not unpleasurable to sleep with him. And she was well short of her reproductive obligations to the colony, so it was easy enough to let herself become pregnant with him. Her people whispered about it. The Wheel was displeased, but Drae didn't want a Jeveni lover who would see her as the River and expect her to follow the Jeveni way in all things.

So, no, she didn't love him. But she loved what he had given her. And now he was wielding it as punishment.

"Lucos," she said, her voice very cold. "Do not tell me how to raise my child."

His expression grew mulish. She thought he would argue, but he didn't. As soon as she became pregnant, she had explained to him how things were. On Kator, his home world, parents shared custody of their children. In Jeveni culture, the parent who gave birth was the only one with legal rights. If that person proved unfit, the community could step in to demand a different arrangement. She pictured Alanye going to the Wheel to argue that they should make the child his—and she nearly laughed. But there was no laughter in her. Not when she could still smell her firstborn, still feel the weight of them in her arms, the way they slept against her chest. They were well loved in the nursery, she knew, but—

"Why have you contacted me?" she asked.

He flushed, embarrassed. She knew how to read him. He tended to bury the lede in conversations, to hem and haw his way around a subject before admitting what he really had to say. She sensed that in him now, and her instincts blared a warning.

"I've had another cast from Sorek. They need my final report... you know...on the depth of the seam." Drae looked at him without answering, a long level gaze that she knew made him nervous. Sure enough, he cleared his throat. "They're, uh...eager to get started on negotiations. Once they have an idea of how much is in the seam, they want to make you a fair offer. Just for leasing, of course. Renegotiable every two years."

"And what if you do not know how deep the seam is?" asked Drae placidly.

He was incredulous. "But I do know. And I can't keep holding things back. I can't keep lying to them, Drae."

"You cannot lie to them because...?" she asked.

His eyes widened a little. "Because if they find out the truth, they'll know that I lied!"

And kill me! he didn't say.

She didn't say it, either; he was too apt to get hysterical. Instead, she stood against the dormitory wall, thinking. When it became evident that Alanye and the Nightfoots would not back off from their search for more jevite, she had decided to feed them information about the Blood Seam, to let Alanye think he was negotiating for access to it. Convincing Alisiana Nightfoot that an operation was underway was the best means to hold her off. And Drae only needed to hold her off for another four years. Gus and his crews had mined much of the Blood Seam for transport to *The Glitch*, but in four years there would be enough left to keep the Nightfoot mining operation busy for a decade.

Give Alisiana all the information now, and she would be greedy and restless and move too fast. Withhold what she wanted for too long, and she would also be greedy and restless and move too fast. The trick was to keep her greedy, but patient and slow. Using Alanye to string her along had worked well for several years. But time was running out. And Drae needed just a little more.

"Tell Sorek the depth of the seam. But explain to him that our crews are dropping mines. We need to study the jevite to determine its purity. Tell him we refuse to consider negotiations until we have a better sense of what is there. In the meantime, our investigation means we are building shafts and tunnels. Tell him our work will establish infrastructure he won't have to pay for. Let him think he is getting the better of us."

Alanye still looked anxious. "Gus says you've mined a huge portion of the Blood Seam. The Nightfoots will notice."

"Leave that to me."

"If they think you're trying to trick them..."

He trailed off. Drae almost snorted. Tricks. As if everything the Nightfoots did from here on out wouldn't be a trick. As if what they had done so far, having Alanye pretend to be a scholar, was not a trick. And this idea of a lease was also a trick. Once the Nightfoots were on the moon, they would take everything they wanted, regardless of what the contracts said. This was what Jeve did. It invited swindlers and crooks. It said, *Keep going. Come closer. Gorge yourself.* And those who gorged would not care about keeping promises.

Quietly she said, "I have known ever since you came to Jeve that you were preparing a way for the Nightfoots." He flinched, ashamed by the reminder of his subterfuge. But she doubted whether he truly understood the danger in his actions. "We can survive their mining campaign. We will relocate the people of Farren Ki to other dome cities, outside their field of interest. They will bring their own miners and spend a decade on our moon, and they will leave us for good. We can survive it. But you must hold them back until we are ready. Do you understand?"

He nodded uncertainly. "Yes, I . . . I'll try."

"Yes," she said. "Try."

She said it in a way that even he must understand, that trying was not enough, that he must succeed. He nodded earnestly now, though of course he would only be thinking of himself, of the risks to his own life. Foolish man. Even as he salivated for a place by her side, among her people, he still thought he could make his fate different from theirs.

That night, or what the station programmed to be night, Drae stood in front of a massive view screen that gave the illusion that the apartment had a window looking out on the Black. The cast properly displayed what was on the other side of the thick station wall of Crisper Node: large swaths of *The Glitch*, and especially the shipyards, where hung *The Hope*. Drae's arms were crossed. She was swaying very gently from left to right. After giving birth to her first child, the months of rocking them to sleep had seemed to rewrite something in her genetic code. Whenever she found herself standing at rest, she swayed, as if the behavior meant to soothe a baby was now about soothing herself. Even when she noticed she was doing it, she couldn't stop. Her body had a tide inside it.

She thought back to the day before she had left Farren Ki. Alanye was off moon visiting his family. The Wheel called on her to give a speech. The spokes were all fine orators, but they recognized that Jeve's population, which trended young due to short lifespans, responded better to Drae. *We are old saan*, the Star told her. *You have youth and the future on your side.*

So she gave a speech. Another well-written, well-delivered speech, about the future of her people and her hopes and dreams for Capamame. She believed what she said, but also she did not believe it. She wondered what would happen if the Nightfoots invaded now, while she was gone. What would they do if they discovered the truth? What would the Kindom do? Most harrowing of all to Drae was a question she ought to be able to answer, but couldn't: What would *she* do? She was not naive; she knew that their enterprise could fail on any number of fronts. Nothing was certain. And yet, she preached hope. What else was there to do but preach hope?

"Drae?" murmured a voice behind her, sleepy and rough.

The view screen cast back a reflection, and in its surface she saw the shadowed figure of her lover sitting up in bed. There was a tumble of dark hair hanging loose, and the shapes of long limbs that had been wrapped around Drae's body just a few hours ago. Yet despite that intimacy, Drae's first thought was to remind herself that she had shut off her cast tablet. No risk of anyone seeing what was inside.

"Stars keep us," Haishik said. "What are you doing up?"

Drae didn't turn around, but she looked to her left. Two feet away was a large crib with two sleeping occupants. The twins were identical, with the same broad noses and the same tufts of dense hair. They looked like their father, but they looked like Drae, too.

"Did they wake up?" asked Haishik, coming to stand beside her and look into the crib.

Drae said, "I thought they would, but it was just a little fussing. My eldest is a terrible sleeper. These two... They have nothing to disturb them."

Haishik chuckled. "They've got each other for warmth. Brothers and sisters need that."

Drae frowned. This was something about *The Glitch* that she had never understood. Here, families gendered their newborns according to sex, rather than using a generic gendermark until the child was old enough to gender themself. Haishik said that children did re-gender themselves sometimes (as Haishik had done), but it carried some taboo on the frontier station, and changing one's gendermark was nothing to be done on a whim.

Yet Haishik, despite their own experiences, had been calling the twins brother and sister, boy and girl, from the moment they were born six months ago on the journey to *The Glitch*. Lucos Alanye didn't know about these children of his, but Haishik knew, because Haishik had been communicating with Drae via cast during her voyage. Hearing the children called boy and girl discomfited Drae, but it also stuck in her brain, a conditioning. *Boy and Girl*, she would think sometimes, in place of their names. *My secret children, Boy and Girl.*

Drae gazed down at them, her body still swaying, and she ached with a love that was like torment, knowing what she must do.

Haishik's arms slipped around her. They put their chin on Drae's shoulder, whispering in her ear, "Let them sleep."

Drae turned in their arms. Haishik was wearing the soft cotton briefs and T-shirt that Glitchers favored as sleeping clothes. For all its presence in the middle of an ice void, *The Glitch* ran hot.

She regarded Haishik, who ran hot, too. Haishik had warm, playful eyes, and wrinkles around their mouth. They had a thickset body, especially in their thighs and in their soft belly. They were incredibly strong, and with their hair down Drae could see the white and dark woven together. When Drae met them, she was sixteen and they were thirty, and all Drae's admiration couldn't so much as turn Haishik's head. It was only during Drae's second trip, when she was twenty-six, that the older saan took any notice of her. Now Haishik was almost fifty. Drae was thirty-four. *Too young for me*, Haishik had teased her earlier. But Drae didn't care. Now she leaned forward, nudging her mouth against Haishik's mouth, swallowing the sound of pleasure and pushing forward into the soft places on their body.

Haishik whispered against her lips, "What did Alanye say? You were happy, until he contacted you."

Drae hesitated. She trusted Haishik. She had confided in Haishik many times, but perhaps that was only possible because their relationship was intermittent. They spoke often enough when Drae was in the Treble, exchanging information about *The Hope*, but they had only been in each other's company three times. And when Drae left *The Glitch* in three months, it would be for good.

"Happy?" Drae repeated, obfuscating.

Haishik smiled and nipped her bottom lip, drawing her away from the view screen and into the small kitchen, where they went about filling a kettle to boil.

"You've been happier, since leaving the Treble. And you were happy earlier when I took you around *The Hope*. But that silly boy cast out to you, and now"—Haishik made a *tsking* sound—"not so happy anymore." Before Drae could respond, they added exasperatedly, "What do you want with a boy like that, hmm? I can tell from how you talk about him, you don't respect him. And he's not smart enough for you. So he gave you some babies. So what?"

Drae was amused. She shrugged carelessly, drawling, "He is a competent lover."

Haishik looked unimpressed. "I have been your lover, Drae sen Briit. You are too good for *competent*."

Drae, who had never imagined such a compliment, went to sit at the kitchen table and scrubbed a hand down her face to wipe away the smile. She balanced her elbows on the table, clasped her hands, and set her chin upon them, watching Haishik at the stove. As the kettle purred, Haishik gave her a soft, worried look.

"Were you ever young, wise Drae? Even when you were sixteen, you had this look about you. Always thinking. Always worrying. Always *calculating*."

The last word stung because it was true. Her relationships were all calculated, interactions and decisions designed to give people enough of what they needed from her that they would trust her and give her what she needed in return. Of course she loved her people. She loved Gus and Dimon and the Wheel. But her actions were always about more than love. She might love having sex with Haishik, sleeping in their apartment, feeling the warm, steady comfort of their nearness— but equally important was that the shipbuilder of *The Hope* was more reliable, more useful, if they loved and were loyal to Drae.

Knowing she had been quiet too long, Drae said, "I have an obligation to worry. It is the office of the River, and mine more than any

River before. We have planned that *The Hope*'s crew would leave Jeve in 1588." She looked at Haishik expectantly, and Haishik's small nod confirmed that the timeline was solid. "I do not think we can do it like that anymore. Tomorrow I will tell the Wheel that I want the last shipment of jevite en route within six months."

Haishik's eyebrows shot up. "Will you have mined enough by then?"

Drae sighed. The Wheel would never be content with how much jevite they sent to Capamame. There would always be the desire to cut more of it from the moon. That was Jeve's terrible seductive power, that it asked you to keep wanting, keep seeking, keep digging your own grave. And the more jevite they found, the longer the Treble would hunt for it.

"My bigger concern is asking the saan across the Treble to move up their trips. These people have been able to visit home over the past few years. Now they will never see their families again. Most of them will never see Capamame. They are making a tremendous sacrifice, and I would be asking them to sacrifice even more."

"So, why do it?" Haishik asked.

Drae's lip curled a little. "We may not be able to hold the Nightfoots off much longer. I am worried that Alanye is...unequal to this work. He will do some foolish thing and they will invade before we are ready."

Haishik nodded musingly. They took cups out of the cupboard and poured a fine golden powder into them—Hasha tea, which Drae had brought them from Quietus. Finally, they said, "Even if your crew escapes, even if they take all the jevite with them, the Nightfoots will still invade Jeve. What will they do to you, when they find the proof of your mining operations?"

Drae exhaled. "Well, the mines are localized outside Farren Ki, but we are leaving Farren Ki for other domes."

Haishik looked confused. "But the Nightfoots can find you in the other domes. They can force you into mining again."

"We hope that they will bring their own miners," she said.

"And if they don't? If they enslave you again?"

Drae studied the table. Not for the first time, she wanted to be completely honest with Haishik, to tell them things that even the Wheel didn't know. But she would not do that.

"We comfort ourselves that mining the remainder of the Blood Seam will take ten years at most. We pray to Sajeven the Nightfoots leave us, afterward."

Haishik narrowed their eyes. "You never seemed like one who left your fate to the gods."

Drae didn't answer. The water boiled. Haishik poured the water into the cups and brought the cups to the table. The tea inside was a deep golden brown.

Haishik said, "You will be in danger, Drae. There's time. Go back and get your son. Bring him here. Either you can join *The Hope* or you can stay with me. Nothing else is safe."

Drae felt an amused, incredulous smile appear on her face, despite the seriousness of the moment. Haishik looked annoyed, more so when Drae laughed.

"I mean it! If *The Hope* is too dangerous, stay here. I'll stand for you and help you raise them. I'm entitled to child-rearing credits. We can live comfortably."

What Drae had taken for an offhanded remark was clearly reflective of deeper thought. The smile faded from her face, but she felt such a depth of tenderness in that moment—and such gratitude—to have been right about Haishik. Even if she couldn't tell them everything.

"No matter where my children are, they will be in danger. If they stay in the Treble, they may be killed, by the Nightfoots, or the mines, or some flu."

"Exactly!" Haishik said. "It's not—"

"If, on the other hand, I take them on the voyage to Capamame, they will be in their sixties before they touch foot to ground again. If they are lucky. The ship might break up en route, or some disaster may strike aboard, or they might reach Capamame to find that the mission is impossible."

Haishik looked at her pleadingly. The look said, *Stay with me.*

"Or...they could grow up here. A frontier station. A place of constantly reconstituting laws, fluctuating centers of power, and conflict. You cannot deny it, Haishik. *The Glitch* is dangerous, too."

Haishik pressed their lips together. Drae smiled sadly at them. She took a sip of the tea. It was too hot, but she let the contradiction of bitter and sweet perform its complex magic on her tongue. Over in the crib, one of the children snuffled and whined and fell quiet again.

"Do you know why I waited so long to have children?" Drae asked. Haishik said nothing. "People looked down on me. We all have certain obligations. With a population as small as ours, we have to reproduce at specific rates or the Jeveni will die out. But I held off as long as I could. The truth is, I did not want to have children. I knew that if I had children..." Her voice trailed off. She realized she wasn't blinking and that her eyes stung. She said emotionlessly, "I knew that having children would change me. That it would become a kind of...illness. They would make me change, give me different priorities. I knew that I would love them *so much*—"

Despite her efforts, a hot tightness filled her throat. She drank more tea, focused on the burn, and didn't dare look at Haishik, though she felt Haishik looking at her.

"I have to go back to the Treble. I am not just the person Drae. I am the River. I am bound to the needs of my people before all else, and that means going back and doing everything I can to protect them when the Nightfoots come. But my children..."

She gathered her courage and met Haishik's eyes. She squashed shame and uncertainty; she concealed all doubts behind an expression of cold intent.

"No matter what I do, I fear not all of them will live through what is coming. Do I not have a responsibility to them? A debt? I brought them into these worlds. They did not ask for it. I must give them a chance." She didn't wait for Haishik to agree. "So, I have made a decision. When I leave *The Glitch* in three months, I will leave my twins here. I would prefer to leave them with you, but if you will not have them, I can pay one of the orphan crèches to take them."

Because orphans were so common on the frontier, the Glitchers had pooled their resources to create a system that raised such children. Unlike orphans in the Treble, who might be thrown into any family, kind or cruel, station orphans were protected and valued as crucial to the survival of the colony. She told herself this. *She told herself this.*

"Drae," whispered Haishik.

"My crew know about the twins. They will take the older one with them on *The Hope.* The other will stay here. I will return to my child on Jeve and do everything I can to protect them."

"Drae..."

Drae felt a flash of anger. She met Haishik's eyes in challenge.

"It is all I can do for them. If I keep them together, I risk losing them all. If I separate them, if I move them away from me, I can give them a chance. It is a question of mathematics. It is a question of odds."

She stared Haishik down. She kept waiting for them to condemn her, to show disgust. Alanye would be panic-stricken over it, if he knew. Just another reason for him not to know.

But Haishik said, in a voice of soft and aching compassion, "How will you bear it?"

This time there was no stopping the burn in her eyes. But though tears slipped free, she kept her face like stone, water tracks making no impact on the facade.

"I will bear it for their sakes. I have borne a great deal already, for my people and my Wheel. And I will bear more. If the Nightfoots try to enslave us, I will bear it. I will not be afraid of the strangers. And I swear to you, Haishik, I will have such a revenge—"

She cut herself off, for rage was simmering in her voice; it had shifted the planes of her face. Revenge, she reminded herself, would come at great cost. Lot 11 was the thing that mattered, the passage-way to freedom. But there was also Lot 12, the strange twin. If Lot 12 became necessary, it would mean that something horrible had happened. However attractive revenge might feel in this moment, she could not wish for it.

Haishik, by Sajeven's own mercy, did not look put off or worried by the surge of vitriol. They did not ask about revenge. Instead, they nodded in validation.

"Leave the twins with me. I will care for them and protect them with my life. Boys have better lives on *The Glitch*. Send the girl to Capamame if you must, though if you change your mind, I will keep them both. And I will raise the boy as my own, but he will always know your face and your voice."

Drae exhaled a harsh breath. She had not realized until that moment how worried she was about having to put the children in the orphans' crèche.

"Thank you," she whispered. "Thank you."

Haishik nodded. Abandoning their cup, they rose and held a hand out to her. "Now come back to bed. You're no River inside this room. Let me comfort you."

Drae went gratefully. As Haishik drew her close, she willfully pushed away her fear and grief. Yet even as hard as she tried, one thought, one image, slipped through her defenses: the figure in the red coat tearing down the walls.

I was ready to believe that the Jeveni Wheel have invited the Redcore twins to the Remembrance Day uprising because of their Jeveni stepfather. Kinship making up for a lack of Jeveni blood, that is, which seemed strange enough given the insular, incestuous nature of those people. Now my cloaks tell me that there are other non-Jeveni joining the scheme, saan without a single connection to the Jeveni. It is a strange development. One assumes the outsiders hold some value to the rebellious intentions of the Wheel. Mercenaries and spies, perhaps? Whatever the case, they will regret allying themselves to such a fool's errand.

excerpt, personal log of First Cloak Seti Moonback.
Dated 1664, Year of the Crux.

CHAPTER THIRTEEN

1665

YEAR OF THE HARVEST

Farren Eyce
The Planet Capamame

Just a couple of weeks ago, Bene was installing plumbing in the galleria in the Market District. Once it's complete it will host dozens of shops and food stalls, a perimeter around a large public square. It'll be the communal center of Farren Eyce, with saan from all over the Treble offering native cuisines that will give the colonists a taste of the Treble. Bene, sitting at a café some hundred feet from the building site, thinks about his life in Najic, the copper mining town on Braemin where he lived after Six rescued him and his grandmothers from Esek Nightfoot.

In the southlands of N'braekos continent, where Najic lay amid coastal mountains, an orange squash called siccup grew wild, and it was crucial to Najic cuisine. It was protein rich, with a sweet, nutty flavor. It was good in soups or roasted or blended with milk to make battercakes. As far as Bene knows, there are no siccup squash in the Farren Eyce farm, so the Market District will never serve siccup battercakes.

In Najic, he was called Ben Lightfoot, and he always wondered if that was some kind of joke on Six's part—some reference to Esek. But he didn't complain about the false name. When he was eight he started working the mines as a waste runner, taking the massive buckets of useless dirt and stone and moving them across the quarry to where a separate team would sort the waste out and sell some of it as building material. At nine he graduated to a sorter, which paid better. At eleven, they put him in the mines, and that paid best.

Manual labor has always been his trade. Life on Braemin was dangerous, the people were dangerous, but the work itself was a release, a thing he could disappear into. Easier to forget his other troubles (his father's death, Grandmi Keena getting sick, the prospect of winter without new boots) when concentration on the task was a life-and-death enterprise.

Working for the construction crews in Farren Eyce was better. The people were kinder. There was camaraderie, and nobody ever threatened him. There was one saan who liked him a lot, and they got into some fun together, just a couple of nights of kissing and groping. A shyness to it. He had felt very young and carefree, doing it all, and then it stopped for no bad reason. Bene started flirting with Effegen. He started watching Masar like Masar was a star that might wink out. His friends on the construction crew teased him. They made up songs about what a lover he was, but it was all good-natured. The Jeveni taught the non-Jeveni old miner songs, and though Bene stumbled over the strange consonants of the Je language, he paid attention and got it right. He treated the happy songs with levity and the serious songs with respect, and his friends liked that.

There was a lot of joy. There was a lot of hope.

A server comes up to Bene's table. "Anything else for you?"

Bene realizes that he's been sitting here for an hour. He ate his sandwich in the first five minutes, and since then it's just been him and a glass of pink juice and Pejun two chairs away. The server probably wants him to move on so other people can have his table.

"Oh!" Bene says, standing up. "Yeah, sorry. Sorry."

He tries to pick up his dishes. The server says, "No, I'll take these things."

There's nothing overtly unpleasant about her tone, but his heart still falls.

"Say," he says hopefully. "Do you need any help in the café? I'm happy to pick up shifts or run errands if you need."

The young woman looks shocked. She at least tries to be polite. "Oh. No. Thank you, Sa. We've got all the help we need." She hurries away.

Pejun stands up with a humorless chuckle. "Nobody wants you serving them."

He says it more matter-of-factly than cruelly, but it stings. Bene looks toward the construction site again, full of longing.

As if in consolation, Pejun hands him a mint reed. "Just be happy you can do good work in the warehouse. Anyway, it's almost time for your visit, and I for one would like to get away from the market. People aren't in the mood to be gracious about you being here."

Bene glances around. Pejun isn't wrong. There's a dark energy in Farren Eyce today, a tension that is different and more powerful than the typical tension of people who did not necessarily want a life on Capamame, and who have lived for several weeks in fear of the avatar wielding tech threats and murderers. Fear of Ujan, that is.

Today, the tension is more specific. Bene was still in his newsnest cell when the colonists voted not to destroy the jump gate. But he has had a front-row seat to the anxiety and stress of this latest vote, which isn't really a vote at all, but a tally. The Wheel gave its populace three days: State your willingness or unwillingness to return to the Treble under the new conditions proposed by First Cloak Seti Kess. No one will receive judgment or reprisal for their decision. No one will be forced to return or stay against their will.

The Wheel promised to publish the numbers on the morning of the fourth day. This morning, they kept their word. The Kindom wants 40 percent of their population. Only 17.9 percent have expressed a desire or willingness to go back.

Pejun curses out of nowhere. Bene looks at him, recognizing that he has received a message on cast. Bene does not have cast access—a condition of his parole. But Pejun tells him, "Revised percentage: 17.1 percent."

Across the market, there are sounds of murmuring curiosity, open despair, and anger. It's likely that those who want to stay in Capamame have been hoping, praying, that their neighbors will take Kess up on his offer. That they will buy the safety of Farren Eyce by indenturing themselves to the sevite trade. Those who want to go must think it is a safer bet than awaiting an invasion. Bene can't blame them for that. On its face, Kess's offer isn't terrible, and maybe the conditions won't be so bad as they were under Alisiana Nightfoot. Maybe it will really be a decent life.

Or maybe Bene is as naive as ever.

"Some of us oughta be forced to go back!" snaps a voice nearby.

Bene looks to find a Draeviin Jeveni glaring pointedly at him. Pejun takes Bene's elbow.

"Let's go."

Eyes watch them leave. Someone hisses a curse, and Pejun moves faster. When they reach the elevators, they get into a car by themselves. Bene anxiously chews his mint reed.

Pejun mutters, "If I get killed saving your ass from a mob..."

Bene doesn't know what to say. A few nights ago, Effegen and Masar welcomed him back into their hearts, into their confidence. Relief is not a strong enough word for what he felt. It was like stepping off a cliff and having someone pull him to safety at the last moment, and he's grateful. He's so grateful, but...

"Look," Pejun says. "Give it time. People will come around when they see that Effegen trusts you." He makes a face. "Though you know it can't help, visiting the prison every day."

Bene doesn't answer. Though Pejun had started out openly resentful of his duty to Bene, and even pointed a gun at him in Effegen's apartment, he's warmed up a little in the past few days. But it's a warmth with limitations, and a lot of snarky undercurrents. How much would Pejun really do to protect him if a mob came calling? Certainly he would do nothing to protect Ujan or Tej.

Tentatively Bene asks, "Did you vote?"

Pejun snorts. "Of course I did. I'm staying." Then a shadow crosses his face. "But my ma...She wants to go back. She worked in the factories all her life. I guess it doesn't scare her as much as fighting a war."

It's obvious what Pejun thinks of this. Bene wants to say something, offer some reassurance, but there's a stoniness in Pejun now. Clearly he doesn't want to talk about it. They ride in silence.

Inside the newsnest on Level 8, sentries guard the cellblock of private offices. A clerk at a main desk nods tightly when Bene approaches to check in. The clerk, who once aided Hyre with the management of colony communication, has taken a strange new role: half warden, half gatekeeper. Bene wonders how much longer the Wheel will keep Ujan and Tej sequestered in the newsnest. What will they do with them if Farren Eyce survives the coming days?

"They haven't caused any trouble since yesterday," the clerk says. "We put Tej in with her. They're both shackled. I know you don't like it, but after Ujan lifted that pen off a sentry—"

Bene sticks the masticated remnants of the mint reed in his pocket. "I understand." He's rather touched that the clerk would even consider his feelings on the matter. But he knows very well the threat that Ujan is.

Inside the cell, his cousins are seated together, wrists shackled to the top of the table. They have some slack, so Tej has folded his arms and rested his chin on them, staring into nothing. Ujan relaxes as far back in her chair as she can, eyes closed. They're twenty-one years old, barely more than teenagers, and if any of this was funny, Bene would laugh at their adolescent behavior: the refusal to look at him, the feigned indifference, their lax posture inviting criticism if only for the opportunity to ignore it. Bene sits across from them, aware of Pejun and another sentry standing against the wall behind him.

"Tej," he says in greeting. "Ujan."

Ujan's eyes flutter open. Her head tips down so she can look at him directly. Features that had once made her look timid (huge dark eyes, delicate bone structure) now only accentuate the malevolence radiating from her.

"Hello, cousin," she says, the soft voice eerily mild. "You look better rested than before. Sleeping like a baby now that you're back in Effegen's bed?"

A shiver runs down Bene's spine, as he remembers Ujan's first few days in the newsnest. The havoc she wrought with her second neural link. From his next-door cell, he had heard the screaming of the sentries as her tech virus attacked their tech, burning through tissue and bone. Does she have access to her neural links again? How else would she know—

Ujan chuckles nastily.

"I knew it. Heart on your sleeve like always. When we met again last year, I thought it must be some kind of act. Optimistic, good-natured, cheerful Bene. Gods, it took me longer than it should to realize you really are this *insipid.*"

Now that he knows she doesn't have her cast access, Bene clasps his hands in front of him. Every day is the same. She finds new insults, new threats, new boasts. And every day he bears it by pretending this is not really her, that the real her is the cousin he called Luja, the one he loved, and that this spiteful creature in front of him has merely trapped Luja behind a mask of disease. Of course, he knows that Luja was the mask, and Ujan is the real one. But his heart has no choice.

He looks at Tej. "How you doing?"

Tej mumbles into his arms, "Fine."

"You sleeping okay?"

Ujan snorts. "When he's not screaming with nightmares."

Tej goes tense, angrily embarrassed and silent. Bene asks gently, "Are you playing your mandola?"

"No."

"What are you doing?"

"Nothing."

Bene sighs, ignoring Ujan's sharp-toothed grin. "Jun fought hard to get you the mandola. You've gotta do something to pass the time."

"Pass the time till *what*? Till the Wheel executes me?"

Bene inhales and lets it out, exasperated. "Tej, you already know they're not going to execute you. That's not how they do things."

Ujan sneers. "They should. If you wanna maintain order, you can't be a coward about it. All this lofty moralism, letting some of us go, offering rehabilitation—it's bullshit. Seti is going to take you all out so easy."

Bene stifles an eye roll. Here they go again.

"It'll be like watching a marksaan shoot fish in a barrel. I mean, yeah, he's gotta bring most people back to work the trade, but Effegen, Jun, the other spokes—they'll all be lined up and executed. You know, Bene"—she leans forward—"it doesn't have to be like that for you. You get your priorities straight, and there may be some role for you on the other side."

Bene pretends that he can see the sickness in her, like a dark shadow, or a layer of grime that could be peeled off a window in one sticky strip. But that's just his naivety, he knows. Because he is naive. There's no getting around it now, even if Effegen has forgiven him and Jun has welcomed him cautiously back into her life. On some level, it doesn't matter. All his good intentions, all his faith in their future on Capamame—it was all born of the naive misconception that if the Ironways could just survive Esek Nightfoot, they would be purified of the toxin she brought on them. They would be saved. He didn't understand, couldn't let himself understand, that as soon as Esek walked into their shop, it was already too late.

To Ujan he says, "You really expect me to believe that after everything, you would protect me from Kess?"

She shrugs. "Well...for a price, anyway."

"I'm not going to help you, Ujan. I tried that already. It was a mistake."

"So you're just gonna let them keep your poor, poor cousins locked up forever?"

"I think that'll be up to you."

Tej rolls his shoulders. "No way we can live in this place. Not after what we did."

"Hey," Ujan snaps. "We did what we had to. We could never trust these people."

Tej glowers, hiding his face in his arms like a child. The past couple of days, he's been anxious but also dull and withdrawn. Today he seems more volatile, itchy. When Ujan speaks, Bene would swear Tej flinches. He remembers when Tej begged her to stop on the shuttle. How he evoked their dead mother and almost shot himself. It was the thing that broke through to Ujan. She became a panicked little girl. She loves Tej, in her way. But Bene isn't sure Tej loves her back anymore.

Bene says, "The one you can't trust is Kess. Do you know what ultimatum he gave us? You claim to be in on things with him. Did he tell you what he planned?"

She snatches at her opportunity. "Forty percent. He wants forty percent of you for the trade. Lemme guess—you're too shortsighted to give it to him? Rather be cut down and culled and taken out of here in chains?"

"You and Tej won't be any safer than me. Your best bet is to help us hold them off."

Tej lifts his eyes again. They look watery, though he isn't crying. "Really think you can hold them off?"

Ujan snorts. Tej twitches like it was a gunshot, his sister crowing, "Kess is the fucking First Cloak. You all don't stand a chance."

Bene says, "For someone who claims to be his ally instead of his patsy, you sure do worship the ground he walks on, Ujan." She narrows her eyes. She looks so mean, so alien, that something mean rises in him. "In fact, I think you're just his copycat. You know, Jun has been through all your casts. She's figured out how your tech virus works, and the neural link torture program you used on Fonu. Apparently it's all adapted from Cloaksaan techniques that Seti Kess implemented when he became the First Cloak. You're not even an original monster. You're just following his lead."

Rather than the furious or flustered reaction he expects, Ujan stares at him for so long that she begins to look like an automaton that has been switched off. Under the table, Tej's foot starts tapping. He really is jumpy today. With a blink, Ujan comes back online, leaning closer, whispering, "Do you remember Esek Nightfoot?"

Tej cringes. He pushes his face into his folded arms again, grabbing at his own shoulders. Ujan ignores him, showing her teeth. This is not the Ujan who Bene and Jun tackled to the ground, who screamed and sobbed and finally collapsed in a catatonia of grief and defeat. This is the Ujan who tortured Fonu into telling her the gate key. Who burned Masar's prosthetic eye out of his head. Who directed Dom ben Dane to murder three collectors.

"Do you? Do you remember her?"

Bene says softly, "I try not to."

She chuckles. "After it happened, I thought about her all the time. I remembered everything I could about her. She was *beautiful*, don't you think? Not in a prissy way, though. She was beautiful like a scythe. She was so sharp and so deadly and she cut your father down"—Ujan snaps her fingers—"like that. Like it was nothing. Death didn't scare her. Killing didn't scare her. She knew what she wanted when she came to our shop and she took it, and we were all a bunch of insects who couldn't stop her. Imagine if she'd just had some *vision*."

It occurs to Bene to point out that Esek *was* stopped. Maybe not by the Ironways, but by Six's operatives who shot down her novitiates on K-5 station, and later, by Six themself, who killed her. He doesn't say this, though. He's too busy trying to keep away the image of his father's brains spraying the shop.

He says, "I see you have a type. Have you always been drawn to psychopathic Hands of the Kindom?"

"Stop talking about it," Tej mumbles into his arms.

"You're not listening," Ujan says. "Esek was ruthless. Brutal. But she was small-time. All she wanted was control of her family. Kess is after the whole Treble. And he can do it, too. I saw that. Back when he first contacted me and I started looking into him and getting my hands on his secrets, I could *see it*. He knows how to get what he needs out of people. He knows how to keep his secrets close, even if it means other people thinking they have one over on him. He even knows how to be who he is, whatever gender he is—unlike *you*, who became a man just to avoid getting beat up and *raped* in Najic." Her eyes glitter. Her voice becomes a hiss. "Seti Kess is gonna be so much more than the matriarch of some fucking family, and if Esek Nightfoot made you piss yourself, he's gonna turn your piss to ice."

Maybe other people could bear this without reaction. Effegen certainly could. Effegen is stronger and more self-contained than anyone Bene has ever met. Bene doesn't have that composure in him. He knows he blanches at his cousin's words. He knows that she can see every blow land, and that it thrills her.

He swallows once, trying to sound assured. "Knows how to keep his secrets, huh? But not from you?"

She scoffs. "Nobody's perfect. I used to track shit down just for fun. Did you know that Kess's father Revel has been fucking his niece for years? Sick, huh? Khen Ookhen Obair? He bought Chono for sex when she was a teenager." Ujan laughs gleefully. "And here Chono's always trying to act so superior and righteous, when really she's just a—"

"You can stop bragging," Bene interrupts. "I'm not impressed. And I'm not interested. All I care about is protecting the people here. That includes you. That includes Tej."

"I don't need protection." Tej sulks.

"You fucking well do," Ujan snaps, and glares at Bene. "Which is exactly what I'm doing!"

Bene exhales, a little shakily, still feeling the ice-pick blow of her vitriol. There's no point to this. There's no point to coming here, to talking to her, to letting her rehearse the same self-important, delusional rant over and over again—

"I'm not weak," Tej growls, his fingers digging into his own arms and pushing his head against them. "I'm not weak...I'm not fucking weak." He hits his head on his arms again. He does it a third time, and a fourth—

Bene urges, "Tej. Take it easy."

"You're always talking about it," Tej mutters. He suddenly raises his head, glaring at Ujan. "Why do you always have to talk about it? I don't want to talk about it!"

Ujan makes a sound of annoyance. "Tej, I've told you—"

"You think you're so smart. You always did. You're not that smart."

Color darkens her cheeks, and Bene can't tell if it's anger or humiliation. She recovers, shooting back, "And what are you? What have you ever done except get in trouble so I have to bail you out? If you hadn't lost your nerve on the shuttle, we wouldn't even be here!"

"Yeah, we would. This is what I'm talking about. You think you're so smart, but you're *delusional* if you think that plan could have worked."

Ujan chokes, spits out, "Fuck you—"

From his place against the wall, Pejun warns, "Settle down."

Tej ignores him. "And you're dreaming if you think Kess isn't gonna kill us, same as everyone else. You're not a cloak, Ujan. You're not *special*. He's not saving you a seat on his moon."

Ujan's red face blanches—she looks so startled that for a moment Bene is too distracted by the expression to notice what Tej has said. But only for a moment. In the silent void that opens up after Tej's declaration, something cold and smooth clicks into place in Bene's brain. His heart gives a throb, half shock, half disbelief.

"*What?*" Ujan's voice cracks, her mask of arrogance gone.

Tej, on the other hand, lights up with vindication. "Yeah. I know about that. You always thought I was too oblivious to know about anything, didn't you? Just because I didn't know you were the avatar, you think I didn't know *anything*? I saw those blueprints you had on cast—"

"Tej," Ujan warns. "Shut up."

Bene says, "Blueprints? What blueprints, Tej?"

"It was a fortress! It could only be one thing."

"Shut *up*, Tej!"

"What do you mean Kess's moon? What fortress?"

Tej floods with self-importance, sitting up for the first time, eyes bright. "What do you say, Ujan? What do you say I show you just how smart I am?"

"Tej," Bene snaps. "Tell me what moon—"

Ujan, paler than ever, pulls so hard at the shackles that the table creaks, and she screams at her brother, "Shut up! Shut up! I'll kill you!"

She rises from her chair and launches forward. They're shackled close together, and she drops her body onto his. The table overturns, Bene barely jumping back as the sentries rush forward, and more sentries come through the door. Ujan and Tej are all mangled limbs on the ground and Ujan is screaming, "Shut up shut up shut up!"

There's a terrible crunching sound, and Bene realizes in horror that she has broken her own wrist trying to get free. The sentries are on her.

Someone—Pejun—grabs him by the arm. "Come on. Now!"

In the hallway, Bene hears them screaming, but it's nothing compared to the scream in his own head as he turns wild eyes on Pejun. "Jun. I have to talk to Jun."

Pejun's eyes are wide; he looks a little pale. "What did he mean? What moon?"

Bene doesn't wait to explain it. He breaks into a run, the screams of his cousins drowned out by a pounding in his brain. Pejun bolts after him. He runs past the startled warden and straight out of the newsnest. He bolts toward the elevator bank. He runs like Som themself is chasing him, and then he remembers that tech exists. As the elevator car plummets him down toward the casting labs, he tells Pejun, "Cast Jun! Cast her!"

Pejun doesn't question him. A moment later Jun's voice fills the elevator car, startled and concerned. "Pejun? Is Bene okay? What—"

"The Silver Keep," Bene gasps, his body shaking with a storm. "The Silver Keep! It's on Jeve, Jun. It's on the moon!"

CHAPTER FOURTEEN

1665

YEAR OF THE HARVEST

Verdant
Sevres Continent
The Planet Ma'kess

It was perfunctory, the beating. No sooner had Six ended their compulsory message to the Wheel than Kess said, "Not the face," and four cloaks set upon them with batons. They led with the electrical tips. Six was instantly incapacitated, blows raining on their prone body. It lasted less than a minute before Riiniana's voice cut through the sounds:

"That's enough."

The cloaks ignored her, but Kess said, "All right. Leave her."

Six lay on the ground, jerking and twitching. The cloaks had pulled their punches. There was pain, but not the agony of shattered bones or damaged organs. They remember now the clip of boots as Kess and his entourage moved away, the First Cloak warning Riiniana, "No doctors," before he quit the room.

Then came the soft-soled approach of Riiniana Nightfoot, who stood above Six for several moments, and finally said, "That was pointless."

The cloaks had indeed avoided Six's face, but Six had bit their tongue at some point. Luckily, they were on their side, so the blood only dribbled out of their mouth rather than drowning them. They couldn't move. They felt helpless but also smug. Confirming that Kess's generous offer was conditional on good behavior would not be a surprise to the Wheel, but at least it signaled Six's loyalty without outright refusing to follow Kess's orders. Hence a non-deadly beating.

Riiniana said at last, "Get her to her room."

Hands fell on them, lifting them onto useless legs. Eventually they were deposited on Esek's bed. Riiniana obeyed Kess to the letter. No doctor, no regeneratives. They suffered their bruises and scrapes and shock burn, and their damned body didn't even have the good manners to pass out.

Now, two days later, they stand in an octagonal room and pull up a sparring program. Riiniana has forbidden them to spar with Verdant guards, but the simulation court allows them at least some opportunity to practice. It's also the closest they can get to the actual casting net, since their neural link remains disabled. A kind of nakedness. An amputation of autonomy.

And the sparring program is dissatisfying. It utilizes holograms and haptics. When the holograms get past Six's guard and strike their body, Six feels nothing more than a tiny buzz. If, on the other hand, Six lands blows on the holographic bodies, those bodies flash red. The bout will continue until the system determines that either Six or their attackers have received mortal injury.

There's no blood. No pain. No human contact or emotion, no

sensation of real danger or success. Annoyed, Six programs three holograms. Six's body is not broken, but it's fucking sore. That helps, actually. They can pretend there is some real consequence to the fight.

Stepping into the center of the court, they watch the human-shaped figures circle them, each armed with a baton. Six themself wields a pair of clubs with spiked bulbs at the end—a pleasurable discovery in the room's armory, except for the fact that they're just hard foam.

The holograms swarm. Wielding the clubs, Six deflects a series of blows. Their side twinges when they rotate, duck, driving the club hard into a glimmering hip. The shape flashes red, but Six's right side is exposed. They feel a series of haptic buzzes—their shoulder, their ribs, their chin—and pull back, cursing. They've got to focus. Push down the pain and remember their forms. Liis Konye could wipe the floor with this program and never break a sweat.

This time they don't work against their injuries. They use their left side for defense and their weaker right arm to attack. Taking the brunt of the violence on their strong side gives them the extra support to sneak in enough hits that the holograms flash and dim by degrees. Six twists and drops to one knee, slamming their clubs into legs that buckle on impact. Six leaps up. The two hobbled holograms vanish in red flashes. Burning down their side, Six turns to the third hologram. This one is tall. As tall as Chono, as broad as Medisogo, as fast and vicious as Esek. Six pretends that it *is* Esek. They stalk each other across the room, trading blows until Six feels another buzz on their arm. A mechanized voice announces that the arm is broken.

Six thinks of the battle with Esek, when she drove her stave down on their forearm, cracking the bone. The taste of her blood, of her *ear*, was still in their mouth, but they thought that she might win now she'd hurt them so badly.

They toss aside the one club, putting their useless arm behind their back. It's a bit of a farce. When Esek broke their arm, the pain was excruciating. It made their skull pulse, made their center of gravity tip. This game of holographic warfare has no cost, no adrenaline spike, no agony. Six drops the other club and draws a foam knife from their ankle sheath, harassing the hologram in circles until it overextends one swing. They slip under its arm, driving the blade into what should be its exposed side, its ribs, its heart.

The hologram pulses red and disappears. The room announces victory, but there was no resistance of flesh and muscle. No crunch of breaking bone. Not like Six's first kill—the weapons merchant, Enye, who ended up with a spearpoint dagger through her chest. Punctured lung. A wet, gasping death.

The door irises open and Riiniana Nightfoot steps inside. Against the stark gray of the room, her flowing shift dress is whimsical, a pale rose, like innocence itself. She has piled her chestnut hair and pinned it atop her head. She looks almost pretty, in a reptilian way. Her thin-lipped mouth does not smile.

Six returns to the cast screen on the wall to program a new battle. Five holographic cloaks. Blades, this time. Six picks a short sword from the racks of fake weapons against the wall and returns to the center of the room.

"I see you've recovered," Riiniana says.

"Never better," Six lies.

The holograms appear, and charge.

Fucking gods, the things are fast. Six struggles more this time with the lack of physical resistance, with the proper distribution of their weight. Their already sore body burns as they twist and shift out of reach.

"We are leaving Verdant this evening," Riiniana announces. Even concentrating on the swarm of attackers, Six's attention points at her. "We're going to a neutral location, where we can speak safely with some important Family players."

Six laughs, throwing themself into a flurry of offensive strikes, carefully avoiding the swords. A baton blow to the shoulder is one thing— a slash with an imaginary blade will rate much more seriously to the cast program. They block three overhead strikes in a row, drop, and slice their blade through a holographic belly. The figure flashes red and vanishes. Six takes a buzz-graze to the hip and hops away.

"This meeting is important," Riiniana says. "For everyone. Kess has entrusted me with persuading the other Families to ally to him."

Six answers without looking at her. "How many spies will he have on the ground?"

"Four," Riiniana says. "And I have bought them. We'll be able to speak to the Families without fear of his interference. Besides, he's distracted. He's returned to the Silver Keep to orchestrate the invasion of Capamame."

Six nearly loses concentration. A sword drives in toward their middle—another comes down toward the gap between their neck and shoulder blade. Deflecting the latter strike, they heave backward to avoid the former. Maybe they shouldn't have been so cocky in programming so many attackers.

Riiniana continues, "The Feast of Sajeven's Dear Friend is in five days. Kess has given the Jeveni that long to meet his terms. If by some miracle they agree to deliver forty percent of their population, I suppose the Cloaksaan fleet will simply offer transportation. But after your little performance, it's less likely than ever that Effegen ten Crost will encourage her people to submit. Which means Kess will invade and crush them."

It's a shade better than luck when Six lands a killing blow to a hologram and manages not to get trapped in a circle of the other three. They're sweating and drained and wondering again if their efforts to help the Jeveni will ultimately have the opposite result.

"Believe it or not, I don't want that," Riiniana says. "Which is why I have arranged this meeting. Or, should I say, *you* have, since Esek Nightfoot is the matriarch of our family."

There's a haptic buzz to Six's ribs. They are driven across the room, like a kai sheep flanked by wolves. They have little breath to speak, and yet no temper for staying quiet.

"Esek was never a good host," they grunt.

Riiniana sounds amused. "But you will be a very good host, as you deliver our offer to the other Families."

The holograms coordinate their next barrage. Six barely avoids being stabbed in the thigh, and then cut through the throat, and then cleaved open at the shoulder. They kick one of the shapes right in the chest, collapsing it onto its back and throwing their body forward into another figure blade-first. They go right through the hologram, feel it flash red and vanish around them as they roll head over heels onto their feet again. Irritated and not averse to cheating, they grab a second sword off the wall.

"And what offer am I delivering to the Families?" they ask. "I thought we had sold our forces to your dear fiancé."

"It is expedient for him to think so," Riiniana allows.

A scoff. "He knows you lied to him about me. He does not trust you."

"I've done what I must to appease him."

A chill travels down Six's spine, considering the ways she might have appeased Kess.

"Here are the terms," Riiniana explains, as bright and no-nonsense as if she were presenting an argument in a public debate. "Kess has limited resources and enemies near and far. He needs at least two Families behind him. Three Families would be preferable."

The holograms seem faster and stronger now. Six's side throbs. They recall when Kess and his cloaks ran them down in the rain-swept streets of Praetima. They were shot in the back, in the shoulder, in the knee. They were bleeding everywhere. They thought Kess would kill them, and instead he tossed them into this girl's web.

The girl says, "If, on the other hand, the Families turned on Kess, they could defeat him. The continental armies would abandon him in favor of loyalty to the Families. The Cloaksaan would not be able to stand up indefinitely."

Six cuts off a hologram's arm. The limb disappears; the figure drops in a pantomime of incapacitation. What did Liis Konye do when Medisogo cut off her arm? She kept fighting.

"I intend you to propose an alliance to the Families. If they side with us against Kess, they will have an equal vote in the installation of the new First Cleric, First Cloak, and the Secretarial Court—as opposed to leaving that decision in the hands of a despot."

Six laughs through their panting breaths. "I thought you hated the Kindom."

"The Kindom is a network of cretins. I don't need hypocritical clerics and backstabbing secretaries. I certainly don't need blood-drunk assassins. Under this new order, the Hands will become extensions of the Families. Which is what the Families have always wanted."

And frequently had, Six thinks. After all, Esek herself only became a cleric to better serve her family. Most of the Hands who come from First Families remain loyal to their Family heads.

"Selecting the new leadership is just part of our offer," Riiniana says. "In addition, we'll give them each a fifteen percent share in the sevite trade."

A buzz against Six's hand. They've lost four fingers, the room announces. They drop the useless blade and square off against the remaining hologram, focusing on their breathing, on control. They think of Chono. Quiet, terrible Chono—the last person they sparred with, in a game like this. She clobbered them for daring to admit that they valued her success above their own life.

"That's quite an offer," Six pants.

The hologram crowds them against the wall, no way to escape. With a last burst of energy, Six bends sideways, away from a swiping blade, rocks inward, brings their sword down toward the creature's shoulder joint—

And feels the buzzing impact in the center of their chest.

The final hologram steps back, pulling its blade out of Six's body. Mortal injury, the room announces. Six is dead.

They stand a moment, absorbing their defeat. When Kess had them beaten two days ago, there was a particularly wicked blow to their hip. They can feel it throbbing now. The pulse of crushed blood vessels. Their body is drenched, and for a moment they imagine blood, or rainwater, but no—it's just sweat.

"You'll present the terms of our offer tomorrow," Riiniana says.

Heaving for breath, Six faces her. Riiniana must see something horrible in them, because for just a moment, her eyes widen, her lips compressing. Her body weight shifts backward. A moment later she reclaims her control, tilting her chin up imperiously.

"And the Jeveni?" Six asks.

Even after all this time, even knowing as they do that Drae sen Briit is their ancestor, Six can never quite think of themself as a Jeveni. Their actions have caused immeasurable grief to this already vulnerable people. Surely that strips them of any right to kinship.

Riiniana sniffs. "We can't change that the sevite trade needs Jeveni. Non-Jeveni don't want the work. The Jeveni hold all the institutional knowledge. They must come back."

"So, you'll enslave them, too?" Six asks.

"No," Riiniana says a bit testily, turning up her nose. "I'm not a slaver. I'm a strategist. Kess made a good start with his offer to Capamame. More money. Better living conditions. Unfortunately, he can't be trusted to keep his word. He's included caveats that you and the Jeveni and everyone in the systems can certainly interpret. I will impose no such caveats. I will let the Jeveni come home, whether they work the trade or not. I will make sure the five thousand currently imprisoned Jeveni are set free—which Kess has *not* done, despite his claims. I will show good faith. The Jeveni will return and take up the work they are best qualified for. Enough of them will, at least."

"And if they do not?"

"They will."

Six laughs at her audacity. They wipe their arm across their forehead. "And the rebels?"

"Will be eliminated, obviously."

Six's nostrils flare. "And Chono?"

A pause. "You won't thank me for lying to you. We can convince the Families to give her amnesty. But if she refuses to stand down, if she insists on continuing to fight alongside this quorum, as they're calling themselves, how can I promise you she will survive? Honestly, *Esek*. In the end, it may be in your hands. Surely she'll take advice from her old mentor."

The thread of mockery is like a splinter under their skin. She holds Six's answering gaze steadily. She's not flippant. Her touch of fear from before has vanished.

"You want me to propose an alliance among the Families," Six says. "But you imagine yourself the de facto leader."

She shrugs. "Not right away, no. But as power shifts and the old Family heads die and give way to their heirs? Yes. I'll be stronger than all of them."

Her confidence is enough to impress Six, though their laugh is derisive. "Do you even *know* the Family heirs?"

"Of course. I've met them several times."

"So have I."

Riiniana blinks in surprise.

"Hejar Paiye. Khen Vorkhen Soon. Giran Moonback. Before I became Esek, I made it a point to meet each of them. To learn each of them, just as I learned their parents. There is a distinct difference between how an heir presents themself to another heir at a party, and who an heir actually is and is likely to be when they assume leadership. Khen Soon is bookish and unwarlike, but he's been trained in strategy all his life. He'll see your power grabs coming. Giran, on the other hand, is spoiled and temperamental. One wrong move from you, and he'll go to war just for spite. As for Hejar, she is far too intelligent and proud to be corralled by an upstart. These saan have been trained all their lives to hold power in a fist. You are just a self-taught pretender."

Riiniana's eyes gleam. "So are you."

Six glares at her, and she smiles faintly.

"Come now, Sa. Don't you see? I'm like you. I cut my teeth manipulating clerics and secretaries. I had my uncle assassinated. Kess's spies are in my pocket. And I have you. It's not a matter of me managing the heirs. *We* will manage them. You and I. Surely you are equal to the task?"

"You think you know me so well. If you get Chono killed—"

"*I* have not done anything that would get Chono killed," Riiniana snaps. "You can't begin to know how much I hate clerics, and yet for *your* sake, I'd spare her. You should recognize a gesture of friendship for what it is."

Six cries, "Friendship? You *sterilized* me."

A wave of her hand. "That was only practical."

"You are using Chono to hold me hostage."

"Only as long as it takes you to see reason. Gods and fire, you spent your life destroying Esek! Don't you see that this is the final step in your revenge? Taking over the Treble with me, doing what she could never have dreamed? Stop obsessing over Chono. She will choose her own path. After everything you've done, do you really want to stand in her shadow for the rest of your life?"

Six doesn't move, doesn't speak.

Riiniana steps closer. "Surely you realize that the more power you have, the more you can protect her. If that really is what matters most to you, help me establish peace before she gets herself killed."

The girl has a point, murmurs Esek. This time, when Six thinks of her, they imagine decomposing skin hanging by threads on a skeleton. A face half eaten by insects and bacteria, and a mouth full of soil and blood. Through the muck, Esek chuckles. *Chono needs proper guidance. Otherwise, she gets herself into all kinds of trouble.*

"Rescue her if you want," Riiniana says. "Keep her safe, if that makes you happy. Keep her comfortable. Have her to yourself. That's what you want, isn't it? Chono safe . . . and yours?"

Six takes one threatening step toward her—and a dozen red lines bisect the air. Six looks down. The lines terminate in their chest. They look up again. High on the walls, the laser lines project from round nozzles identical to the ones in the other rooms.

"This is my house, Esek," Riiniana reminds them coolly. "It watches over me. Obey, and it'll watch over you. It'll watch over Chono. That's a promise." She flits her eyes up and down their body. "You need to bathe. We leave in three hours."

Not waiting for a response, she strides from the room, her dress swishing like a cloak.

CHAPTER FIFTEEN

1665

YEAR OF THE HARVEST

Kel-Ma
Trini-so Continent
The Planet Teros

The quorum disperses in the space of a day, the Kel-Ma farmhouse abandoned but for its usual denizens, snipers melting off the roof, lookouts vanishing from the fields. As he stands in the lot beside Zemit, Masar wonders where the representatives of the foreign insurgencies have gone. What their next moves will be. If they really will follow Chono's plan.

Zemit gives some form of an answer. "General Ashway is a

reasonable saan, and a damned good war strategist. He knows we all need to help one another. If Chono is successful, he'll follow her lead, even if it means working with the Families."

Masar gives Zemit a skeptical look. General Ashway of Ma'kess has yet to show himself, and Siltmire and Goodrite, his representatives and so-called lieutenants, don't seem particularly dedicated to the quorum. Or to Ashway himself.

Instead of saying so, Masar mutters, "Chono is reckless. She's probably dead. Or worse."

He was furious when Chono stated her intention to go to Oyun Paiye. The others in the quorum tried to dissuade her. Only Yantikye wore a look of impressed approval.

"Don't lose faith," Zemit says. "Chono knows what she's doing."

Masar warns him, "You should move your people out of Trin-Ma. Kess is gearing up to something. He'll make an example of you."

Zemit looks determined. "That may be. But Trin-Ma is a beacon to those in the Treble who want to believe we can stand up to the Kindom. We can't retreat now."

Masar wants to scream at him that they won't be much of a beacon if they're eradicated. But he thinks of Liis Konye and her band of warrior recruits in Farren Eyce, and grunts. "I would probably do the same."

Zemit smiles like a child getting praise from an elder, and he's just so damned young. Masar imagines his own young collectors who died at Nikapraev, and Qlios and Layez standing by, waiting for orders. He looks away from Zemit, relieved by the distraction of Yantikye swaggering out of the farmhouse. The knives crisscrossing his chest glint in the sun.

"I'd better go," Zemit says. "Gods keep you well, Masar Hawks."

He boards a ground shuttle bound for Trin-Ma. Masar and Yantikye climb into a warbunny, which turns east, off the beaten road onto red dirt plains. After two hours of silent travel they come to a clearing where Graisa the Honor has set down Yantikye's shuttle. As they come aboard, Masar can't help a grin at the sight of his third collector, Siel, who was injured at Nikapraev and recovering when the rest of them went down to Trin-Ma.

Siel grins back at him. Layez grabs her in a bear hug. Qlios ruffles her hair. They're all as young as Zemit. And just as likely to die in the near future.

From the cockpit, Graisa calls, "Everybody strap in."

As Masar obeys, he has an unwelcome memory of Tej zip-tying him to his flight seat. Of the stunning pain in his eye as Ujan's tech overheated and destroyed his prosthetic. He's adapting well enough to the change, but there are moments of disorientation, fluctuations in perspective that make him question the position of his body. Despite this, he doesn't miss the glitchy prosthetic eye. He only wishes that when the doctors had taken it out of him, they could have excised some of his memories, too.

The shuttle lifts off.

Siel bumps him with her elbow. Startled out of his thoughts, he bumps her back. "You doing okay, kid?"

She nods, all earnestness and pride, as if the fear alone couldn't have killed her when she was gut-shot twelve days ago. *So young.*

They are well into the Black when a message pings in his ocular:

You out?

He answers Jun:

Yeah, we just lifted off.

Chono?

No word yet. Have you seen anything?

Not since she went into Yeyankatayan. She was alive at least. Look, we need you on cast. Whole team is here.

Masar opens a view in the air above him. His collectors sit up straight as the Farren Eyce council room appears. About a dozen figures sit around the table: the gate engineer, and a couple of senior casters; the spokes of the Wheel, including a sunken-eyed Fonu sen Fhaan; Jun and Liis and—

The sight of Bene takes Masar off guard, but he has no time to question it before Effegen greets him in a no-nonsense voice. "Masar."

Masar stands from his seat and bows over his open hands, the collectors around him quickly doing the same. Effegen, noting the collectors, smiles warmly.

"Layez, Qlios. It's good to see you. Siel, how are you feeling?"

"I'm well, my Star."

"Stay that way," Effegen orders. She looks at Masar again. "Who else is on the shuttle?"

As if he has been awaiting his cue, Yantikye saunters into the cabin. He stops beside Masar and crosses his thick arms, a gesture that is somehow more jovial than aggressive. Effegen takes him in shrewdly.

"Sa Honor, I believe?"

Yantikye bows. "As you say, Sa Effegen. You'll forgive me if I don't call you my Star, won't you? We'll have to get to know each other before you're my anything, nah?"

Masar shifts irritably. Effegen looks amused. "A reasonable assertion. On that note, I hope you'll forgive me for not automatically trusting the person who betrayed Chono and Six."

He shrugs. "No hard feelings. Though I would expect a woman like you to understand that sometimes we have to sacrifice people, even if we like them perfectly well."

Effegen folds her hands on the table, raising her eyebrows. "A woman like me?"

"Of course. I've heard this and that of you. You're no wilting princess, I gather. That'll serve your people well, in these martial times."

Effegen smiles again, but it's icy. "I come from a long line of survivors, and we haven't gotten that way by bowing to flattery or welcoming strangers into our confidence. If you'll excuse me, I'm going to direct the remainder of this conversation to Masar's aural link."

"Privacy!" Yantikye grins. "Can't get enough of it. But let me say one thing, Sa. A little isolationism is good for the soul. But if a wolf pack shows up at your door and starts prying apart the hinges, you'd do well to have good neighbors."

Gaeda ben Kist, austere in her bright green robe with its glittery threadwork, asks him, "And you are a good neighbor, Sa Honor?"

"I am the best kind of neighbor, if our interests align."

"Nice caveat," says Jun.

Yantikye looks at her, delighted. "Kata's tit, if it isn't the famous Sunstep. And am I wrong, or is that woman at your side the cloak that escaped the Cloaksaan? Liis Konye! I am always eager to meet kin troublemakers."

Liis gives him a distinctly bored look.

Masar has had enough. "Stop flirting with everyone you meet. Get back in the cockpit and let me speak to the Wheel alone."

Yantikye holds up his hands. "Of course, of course!" He looks at Effegen again. "But remember what I said."

Once he's left the cabin, Effegen's words go directly to his aural link. "Masar, please use text comms to respond going forward. Jun has locked in and secured your cast connection."

Masar smirks at Jun.

Getting inside my head?

She smirks back, glancing at Effegen. "I'd rather not."

"Enough chat," barks Tomesk. "Masar, where are the rebel leaders?"

Zemit has returned to Trin-Ma. The others are keeping their locations secret, and everyone is waiting to hear from Chono.

"Chono is a lost cause. She's probably dead."

Though Masar said the same thing to Zemit, Tomesk saying it makes his hackles rise.

It is Liis, however, who shows rare annoyance when she says, "That's not a foregone conclusion. Oyun Paiye is a shrewd person, and she won't be in a hurry to bow to Kess. Chono may succeed."

"We can't pin our hopes on her."

"Nor can we afford to ignore such a significant weapon in our arsenal," Liis says.

Gaeda snaps her cane against the ground. "Moon arise! It won't matter what sort of weapon she is if we don't know what we're aiming at. Masar! Can these Ma'kessn rebels get you to Ma'kess System?"

Masar pauses, confused by the question.

I doubt it. Even with our Hoods it's too risky. Chono had to make a deal with Khen Obair to get to Kator System.

Gaeda scowls. "But I presume that there are Ma'kessn rebels *on* Ma'kess."

Yes. Two of the quorum members report directly to a general who defected from the Kriisturan army. He's leading a number of offensives on Ma'kess.

"Can we trust him?" Hyre asks.

I haven't met him. I'm not particularly fond of his agents, but that doesn't mean he won't listen to me.

"We can't trust Treblens who are no doubt prejudiced against us," Tomesk says.

Masar surprises himself with his answer:

In this quorum, Braems are working with Terons. Katishsaan are sharing intelligence with the Ma'kessn. The only prejudice they seem to care about is a prejudice against the Families and the Kindom.

Tomesk and Gaeda scoff in unison, which Masar can't fault them for. He's not inclined to trust in the goodwill of these non-Jeveni, and yet he's not ready to naysay them, either.

Effegen says, "Right now the most important alliance we can strike is with the Ma'kessn rebels. If you can't get there, Masar, we need someone else who already is."

Why? What's in Ma'kess System?

In answer, Effegen looks over at Bene, nodding shortly. Bene seems a little small among the giants of the council table, and Masar feels a surge of protectiveness toward him, knowing that some of these people view him as a traitor. But his voice is steady. "Masar, we've had a breakthrough with Ujan. Or I should say, with Tej. We think at some point he got a look at her cast programs. He saw blueprints of the Silver Keep."

Taken aback, Masar doesn't respond for several moments. That is until he catches sight of Jun, shifting restlessly in her chair. Jun has been all over Ujan's cast records, stripping her firewalls down and plundering the secrets inside. Masar asks:

Did you find blueprints in Ujan's files?

Gaeda sniffs. Tomesk glowers at Jun, who for her part looks defiant—and then defeated.

"Not until Tej told us about them," she says.

There's something more to that story, but Masar senses that pressing the matter would hurt Jun in some way. From Tomesk's look, Masar can guess who would do the hurting, and he wants no part in it. He looks at Bene again.

These blueprints. They show that the Keep is on Ma'kess?

Bene says, "They have topographical signs of a moonscape."

Masar doesn't understand at first. Then a slap of shock hits him. It's Liis who voices his realization. "We think the Silver Keep is on Jeve."

His ears whistle, high-pitched as mortar fire. The feeling somehow

combines repulsion and excitement, but after so many disappoint-
ments, he won't get ahead of himself. He looks at Jun, trusting her to
know the files best.

These topographical signs—could they apply to other moons?

"She probably hasn't had time to find out," Tomesk says waspishly.
Effegen's voice is lethal. "That's enough."
"Tomesk is right to be frustrated," the gate engineer says, though
he's not looking at Jun. "If we had found these records sooner—"
Bene interrupts hotly, "Do you know how much fucking data Ujan
has in her—"
"Jun has an entire casting lab at her disposal," Gaeda says, not cruel
but stern. "If she weren't trying to assess the data by herself on top of
all of the other work she's doing, this could have been avoided."
"Or her casters would have walked right past the blueprints," says
Liis, "and dismissed them as just one set among thirteen hundred *other*
blueprints."
That shuts the room up. Masar wants to laugh from sheer
incredulity.

Ujan has thirteen hundred blueprints in her records?

Jun meets his eyes, and through her bravado he sees the guilt that
has haunted her since they first watched Ujan Redcore replace Luja
Ironway. "She's a bit of a hoarder."
Masar knows this can't be the focus right now. He returns to his
earlier point.

There are several moons in the Treble.

"But none of them are as isolated as Jeve," Bene says. "None of them
are unpopulated. Think about it, Masar. Why did the Kindom only let
your people visit Jeve once every twenty-five years? Why did it take so

long to get permission in the first place? Why were you never allowed to go to the surface, or visit it out of season? It's against the law for any Treblens to go to Jeve. *Why?*"

To stop scavengers hunting for leftover jevite.

"The Kindom has never said that," Jun points out, seeming to shake off her humiliation. "They've always said it's out of respect. That the moon is a memorial. But that's bullshit."

Masar lifts his eyebrows.

Bullshit? Of course them caring about a memorial is bullshit. But that's a far cry from going to the trouble of relocating your fortress to a moon.

Liis says, "The Cloaksaan relocate the Silver Keep at least every hundred years."

Taken aback, Masar looks at her stolid face. He has the random thought, *That's interesting and creepy*, then he shoots back:

By the time of the genocide, only three dome cities were left standing. Ninety percent of the moon's surface was so destabilized from the effects of the trade, it would be impossible to build anything. If the Keep is there, it'll be on the bones of one of the cities. Why bother?

All eyes shift to Liis Konye. She rests her prosthetic arm on the table, two fingers slowly tapping in a rare hint of restlessness. Though she was ready enough to share the snippet about the Cloaksaan's relocation habits, now she hesitates, as if some old instinct for keeping house secrets has waylaid her. As Masar watches from his vantage, he sees Jun's hand shift under the table to gently rest on Liis's knee. Liis gives an almost imperceptible start. She isn't looking at any of them when she begins to speak.

"In the city where I grew up, I knew of four assassinations by the time I was five. Politicians and businessaan who got taken out by cloaks in the night. When I heard people say that the Cloaksaan go unnoticed, I believed it. The trouble is they don't go unnoticed, do they? Oh, they can hide in a crowd. Sneak into your house and cut your throat without anyone being the wiser. But the whole Treble notices them, watches them, fears them. And in their own way they have always been"—she pauses, and Masar sees a tiny, bitter smile cross her lips—"theatrical." She looks up at last, eyes as dark as pitch and full of the shadowed past. Indeed, it's never looked so near the surface of her before. She wears it like a shroud. "They have a weakness, like every Hand. They like their symbols. When I became a novitiate, my mentor told me about the previous locations of the Keep."

She holds up one finger.

"In the first century, they built it in a mountain pass overlooking the valley where the original Kindom and *The Risen Wave* colonists first set down. The generation ship *The Black Harbor* tried to fight the Kindom for Ma'kess, and failed. It had to flee to Teros as punishment."

She holds up another finger.

"In the fifth century, before the discovery of jevite, a nomadic tribe on the polar caps of Kriistura found several trillion tons of oil, enough to fuel the entire planet for a century. The Cloaksaan rode in, wiped out the tribe and all its claims to the land, and took the oil. They put the Keep inside a nearby glacier."

She holds up a third finger. "In the ninth century, the first Quietan homesteaders tried to create a republic apart from the Kindom. The Cloaksaan decimated them. It was the biggest slaughter in a millennium, and it reasserted the primacy of the Brutal Hand, who proceeded to put their Keep *under the ocean floor*."

She holds up her fourth and fifth fingers, and all five of the other hand.

"The Cloaksaan relocate as a security measure. And they use it as an opportunity to celebrate the locations of their best kills."

Masar's skin prickles. The table is quiet for several moments. Eventually Hyre asks, "But have you ever heard that the Keep is on Jeve?"

Liis shakes her head. "My mentor was chatty, but he didn't know the current location of the Keep. Only the top commandants and special clearance officers know where it is. Cloaksaan who are stationed there never leave. Cloaks who are brought there temporarily are incapacitated first. I've been there twice, and I could never have told you where it was."

Masar casts:

So how do we confirm its location?

"Not from here," Jun says. "The cast satellites around the moon are limited, and if the Keep is there, I won't be able to hack those satellites without someone noticing. We need to send someone there under Hood to scan the moon for evidence of a structure, probably underground and close to one of the dome cities where the rock foundations are strong enough to sustain something as big as the Keep. If we find it, our best option is for me to jump through the Jeve gate and cast into the Keep manually."

Masar is astonished.

You want to infiltrate the Silver Keep?

"Sure," Jun chirps. "How hard can it be?"

"Very hard," Liis says. "A single caster can't do it. Not even you."

Effegen says, "We understand that there are representatives for the Ar'tec Collective in this quorum. With their help, we might be able to—"

"And suppose the Ma'kessn strangers do find it," Tomesk interrupts. "And suppose a bunch of caster criminals manage to get inside its casting net." He gives Jun a doubtful look. "Then what?"

"We fuck it up," Jun says.

Tomesk rolls his eyes. Gaeda says, "This is no time for your boasting."

"Perhaps we should try to negotiate with Kess instead," Hyre hems. "Perhaps he'll be content with a smaller percentage of our population."

"We should focus on our armaments," Gaeda declares. "Hold him off."

"For how long?" Jun demands.

"If Kess catches us trying to invade his Keep, he'll kill us all."

"No," says Hyre. "He wouldn't!"

"Of *course* he would!" Tomesk snaps.

"Listen to me." Liis's voice is sharper than usual, commanding silence. "This is the most important piece of information we could possibly have discovered. The Silver Keep is the centerpiece of the Brutal Hand's command infrastructure. From there, the cloaksaan have access to the navigation and armaments of their fleet."

Jun says, "If we got inside, we could cut off communication between members of the fleet. We could infiltrate their private cast network and hobble Kindom ships. They wouldn't be able to keep us from using the gates. That's to say nothing of the fact that if we could lower the Keep's shields, we might be able to destroy it with an aerial assault."

"Let's not get ahead of ourselves," says Effegen. "We still haven't confirmed the Keep is there. Masar, can you persuade the quorum members in Ma'kess System to do this? Surely it would align with their interests, to destroy the Keep."

Masar rubs a hand down his face. He doesn't even know if Siltmire and Goodrite have returned to Ma'kessn space, let alone if they have ships capable of this reconnaissance. Ashway, perhaps? But Masar's never met the man.

Most of the quorum members seem all right. But the two Ma'kessns I've met weren't particularly friendly to me and Chono. I don't know if we can trust them, or even if they'd want to help us. This is a big secret to give them if we're not sure.

Jun looks restless. "We can't just sit on it. The new gate key isn't done. It won't be done before the Feast Day."

Tomesk gives Jun an accusing look, but he doesn't understand the labor of creating a key. Masar wants to voice some support for Jun, but another voice speaks up:

"We must do whatever is necessary to find and dismantle the Keep."

It takes him a moment to realize who said the words. It seems to surprise the others as well, gazes shifting toward Fonu sen Fhaan. The River looks small and haggard in their chair at the fringes of the council, but their voice is strong.

"We have no more time for half measures. This is the moment for which Drae sen Briit sent the Draeviin to Capamame. She said that one day the Kindom would tire of nibbling on our edges. That one day, it would try to swallow us whole. And now, here it is. We are on the verge, and we do not have time to chase after Kess when we may have his entire Hand in our grasp."

Fonu looks directly at Masar. Masar is thrust back into the moment when Tej and Bene led him aboard the shuttle on the surface of Capamame and he saw Fonu stripped and zip-tied. Broken hands and feet and teeth. Their ear carved off in some grotesque homage to Six. And yet that isn't the worst scar Ujan left on Fonu. The worst scar must be their knowledge that, when torture came, they gave away the Capamame gate key.

Now, prosthetics replace their missing ear and amputated foot. Their mouth has new teeth. The internal injuries must be nearly completely healed, and the outward marks have faded with the use of regenerative meds. But that other scar—it burns in Fonu's eyes.

"We must go to Jeve. You must convince *someone* on Ma'kess to go to Jeve."

Masar has never loved Fonu as he loved Nikkelo sen Rieve. But he feels now the deeply ingrained loyalty to Fonu's office. He nods.

I can try.

The River's expression declares that this is not enough. "We cannot afford for you to fail. What about Sa Honor? Could *he* convince the Ma'kessn to go?"

Now there's an idea—more astute than Masar would have expected. Zemit brought Yantikye to the quorum meeting to vouch for Chono because he knew the quorum would listen to Yantikye. Yantikye's betrayal of Chono was not enough for the quorum to oust him.

Goodrite and Siltmire may not listen to Masar, but they might well listen to the Quietan. Still, if Masar trusts the wrong people—if he lays their fate in the hands of traitors—he will never forgive himself.

The reluctance must show on his face, for Liis interjects.

"I'm doing everything I can for Farren Eyce. I know that we can hold the Kindom off for a time. But Masar"—she meets his gaze, one warrior to another—"we need more than that. If we are to *win*...we need more."

She's right. Caution is now more dangerous than an act of hope. Suddenly Bene says, "Six trusted Yantikye, didn't they?"

Masar almost laughs. Six, the fucker who got them into so much of this mess. A saan for whom trust is too extreme a concept but who nonetheless appears to have had a certain wisdom when it came to winning their gambits.

Masar sends a comm into the cockpit of the shuttle. Some needless delay later, Yantikye walks in looking pleased as can be.

"Why, hello again, my darlings," he says to the people on cast. "What can I do for you?"

The arrival of her child does not seem to have mellowed Melicini Nightfoot's ideas about herself. She continues to insist on the inappropriateness of her female gendermark, a position that will ultimately make her ineligible for the matriarchy, much like her mother. As for the child Riiniana, she suffers from respiratory and other illnesses, which don't respond normally to medical intervention. While it's likely the Nightfoots will keep the girl alive, she seems as unlikely an heir to Alisiana as anyone else in the matrilineal line.

excerpt, report to First Cloak Xer Ooxer Ang.
Dated 1651, Year of the Level.

CHAPTER SIXTEEN

1665

YEAR OF THE HARVEST

M-4 Station
Orbiting Ma'kess

Riiniana Nightfoot is the future of the Nightfoot family. This is not arrogance or wishful thinking, but rather the only logical conclusion to the circumstances in which she finds herself. She's not like her mother, too concerned with her own petty needs to serve the family. She's not like her grandmother, addicted to sensation and stunningly obtuse. She's not even like Alisiana, for Alisiana was insular. She kept her own counsel, held her lieutenants at bay—barring a couple of exceptions: her uncle, Caskori, the foppish playboy. And, of all people, Esek, her self-interested wolf of a favorite. Neither of those worked out for her.

Nor, in the end, did her economic strategy. Oh, yes, Alisiana raised the Nightfoot fortunes astronomically. She committed her tenure to expanding the trade, and succeeded. She milked the Jeveni refugees for all they were worth, tempering their bad circumstances by giving them unions and self-determination, or at least a semblance of it. And she held back the Kindom and the other Families, making herself a single-woman bulwark against encroaching storms.

That was her mistake. Her entire strategy relied on *her*. Her methods, her insight. Her survival. She trusted Caskori, but in the end he sold her secrets to the Kindom. She waited too long to pick an heir, and when she did, she handed the family over to a trickster. All of which could have been avoided if she had only seen a little further than her own tower rooms.

No. Riiniana is not like her. Riiniana will accomplish more than she ever did.

As their shuttle coasts into the bay of M-4 station, neutral ground with no affiliation to any Family or planetary power source, Riiniana takes note of the Moonback and Khen shuttles already docked. A quick cast indicates that Oyun Paiye is only a few minutes away. All four Families have military entourages, and she can only imagine the hostility suffocating the meeting room where Revel Moonback and Khen Ookhen Obair are waiting. While Obair has always had a civil relationship with Oyun, the Khens and Moonbacks hate each other, just as the Moonbacks and Nightfoots hate each other, just as the Nightfoots hate the Paiyes. The Paiyes, on the other hand, are content to turn up their noses at everyone. Riiniana recalls a time when she proposed to Alisiana that they should bring the First Families together under a single head, unify them at last, and dwarf the power of the Kindom. Alisiana seemed surprised and amused. Later, Uncle Torek spent the flight back to his estate on Coral berating her for bringing such an idea to the matriarch.

"Arrogant," he'd said. "Naive. You have *no* grasp of history. What were you thinking? You will spend tomorrow at temple, first Makala's and then the Godfire. Maybe one of them will see fit to give you a little wisdom."

She bore his abuse silently, and hid curses inside her prayers, until he was certain of her regret and piety. This was the strategy that had worked best for her throughout her life. In the childhood years of sickliness, she cultivated a reputation for being mild but not insouciant, intelligent but not ambitious. Obedient. *Shy*, even. Efforts to assert her voice or her will too aggressively never succeeded. Torek always shot her down and looked at her with distrust, as if to say, "You will not rise above me, heir or not."

And being young, and physically vulnerable, and without Alisiana's support, Riiniana learned quickly not to rise above anyone. At least not in the way that they might recognize. She rose behind the scenes. She learned to manipulate. Her attendants. Her doctors. Her secretary tutors and, finally, Torek. After so many years of convincing him of her submissiveness, it was easy to twist him toward her will, to make him think her ideas were his own. An innocent comment at dinner. A cast program about some specific investment left hanging in the air. A word of curiosity regarding a potential study partner—whose parents Torek would have to investigate first and who, it turned out, would be a lucrative connection. Riiniana, always poised to benefit from Torek's financial decisions, padded her coffers in secret. Then it was just a matter of buying investigators and secretaries. Buying the guardsaan and servants of the Coral estate. So on and so forth, until it was Riiniana who decided last year that they must put a contract kill out on Esek, but it was Torek who made the deal and considered it his own.

And now Torek is dead. He had been a good mask, all things considered. But once she learned about Esek's little doppelgänger, it was time to graduate to a new puppet. Terrible tragedy, Torek's heart attack in the middle of the night. No chance for a doctor to save him.

On the M-4 docks, she disembarks, Esek in tow and both of them flanked by Verdant guardsaan. The station governor is waiting for them, all solicitude as he guides them through the station. Well, he ought to be solicitous for all she's paying him. He keeps up an end-less barrage of chatter, describing the station's history, but Riiniana, affecting meekness, does not react. She is more interested in gauging the Riin Matri, a woman who she refuses to call anything but Esek, even to herself. The female gendermark stamped on her person is good enough for Riiniana, who cares nothing for a street urchin called Six, who, according to Riiniana's research, used some vague Katish gender-mark before turning herself into Esek. Well, Esek they will be. Esek she is.

Riiniana certainly likes her better than the first Esek. The first Esek was myopic. She was born to a minor branch of the family tree, which was the same as born to nothing, and not surprisingly she wanted her own bloody mouthful of the worlds. But rather than taking sly, deli-cate bites here and there so no one would even notice her filling up with power, she ripped and gnawed and guzzled anything she could catch, till she was a spectacle, and a detested one at that. Easily tracked and positioned and replaced by the one-time kinschool student.

The new Esek is like Riiniana. A quiet tactician. Ruthless but con-trolled, brilliant but smart enough to wear a shade, so it's no easy feat to see her for who she really is. Yes, of course, now that she is Esek, she must be the same gregarious spectacle as her predecessor, but that is why she and Riiniana will be a powerful team. The new Esek will use the first Esek as a mask, and Riiniana will use the new Esek as *her* mask, and behind their layers of subterfuge and theater, they will take the Treble for everything it is.

"Sa Khen and Sa Moonback are taking refreshments now," says the station governor. "We've reserved you a secure conference room. You can be assured of its privacy."

Esek chuckles, and the governor is clearly unnerved. He knows Esek's reputation. Riiniana hides a smile of satisfaction, watching her puppet do her job, and marveling, not for the first time, at the effec-tiveness of the illusion. Dressed in a ruby-red suit, New Esek cuts a striking figure, her hair pristinely braided into a crown, and the jacket hitting mid-thigh in a way that cannot help but evoke her one-time cleric's coat. She looks serpentine, beautiful, exactly how people would expect Esek to look.

The hall opens into a hexagonal foyer, with a door on the far side. Khen and Moonback guards stand at either side of the door, looking surly.

"Here we are," says the governor, badly hiding his nervousness.

"My favorite kind of reception," Esek says. She gestures dismissively at the governor. "You can go." He hesitates long enough for her to lose patience. "*Go.*"

He goes. The Nightfoot guardsaan take up position against another wall. Part of the agreement of the meeting is that all guards stay outside. No weapons in the conference room.

"Play nice," Esek orders them, and marches toward the door.

It irises open to let them inside, and Riiniana scans the room as thoroughly and surreptitiously as she can. Obair and Revel have each taken a seat at a square table that dominates the room—short, sweating Obair in a green toga typical of Teron aristocracy, and tall, narrow-eyed Revel in a black suit. Obair is alone, but to Revel's left sits his niece and chief strategist, Karix Moonback. Nearly as pale as a Braem, nearly as thin as Riiniana, she has sharp, observant eyes.

"Hello!" Esek brays. "Have I kept you long?" Both men glare at her. "Congratulations on not killing each other! I see the spirit of friendship is already growing among us."

"And *I* see you're as obnoxious as ever," Obair says. "What Alisiana ever saw in you, I don't know."

"It's true," says Esek. "I am quite unbearable."

Obair looks past her to Riiniana, declaring, "She would have been better served following tradition and appointing you, Bright Daughter. At least you took good counsel from your uncle Torek. He was a reasonable and righteous person. My sincerest condolences to you for that unexpected tragedy."

"What about me?" asks Esek. "Don't I get your condolences?"

"You are a circus performer," says Revel Moonback spitefully.

"Oh, no," Esek assures him. "Circuses are far less dangerous, for one."

Riiniana fights not to show her annoyance. Yes, of course, Esek must play her insufferable self, but she's not meant to openly antagonize them! This meeting is to bring them all together.

"Now," says Esek, "let's not be rude. Revel! Isn't this your niece? Why, last I saw her, she was half your age!"

Esek bows over her open palms to Karix, a gesture infused with mockery. Karix smiles as if through a nasty smell. Raised up from her youth to be a policy adviser, she is leagues smarter than Revel's actual heir, Giran. Tellingly, Giran isn't here. Neither is Khen Vorkhen Soon.

"Esek," Karix says in greeting, then she inclines her head to Riiniana. "You're looking well, child. I'm sorry for the loss of your uncle. I would have thought you would be at home, in mourning."

Riiniana says in her most demure voice, "I grieve every moment, Sa Moonback. But the Riin Matri believes this meeting is essential to all our futures, and as my new guardian, she is responsible for my movements."

Karix's eyes glitter. "I'm sure."

"But where are the other heirs?" Esek asks. "Soon. Giran. Aren't they interested in our business?"

Obair scowls but looks cagey. "My son has other burdens on his time."

"As does mine," says Revel.

Karix sniffs, the only hint at her spite for Giran.

Esek tuts at them. She pulls out a chair on the opposite side of the table, dropping into it and snapping her fingers at a station attendant who stands beside a sideboard laid with food. The attendant rushes forward with a pitcher, filling a cup that waits on the table.

"And bring me some of that food. Riiniana. Don't be rude, girl—sit down."

Riiniana, aware that Esek will take great delight in demeaning her, placidly sits in the chair next to hers. The attendant fills her glass as well, then rushes to the sideboard and comes back with a plate of artfully arranged cheeses, dried meats, pickled vegetables, and some type of puff pastry that oozes a red sauce. Riiniana gestures the attendant away, then lifts her glass to sip, fruity, acidic flavors rolling over her tongue.

"Now, mind you, don't get drunk," Esek warns her, wrapping a sliver of cured meat around the tines of her fork and placing it in her mouth. She moans gustily, popping a cube of cheese in her mouth. "Wonderful. Glorious. *Funky.* Won't any of the rest of you eat?"

"I'd rather get on with whatever this is," says Revel.

"Now, now," Esek chides. "We can't leave dear Oyun out of it."

As if on cue, Riiniana receives a notification that the Paiyes are on station. Revel harumphs his impatience while Obair picks up his glass and drinks. Esek bites off one side of a puff pastry, sauce dripping onto her fingers. Riiniana catches Karix watching with a curled lip. They all sit around, not talking, tense and moody.

Five minutes later, the door opens again. Oyun Paiye, gorgeous in lavender robes and hair glittering with silver beadwork, strolls into the room with all the pomp of an unrepentant late arrival. Behind her comes her proud, straight-backed daughter in military whites, breast appliquéd with metals. Displaying none of the anger and pique of the other family heads, the Paiyes are a striking picture of composure.

But Riiniana barely sees them, her gaze locking on the figure in their wake. Her blood runs cold and she blinks to clear her vision, hoping it's an illusion.

No luck. Cleric Chono is in the room.

Shocked into stillness, Riiniana tries to parse the avalanche of thoughts that breaks over her—that her spies did not tell her this was happening, that Chono's presence is an implicit threat, that Paiye is even less predictable than she thought, and that Esek—

With an internal jolt, Riiniana snaps her gaze away from the cleric to land on Esek. Dread pitches and yaws in her stomach as she watches her carefully managed puppet look at Chono. What will Esek do? Some utterly irrational, dangerous thing, surely? Some explosion of violent revolt? But Esek, to her surprise, does not erupt. She looks at Chono with a flat, shuttered expression that Riiniana cannot read, that Riiniana instinctively fears. Riiniana looks at Chono again, watches her stare at Esek. But she, too, looks utterly stoic.

Fighting back hysteria, Riiniana wonders how these two unfathomable people even know they care about each other.

With a cry, Khen Obair is on his feet, shrill voice punctuating the stunned silence. "What is this?! What is this?!"

Revel growls, "Oyun, do you have a death wish?" He looks at Esek. "Did you *plan* this? Are you trying to ensnare us?"

"Arrest her!" Obair shrieks, as if there were guards in the room.

"Cleric Chono is my guest," says Oyun. "No one will touch her."

Karix hisses, "She is a *fugitive*! What are you thinking, bringing her here?"

"If you would all stop being dramatic, perhaps I could properly introduce—"

"I want no such introduction!" Obair cries. "I want her out of this room. I want her—"

Esek bangs her fist down on the table. "Everybody calm down, right now."

Perhaps it is the authenticity of her anger that makes them all obey. Three seconds pass. Five. Riiniana, who can't stop looking between Esek and Chono, trying to comprehend how this happened, carefully modulates her breathing. This is just a complication. She has dealt with complications before.

"Good," says Esek. "Now, sit down, all of you, for gods' sake. You'd think you'd never seen a cleric before."

Slowly, everyone obeys, and the station attendant, now quivering with fear, manages to pour out the drinks without spilling. Oyun, who looks perfectly at ease despite the ruckus, takes a dainty sip. Her daughter follows. Chono, sitting beside Oyun Paiye, ignores her drink completely.

Esek barks a laugh. "Come now, Chono. I raised you better than that."

Riiniana watches them meet eyes across the table. She's only ever seen Chono on cast view, and that did not prepare her for the real thing. Clerics who haunted the Coral estate told Riiniana that Chono is dull, ponderously self-righteous, and completely uncharismatic. Of course, she knew that was nonsense from the start. She has seen the cast recordings, heard the voice like a deep bell. Even so, Chono in person is far more arresting than Riiniana expected. Her tall, broad-shouldered body seems to take up space without trying. Her severe expression rebukes anyone foolish enough to dismiss her. She may not be a beautiful person, but looking at her is to realize that beauty doesn't matter. She is *affecting*, attractive like a magnet rather than a flower. Her eyes have the ominous intensity of a hurricane sky.

Chono lifts her glass, sips, and puts it down again. There is a finality to the gesture that seems to snap everyone to attention.

"Well," says Oyun brightly, "now that we've all remembered we're not overexcited children. Esek, this is your meeting. I suppose you've got a mouthful of Kess's promises to give us? Honestly, I never took you for the collaborative sort."

"Collaborative!" says Obair, nostrils flared. "This is a very bad start, very bad."

He looks downright frightened. Even Revel, who grumbles, "Agreed," does not seem as wrong-footed as him.

Riiniana watches Chono flick a glance at Obair. Something shifts in her expression, just a moment of unreadable emotion, and then it's gone.

"A very bad start to what?" asks Esek. "Perhaps you'd better hear what I have to say before you make pronouncements about what serves and doesn't serve our purposes."

"Our purposes?" says Revel with a dark laugh. "You can't be serious."

"Not usually, no. But my overtures are sincere. And what I'm going to offer you—"

Obair can't hold back the tide of vexation. "You've brought a terrorist into our midst!" He throws a gesture at Chono, though he can't seem to quite look at her. "You associate us with Seti Kess's sworn enemies!"

Esek laughs. "*I* did not invite Chono here. That was dear Oyun. Though I admire the audacity."

"Then you're just going to let her sit there?" Obair cries.

Karix Moonback says icily, "Of course she will. We all know Esek is irrational when it comes to her." She looks at Esek. "It's been a marvel to watch, I must admit. Chono turned you against your family and the sevite trade. She drove you to ally with Jeveni malcontents. How did she do it?"

"Obviously she has her on some kind of leash!" Obair declares. "A—a spell! You may as well be a dog chained to her chair!"

Esek clucks her tongue. "Kinky."

Obair's voice rises to a shriek. "She *murdered* my uncle!"

There is a pregnant pause, finally interrupted when Chono says quietly, "Your uncle was a rapist of children, Sa Khen." As if drawn unwillingly by that magnet inside Chono, Obair looks at her. His skin is blanched white. Chono doesn't blink. She asks in that smooth, resonant voice, "Do you think that rapists of children deserve my mercy?"

A shiver runs down Riiniana's spine. She senses it—some history between them that goes beyond Chono's murder of Khen Caskhen Paan. Obair looks on the verge of a heart attack as Chono stares at him with what looks like carefully controlled hatred.

Obair gulps for words. "I will not be intimidated by you!"

"No," Chono says. "You will simply try to have me assassinated." She looks at Esek. "Both of us, at the praevi farm."

Riiniana blinks. She thought she was the only one who tried to assassinate Esek.

"Oh-ho!" Esek laughs, incisors flashing. "Truly? And here was the Kindom telling us Teron rebels did it! You are sneaky, Obair, I'll give you that. But alas, we survive, and you will have to live with that failure. For a while at least."

Obair looks from Esek to Chono to Esek again. "I have more guardsaan on my ship."

Esek rolls her eyes. "This is tedious. Shall we proceed?"

"Yes, let's do," Oyun Paiye says. "I assume, given the fact that you have lent your forces to Seti Kess, you intend to argue for us to do the same."

Esek laughs. "Do you think so, Regal Paiye? Isn't it rather well known that Kess hates me and I hate him?" She looks at Revel. "You and I have very little in common, Sa, but I think we concur on one thing: Seti is an insufferable prick."

Revel's nostrils flare. It's Karix who says, "There may be no love lost between my uncle and his son, but it behooves the Moonback name to remain allied to one of our own."

"One of your own!" scoffs Oyun. "Honestly, Karix. He's taken a different name!"

"That's because he's an ingrate," says Revel.

"Nonetheless." Karix sounds firm. "If you are done showboating, Esek. You must mean to bring us to Seti's side. Why play games about it?"

"I have no intention of bringing you to his side. I myself have only lent him Nightfoot forces as a feint. His reliance on those forces will make it more devastating when I pull the rug out from under him."

Obair's sweaty brow furrows, and Revel and Karix glance at each other, distrustful. Oyun looks contemplative, and says something indiscernible to her daughter, who nods. Chono does not react at all.

"This *is* surprising," Oyun says at last. "Do continue."

Riiniana's heart flutters, knowing that all her schemes may be about to pass a crucial hurdle. Anticipation makes her palms clammy. Which is why it hits her harder than she's expecting when Esek turns a smiling look on her.

"As to that, I thought I'd let my dear cousin give you the details."

Riiniana's eyes widen. This is not what they agreed to. It is absolutely essential that Esek makes the case, and that Riiniana remains a timid observer. If the First Families turn on Esek, Riiniana must be able to argue that the entire thing was Esek's idea, and she had no part in it.

"I . . ." she says.

"Don't be shy! After all, the germ of the idea was yours. Don't you think you deserve credit?"

Riiniana feels the blood drain from her face.

"Don't let her bully you, girl," says Revel. "Just tell us what all this is about."

Meanwhile, for all Esek's outward performance, it is the street urchin, the trickster, who smiles mockingly at Riiniana.

Swallowing, Riiniana addresses the people at the table. "My matriarch would like to propose a—well, a—an alliance, among the four of us, against Seti Kess."

The Families don't look surprised, exactly, but she can see how discomfited they are. Karix shifts back in her seat. Obair searches the ceiling for a cast camera. A trap, they're thinking. But it's too late to go back now. Riiniana is no orator, and all her thoughts as to how the plan should be presented required Esek to present it. Now, presenting it herself, she has a fleeting image of Torek's disapproving glower, and Alisiana's mocking smile.

But her voice steadies as she speaks. She knows the details, after all. She has pored over them and crafted them herself. She explains the numbers: Kess's forces and strongholds, the forces and strongholds of the Families, the difficulty proposed by the overly defended gates, and the opportunity inherent in Kess's failure to properly defend other sites. And why it is possible for the Families to defeat Kess. She speaks in as timorous a voice as she can, trying to convey that she is merely reciting someone else's ideas. But it may be too late to persuade the room of that. She sees their expressions changing, the slow recalibration, as they look at her anew.

After Riiniana has finished, Oyun asks, "And then what? If we band together and crush Kess, what comes next?"

Riiniana swallows, wishing that Esek would take over. But Esek only smiles that infernal, charlatan smile.

"With Kess and his cloaks defeated, the Kindom will have no leadership left. We can step in, appoint our own leaders, and assume governmental control over the Treble."

Revel chortles disbelievingly. Hejar murmurs something to her mother. Esek grins like a skull. And Chono watches without expression, without comment. Annoyed by the doubt in the room, Riiniana raises her head. It's an effort to maintain her docile affect as she lays out the details of her offer. The particulars are so specific, so brilliantly thought out, that she wants to brag. She wants to shame them for their doubt. Instead, she stays humble, outlining everything from infra-structural reorganization to the concessions and sacrifices the Families will have to make. Of course they don't like that part at all. But then she wields the carrot:

"As a gesture of goodwill and partnership, the Riin Matri will offer each of you a fifteen percent interest in the sevite trade."

This time, no one chortles. She can taste it instantly: intrigue and greed. The other Families have always wanted a piece of the trade. It has hurt their pride and their coffers, to have to go to the Nightfoots for sevite. But the Kindom always defended Nightfoot sovereignty in this matter, facilitating the trade and conceding the profits to Alisiana. Riiniana suspects this was a self-preservative measure. If all the Fami-lies shared control of the trade, what would stop them from turning their monopoly against the Kindom? Just as Riiniana now urges them to do.

"This is ambitious," says Oyun, but she doesn't dismiss it outright.

"And probably impossible," says Revel.

Esek asks merrily, "You think so?"

"Kess has control of the trade right now. What trade there is, I should say. When he realizes that we've revolted against him, he'll put considerable force into choking off our access to sevite. We can't win a war—we can't even start a war—without sevite."

"The sevite vaults are on Ma'kess," Riiniana says, forgetting to sound meek. "If we begin our campaign by securing Ma'kess, he'll be the one cut off from the resources he needs."

They all look at her, reassessing her once more. Riiniana lowers her eyes, wishing she could blush on command. This entire thing is threat-ening to unmask her. The moment they register her as the force and threat behind her family, she is in danger.

Unsurprisingly, Obair is the first to lose his nerve. "This is absurd. If Kess finds out about this plan, he'll have us all assassinated."

Hejar Paiye grunts her contempt. "Kess slaughtered his own kin Hands and tried to blame it on Cleric Chono leading a revolt. Isn't that right?"

Chono says, "It is. Esek and I were prisoners. Kess massacred secretaries and guardsaan alike, even after the Secretarial Court surrendered."

"You're proving my point!" cries Obair. "If Kess learns of this meeting, he'll—"

"You misunderstand my meaning," Hejar interrupts. "The threat of Kess assassinating us is little better than the threat of allying to him. If he could turn on the Clever Hand, he could certainly turn on us. Suppose we lend him our forces. Do you think he'll give them back? No. Consider the name he chose. He wants to set himself up as akin to a god. I never knew him well, but I know him better now. He's a blood-drunk tyrant."

"Hear, hear," drawls Esek.

Riiniana feels a spark of hope, feels the tides turning in her favor—

Oyun addresses Chono. "What do you say, Burning One?"

Riiniana stiffens. She is reminded of a hundred visits to the temple in Coral, and Uncle Torek bringing her before the clerics to bow and scrape, and always he would ask them, "Well, Burning One? What do you think of my niece?"

And they would offer pandering praise to him, and subtle threats to her.

Chono, far less expressive than those clerics, says nothing for several moments. Obair looks as nervous as if he expects her to draw a gun on him, but the Moonbacks and Paiyes (not to mention Esek herself) watch with interest.

"I agree with Hejar. Kess won't be content until he has eliminated every possible threat to his authority. That will doubtless include you all. I also agree with Sa Riiniana." For the first time, she looks Riiniana in the eye, giving a little nod that makes Riiniana clench with her inborn distrust of all clerics. "You have to work together. The Brutal Hand is strong enough to take out two Families, but not three.

Certainly not four. And if any of you chose to side with him against the others, it would produce nothing but bloodshed and destruction. Your very survival requires you to collaborate."

Despite all her distrust, Riiniana's heart leaps. Can it be possible? Is Cleric Chono really going to lend her voice, her influence, to this cause?

Chono says, "However..."

And the air stands still.

"Even if you defeat Kess, you will fail."

In the answering silence, a deep pit opens in Riiniana's body, one part shock, one part despair, but all of it is rage.

"Go on, Chono," prompts Esek. "Fail at what?"

"At holding the Treble. At maintaining your fortunes. At surviving."

"And why is that?" asks Revel distrustfully.

"Because the only way to establish long-term peace and prosperity in the Treble is for you to stop attacking the rebels, and work with them to find common cause."

She may as well have told them to get on their knees and drink from a pig trough. Revel's lip curls in disgust. Obair laughs aloud, though it sounds strangled.

"You can't be serious. These people are as fanatical as Kess. They kidnapped my son, they drove me out of Trin-Ma, and they'd see us all spitted if they could."

"They are not fanatical," says Chono. "They are a quorum of like-minded saan. They want an end to tyranny, and to have influence over the Treble. They want a better life."

"They owe us for having life at all!" cries Revel. "It's *our* industries that give them work and pay enough to survive in these worlds."

"And it's their labor which keeps your industries running," Chono replies.

"They're thugs," he says. "We'll exterminate them."

"Forgive me," says Oyun Paiye. "But isn't it true that Ma'kessn rebels have seized the city of Teveet? An important manufacturing center, isn't it? And I hear they took Reveñon Manor just last night."

Stymied, Revel opens and closes his mouth. It's Karix who says,

"We have already called the Kriisturan militia to arms. We'll have Teveet and Reveñon back in a week."

"You've only called up the militia because the general of the official Kriisturan army has sided with the rebels," says Chono. "Your own forces are turning against you."

Karix flares her nostrils. "General Ashway may have betrayed his office, but we retain control of the majority of the military in our territories."

"Yet you've made no headway. Neither has Teros. The Trin-Ma rebels have had the upper hand for weeks. And now uprisings in Khenphasi, Lo-Meek, and Aniso are gaining ground. The Khens may lose Teros entirely." Though Khen Obair looks apoplectic at this pronouncement, he doesn't argue. Chono faces Revel again. "As for your own continents, you have never had the benefit of numbers. If the rebel forces in Ma'kess territory set their sights on you—"

Karix interrupts, "You are grossly underestimating our resources."

"But I do not underestimate the losses you will take. If you serve Kess, you'll still have to fight the rebels. But on top of that, you'll have a despot lording over you. If you fight against Kess, you'll take losses, all while another enemy attacks you from behind. If, on the other hand, you and the quorum band together against Kess, the fight will end faster, with fewer casualties. Not just human casualties, but the casualties to your industry and strongholds."

"The rebels want us eradicated," Obair says. "They send out casts and pin up bulletins calling for my head. And you expect me to partner with them?"

For a strange moment, Chono's eyes grow distant. Is it Riiniana's imagination, or does some color drain from her face? It looks like memory. It looks like haunting. Obair, unnerved, leans farther back in his chair, as if he could sink through it and away from her.

Esek slaps a hand on the table, startling everyone. "Chono is a deadly serious actor, and not fanciful. Besides the fancy that gods are real. She wouldn't make these kinds of statements if she didn't believe that she can persuade the rebels to abandon lusting after our heads."

Chono, seeming to flutter back into the room, to blink out of whatever fugue she'd entered, nods. "Yes. I have the ear of the quorum leaders. They supported me in going to Oyun Paiye to make this offer. They gave you back your son on my word, Sa Khen, though he was a very valuable prisoner. If you listen to them, if all sides can come to an agreement, you'll save your own lives and eliminate Kess in the bargain."

Riiniana's spies never told her Soon was a prisoner. What else have they kept from her? She feels unmoored. She has no objection to leveraging the rebel armies toward the end of killing Seti Kess. She's even willing to throw them some little power, if it will keep the peace. But she does not like how Chono has seized control of this meeting—*Riiniana's* meeting!—so quickly. Everyone is listening to her. When Riiniana looks sidelong at Esek, when she sees the fierce, intense way that Esek is looking at Chono, she feels her tether on her captive strain and fray. How can she control Esek now? And what does a freed Esek mean for her?

Revel makes another of his huffy little noises. "And what about you, Cleric Chono? I don't trust anyone who claims to want peace for its own sake."

"Peace has enough merit to satisfy me," Chono returns. "More than that, bringing down Kess will save the imprisoned Jeveni on Ma'kess. It will also save Farren Eyce."

Riiniana's ears ring. The Jeveni. She will need them to rebuild the trade.

Revel mocks her. "So selfless. Where do you see *yourself* fitting into this glorious, better world you imagine? Don't give me platitudes, Sa. I know how the people of the Treble revere you. And I know what Aver Paiye has said about you for years. You beat a Hand to death, a First Family scion, and yet no cloak darkened your door. You were protected. I know what you expect to get out of all this."

"And what is that, Revel?" Oyun interjects.

"First Cleric," Revel says coolly. "And by default of the Treble's love, the most powerful Hand in the Kindom. With your influence, it won't be us operating the Kindom. It'll be *you*."

The ringing in Riiniana's ears gets louder. Clerics flouncing around her with their poisonous smiles. Secretaries nipping and gnawing at her edges, trying to make her in their own image. Cloaks, lurking in her doorways, as Kess does, as Kess always will, if he has his way, if he has her for his wife and trophy.

Oyun says, "And would that really be such an unreasonable concession? Surely you are savvy enough to recognize that these people will want a representative in the highest echelons. Why not a known quantity? And someone sympathetic to keeping all of us alive."

Riiniana blinks rapidly, too rapidly; she can barely see. She forces herself to focus, staring across the table at Chono. Chono's mouth is a thin line, but it's a trick. It must be a trick. There was never a cleric in the history of the Treble who did not pant and whine for power.

"She can't be trusted," Obair snaps, eyes wild with fear again. "She is an avowed enemy of my family. She is full of vendettas."

"And yet *you* are the one who tried to assassinate her," Karix points out, voice flat. If Chono wins Karix over, Karix will win over Revel.

"Honestly," says Oyun, "it's as if none of you grew up going to temple! The vast majority of saan in the Treble are devout. Maybe to varying degrees, but it *is* devotion. What better method to restore order and appease the common saan than to give them Chono?"

Esek laughs. "Ah, Chono. It's everything you ever dreamed."

"I am not interested in being anyone's religious cudgel," says Chono sharply.

"But you are interested in ministering to the Treble," Oyun points out. "And I, for one, can think of nothing better than to have an actually righteous cleric take the reins of the—"

"There is no such thing as a righteous cleric!"

Riiniana hardly believes she has said the words out loud until all their eyes snap toward her. Her throat is tight, her body burning. She tells herself, *stop stop stop*—but she can't.

"Cleric Chono is a distraction!" she cries. Is someone else controlling her voice? "The Hands are bloodsucking hypocrites! They prevent us from seizing what's rightfully ours. They're corrupt, self-interested thieves who feed off the product of *our* industries. I'd rather the Night-foot name disappeared than see us scrape for the Kindom any longer!"

The faces around her shift in disorienting ways: Revel and Obair look confused; Paiye's eyes light up with revelation; Hejar turns away in distraction, speaking to someone on cast; Chono looks surprised, then concerned. Unbearable, intolerable gentleness in her face—disgusting. Riiniana rejects it. She reviles it. She looks at Esek just so that she will not have to look at that softness in Chono's eyes. Esek's expression is worst of all, that beautiful face transformed, the mask of her predecessor stripped away to reveal the animal underneath. Teeth and eyes and all of her gleaming with victory—

"What do you mean?" a voice says. "Where are you—"

It's Hejar speaking into a comm. Suddenly she stands, reaching for a sidearm that isn't there—no weapons in the conference room, they'd all agreed. Obair cries out in alarm, and suddenly gunfire explodes on the other side of the door. Gunfire, and outcry, and something louder, shaking the room, forcing Riiniana to grab the arms of her chair. Oh gods, what is this? She hears the Family members *shouting shouting shouting*. Oyun grabs Hejar to stop her leaving the room. Chono says something about taking cover, and Esek leaps onto the table and jumps off on the other side, standing with Chono nearest to the door. It seems to Riiniana that the cacophony of battle outside goes on for hours. The world shifts. Her plans collapse—

The gunfire stops, leaving behind a hollow silence. The door sweeps open.

CHAPTER SEVENTEEN

1665

YEAR OF THE HARVEST

M-4 Station
Orbiting Ma'kess

Chono thinks at first that one of the Families has turned on the others. Maybe Khen Obair, unwilling to tolerate her presence, has signaled his forces to take them out, to capture or kill her. Maybe Riiniana, clearly the engine behind this Nightfoot plot, lost her nerve and decided to simply assassinate her rivals. Or maybe—

A party of armed saan storm the room, rifles steady, shouting commands. Chono, suddenly with a muzzle in her face, steps back. Six steps back with her, and she can barely process the relief of their near-ness through her alarm at the armed strangers.

"Sit down! All of you fucking sit down! Now!"

A few more scattered shots sound from the outer room. Chono drops into a chair, and Six takes the one next to hers, their body a tensed spring. A moment later everyone is seated, except Hejar, who stands glowering at the saan.

"Whose treason is this?" she snarls.

"Sit down, bitch, or I'll make you," a riflesaan warns her.

Oyun, sounding remarkably calm, tells her daughter, "Sit."

Hejar reluctantly takes a chair that partway shields her mother.

"Which one of you is responsible for this?" Moonback demands of the other Families. "Who?! I'll have your tongues cut out of your—"

"Be quiet, Revel," Oyun hisses.

Khen points wildly at Esek. "You said we had protection here! Security!"

"Shut up, all of you," another riflesaan orders, before calling over his shoulder, "Clear!"

Moments later, a new figure walks into the room. Chono's blood runs cold. It's Cly Siltmire, the Ma'kessn rebel she met on Teros.

"Nice work," Siltmire says, looking insufferably pleased with her hands clasped behind her back and her chin tipped up.

Things only get worse when Sikrt Goodrite follows her, less smirky but just as vindicated. The last time Chono saw these two, they were representing Ma'kess and General Ashway at the meeting of the quo-rum. They were hostile and unimpressed with her, and quick to insist on the loyalty of their armies. She didn't trust them when she shared her plans to parlay with Oyun, but she never expected—

"What is this?" Chono asks softly, though she fears she already knows.

Goodrite looks at her with a guarded expression, whereas Siltmire is all bravado.

"Cleric Chono! How wonderful to see you again. I thought that Paiye would throw you into a cage. I certainly never expected this!

An audience with the whole lot of them. Thank you. You've made this enterprise much easier."

Khen Obair shrieks, "I told you! She led them straight to us!"

"Oh, shut up," Siltmire huffs, as if dealing with rowdy children. "She's not that devious."

Realization dawns on Chono. "You tracked me here."

"Did I? Well. Why don't you ask the little Nightfoot spawn about that?"

A dozen eyes shift toward Riiniana, who looks white with shock and disbelief. What can this girl have had to do with—

"Somebody explain to me what is going on," orders Oyun with high-handed impatience.

"Easy, old girl," says Siltmire. "This can all go very smoothly, if you like. Now, everybody up. We're going on a trip."

"I'm not going anywhere with you," Hejar growls.

Siltmire raises her eyebrows, looking around at the other mutinous faces before saying to the riflesaan nearest her, "Next one of them that argues with me, shoot them in the leg."

"Siltmire!" Chono cries. A dozen guns fix on her. She hears Six's hiss, their body leaning forward, and she raises an arm against their chest to hold them back. Blessedly, nobody fires, which seems to annoy Siltmire. Chono reminds her, "The quorum agreed that I would speak to the Families. That I would seek an alliance."

Siltmire shrugs. "The quorum obviously doesn't know what's good for them. Do you know how relieved they'll be that I've taken the decision off their hands?"

"By forming a separate faction? By taking the Family heads hostage? Did General Ashway agree to—"

"Ashway isn't my *keeper!*" she answers scornfully. "We've done what's best for our own. If any of the rest of you have any sense, you do as we say."

"We don't have time for this," Goodrite says. "Get in line or we start shooting kneecaps."

Chono feels the eyes of the Family members on her, perhaps thinking she can do something, will do something. But what can Chono do? Helplessness fills her. As everyone slowly rises, the rebels are on them, binding their wrists. There are many sounds of disbelief and pain at the rough treatment, though Hejar remains malevolently calm.

When a rebel approaches Chono, Siltmire orders, "Not her. So long as she doesn't cause trouble, there's no need to mishandle a friend."

"Esek is our ally, too," Chono says, stepping between Six and the rebels.

Goodrite scoffs. "She's working with Kess. Stand aside or I'll make you."

Six reassures her, "It's all right," and actually presents their wrists to be lashed together with zip ties. Once it's done, they look over their shoulder at a wide-eyed, trembling Riiniana. "Don't worry, little cousin," they say. "This is all a misunderstanding, I'm sure."

Goodrite nods toward the door. "All of you. Out."

The riflesaan march them into the outer room. It stinks of blood and gunfire. First Family guards lie dead, some with limbs blown off. Chono was right about the crowd-killer grenade she thought she heard. At least two dozen Ma'kessn rebels make a circuit of the room, and she is darkly reminded of the massacre at Nikapraev when cloaks disguised as guardsaan seized the perimeter of the Centrum and swooped down like hawks to decimate their prey.

Goodrite and half the rebels take point, followed by the Family heads, including Six. Riiniana, Hejar, and Karix come next, while Siltmire and Chono walk a few feet behind them, and the rest of the rebels take the rear. The hallway is empty. Chono wonders what happened to the solicitous station governor.

"Is Masar alive?" Chono asks.

Siltmire gives her a wounded look. "Why wouldn't he be?"

"Does he know about this?"

She clucks her tongue. "Once we realized that you had left Kator with the Paiyes, there wasn't time to sit around a table and debate the pros and cons."

"And tracking me? Did you debate the pros and cons of that? Or of working for Riiniana?"

It seems absurd that either Siltmire or Goodrite would ally with a First Family, let alone *spy* for Riiniana.

Siltmire laughs. "That little brat? Please. She's like every other First Family snob who thinks they can buy people. She had some idea about us helping her take the sevite factories from Kess, and some other idea about us watching you and killing you on her say-so. It was easy to feed her tidbits and make her think we had you on a leash."

If Riiniana thought she could use Siltmire as an executioner, and if she used that belief to threaten Six, it would explain why Six has been playing Riiniana's game. But while Riiniana may not have known who she was dealing with, Siltmire and Goodrite are just as delusional about their position.

"How did you track me?"

Siltmire grins. "Just a little homing chip under the skin. Nothing dramatic."

"You never got close enough to me to—"

"We hacked Yantikye and found it in his neural link cache."

Rage isn't a strong enough word for the emotion that boils up in Chono. It was while they were fleeing Nikapraev, she realizes. Six was missing, and she refused to leave without them. She tried to fight her way past Masar, and Yantikye slammed a rifle stock into the back of her head. He must have put the tracker on her then. A spy, under her skin.

"Oh, don't hold it against him, Chono. Like I said, we took it off him. I'm sure he only meant to keep an eye on an asset. Though I'll say, he hasn't peeped about it to the rest of the quorum, even with them desperate to know where you are. I'm guessing he's still not quite sure what to do with you. Honestly, neither am I! A great valuable thing like you!"

Chono considers that she is taller and broader than Siltmire. It would not be especially difficult to break her neck—

The hallway before them turns left. They're headed toward the bay, where the Ma'kessns must have neutralized the Family ships.

"Where are you taking the Families?" Chono asks.

"Never mind. It'll all be fine, I promise you."

"This is a mistake. How in the worlds you don't see that is—"

"And how in the worlds *you* can think that we would want to ally with these fatuous, spoiled tyrants is beyond my comprehension. Do you think I'm fighting the Kindom only to bend over for Khen Obair or Revel Moonback?"

"If you think I love the Families, you're wrong."

"You love *one* of them. I can't trust anyone who's knit their fate with Esek Nightfoot. You should have told us you were still working with her."

Chono grinds her teeth in frustration. "It's more complicated than you realize—"

"Spare me."

The lead riflesaan exit the hallway into the station's atrium. Chono would expect to hear a crowd of stationers, perhaps crying out in alarm or confusion, but instead there is quiet. Did the rebel forces come through here and scare the stationers away?

"And what will you do if the rest of the quorum doesn't agree with your actions?"

"The rest of the quorum have their own planets," she answers coldly. "They can manage their own affairs. This is *my* system."

"M-4 station is neutral ground. It doesn't belong to Ma'kess."

Up ahead, Six walks into the atrium.

"There's no such thing as neutrality," Siltmire says philosophically.

The atrium is a square expanse of metal courtyard with shops on the borders. The high ceilings reveal a mezzanine with round balconies jutting out into the open.

"There's such a thing as restraint, though," Chono warns. Something glints on one of the balconies. "Siltmire, I—"

"Shut up, would you?"

Another glint, and figures emerge from the shadows. Chono has less than a second to process the rifles—

"Down!" she shouts. "Get down!"

No sooner has she shoved Siltmire aside than something sharp as a razor slits across the ball of her shoulder. She stumbles, and the atrium erupts.

There's no time to wonder what the fuck is happening. Chono has half collapsed to one knee, spun off-balance by what she hopes is only a graze. But she won't be that lucky for long. The Ma'kessn rebels begin to fire on what must be Family guardsaan in the balconies. The windows and doorways of the ground level shops spring open, and more guards appear. She can't tell how many there are, can't see from her kneeling position. Gunfire spatters the ground nearby, and she stands—only to be grabbed and hauled backward.

Suddenly pressed against the wall farthest from the fighting, she gasps Six's name.

"Get these fucking things off me," Six growls. "There is a knife in my boot."

Chono doesn't bother to ask how Six got into the conference room with a weapon. She drops to one knee again, ears ringing with the shouts and battle sounds in the atrium. The knife is made from what looks like broken ceramic, sharpened to an edge and fitted into a grip of wood. She stands again, and Six shows her their hands. She's barely started sawing through the ties when Six gets enough give to snap them off. They grunt in satisfaction, look up at her, and a moment of absolute stillness blooms between them—

Out in the atrium, a voice screams, "Khen! Don't!"

Chono whips toward the sound, just in time to see Khen Obair making a wild break from the rebels circling him. He seems to be running toward one of the shops, but he doesn't get far. His body suddenly jerks, tripping sideways and hitting the ground out of sight.

Siltmire screams above the fray, "Hold them, damn you, hold them!"

Someone from the rebel side throws a grenade up toward the balconies, but in a moment of complete absurdity, it bounces off a column, falling among the rebels and the Families.

"Oh gods." Chono steps away from the wall as if she could possibly do something. Six grabs her arm.

"Chono!"

The crowd scatters in a chaos of broken ranks, and among them Chono sees Hejar—Oyun—Goodrite—

The crack of the explosion deafens her. The force of it hurls her body back against the wall. She crumples, vaguely aware that Six has fallen, too, and aware a moment later of a second explosion, farther away. She lies on the ground choking on a sudden flood of debris smoke and extinguisher mist. She blinks dazedly up at the ceiling, trying to read her body. There's the bullet graze burn in her shoulder cap, and something new stinging on her forehead. Past the feeling of rattled bones, she realizes that her chest is pinned down.

"Godsdamnit," someone wheezes nearby. "Godsdamnit."

Chono keeps blinking, afraid the extinguisher mist will coagulate in her eyelashes and blind her. She tries to sit up, but the heavy feeling holds her down. Gunfire that had vanished suddenly comes back in fits and starts. She senses movement to her left. Six is on the ground beside her, furiously trying to lift something off their body. Both their bodies, she realizes—the pressure on her chest. Some sheet of something—metal? Anything heavy enough to trap them both is enough to kill them with crush injuries. Except she can still breathe. And she can—

She looks down her body and sees that one of the rebels lies dead on top of the lower half of the sheet, effectively pinning them.

"Six," she chokes, "Look. Look." Six looks. She catches a glimpse of sheer Esek-like annoyance. "Hold on," Chono says.

She inches her body to the right. A bullet ricochets off the metal sheet. Somewhere in the atrium a high voice is screaming, "Get help! Get help, now! He's dying! Get help!"

Chono keeps going, wiggling out from under her half of the sheet and getting onto her knees. She grabs the dead rebel by their shoulders, trying not to see the gape of the obliterated face, and pulls them clear of the sheet metal. With a curse of gratification, Six throws the sheet off themself. They and Chono stand at the same time, and she suspects she looks as stunned as they do.

"You are bleeding," Six says.

She wipes at her forehead, feeling a sharp pain near her hairline. Her hand comes away bloody. Six stares at her. *Six Six Six . . .*

The gunfire has stopped.

She looks around, expecting to find a bloodbath of rebels, certain that the force of the ambush and the effect of the grenade will have completely decimated Siltmire's forces. But after a few bleary moments, a different picture unfolds. Yes, there are bodies on the ground, several in pieces, but many of them seem to have fallen from the balcony, which has collapsed inward under what must have been that second explosion. Another crowd-killer grenade hitting its target this time. Amazingly, most of the rebel riflesaan appear to have escaped the worst of the explosion radius. As she watches, many emerge from the shops. They must have turned the retreat into an impromptu offensive, going after the guardsaan in their hiding places. When those guards don't follow the rebels out of the shops, the outcome of the fight is clear.

Cleaving through Chono's shock, the frantic shouting starts up again. "Help him! By the gods, help him!"

It's Karix Moonback.

Chono rushes forward. The riflesaan are getting their bearings back, and she glimpses Goodrite on one side of the atrium, and Siltmire to her right. She is viciously disappointed that they weren't killed, but she ignores them both to skid onto her knees beside Karix, who is holding Revel in her arms. The old man's eyes are wide with shock, blinking sluggishly. A wound gapes in his stomach, and he can't seem to move.

Karix looks at Chono wildly. "Do something!"

After a moment of numb shock, inspiration strikes. Chono scrambles for her pocket, amazed to find that the little packet of ash-smelling herbs she took from the folk pharmacy in Trin-Ma is still there. She never imagined using it to save a First Family head, but she doesn't hesitate. She pours the contents into Revel's wound, not knowing the proper amount but relieved when it starts to gum up like glue. It won't be enough, though.

"Siltmire!" she shouts. "Where's your medic?"

Siltmire staggers over to them, her expression stunned. She shouts a name, voice laced with panic to rival Karix. From amid the disorganized chaos, a young saan appears, kneeling beside Revel.

"Put him down, Sa, and let me look at him."

Siltmire bends over the scene, hissing, "Save him. Do you hear me? Save him!"

The medic starts wiping at the blood on Revel's torso, clearly to see what he's working with: a smattering of shrapnel wounds, deep wells of blood gone sticky and thick from the coagulant. He puts some fingers inside one of them, probably feeling for the artery. Revel cries out and faints. After a moment the medic withdraws his fingers and shoves gauze in their place. He slaps a thick square regenerative bandage down over the holes. Only a stopgap. Will the rebels have a surgeon on their ship? She is almost certain they won't be willing to stay and use the station hospital. Can Revel possibly survive otherwise? Chono meets eyes with Karix, whose face is caked with extinguisher mist and dust, but not tears. She's obviously too furious to cry, but her expression is also desperate, baffled, pleading—

"Drop it!"

The shout from nearby startles Chono out of the staring contest.

"Drop it now!"

There are at least five voices shouting threats and orders. Chono rises unsteadily. Six is with her again, and together they look through a scrum of bodies to find Hejar Paiye—who has a gun.

"Stay back," Hejar snarls. "Don't *touch* her!"

Goodrite and Siltmire join the group of saan surrounding her. Siltmire holds out her hands in a placating gesture. "Hold it, hold it! Don't make things worse. Take it easy."

"Don't you fucking tell me 'easy'!" Hejar's teeth are red, a shrapnel graze oozing from the side of her mouth. Her voice is slurred with blood. "Don't you fucking come near her!"

"Put the gun down," Goodrite says. "There's no way out."

"These fucking amateurs," Six growls under their breath.

Chono rushes forward, stepping around the empty-eyed body of Khen Obair, his throat a bloody maw. She doesn't have time to think or feel anything about it, shouldering through the rebels until they are all so surprised that no one stops her from putting herself between them and Hejar. She holds up a hand to either side of the showdown.

"Stop! Stop this!"

"I'm going to kill them," Hejar pants, dribbling blood. "I'm going to tear their hearts out—"

"Stand down," Chono speaks over her. She ignores Goodrite and Siltmire, their faces blanched. She makes contact with the common rebels instead, looking into their faces, into their eyes. Through the dust in her throat she rumbles, "Lower your guns." They look uncertainly at her and one another. "I am a cleric of the Righteous Hand!" she thunders. "I am a steward of the Godfire. As you fear to burn alive, I order you, lower your guns, *now*!"

Siltmire and Goodrite, remarkably, don't say anything. Perhaps they are too shocked by what has happened. Goodrite looks almost befuddled, his brow knit, whereas Siltmire's eyes are wide-rimmed and disbelieving. Slowly, cautiously, the rebels lower their rifles.

In a breath, she feels it behind her. Hejar, tensing, shifting forward, arm straightening out. Chono spins toward her. Six is there. They bring her down as one, wrestling the gun from her grasp as she fights and spits and screams. Only now, in this new position, does Chono see the body that Hejar was shielding. Oyun Paiye looks far more dignified than either Khen or Moonback. Her eyes gaze upward, her lips pressed together in disapproval. Chono can't see where exactly she's been hit, but thick blood pools around her. The image of Aver flashes in Chono's mind. The broken body. The staring eyes.

Hejar keeps fighting, keeps screaming in a fit of grief and rage. Six and Chono hold her down. Chono bends close to her, speaks near her ear. "Breathe, Hejar. Breathe."

Hejar makes an animal noise that turns into one sharp sob.

"Breathe," Chono whispers. "Listen. *Listen to me.* 'I bring her to Kata, bathed in the glories of her life. Sigh, you that grieve, and abide. Kata is not cruel and they are not tender, remember this. They are honest like the wind and the wave and the rock.'" Beneath her, Hejar's struggle begins to lose some of its energy, as if her strength is going out of her. She still makes those animal sounds. Chono prays, "'So I bring Oyun to Kata, to be seen. Perceive, my god is keen and wise. They will welcome her into their Many. They will make her a spy in your life, to watch and compel and comfort you.'" Hejar is only whimpering now, her lips moving, though no sound comes out. "'So peace, Hejar, peace. Kata's Many protect you. Peace, Daughter, peace. Kata's Many protect you.'" Then Chono hears it, the broken whisper as Hejar joins the final refrain, "'Peace, Warrior, peace. Kata's Many protect you.'"

Finally, there is no need for Six or Chono to hold Hejar down. Six melts away, and when Chono stands and tries to help Hejar up, Hejar only turns on her knees to kneel over her mother. She presses her forehead against the old woman's chest, her shoulders shaking. Chono watches. She knows that the comfort of the death rite won't last. She looks at Siltmire and Goodrite again and hopes they can see that Hejar isn't the only threat here.

The medic appears.

"Sa, I have Moonback stabilized, but only barely. We must find a surgeon."

Goodrite says shakily, "Those guardsaan will have sent for reinforcements. We have to go."

Siltmire, still looking shocked by the collapse of her plans, blinks rapidly. She tells the medic, "Reveñon is closest. We have surgeons there. Will he last that long?"

The medic grimaces. "I don't know. The longer we wait, the less likely."

"Fine. Gather up the bodies and the prisoners." She looks over at Hejar. "Let her carry her mother. Chono, will she let you help?"

Chono, relieved that Siltmire would show this much tact, nods.

"Good. Let's get moving. If anyone sees that governor, I want his throat cut for a traitor."

The surrounding riflesaan move immediately into action, but they have hardly broken ranks before Six speaks, voice mellow and light with mockery.

"One problem," they say, and wait until all eyes are on them before offering a small, twisted smile. "You seem to have misplaced Riiniana Nightfoot."

CHAPTER EIGHTEEN

1588

YEAR OF THE MAZE

Farren Ki
The Moon Jeve

Swaying. Always swaying. Feet planted apart but hips and upper body moving slowly back and forth, like an interminable tide. Drae saw an ocean up close only once, when her dealings with pirates took her to Braemin. It had frightened her more than the Black Ocean ever could. The Black Ocean had an endless, reliable sterility, a nothingness, even though it contained so much. But the ocean on Braemin churned with life. It was unbearable. It moved to the beat of some internal heart both wiser and more indifferent than

Drae could imagine, and she feared it, just as she feared all inevitable things.

And now, standing under the dome of Farren Ki, rocking with the newest baby in her arms, she felt as if the ocean was inside her, pulling her into depths from which she could never emerge. She had to be careful not to hold the baby too close, too tight, or she would hurt them in her helpless desire to protect them from the encroaching waves.

This fourth baby had been an accident. A consequence of bad timing, carelessness, and the very specific lust that Lucos awoke in her—the lust of the conqueror, of the dominant. Her first child and the twins were planned. Not by Lucos, of course, but by Drae, who knew her obligations to the survival of her people and thus did everything she could to make sure some of them survived. She had not known, when she birthed the twins, that she would give them away to *The Glitch* and to Capamame. It was only the months en route to *The Glitch*, and growing unrest back home, that persuaded her at last. And though it broke her heart, she saw a symmetry in the fates of her three children. One for the unstable Treble. One for the dangerous frontier. And one for the unknown, for Capamame.

Now *The Hope* had departed *The Glitch*, carrying in its hold the materials that would build a new colony, a new gate, including the vibrant, dangerous Lot 11. *The Hope* was six months out from the frontier station. There was no turning back. There was no chance Drae would ever see that first twin again. And unless she made her way to *The Glitch*, she would never see the second twin again, either. Until very recently, she had comforted herself that she would have Kati, but now it was becoming clear that he must go away, too.

And on top of everything, there was this new, fourth child to consider.

She squabbled sometimes with the semantics. An accident? A mistake? A blessing? None was entirely accurate or inaccurate. It *had* been an accident. And it *was* a blessing, to stand alone under the stars and feel this snuffling, trustful weight in her arms, to rock like the ocean and smell the baby's smell, that was not like the city and not like the mines.

But it was also a mistake. Whatever soul had gone into her baby, it would have been better given to some other child, some other parent. A Ma'kessn seamsaan, or a Katish engineer, or a fishersaan on Quietus. Even a pirate might have been better. *Yes*, Drae thought. *I wish that my baby had been born to a pirate. Then they could grow up and be a pirate themself, and have great, reckless adventures. They could braid their power into their hair, and gather riches, and be nobody's victim.*

Instead...Instead...

She rocked the baby and let the week's revelations rock over her. Gus could be wrong, of course. His preliminary findings were just that: preliminary. It would take weeks to confirm what his initial scans implied, and perhaps this would all be some illusion of the deep rock, some joke that she could laugh at later. But Drae knew he wasn't wrong. Already miners were whispering, calling it the God Seam.

It had been almost ten years since they found a new seam, and the last one had been merely an offshoot of the Blood Seam. Drae had comforted herself, after Lucos arrived and the return of the Nightfoots became inevitable, that the mining operation would last ten years, fifteen at most. Her people could survive fifteen years. But this God Seam cleaved through her hopes. It was much longer and broader than the Blood Seam. Most importantly, it was deep. It might go as deep as the moon's mantle, for all she knew. This was a seam that couldn't be exhausted in fifteen years. This seam would revitalize the jevite trade for a century. But it would be different this time. The other Families were stronger than ever. The seam would wake their unfathomable hunger. There would be war. If the Kindom intervened, it would be to occupy the moon as a protectorate, an excuse to tap the seam itself. Even if the Jeveni could flee—to where? What could they have out there in the Treble but the contempt and abuse of those who did not even think they were fully human? What had Captain Wolf said? *Those bastards carry more disease than rats.*

Yes, Drae thought. *We carry disease. We are infected with the disease of the seams, with the curse of this moon. And just as we are prepared to flee it entirely, it finds a way to trap us.*

For how could the Jeveni flee to Capamame in sixty years if they were surrounded by the Kindom and the Families? If they were enslaved to the trade again? Or if they had been eradicated altogether?

"Sajeven," whispered Drae, trying to taste the name, to feel it. "Sajeven, beloved, come here to us and create a path for our hope." The prayer tasted like brine in the back of her throat. She held the baby closer, but her voice was shaking now. "Dissolve our weariness and shine a light to live by, we entreat you, Sajeven, beloved—"

She couldn't continue. She had done little honest praying in her life. How many times had she tried in desperation to love her goddess? But now she felt no love. She felt bitterness, and hate, and shut her eyes. She tried to believe, not in the goddess, but in chance. In luck. She wanted in that moment to be the penitent of Terotonteris, wily and clever. Under his playful gaze, perhaps her twins would be safe and happy. Perhaps they would thrive. Perhaps Kati would, too, and this new infant in her arms. Despite everything. Perhaps...

She sensed someone behind her, and though she knew she was safe among her own people, she felt a spark of panic. She whirled around, exhaling to find Lucos there. He showed no concept of having startled her.

"I just got back. I went to your office, but you weren't there. So I picked up Kati from the crèche and we spent about an hour in the Game Commons. His Katish is coming along so well! He says he wants to learn Teron next."

Drae said nothing. Kati was not even his name, and yet it was the name he told everyone to call him. Seven years old, gendered, he had that right, she supposed. And he had the same gift for languages that she did. But whereas Lucos was there to teach him Katish, Drae did not have access to any Teron tutors. She supposed she could teach him herself, so long as his other studies didn't suffer. He was a boy of whims, constantly jumping from one interest to another, forgetful and distractable and *so smart*, smart in a way that Drae could never be. Her mind was all straight lines, one task to the next, each duty in its proper place. And she did not smile the way he did.

Lucos bent over the sleeping baby. He smiled and touched their little hand that was poking out. Kati had that smile, wide and delighted. Lucos had seen the baby just a week ago, before his most recent trip to his legitimate family in Kator, but he acted as if they had spent months apart. Drae thought of her twins and swallowed a sob.

"Do you have any ideas about names?" Lucos asked. "I swear I'll never understand the way you Jeveni wait for weeks to name your children. I was thinking, maybe—"

"I have not decided on a name." She hoped he would read her meaning: that his ideas didn't matter, and *she* would name her children.

He sighed, then asked hopefully, "Can I hold them?"

The thought of relinquishing the baby into his arms felt like a fist around her heart. It would have been easier if he was indifferent to the children, but he had loved them from birth. If he knew about the twins, about how she had hidden them from him, he would never forgive her.

She carefully transferred the baby into his arms, and he stood gazing down at them joyfully. But he wasn't rocking, so the baby woke up. Drae thought they would begin to cry, but after some noises of distress, those impossibly large eyes blinked hazily and fixed on his face.

"There you are," he whispered. "There you are, my sweet."

He said it in Katish, and the 'sweet' he used referred to a Katish dessert, a delicacy to be relished. Drae's heart hammered. She wanted to take the baby back, to rescue them from the devouring world. After a little bit Lucos looked up at her, beaming. If he was just a little bit different, she might have been able to love him. But his differences were too significant. He was naive and ambitious—a terrible combination. He was sulky and presumptuous about what he thought was his by right. He was, underneath his charm and his years of guardsaan work, fundamentally cowardly.

How long before he, too, knew about the God Seam? And what would he do when he knew? He wasn't brave enough to hide it from the Nightfoots, not even for her sake. This was why she had never told him about *The Hope*. His love for her was the shallow, romanticized love of a boy. But his desire to protect himself had the strength of ages.

"When is the last time you spoke to Sorek Nightfoot?" she asked.

His happiness melted into a scowl. "Can't we enjoy our family for two minutes—"

"No. We cannot."

"You worry too much. Everything is fine. They'll pay a good lease for what's left of the mines and get in and get out. They've got no reason to shake things up now."

She had never hurt a soul with her own hands, but if he wasn't holding her baby, she would claw his eyes out for his gullibility. Her voice was glacial. "You are an utter fool."

He blinked, head darting back as if she'd slapped him. "Drae. Come on. The money on offer here is astounding!"

"Fuck your money," she hissed. He flinched again. The baby wriggled restlessly. "Fuck Ma'kessn ingots and Katish plae and all the streams of income flowing with our blood. After everything you have learned, everything you have seen, you still harbor a dream of riches—"

"For our *family*, Drae!" he beseeched her. She glowered at him. She was sure he saw the hate in it, for his entreaty vanished. All at once he sneered. "Oh, I see. You want to pretend that living and dying on this rock is all you've ever wanted for yourself."

This time Drae felt the slap. "What?"

He laughed without humor. "I *see you*, Drae. You're never more relieved than when you get to leave this moon on one of your mysterious trips. You're never eager to come back, not even with your own son growing up here!"

"Give me the baby," she said, for they had started squirming more, and made a little unhappy sound when Lucos raised his voice.

"No! Admit it! If you had your freedom, you'd run away from all of this and spend the rest of your life owing nothing to anyone. Admit it!"

The baby wailed. Lucos was startled. It made it easier to take them from him, to step back from him and rock her child, murmuring comfort and glaring daggers. Her breathing was unsteady. He had cut through her like a blade, and even though she knew he was wrong about her—oh gods—he was right, too. But whereas he imagined them escaping Jeve together, setting up on some beautiful estate with all the wealth they could carry, Drae imagined something very different. Maybe Riin Kala, or Barcetima. Some big, bustling city into which she and her children could disappear. Or maybe a fishing village on Quietus, a place to rest and work and learn how to love the ocean.

"I'm sorry," Lucos whispered. She didn't look at him. "Drae, I'm sorry. I know how selfless you are."

Selfless? she thought. *I am the most selfish person who ever lived. It does not matter what anyone says to me, it does not matter whose heart I break. I will have my way.*

In time the baby was quiet, suckling on Drae's pinkie finger. Gazing into the beloved face, she said, "The children have to leave Jeve. It's not safe for them here."

She heard his soft indrawn breath. He had wanted this ever since Kati was born.

"Agreed. Someplace out of the way, just until things settle down."

She said nothing. She detested the eagerness in his voice.

"I'll speak to Ledra. She'll take care of them."

His wife's name almost made her lip curl, not because of jealousy, but because she knew what the daughter of a Katish governor would think of her husband's Jeveni bastards. At best, they would be accepted as charity cases and curiosities. At worst, they would be abused and demeaned until even Kati's light went out.

"We are not sending them to Ledra," Drae said.

Lucos sighed, and said in an infuriatingly gentle way, "Drae, she knows about them both. She's *always* known about you. I never hid it from her. And she doesn't hide her lovers, either. There's no ill will, no competition."

"Competition?" Drae repeated, looking at him again, showing him the full force of her contempt. "Competition? It has nothing to do with that. They cannot go to Ledra because if the Nightfoots discover that you have been collaborating with the Jeveni, the first thing Alisiana will do is go after your family. Is it possible you are so naive that you do not understand that?"

She kept her voice level and swayed back and forth as the baby fell asleep. Lucos's initial expression of anger slipped as he realized that she was right. He turned away from her, rubbing the back of his neck in a gesture so youthful that she was reminded of him when they met almost ten years ago. He faced her again, and he was older. Weary and resigned.

"Where will you send them?" he whispered.

Drae thought spitefully that she had no obligation to tell him. "Our children pass for Katishsaan. I have allies on Kator. They are comfortable but low-profile. Farmers and drovers. It will not be a *luxurious* life, but it will be safe."

He thought about it, then nodded. "All right. What do you think? A year or two?"

She just looked at him. She looked at him so long that his expression shifted from waiting to confused to annoyed and then—the color drained from his face, till he was gray. He stood several feet away and the gulf was uncrossable.

"No," he said. Drae didn't answer. Her eyes were dry. He shook his head. "No. No. Absolutely not. They're our *children*, Drae. I'm not giving them up forever just because you—"

"It is the only way to protect them. If you love them, you will protect them."

"I won't let you do it!"

The words were half bark, half growl. It had been some years since he stopped putting on his affected growly voice around her, and now he was trying to use it like a weapon. She felt the lightning flash in her own eyes. "You have no legal right to them."

"They're my children!"

Her control snapped, all the fury, all the loss and sacrifice strangling her voice as she told him, "They are *my* children!"

Rage flushed the color back into him. He stepped toward her, and for the first time ever she was afraid of him. But before he could get more than two steps closer, the sound of a rifle racking split the air almost as loudly as a bullet.

"Stay as you are, Alanye," a low voice said. Dimon stepped out of the shadows. Drae had had no idea that he was there. "You would probably do well to go and walk it off."

Lucos was stunned. Dimon had always done a good job of being welcoming to him, waving off their first hostile meeting with false acts of friendship. There was no friendship in his eyes now. If Drae told him to, he would shoot Lucos dead.

"Dimon," she said, stern.

He glanced at her, lowered the gun, though not all the way. Emboldened, Lucos said, "We have to talk about this, Drae. Please, let's talk about this. I know you. Do you want us to never see them again? How could you do something that cruel? There must be another way."

Cruel. How could she do something so cruel? How could she leave her children with Haishik? Send one to Capamame? Abandon another on *The Glitch*?

"It is done," she said.

"Let me take them!" he exclaimed, desperate and irrational. "I'll take them far away, I'll take them so far, no one will find them! Fuck, I'll take them to a frontier station!" She almost laughed, but it would feel like drowning. He must have seen the resolution on her face because he cried, "I won't let you do this!"

"Lucos," Dimon said, his voice a warning rumble. "Walk it off."

Wild-eyed, Lucos looked back and forth between them. Then he stormed away, off into the darkness of the city. After a few seconds of watching to make sure he wouldn't turn back, Dimon said, "We will watch him more carefully now. He will have to accept what you are doing."

"Even the Wheel would not accept it, if I told them," Drae said with a bitter laugh. "Giving a Jeveni child away is a crime against the goddess."

"You are not defying the goddess. You are handing your children over to her protection. These are holy choices."

Drae said nothing. She watched Lucos's figure disappear, knowing she would have to speak to him again. Leaving him like this meant leaving him volatile, a threat to her plans.

Dimon said, "I will make holy choices, too, my River. You can rely on me."

Drae gave him a long look. Her parents were dead. His parents were dead. Their siblings were dead, and Dimon had lost his ability to have children after an illness in his childhood. Sen Briit was an old name among the Jeveni, but now it was just Drae and her children and Dimon. This blood belonging meant less to Drae than to Dimon. Dimon viewed it as an oath between them. It would grieve him to think that all her children must adopt new names.

"Thank you, Dimon," she said quietly. "I hope you know how dear you are to me."

Though he rarely smiled, she could see that the words pleased him. He admired her. He trusted her. She wished she had such faith in herself.

She looked up into the Black, imagining *The Hope* in courageous flight. "Tomorrow I will speak to the Wheel. I want the Farren Ki population relocated within four months."

She could feel the way the air changed around them. His words were hesitant, as if he wished not to offend her. "My River... it no longer matters if we go to the other domes. The Nightfoots will bring us all back to mine the God Seam."

"Our people do not know about the God Seam, yet. They do not need to know. In the meantime, we must proceed with the evacuation."

Several seconds passed. To her surprise, Dimon said, "Is this about Lot 12?"

She looked at him sharply. Dimon had never been one to probe her for information. He never asked questions like this. But he was one of only a few people who knew that Lot 12 existed, and he was smart. Drae remembered buying the lots from Captain Wolf. She had been younger then. She had been cocky, so proud of herself for the scheme that prickled in her imagination. It did not feel clever anymore.

Though she didn't answer Dimon, he seemed to understand and, more than that, to accept it. "It will cause anxiety, moving up the timeline. Saan will wonder what it means."

"Yes," she agreed. "But I will speak to our people. I will comfort them."

There should have been hesitation in him now. Doubt of her. He should have asked more questions. Instead, he nodded, a short soldierly nod of acquiescence to her leadership. He believed in the power of her speeches.

Later, the children slept.

It took a while to get Kati to settle down. Ordinarily he would be in the dormitory with his age-mates, but Lucos had gotten into a fistfight with a sentry who stopped him from taking Kati. Even though Dimon and the others could have protected Kati as easily in the dormitory as elsewhere, Drae wanted her children to stay with her tonight. Instead of bringing them to her own dormitory, she was in her office, one of those rare private spaces in the city. The baby slept in a crib. Kati was splayed out on a cot with his favorite doll, the one Lucos had given him three years ago, a simple baby doll with thick cotton hair. Kati loved it.

Sitting at her desk, Drae read and wrote by the dim light of a lamp, but it was hard to concentrate. Her mind swam with the things she had heard tonight. Kati asking why he couldn't stay with his friends, and Lucos telling her how cruel she was. She put down the stylus she'd been using on her cast tablet and rubbed her eyes. A year ago, just after her return from *The Glitch* and the abandonment of her twins, Lucos had come to this office and found her writing. She had been avoiding him more than usual. He was at his best that night. Funny and sweet in a way that somehow breached her defenses. He stood behind her at her desk and rubbed her shoulders as she tried to focus on the account she was giving of the day's events. He couldn't read Je, but it still made her nervous to feel him looking at the journal.

He said, "These will all be famous, someday. The great Drae sen Briit. They'll study you in the crèche."

She grunted wordlessly, irritated that he was right. People had begun printing and circulating little pamphlets that transcribed her speeches. A month ago she had been walking through a trade district and seen a maxim painted on a wall:

OUR HOME SHALL BE OUR SANCTUARY. AND OUR WEAPON.

That speech had gone particularly well, rousing the Jeveni with the thought that *The Hope* was not just a means of escape but a symbolic weapon against tyranny. They had not known that Drae was speaking of a different home, and a different weapon, and it was not symbolism.

Lucos massaging her shoulders brought her out of the memory. She was startled by how good it felt, and mortified to feel tears in her eyes, as if physical touch had opened a well in her. All the months of agony and grief since returning from *The Glitch* overwhelmed her. To keep from crying, she turned in his arms and drew him closer. He was surprised but happy, his mouth sweet with the taste of a mint reed. She kissed him and bit him and raked her nails down his back, insensate with lust. She took him into her body with the desperation of someone reaching for an oxygen mask. It was hard and desperate, and she sobbed with need so she wouldn't sob with sorrow, and he told her he loved her, which made her hate him.

The memory was a complicated one. She conceived her fourth child that night. But in conceiving them, she gave Lucos another thing to want. To think of as his own. And in taking the baby from him, in taking Kati from him, she made him dangerous. If he turned on them now, every fragile thing would crack apart. She would have to give him something. Some peace offering. *I'll tell him I changed my mind*, she decided. *I'll let him think he can have them back afterward. Once he's exhausted his usefulness, I'll hide them somewhere else.*

She looked down at her journal again. Someday it would enter the official archive, and future saan might read and study it just as Lucos had said. They would come across the errors, the little hiccups in language, and think, *Drae sen Briit was human like the rest of us. She misspelled words. She left typos.* It wouldn't occur to them that the mistakes indicated something unseen. Not unless someone made it occur to them.

That thought turned her stomach. It was the nausea of premonition, the knowledge that she was putting something off that could not be put off any longer. She recalled what the Kai Sheep had said to her, when its agents brought Lots 11 and 12 to the rendezvous point all those years ago. It had encouraged her to name "a second."

"As in duels!" it cried, the grin uncanny on its sheep face.

As she had said to the Ar'tec Collective before, she said now, "That is my affair."

"We are excellent seconds! Could second you beautifully."

"No. You could not."

It made an offended sound that was also mocking. "But we can be trusted! All it takes is a contract! The contract, you know. It is the law for us! It is our Godtext. We are holy, we are law-abiding. Look to our works, nah?" It sniffed at her silence. "And if you die? Who shall you trust to hold the key? You, who trust nothing, no one?"

Drae bristled just at the memory, at the implication that she had not thought this through. Lot 11 was already in the power of *The Hope*'s engineers, but only Drae could control Lot 12. She knew that she must give that control to someone else, a "second," as the Collective said. But the question of trust—it was like a different language to her, something she could never speak fluently. So in the seven years since buying Lot 12, she had kept her own counsel on the matter, and let her journal alone hold those secrets in trust. She had hoped that there would never be any need for Lot 12. She had fooled herself.

You who trust nothing, no one…

But that, in the end, was not entirely true.

She throttled her uncertainty, and sent out a new cast.

When Haishik appeared on the view screen, bleary-eyed and half in the dark, Drae realized it was nighttime, by *Glitch* standards. She had woken Haishik up, but they seemed more confused than irritated. Drae gave them a few moments to collect themself, but there was no putting this conversation off. Like someone throwing themself over a cliff, she surrendered to the wild hope that there was a soft landing beneath. She explained it to Haishik, probably talking faster than she should, though in only as much detail as was necessary. She described the contents of her journal, explained the cypher, as well as the conditions in which it would matter. She kept expecting Haishik to ask why she was not having this conversation with the Wheel, her equal in government, her supposed partners in the protection of the Jeveni. But Haishik never asked this question. After Drae had said everything, the shipbuilder was quiet for some time.

"So," they said at last, "just your journal, then."

Drae exhaled shakily. "And the means to crack the cypher."

"All right... But if the journal ever comes to me, it will mean that you are—"

"It is just a contingency."

Haishik knew what that meant. Their face was grim. Drae thought she would have to convince them, plead even.

"All right," Haishik said. "Will I be the only one with the journal?"

"No," Drae admitted. "The original will remain in the possession of my people. But my people will not have the cypher."

"And what if they decode it anyway? Or what if someone else in the Treble does?"

Drae set her jaw. This was a possibility, of course.

"People in the Treble do not... care about unrecognizable languages."

Understanding showed in Haishik's eyes. They nodded, more in contemplation than agreement. Drae thought for a moment that she was going to vomit. After so many years, so much anxiety and resistance, the whole conversation had taken very little time, the resolution of this matter happening with no fight, no struggle. Drae thought of Kati, who would sometimes put off a chore for hours and hours only to finish it in five minutes. The feeling of nausea passed, replaced by cool air in her lungs, as if she could breathe again.

Haishik, as if they had not been talking about anything else, said, "He's asleep, but...do you want to see him?"

Him. The second of the twins. Too young to have gendered himself, yet Haishik had always called him a boy, and it stuck, for Drae. Her heart leapt, and dropped. Her child, close at hand. Safe, in Haishik's home, and she could see him if she wanted, could feast on his small face and curious, shy eyes.

She glanced over at Kati and the baby. Kati had rolled onto his stomach and was sucking on the knuckle of his thumb, an odd but endearing habit. She dragged her eyes away. She must lose him soon, probably forever. She looked at Haishik, and broke her own heart to whisper, "Not this time."

CHAPTER NINETEEN

1665

YEAR OF THE HARVEST

Farren Eyce
The Planet Capamame

Thousands of Jeveni gather to the open promenade of the Market District, and tens of thousands more watch and listen from levels above and below, as Effegen describes, in calm, precise language, exactly what their options are. Jun is in her office watching the events in private. Effegen and the rest of the Wheel stand on a dais where, just a few weeks ago, they presided over the funeral of a woman named Kereth ben Dane. Kereth, the wife of a collector, had been killed by a pipe bomb in her own home. Just one of the tragedies instigated by

Ujan, just one of her brutalities: tech-frying software and murdering collectors and risking brain damage with a second neural link. Was Esek Nightfoot even that dangerous?

Where is Bene? Jun wonders, anxious about him being out in public right now. There was a time when everyone who knew Bene loved him. But now he's the object of suspicion and bitterness. After this speech, it won't be any better.

Gods, but Effegen is a talented speaker. As good as Chono. She somehow projects the gravitas of her high office while remaining approachably human, as if each of her listeners is a friend with whom she is having a private conversation. Even without being among the crowds, Jun can sense Effegen's command of them. Every saan in the colony waits, listens. Silent as the Black. Still as a stone.

There's no point pretending things are better than they are. With Yantikye's help, a contingent of General Ashway's soldiers have traveled to Jeve under cover of Jun's Hood (fuck but she's tired of everyone and their godsdamn mother having access to that program). Even hoping for a result, Jun was still shocked when, just seven hours ago, the rebels confirmed evidence of a structure several hundred feet under the surface of Jeve. It sits beneath Dewbreak—no, Farren Ki—and has for its protection not just the rock and the ruins, but an invisible holo shield.

Jun would like to think that confirming it's there has changed the game in their favor. But of-fucking-course it's more complicated than that. The Jeveni are stung by this defilement of their moon, the Wheel have no way to use the information, and the rebel quorum refuses to take further action until they learn if Chono has secured the help of the First Families. No one has heard from Chono in three days, and the Families themselves have gone quiet, barely any chatter on the casting net. With Kess still heavily guarding the gates, it's uncertain how successful an offensive on Jeve would be right now. If Jun had found the Silver Keep's blueprints sooner, they might have been able to act before Chono went on this fool's errand. But Jun wanted to do it herself, she wanted to do all of it herself, and now they're paying the price. Farren Eyce may yet receive help, but if that help doesn't come before Kess's deadline, it could be too late to do any good. Jun and her casters are working around the clock, but there is no hope of completing the new gate key in the three days between now and the Feast of Sajeven's Dear Friend.

Effegen explains these things to the colony. She explains without false promises. The silence in the market gives way to a growing murmuration of fear and despair. Effegen's voice, already cast-projected, gets louder, fiercer.

"Most of you had no choice about coming to Farren Eyce. Many of you have resented your place here, and I understand why. You asked us not to destroy the Capamame gate, and so we have not. But nor will we capitulate to the Kindom's threats." The rumble grows. Some anonymous person hollers, a cry of excitement that moves through the crowd like a pebble skipping over water. But that exaltation won't speak for everybody, and as if to say she knows so, Effegen continues. "I will do everything I can to protect you. And that means giving you choices. Liis Konye has a plan for our defense. If you wish to fight under her leadership, then Sajeven bless you for such a sacrifice." Effegen pauses. The crowd is dead silent again. "However... many of you will not want to fight. Many of you can't fight. We won't force anyone. So now we must also consider your protection. Liis Konye believes that a ground assault from the Cloaksaan could reach as deep as Level 7 within one or two hours."

Fresh sounds of alarm fill Jun's ears. How many of these saan have seen their homes destroyed before? Have had to run for their lives? What memories must be coursing through them, even as they imagine cloaksaan flooding their neighborhoods? Decimating the hospital on Eight? Burning down the farms on Nine and Ten?

Effegen holds up her arms, speaking over the voices loudly but with patience. "Sa Konye has no intention of letting them take us so easily. Her defense has the potential to hold them off for much longer, and even to stop them in their tracks. But as a safeguard, we want to move residents above Level 5 deeper into the colony. The farther you are from the surface, the more protected. To that end, we're retrofitting our warehouses into bunkers. Leaders of the black market will find shelter for many of you on Level 2, as will the community leaders on Level 3."

Jun tilts her head a little, smiling for what feels like the first time in days. Effegen could have just said "community leaders." By evoking the black market, she unites the various populations of Farren Eyce. No one is an outsider, and everyone shares the mission to survive.

"So, we have a route for those who want to fight, and a route for those who want to take shelter. But there is a third route. A significant number of you want to return to the Treble under the conditions laid out by Yorus Inye. Now that you've heard what I have to say, some of you may have changed your mind. You might want to stay here—or you might want to go. There is *no shame*, in either decision! If you wish to accept Kess's offer, we will relocate you to the trade hauler *The Brute Crane*. It's not a residential ship, but it has enough space to temporarily contain as many as twenty thousand people. We can commission another ship, if necessary."

There had been some talk of using *Drae's Hope* for this, but it is in fact too small for those numbers, and Fonu sen Fhaan urged their kin spokes not to permit this insult to the Draeviin. So *The Brute Crane* it is.

"If Kess and his forces jump to Capamame," Effegen says, "you can surrender to him, and you'll be well out of range of any fighting. Please believe me—he will *not* attack you. He needs factory workers; he'll want you protected. If you choose this route, you go with my blessing and wishes for a happy life."

Effegen's voice cracks on the last words. Always a pillar of control, now she lowers her head, as if collecting her thoughts. Jun watches her, the straight shoulders and emerald robes, the deep dark hair pulled up into a modest, dignified crown. She raises her head again, and her rivermoss eyes are bright, but it is more ferocity than tears.

"I wish I could say that these are unprecedented times. But this decision has been forced on us, over and over again. Where to go. How to survive. When to fight and when to wait. You are the only one who can make that decision for yourself. If I had the liberty, I'd give you a week, a month, to pray and search yourself. But we don't have that much time. Whichever direction you choose, you must choose now. Depending on your decision, you'll receive immediate instructions, including a schedule. We need to begin relocating colonists to *The Brute Crane* no later than midnight."

Jun silences the cast. There will be more—logistics, instructions. She already knows it all. She sat with the Wheel and some others last night, as they prepared this statement and finalized their options. Jun knows the details of Liis's planned defense, and every crook and cranny into which she can fit an able fighter. Jun knows how they'll make use of the different levels. And she knows about the shuttle schedule, by which they'll use every ship they have to relocate the volunteers off world as quickly as possible.

Three days till Kess's deadline. It may not be enough, but it's all they have.

Jun recalls the predawn moment when Fonu lifted their hand. No one had slept yet. The Treble quorum had already told them that it was holding off on action. Jun and the other council members talked for hours, making plans. Jun was so tired she could barely keep her eyes open, and the thought that Fonu had more to say made her want to scream.

"Yes, Fonu?" Effegen asked.

The slender saan put their hand down. Their eyes were shadowed and their injuries still healing, prosthetic ear shiny on their head, rebuilt foot shifting against the ground as if with phantom pains. But they spoke in a surprisingly clear voice, "There is one thing we have not acknowledged yet. And that is that each of us must also make a choice."

The room grew quiet, saan looking at one another in confusion. It was obvious what their decisions were.

Hyre said with a light, nervous laugh, "Well, I may not be fighting stuff, but I hope you'll find a use for me, Liis."

Liis smiled kindly at the Gale, inclining her head. "I can use everyone. But you are a member of the Wheel, Sa. We must protect you. You'll do more for the colony by going into the bunkers. All of you." She looked at the spokes of the Wheel. "You can raise people's spirits—"

"We cannot all go into the lower levels," interrupted Fonu.

They looked at the River again, Jun asking with less respect than she could have shown, "Are you asking for a gun, Sa?"

Fonu's strained smile gave way to a look so serious and intent it sent a chill through her. "No. I could not even fight off a little girl. I am no good in that way." Jun probably wasn't the only one who felt a surge of embarrassment at their words, but Fonu went on indifferently. "I am speaking of the third choice."

Tomesk ten Ruvo exclaimed, "Are you asking if any of us wants to surrender to Seti Kess?!" He barked a scornful laugh. "That is preposterous. That is—"

"I am not speaking of what any of us wants," interrupted Fonu, cold as a storm front on the surface of Capamame. "I am asking... which of us will *choose*... to go back."

The saan at the table rustled uneasily. Some looked confused, like Hyre. Others offended, like Tomesk. But Jun understood at once what Fonu meant, and she could see that others, like Liis and Effegen and Gaeda, saw it, too.

"You mean that some of us must go back," said Gaeda. The old woman who always threw such strength into her voice sounded raspy now.

Fonu inclined their head. "Yes."

"What?!" cried Tomesk. "Moon arise, what are you—"

Effegen interrupted, "If Farren Eyce is conquered, Inye will seek out the spokes of the Wheel and execute us. But he doesn't know your faces. Some of you could hide on *The Brute Crane*. Then there would be a Wheel on Ma'kess, in the factories."

"No," said Tomesk, looking horrified. "Become slaves? No!"

"It is not about what we want," Fonu repeated. "It is about necessity."

Liis said, "We may win. It may not be an issue."

"But we must be prepared," Effegen said. She thought for a moment, and repeated, "He doesn't know your faces. You should all go. I will stay—"

"No!" Tomesk declared. "I will *not* go, nor let you play some solitary martyr!"

Fonu said, "At least two of us *must* go." Breathing in and exhaling slowly, they added, "I will go."

Jun's heart squeezed. Fonu was Draeviin, descended of the original crew that brought *Drae's Hope* to Capamame. Fonu had never set foot in the Treble, had never dreamed of it, pinning all their hopes on the new world. To offer this thing was not cowardice, nor some attempt to avoid execution by Kess's marauding cloaks. It was a sacrifice beyond conceiving. For going back would be worse for them than staying and dying. Everyone in the room knew it.

After some silence, Tomesk said with no hint of his usual temper, "You must go, my Star. We will find a way to hide you."

Effegen shook her head emphatically. "No. I can't leave the people here. I am the Star."

Tomesk looked mutinous. Tears had begun to leak down Hyre's face.

Gaeda, who had sat quiet and bowed under with her thoughts, gazed across the table at nothing. She fisted the pommel of her cane, and spoke: "I was born the year that *Drae's Hope* left the frontier station. I was the youngest of six. A year later, when the Kindom attacked Jeve, one of their first missiles struck the dormitory where my siblings slept. I was in bed with my mother, in an adult dormitory. When I was a young woman, she told me about her and my father, running to the children's dormitory. It had been bombed, and my father went into the ruins. My mother told it to me this way. She said he came out carrying ash. The explosion had been so hot that there were no bodies left. All those children—dozens and dozens of children—and all that remained was ash."

Blood beat in Jun's temples, a hot frantic river in her veins. She pictured her family in the Ironway shop, and Esek Nightfoot a missile that burned them up.

Gaeda, as if snapping out of a dream, looked around at them again, saw them again.

"Our people will need a Stone to stand on. By Sajeven's own mercy, I will go back." Her voice broke, just as Effegen's would break when she spoke to her people hours later. "But it is *bitter* to me, my friends. To send my mother's final child into the factories. What a bitter thing."

Someone knocks on Jun's office door, startling her into the present. She's been sitting against the edge of a desk, watching the views, but in these past few moments she may as well have dropped into a cast for how much her mind went away. The door opens. One of her casters, an older woman called Maiye, looks in on her. Something about her has always reminded Jun of Grandmi Hosek—or Hosek as she was when Jun was young. Round, stocky, grave.

"Jun," Maiye says, for Jun has, after all these months, trained her casters to call her Jun instead of Sa. "The rewrite just hit another marker. We're at fifty percent now."

Jun, despite everything, despite the pure futility of it, smiles at her. She hopes that her despair doesn't bleed through.

"Good. Show me."

She goes out into the larger lab. The casters at their stations look frozen. They watched Effegen's speech. They must have been sitting with the gravity of it when the rewrite program pinged at them. But even the success of the 50 percent marker hasn't sent them back to work.

"All right," Jun says. "Tell me what we've got."

A couple of them take the lead, explaining what she already knows, what she doesn't need to hear but what they need to tell her: the recalcitrant gate key that Drae's casters wrote decades ago is like a snarled length of string, and by Jun's guidance and their own tenaciousness, the Farren Eyce casters have untangled half of it. And to every reclaimed inch, they have bonded the new string of their rewritten code. Give them another three weeks, and they could have the whole thing finished.

But they don't have three weeks.

When the casters have finished their explanation, Jun nods silently. She smiles. She is not given to sentiment, and yet she says, "I never knew a casting corps like this."

The casters are surprised, even confused.

"A year ago, the Jeveni had a casting corps that was three hundred strong. Well educated, experienced, ready for their mission on Farren Eyce. And the Kindom killed them. Nikkelo sen Rieve asked me to come in their place, to build a new corps. If he were here today...by the gods. The pride he'd feel in you all."

Now those uncertain looks give way to shy pleasure, and to the intense, determined pride of the warrior among kin warriors.

"You all have a decision to make. Go home to your families."

Instantly they're confused again, rattled; some of them even look angry. One says, "Sa, I'm staying here. I'll fight back from the labs."

Dozens echo her. Others are quiet. Jun nods. "Just...take the day. That's an order."

They still hesitate, and she rolls her eyes, giving them the comfort of her normal, irascible self. "You think you can win a stubbornness contest with me? Get lost!"

This time, they go, some more eagerly than others, some dragging their feet and looking back at her like lonesome puppies. She almost laughs. Then she does laugh. But the door shuts after them, and she is alone in her casting lab.

"Gods and fire," she whispers into the rafters, the high dark ceilings like a version of the Black where she cut her teeth and made her life. "Could we ever have dreamed it, Great Gra?"

She looks at the cast program, the snarled string half reclaimed. She'd told Effegen and the Wheel from the beginning. Weeks, she'd said. It'll take weeks to rewrite the gate key. But she'd hoped she was wrong. She thought, *I am Sunstep. I escaped the Cloaksaan and Esek Nightfoot. I robbed the Paiyes. I rescued Liis Konye by the skin of her neural link. I wove a Hood, and threw it over the entire Jeveni fleet, and bore them to safety.*

A sudden ping from Liis snaps her back. She raises the cast, and Liis appears before her, dark twists peeking out from under her cap. Her serious, scarred face is as beautiful as ever.

"Hi," Jun whispers.

Liis says, "I'm in the market. Thousands are volunteering to fight. I don't think I'll be home till late."

Jun smiles mirthlessly. "Me neither." They stand in silence for a few moments, and Jun says, "Don't let any of them accidentally shoot you."

Liis chuckles, warm and sad at the same time. She has been sad, these past few days, even anxious sometimes. She has radiated a deep grief of memories that will never go away. Jun feels such tenderness for her, such desire to comfort her as she faces her cloaksaan enemies again, as she contends with the specter of her old master, Seti Kess. Now she says with composure, "Today is about assessing our assets. I'll evaluate skill sets and experience and run test drills if necessary. Once I have a grasp of the talent, I can begin making assignments and sorting the useful from the liabilities."

Her clinical tone sends a shiver down Jun's spine. This is Liis the soldier, the strategist, the one who could have been a Cloaksaan commandant. Or the First Cloak themself.

"You okay?" Jun asks uneasily.

Liis blinks, looks at her, and it's *her*—her eyes. Her scars. Her small grim smile. "This will be bad, Jun. A lot of people will die."

Because I can't finish the gate key, thinks Jun bitterly. *Because I couldn't see Ujan for who she was.*

"I know," she says.

"I want you in the casting lab the whole time. It's where you can do the best work anyway. I don't need scrawny casters lobbing grenades on the upper levels."

"And I don't want you on the front lines," Jun shoots back. "The cloaks will recognize you; they'll target you. You're no good to anyone if you get yourself killed in the first wave."

They glare at each other. Two, three, four seconds.

"How's your arm?" Jun asks.

Liis sticks her tongue in her cheek, narrowing her eyes. "Sore."

"I'll look at it in the morning. Do *not* leave the apartment before letting me look at it."

"Fine," Liis says.

"Fine," says Jun.

"I love you."

Liis's words, fierce and tender at the same time, soften Jun's body. She whispers back, "Same."

Only when Liis is gone does Jun allow a sharp sob to climb up her throat. But a switch flips, and it becomes a sound of anger, almost animal. Her instincts are old and deeply ingrained, and so when she drops down into the net, it rushes over her like cool water.

In this pristine re-visioned version of her casting lab, the gate key still circles overhead. It is a glowing blue-white snake that eats its own tail, little code creatures affixing themselves to its scales, one by one, inch by inch. How many times has she grabbed one of those creatures? Made it bigger and faster? And now the things are paper-thin and move at the speed of light, and there's nothing more to be done, no way to shorten the timeline. She doesn't even try. The gate key offers no immediate solution. It's as good as a dead end.

So she turns away. She envisions Jeve instead, that dark moon with its underground secret. She flies down to its surface and sees the Silver Keep glowing red under the rock, a stark, detailed stamp of rooms and corridors and bays. It is just a model, just an extrapolation of the data they have and what Liis thinks will be there. It's also a deception. To look at that shape is to imagine Treblen rebels descending upon it in fleets of warships. But despite their initial hopes, they know now that the Keep is holo-shielded, and too far underground for an aerial assault. The ruins of Farren Ki above it are like an impenetrable camouflage. The only possible way to war on the Keep is to war on its casting net and hopefully disable it.

She engages the practice program she has written, built on theory and hope. Fifty-foot waves circle the Keep, full of snapping gaba sharks and sea elks with razor tusks. Silt like quicksand. Salt like acid.

Jun steps up to the wall, the mighty boundary that protects the Keep from outside attack. With a scythe made of air, she parts the waves, cutting a path into the depths. She sprouts harpoons, skewering the sea creatures around her. She carves her way through, driving toward the Keep.

But a thousand tons of water conspire to crush her. Her initial assault staggers under the power of the ocean, momentum broken. Her ears pop and her muscles strain, the harpoons disintegrating in the tide as her pace slows to a crawl and the pushed-back waves begin to crest over her head.

At her periphery there come the shapes of tall figures wearing white. The archivists of her academy days, storied saan who taught her theory and technique. "Use your ocular to envision the stories," they say. "Use your aural link to hear the code. Become one with the cast."

"I am," Jun snaps, but deepwater snakes are lashing through the gap, sinking their teeth into her, venom flooding her veins. She grits her teeth, pushes forward, but it's like setting one's shoulder against a mountain.

"Try Silvani Silomye's power extraction technique," says one of the archivists.

"Recall the Kian Dustrow theory of net repulsion," suggests another.

"Do not forget Dev Whiteclash's six-step methodology for system override."

Jun screams through her teeth, watches her path grow narrower and narrower, until she is flung onto her back. The wall of water pours in again.

Breathless and sweating, Jun reads the result of her program. Two minutes. Based on her best guess for the firewalls and counterattacks, she managed to maintain an assault for two fucking minutes. She runs a calculation for how the assault would fare if she were not alone—if brilliant casters like the Ar'tec Collectivists joined her, maybe a hundred of them, everybody going up against the wall at the same time. Fifteen minutes until failure, the program predicts. Fifteen.

It turns out that knowing the location of the Silver Keep is about as useful as knowing she could finish rewriting the gate key in three weeks. If they can't break through the Cloaksaan casters and damage the Keep's internal systems, they'll achieve little more than alerting Kess to their presence. Surely he'd retaliate. Kill the five thousand Jeveni prisoners on Ma'kess, maybe?

Jun has never been one for despair. She's the seething-fury type. Still standing in the amphitheater of her cast, she reaches beyond its borders and yanks a figure into view. Drae sen Briit is compiled from the three known images of her. She is a woman of average height, of average build, but with striking auburn hair in a braided plume down the center of her head, shaved on the sides like a half version of Teron mourning. Her skin is dark and cool, her eyes just the same. Her expression has the unsettling quality of one who can see more and further than the common saan. As in her historical images, she does not smile. As in her journal, she projects something grim and secretive.

Since Jun began to read that journal, she has come to view Drae as somehow similar to herself. Before Liis, Jun lived by the genius of her cons alone, casting her way through businessaan and bank accounts. To do it, she needed more than technical skills. She needed more, even, than her fat, expansive, enviable brain. She needed a sense for things, the ability to look at a situation, or look at a saan, and know how they could be maneuvered. Should she trust them or should she run? She relied on those senses for so many years. Then Ujan and Tej happened. Then Bene chose not to warn her, not to trust her. Then she missed the blueprints Ujan was hiding. She has failed so badly, and all when it matters most. Maybe her past successes were little better than luck.

Yet, despite all of it, there is some low, perpetual song in her ear, a faraway tune that coaxes her to keep going, to come closer. She stares at Drae's hologram and feels her old instincts pacing restlessly. Drae is like her. Broad thinking, a schemer, a woman of contingencies.

"You had a plan for everything," Jun tells her. "You must have had a plan for this."

Even fed through with the texts of Drae's life, this creature before her isn't alive. Anything it does or says will be nothing more than a projection of the data Jun has put into it. And because the data that Jun has put into it depicts a woman of stony reserve, the hologram just stares at her, not answering.

"You were too smart to think the Kindom risk would disappear when *Drae's Hope* left the Treble," Jun says. "You must have had a plan for that!"

Drae sen Briit doesn't answer.

"I am trying to save them. Again!" She waves her arms. "But there's nothing left in me, okay? I've dug as deep as I can, spread myself as thin as I can. I've twisted myself into knots. For you! For *your people!*" She loses control, screaming the final words like a tantruming teenager. She has always been a tantruming teenager. "My casters are going to die! My family is going to die! *Liis* is going to die! Give me *something!*"

But Drae sen Briit, dead these seventy-six years, cannot answer. Exhausted, Jun sits down on the floor, crisscrossing her legs and holding her face in her hands. It is either moments or hours later that, like a breeze sneaking in through a cracked window, a new voice comes.

Now, now, soothes Great Gra. *No use getting frustrated.*

Jun sobs into her hands. It's just a program. Another projection compiled from data points and sense memories. That is all a cast fugue ever is. The thin line between concrete action and hallucination.

Go on. Listen to your instincts. Tell me what you've seen.

She tells him, "I haven't seen anything. That's the problem. Just a bunch of dull journal entries full of typos!"

And why do you keep coming back to that? Great Gra asks. *Why do the journal entries matter so much to you?*

"I—they don't. I'm just being neurotic. They don't matter."

Listen to your instincts, he says again.

Her brow furrows, but she doesn't raise her head from her hands. If she does, she will see his hologram, and it will remind her that he isn't real, that he isn't coming back. And she'll be grateful—because she never has to look him in the eyes. Never has to apologize for failing their family.

Look, Ricari's voice beckons her.

Like the child who was so hungry for his lessons, she raises her eyes. Something appears in the air before her. It's a circuit board. The first one Ricari ever trained her on. It looks like the blueprint of a station. The electronic components are like community hubs and private domiciles connected by hallways. A little light bulb pops out of the top-left corner, and in the bottom right is an on/off switch.

You know how it works.

She pushes the little switch, and the light comes on. She remembers when she completed this circuit board and the light came on for the first time. All her thinking and arranging and soldering, come to fruition in a spark.

It's that simple, Great Gra says. *If you've got the components, and you know how it works, it's that simple.*

"I don't *have* the components."

He says, *When the circuits don't work, they have to be fixed. When pieces are missing, they have to be built. All those errors in a journal, demanding to be fixed.*

Of all the fucking things to harp on. She sighs in exasperation. "It's just bad writing!"

Does Drae sen Briit seem like a bad writer to you?

This is not real. This isn't a cast projection. She's dreaming or something. She imagines stomping her foot at him. He was always the one who dealt with her tantrums. He saw her, as the rest of her family couldn't. Maybe if Ujan and Tej had had him in their lives a little longer, that force of gentleness and strength, it all would have turned out different. Instead, her cousins are a code full of errors, like Drae's journal. Errors that Jun couldn't see, couldn't read, like a foreign language—

Something very like an electrical shock bursts across her skin and nerves. She looks sharply in the direction his voice came from, but Great Gra isn't there. Nearby, Drae stands just as she did, stern and watchful in the blue glow of the lab.

"What languages did you speak?" Jun asks.

This is a question that the hologram can answer.

"I was a polyglot. I spoke Je, Braemish, Ma'kessi, Teron, Katish, and Qi. I also spoke several stationer and moon dialects derived from those languages."

"What dialects?"

Drae lists a half dozen. Working on whim alone, Jun runs the journal through her translation program, looking for some correlation between those languages and the original Je entries. Nothing comes of it, and yet...

"No other dialects?" she presses.

This time, Drae blinks once, slowly, almost like she is bored by Jun's question. "Not according to my records."

There's something about it—almost mocking. Jun stands up. She begins to circle Drae, slowly, assessing the figure that seems now like a giant egg on the verge of hatching. She reaches into Drae's pixelated body, pulls from the heart, and tosses star maps into the air. She scatters the maps with pinpoints, places where she knows Drae had been. Xa Cosas on Braemin. Riin Kala on Ma'kess. Lo-Meek on Teros. But these are not what catches her attention. There, far beyond the muzzy borders of the Treble, is a frontier station called *The Glitch*. The station where *The Hope* was built, before its sailors changed its name to honor their murdered founder. Drae visited *The Glitch* three times in her life. Jun herself once imagined evacuating her family there, if she could only save them. If she could only *see*—

That electric shock sensation comes again, like a lightning strike, surging from her skull down to the flats of her feet. She has a memory of lying in bed with Liis, during one of their early nights together. She was sleepy. She was telling Liis about her dreams of the frontier station.

"They have their own languages, you know," Liis had said, one of her hands trailing up and down Jun's spine, a tenderness she was just beginning to allow herself. "You'll have to program your fancy translator bot to speak pock-pock, if you want to go to *The Glitch*."

"That's a ridiculous name for a language," Jun mumbled, and fell asleep, and now—

Jun reaches out with her hands. With more than her hands. With new hands, full of magnets. She draws iron bits of data to herself, sucks them from the furthest corners of the casting net. The data flows into her like a river. She reaches and reaches and reaches, for every piece of writing there is: formal histories; business ledgers; poetry; contracts. She finds every known recording, the voices *click clicking* with hard consonants, hardly a vowel in sight. She pulls out her translator bot, making it big with a mouth like a feeding bird. How it glitters, each feather iridescent as a gem. She pours knowledge into it, siphoning language through her own body and into the bot. Its hungry, hungry mouth gobbles up the words, the sentence structures, the grammar.

Nearby, Drae sen Briit watches.

A voice says, "Jun?"

She snaps out of her fugue to find that two hours have passed. Bene is standing in the lab, looking at her curiously. He's got something in his hand. Oh, a sandwich. He holds it out to her with a perplexed look, and for some reason she starts laughing. His eyebrows shoot up.

"Have you cracked?" he asks.

"No," Jun gasps. "No!"

It will be hours before her translator speaks pock-pock fluently. But already the program has begun eating Drae's journal, searching it. It may come to nothing. *Drae sen Briit was human like the rest of us. She misspelled words. She left typos.*

And yet...

"What are you doing?" Bene asks.

She holds up a finger, watching the translator work. As Je, the grammatical glitches in Drae's journal mean nothing. Now, translated from Je to pock-pock, those same errors reveal a pattern too distinct to be meaningless. Jun's heart gives an erratic leap.

"Code," she breathes. And then, as the code begins to unravel, "Cypher."

The code is elegant. The cypher more so. A linguistic sleight of hand to rival anything Jun has ever done. But when the cypher starts unveiling its prize, when the trick of it is revealed, something slender and gold looks out at her. All this time it's been right in front of her, niggling her, bringing her back to the journal over and over like a euphorics fiend. An itch begging her to scratch. The sight of it unveiled fills her with terrified wonder.

Bene asks, "Jun? What is it?"

She laughs again, a sound of jubilation and disbelief. She knows what it is. And it is everything.

CHAPTER TWENTY

1665

YEAR OF THE HARVEST

Reveñon Manor
Torznol Continent
The Planet Ma'kess

If there is any pleasure to be taken from these circumstances, it's the way that Karix Moonback grouses and sputters when the rebel ship alights on the private tarmac of Reveñon Manor. Though not the Moonback capitol, Reveñon is a second home to the family's upper echelons, who have been forced out by a ground invasion of Ma'kessn rebels. What better insult to Karix Moonback than to flaunt her family's losses?

Six, feeling a very Esek-like cackle rising in their throat, takes one sidelong look at Chono's grim, troubled face and controls themself.

Nearby, Hejar Paiye says acidly, "Pure self-indulgence."

This time Six does chuckle, because Hejar is right. Reveñon Manor is a mere country house. It has few battlements, no holo shields, and limited evacuation points. There's a reason why the Ma'kessn rebels took it so easily. The same reason why the Moonbacks will be able to take it back. More importantly, it has no military value beyond symbolism. A useless acquisition.

On the tarmac, Goodrite and Siltmire have overcome the shock of their failure on M-4. They lead the way like conquerors on procession, their soldiers hustling the captives forward. Karix and Chono walk alongside Revel Moonback's float stretcher. The man is barely hanging on to life, and Karix, holding his limp hand, looks pale and rigid, though it might be more from anger than fear. Six, who has known for almost twenty years about the incestuous relationship between uncle and niece, wonders if his death will transform Karix as Oyun's death has transformed Hejar—how deep the hunger for revenge will go.

As they approach the main entryway to the manor grounds, a pair of medics jog out. They shoulder Chono and Karix aside, quickly assessing Revel and guiding his stretcher back inside. When Karix tries to follow, soldiers block her.

Siltmire says, "Don't worry, Sa Moonback. We have a talented surgeon. Your uncle is in good hands."

"Fuck you," Karix spits.

Siltmire gestures at Karix and Hejar to her soldiers. "Take them inside."

As the saan obey, Goodrite mutters something to Siltmire, who nods and gives Six a shrewd look.

"She stays with me," Chono warns. The chosen pronoun confirms what Six already assumed: To the rebels, they will remain Esek Nightfoot, for now.

Siltmire chuckles without humor. "All right, then. A gesture of goodwill. Come on."

They're led down a path to the large manicured grounds behind the manor. It's the end of spring on Ma'kess, the hedgerows and gardens in full bloom. At the center of it all, a large gazebo filigreed with flowering vines stands like a throne. Six immediately clocks the monarch, a figure sitting in a cushioned patio chair reviewing something on a cast tablet. Six recognizes him at once: Exani Ashway, the one-time general of Torznol's continental army. He is a grizzled saan of around sixty, copper skin leathery and creased. His noticeable paunch and broad, muscular upper body, his thick dark hair and beard, give him a bear-like appearance.

When they walk up the steps into the gazebo, Ashway goes on reading his tablet, but he says with a voice as deep as a gong, "I see you come back bearing trophies."

Siltmire's voice is cocky. "Good afternoon, General. You seem well situated here."

"Not for long," says Ashway to his tablet. "Revel Moonback held off on a counterattack out of sentimentality. Giran Moonback is erratic and destructive. If he decides he's the Family head now, he'll undoubtedly move to blow the manor off the face of the continent."

Siltmire answers without a trace of deference. "It's a symbolically valuable location. We made the Moonbacks run away like children. It's as good as when the pirates sacked Verdant." She tosses a sneering glance at Six, who grins so widely back at her she looks startled.

"You did it without my permission," Ashway says flatly. "Just as you attacked M-4 station without my permission."

More and more interesting...

Siltmire bristles. "You're not leading a continental army anymore, General. My fighters came together under your command because you promised to be our equal. Goodrite and I have plenty of saan between us, and if you won't listen to them, I have to do it for you."

The old general's face shows no reaction. "And tell me: Was murdering two Family heads, mortally wounding a third, and losing Riiniana Nightfoot what your saan wanted?"

For the first time, he looks up. He has the eyes of a hawk. Six thinks of little Riiniana slipping away into the shadows on M-4 like a rabbit disappearing into her warren. Will the hawk catch her? Will anyone? A girl like that has contingencies.

Goodrite says, "There was no time to search for her. We had to move quickly. She's just a child. We've brought you the real matriarch."

Six blurts a laugh. "If you think she's inconsequential, you're worse fools than I thought."

Goodrite glowers at them.

Ashway gives Six a long, considering look before shifting his attention to Chono. He puts the tablet down at last and bows over his open palms. "Burning One. I haven't had a chance to speak to a cleric in some time. Would you bless me?"

This is clearly the last thing anyone expected, especially Chono. But those old habits of hers stick, Six observes. Ashway levers his giant body out of the chair and bows his head to her. The gazebo may as well be on fire for how tense Siltmire and Goodrite become. Chono's prayer to Makala is full of sweetness and the promise of new life, and afterward, Ashway raises his head with a tight smile.

"Thank you, Burning One. I hope it goes without saying that you are most welcome here. And many of my saan would gladly receive your blessing, too."

Chono says, "Thank you, General. But coming here like this is the last thing that I wanted. Before your lieutenants attacked, I was making progress with the Families. They—"

He holds up a hand. "Let me spare you having to tell it twice. We're meeting with the quorum in two hours. Has the Wheel briefed you on recent developments?"

Chono nods. "Yes, luckily enough, I spoke to Effegen ten Crost during the flight here. It was very good of you to send the reconnaissance mission to Jeve. This gives us a huge advantage."

The old man clucks. He's not taller than Chono or Six, but his bigness makes Six feel like a kinschool student gawping up at a master for the first time.

"The Keep is shielded and well underground, so there's very little a surface assault can do. But come, we can save this discussion for another time. Go inside, have some food. We'll find you a room to rest in. I need a moment alone with my... lieutenants, as you call them."

Goodrite blanches at his tone, but Siltmire's eyes are defiant. Six doubts they will reach much resolution with their general.

Over an hour later, Six sits on a divan in one of the manor's private bedrooms, watching Chono pace a hole through the expensive woven rug. Though Six has washed and eaten, they note with displeasure that Chono has ignored her own portion of food.

"I'm not hungry," she says.

Six rolls their eyes. "You are behaving like a sulky child."

She nearly squawks, stopping to give them an incredulous look. "Sulky?"

"It is sulky to deny your basic needs because you are upset about how things are going. You have not even treated that cut on your face."

"It's a graze. I washed it with disinfectant."

"It needs a stitch patch. I have some. Come here."

She huffs with impatience, but as they stand she comes to them, and they are face-to-face as Six reaches into their pocket and retrieves the little medical kit they accepted from one of the rebels in the foyer head-quarters. They withdraw the stitch patch and ignore her outstretched hand, assessing the two-inch cut right where her natural hairline starts. The beginnings of a fine black stubble on her head distracts them for a moment. They consider the still-open cut and unwrap the patch. At least she let a medic treat the deeper wound on her shoulder.

"I can do this myself," Chono complains, though she doesn't try to stop them.

Six carefully and gently applies the patch, picturing the microscopic medical bots zipping into action at the trigger of human skin, knitting her back together. They recall the time she nearly died on *The Risen Wave*, and how in a desperate panic Six injected her with other bots, hoping the creatures could hold her heart and arteries together long enough to get her to the Jeveni surgeons. How pale she was. How close to death...

With the patch in place, Six meets her eyes. Some of her anger seems to have abated, but she looks back at them with a hollow expression. They take this moment to appreciate the striking depth of her eyes, which they have had rare occasion to look into so closely. A touch of blue amid the gray, they decide. Flecks of slate. Their hunger for her well-being is like a stomach cramp. Their relief, that she is safe, aches deep in the center of their body.

She suddenly puts her hands on their face, and the press of her forehead to theirs washes them in warmth. They stand like that for some time, until Six feels the curious brush of her thumb, tracing their repaired ear.

"It's fixed," she whispers.

Six shivers and tries to hide it with a mirthless chuckle. "There was a lot that needed fixing."

Chono pulls back, looking fierce. "Tell me what happened to you."

Six smiles, unsure where to start, and chooses the cowardly way out. "You first."

She scowls, but accepts, and tells them a tense story of fleeing Kator and near death on Teros and calculating a truce with Oyun Paiye. When she is done, Six shares their own tale. Neither of them goes on about it. They're economical, relaying the facts of their experiences and how they got where they are. Six doesn't lie to her about anything, which they vaguely recognize is a feat. They sense, and are sure that Chono senses, that there are much longer versions of each other's stories. Perhaps after a year of retold details and new asides, they really will know everything. But for now, there is only one piece Chono dwells on—

"She *sterilized* you?"

Chono's voice is a rasp, her stoic face transformed with disbelief and something Six didn't expect: grief. Grief on their behalf. They are discomfited, as much by her concern as by the way that it wakes up some curl of grief in them, some feeling of violation that they have mostly pushed to the side. Being captured by Kess, imprisoned in Verdant, stripped of their neural link access, and yes, sterilized... They spent their life guarding against these kinds of attacks. But they were vulnerable in the end. And it hurts more than them. It hurts Chono.

Still, awkward with the facts, Six shrugs. "I never wanted children."

"Yes, but—to take it from you," Chono says weakly.

There is such tenderness in her, more than Six has received from anyone since Da died. They don't answer. What answer is there? Eventually, Chono seems to understand, and lets it go. Several moments pass in silence, but there is a subject that Six must raise:

"Khen Obair is dead."

Chono stiffens. It's no use Six pretending that they don't know what they know. If circumstances had been different, if Six had had the opportunity, they would have tracked down and killed all the saan who purchased Chono. But they were too busy with their Esek mission.

Chono looks pale. Should Six not have brought it up? They knew, when she stepped into the meeting room on M-4, that she was seeing Obair for the first time since her assault. They had felt a combination of anger, grief, and pride, for she was so composed in the face of that horror. But she should not have had to be. And now Six has made her remember again.

"We've lost the Families," Chono says, bypassing the conversation altogether.

Six allows her that. But the low despair in her voice will not do. They look at her steadily, asking, "What would Esek say?"

Chono furrows her brow in confused surprise, before her face smooths out with understanding. Her lips twitch, though there is that sadness in her eyes that she always gets when she thinks of her old mentor. "Esek would say... it's not over till we're dead."

Six is just nodding their agreement when someone knocks at the bedroom door. A Ma'kessn in the colors of the Torznol military asks to escort them to the war room for the quorum meeting. As they follow him down a gilded hallway, and down the wide staircase onto the first floor, Six looks through a south-facing doorway into what appears to be a reception hall of some sort—full of cots and rebel fighters. Six wonders how many soldiers Ashway is billeting here, and if Siltmire's rebel forces would stand against him for her and Goodrite.

They head into the west wing of the house, which terminates in a large dining room. Ashway has already taken a seat at the head of the square table, and there are about a dozen continental soldiers stationed around the perimeter of the room. Siltmire and Goodrite are seated at the opposite end of the table, as if to assert an equal position to Ashway. Six follows Chono's lead when she sits down just one chair over from Ashway, separated only by a soldier who seems to be another one of Ashway's lieutenants—and a more loyal one, Six guesses. Without a word to any of them, Ashway makes a sweeping gesture over the table. Weaves of light resolve as holograms start to pop up, the cast program putting a dozen seated figures at the table, until Six is surrounded by faces they don't know, and a couple they recognize.

"Yantikye," they say.

Yantikye grins his wide irreverent grin. "Hey there, little killer."

Chono's body beside theirs is as hard as a stone. Graisa is on Yantikye's left, Masar Hawks on his right. The latter looks at Six about as coldly as Chono looks at Yantikye. Well, Six got many of Masar's collectors killed. He's entitled to his bitterness. Six holds his eye only long enough to show respectful acknowledgment before assessing the others at the table. Some Braemish pirates, one looking like an everyday scrapper with kin scrappers on either side, and one obviously a captain, with his second on the right. There are also two ragtag Teron rebels, as well as a Quietan sailor. And, surprise of surprises, Six recognizes Imicanta Oninye: the headsaan of engineering at the University of Hestos. What a peculiar congregation...

"Cleric Chono," says one of the Teron rebels, a youth with a topknot and earnest eyes. "Thank the gods you're safe."

"It's good to see you, Zemit," Chono says, sincere but unsmiling.

"I only wish the circumstances were different," Zemit replies, and casts a glower at Siltmire and Goodrite that could freeze the ground. "This certainly isn't what any of us wanted."

Siltmire rolls her eyes. "Relax, Zemit. We can all talk about this rationally."

Imicanta Oninye says with a bite in her voice, "We spoke rationally, days ago, when we agreed to send Cleric Chono to parlay with the First Families. We spoke rationally *again* when we held off taking action against the Silver Keep to await Cleric Chono's word."

Siltmire retorts, "This was an opportunity to take high-value targets and use them to force the Families' hands—"

A Quietan named Melosi the Grave repeats angrily, "High-value *targets*? If by 'targets' you mean target practice. Khen Ookhen Obair and Oyun Paiye are dead. Revel Moonback is dying. Riiniana Nightfoot is missing. All you have is a Paiye heir with a vendetta, and a Moonback adviser who is unlikely to hold sway over Giran Moonback."

"Don't forget me," Six drawls.

Melosi glowers at them. "You've been collaborating with Seti Kess. Sa Yantikye speaks for you, but I won't take that at face value."

"I'll tell you what," says Yantikye jovially. "She's a self-interested fucker." The "she" confirms that Yantikye will keep Six's secret, too. How interesting. "But she's far less likely to betray Chono than any of the rest of you. And am I wrong, or is Chono not a bit of a linchpin in this whole enterprise?"

Chono looks at him hatefully. "Feeling protective now? These two"— she points at Goodrite and Siltmire—"say you put a tracker on me."

Eyes widen around the room. Yantikye looks surprised and impressed, laughing at the culprits. "Did you rob me, you little fuckers?" Not waiting for an answer, he holds up his hands. "Now, everybody catch your breath. There was nothing nefarious about it. How was I to know someone would use it irresponsibly?"

Chono's lauded self-control has practically vanished. "You cut me off at the knees. Negotiating with the Families was our best shot, and I was making progress. Now, we've killed half of them. We've lost our chance."

"We haven't lost anything," Siltmire insists. "The Families won't lend their support to Kess while we have these hostages. The Paiyes need Hejar back, Giran Moonback hates Seti, and Khen Soon is a recluse."

Chono says, "Khen Soon might have trusted me and pushed his family to help us. Instead, you killed his father! As for Hejar, you'd be a fool to underestimate her."

"Or Riiniana," Six adds.

"Listen to them!" Siltmire cries, looking around the table. "Cleric Chono would rather ingratiate herself to the Families than see real change. By the gods, of course she won't rise up against the Night-foots! Esek Nightfoot is her *lover*—and we think we can trust her?"

Chono makes an exasperated sound. Six gives Siltmire a wink.

Masar speaks up. "I've worked more closely with Chono and Esek than any of you. They returned to the Treble with the express purpose of freeing five thousand Jeveni prisoners. My Wheel believes in their loyalty to us. As do I."

Well. Six wasn't expecting that.

Chono says, "There is no question of my loyalty to the Jeveni. But this is about *alliance*. We need the alliance of the Families, and now we've lost it."

"We *don't* need it!" Goodrite shouts back. "We've got insurance with the Family heads. We have weapons and fighters across the Treble. We don't have to *compromise!*"

The pirate captain Vikar Wren laughs. "Compromise, is it? You know, I've got no love for any First Family. But in *my* family, when we decide where to send our ships, none of us goes haring off in the opposite direction. We especially don't lie to one another's faces about it." He looks at Ashway. "And if we do, we get punished."

Siltmire says disdainfully, "I'm nobody's dog to be swatted for misbehavior. I have my own army. If this quorum wants me out, I'll take my fighters and resources elsewhere."

"Do you not understand what *alliance* means?" Oninye demands.

Siltmire retorts, "Alliance is obligation. I'm obligated to my troops."

"You're damning your troops," Chono warns her.

"And I'd rather we *were* damned than spend a single second at the same table as the fucking Families!"

No one speaks. Goodrite looks a little startled. Six thinks about

Riiniana, and her rare expressions of emotion. *I'd rather the Nightfoot name disappeared than see us scrape for the Kindom any longer.*

General Ashway exhales gustily, draws himself up, and seems about to speak—but a new hologram materializes at one of the only open chairs at the table.

"Forgive us our lateness," says the newcomer. Absurdly, it resembles a minkat, though with the mannerisms of a human. "All this family trouble. Badly done, utterly inexcusable. Ah! And the Righteous Hand is back, with her hanger-on, no less. Excellent, excellent."

Six speaks aside to Chono, "Did that cat just call me a 'hanger-on'?"

Chono tells the Minkat, "Sa, it's good to see you."

"Better than you know!" the Minkat declares. "Or, could be worse, nah? Asks a question: If a sa brings you bad news, do you rather it come sooner, or later?"

Imicanta says impatiently, "Out with it."

"Oh, we will out, most certainly. Though it's not us, I should say, that wants to chat. My kin and me caught a little bit of something, cast off from a Cloaksaan ship this past hour. May be of interest, nah?"

The Minkat tosses a cast into the air above the table, and Riiniana Nightfoot appears.

She is seated at a desk, her hands folded before her, her expression tranquil. Or it would be, Six thinks, except that there is a tiny shine of sweat on her hairline. Six sees a trace of something in her eyes: fear, perhaps?

"Sa Khen," she speaks to the camera. "And Sa Moonback. I'm sorry to be contacting you under these circumstances. By now you will know from your own people that the peaceful meeting on M-4 station was ambushed by rebel forces under the authority of Cleric Chono. I was lucky to escape alive and have been rescued from the station by First Cloak Seti Kess."

Six can practically hear Chono's teeth grinding.

"It pains me to do this, but I must confirm what I saw. The rebels slaughtered your fathers in cold blood. They also killed Oyun Paiye, and have Karix Moonback, Hejar Paiye, and my matriarch in custody.

The meeting on M-4 was our attempt to convince the family heads to lend their support to Seti Kess. Now we have suffered unimaginable losses at the hands of this renegade cleric.

"I'm calling on you to avenge your families in the only way that makes sense: by eradicating these rebel factions. To that end, I beseech you to join your forces with ours, which, done sooner, could have avoided all of this in the first place. In exchange for your alliance, we will reclaim the Treble and share the sevite trade among our families. Not only will you have your revenge, but your riches and glory will pay homage to your dead. Please, do not delay. The gods call us to action. I pray you will listen."

She vanishes. In the silence, Six *hmms* thoughtfully. So, this is her contingency. Prevent any alliance between the rebels and the Families, and by that action prevent Chono, a cleric, from rising any higher. Meanwhile, she throws her lot in with Kess, and must—what?—hope that she can lead a coup against him someday? Well, it's not the worst plan in the worlds.

Captain Wren glares at Siltmire and Goodrite. "You have well and truly fucked us."

Goodrite looks pale, but Siltmire answers defiantly, "That girl is no general."

"No, but I am," says Ashway. "And I know what happens when kings go on crusade."

Siltmire retorts, "Giran and Soon are barely even *princes*!"

Six had thought that Siltmire was the smarter of the two, but maybe she is only the brasher, for Goodrite seems to understand the gravity of the situation far better than she does. His eyes shift from one saan to the next.

Ignoring Siltmire, Ashway gestures to one of his soldiers. "Bring Hejar Paiye and Karix Moonback here."

"What?!" cries Siltmire. "Why?"

Ashway looks at Chono. "Speak to them again. Appeal to them again." Chono's jaw flexes. She doesn't answer. "There's a reason why you thought they would ally against Kess. You said it was going well."

"That's like saying the ground was dry before a monsoon. It doesn't matter anymore."

"You have to try, Cleric Chono," Imicanta Oninye says. "Otherwise, we will have such a storm coming down on us—"

"This is ridiculous!" Siltmire gets to her feet. "We've been fighting the Families from the beginning. What does this change? One setback and you turn into cowards?"

Ashway makes another gesture. Siltmire doesn't even have time to reach for her sidearm before she and Goodrite find themselves on the wrong side of a dozen rifles.

"Are you *suicidal*?!" Siltmire shrieks, even as hands yank her arms behind her back. Goodrite gets the same treatment, his eyes wide and scared. The soldiers push Siltmire back into her chair as she lobs profanity and threats. "My saan are in this building! When they find out what you're doing—"

"Unless you want to be gagged," says Ashway stonily, "you will stop talking, now."

To Six's surprise, she does. She looks stunned, disbelieving, but not yet humbled. Six considers what they've seen in the manor so far—plenty of Ashway's soldiers, but ragtag rebels, too. If Ashway isn't careful, he'll have a civil war breaking out under his roof.

"Cleric Chono," Ashway says. "Will you speak to Paiye and Moonback?"

Chono shakes her head, not in denial but in doubt, until suddenly Masar Hawks barks at her, "Chono! Tomorrow is Feast Day. By the gods, *try!*"

She blinks at him, chastened. Her expression shifts from one of open despair to grim resolve. This is what they came back to the Treble for. And they are out of time.

A door opens. Bound at the wrists and surrounded by guards, Hejar Paiye and Karix Moonback enter the room. Six takes note of their clean clothes and washed faces, and the stitched cut near Hejar's mouth. Karix, who was not wounded in the fight, wears an expression of arrogant fury. But Hejar is the frightening one, so calm and murderous.

Imicanta speaks first. "Regal Paiye, my deepest condolences for your loss. Sa Moonback, I understand your uncle is still alive?"

Karix scoffs without answering. Hejar addresses Chono. "Where is my mother?"

Ashway answers, "We have both Oyun Paiye and Khen Obair in a safe location. Their bodies are being treated with all respect."

"My mother is a penitent of Kata," says Hejar, that chilly voice enough to make Six itch for the weapon these rebels have denied them. "By the terms of our faith, I need to burn her on Kator within ten days."

"That can be arranged," Ashway says.

"Indeed?" Hejar replies. "You mean to return me safely home now, do you?"

Ashway says, "I will. I will treat you justly."

"You're a traitor to Ma'kess," Karix spits. "You led half the Torznol army into rebellion."

"I am a servant of the Godfire. And the Godfire burns justice into everything."

"It will be justice when I have you *executed*," Karix promises.

Hejar looks around at the faces at the table, pausing on Siltmire and Goodrite to observe their bindings and their guards. She looks at Chono again. "When you asked the Families to ally with you, you forgot to mention how fractured your supposed quorum is."

Chono speaks softly, without pride. "Siltmire and Goodrite defied the quorum. Those assembled here all gave me their blessing to seek an alliance with you. They still give it."

"Their word means nothing to me."

Chono pauses, and asks, "What about Oyun's word?"

She may as well have lit Hejar on fire for the rage that suddenly burns in her expression. "You *dare*—"

"I don't dare. I beg. I beg you both. Please consider what is best for your families. Internment to Kess, or a more just and secure Treble."

"The Treble will be secure when all of you are dead," declares Karix.

"It won't. You're an intelligent woman, Sa Moonback. I know you saw it as soon as I began to make my case—Kess is *not* the future that your family wants. And you"—she looks at Hejar—"your Regal brought me to M-4 because she wanted this alliance to happen. She wanted me to persuade the Families to work together and take Kess down. She was a wise and reasonable woman. Would she want you to roll over for Kess now?"

"You have some nerve," Hejar breathes.

"It's not nerve," Chono replies. "Look."

She nods meaningfully at the Minkat, and the recording of Riini-ana starts again. Six watches Karix and Hejar. Karix, who Six expects to look smug and vindicated, instead goes slowly paler and paler, fear clouding her eyes. Giran, Six realizes. She is thinking of Giran, Moon-back's unmanageable, erratic son, and what he will do now that he believes his father is dead. The idea seems to terrify her.

Hejar, on the hand, remains composed. When the recording ends, she looks at Chono again. "My family will wait for my word. And Khen Soon won't jump into bed with Kess."

"But Giran will," Six says, looking at Karix. "Won't he? And with glee."

"Kess will have both the Ma'kessn Families, and the Brutal Hand," Chono says. "He'll outnumber you."

"Then perhaps I'll ally with him," Hejar says.

"You won't. I know the respect and love you bear your mother. You won't act against her wishes in that way."

Hejar flares her nostrils, clearly caught between anger at Chono's presumption and anger that she's right.

The Teron called Zemit speaks up, voice earnest. "The rebels that attacked you are a minority in our number. They were misled by self-interested people."

Siltmire makes an apoplectic sound.

Hejar snorts. "A minority can do a lot of damage. Especially to goodwill."

The soldier next to Chono, Ashway's lieutenant, says, "My saan are arresting those rebels as we speak."

Goodrite's voice is faint with shock. "What?"

"You traitors," Siltmire hisses. "I am an *equal* representative of this quorum! You can't arrest my people because I disagree with you! You're as self-serving as the Families!"

Surprisingly, Hejar laughs. A short, glacial laugh. She tells Chono, "This... *murderer* has a point. You say they worked apart from your alliance. Yet here they are, sitting at your table."

"They will be punished," Ashway says.

"I don't believe you," Hejar replies.

"We are not animals!" exclaims Zemit. "No one is above justice."

"Pretty words," says Hejar.

"How can we persuade you?" Imicanta Oninye asks.

"Execute them," Hejar goads. "Kill them as they killed my mother. Ha! You see? None of you is willing to do that. None of you would ever—"

And then something extraordinary happens. Chono stands. Chono has a sidearm. And Chono—as grim and calm as Som themself—shoots Goodrite and Siltmire in their heads.

I do sincerely apologize for any misunderstanding that has occurred. Given Esek Nightfoot's propensity for training cloaks, and given her reports on this novitiate, I can understand why you want the girl for your kin. But Esek is a cleric, and so it is the Clerisy that has first rights to her novitiates. I find, on careful study and reflection, that this Chono is far better suited to the ministry of the Godfire than she is to the bloody—though needful—mission of the Brutal Hand.

excerpt, letter from First Cleric Aver Paiye to First Cloak Xer Ooxer Ang. Dated 1653, Year of the Flight.

1665

YEAR OF THE HARVEST

Reveñon Manor
Torznol Continent
The Planet Ma'kess

Cries and shouting ring out, and a scream from Karix Moonback. The soldiers in the room have their rifles raised in an instant, and Chono hears authoritative voices telling her to put the gun down. She sets it on the tabletop. Soldiers move in, but from the corner of her eye, she sees General Ashway raise a hand to stop them. Many of the quorum's holographic figures have risen in alarm. Six remains seated.

After the first moments of chaos, silence descends on the table. Siltmire and Goodrite, killed instantly, have fallen out of their chairs and Chono can no longer see them. She can, however, see the expressions of the saan around her.

In the end, it is Ashway who stands, leans over the table, and picks up the gun. He considers it thoughtfully, and says, "Lieutenant Brightlock...Sa Chono took your gun."

The lieutenant next to Chono looks stunned. "Yes, General. I—no excuse."

"Hmm," Ashway says.

He makes a few quick gestures at the soldiers nearest to Goodrite and Siltmire, and they swing their rifles back over their shoulders, moving into action. As the bodies are carried out in a wake of shock, Yantikye suddenly whistles.

"Som's ass, Cleric. You certainly know how to make a point."

"This is unacceptable," Imicanta Oninye says, her face ashen.

"Nah!" says Vikar Wren. "It's well done. Took care of the problem."

"But—" Zemit is wide-eyed. "But—we have to have some rule of law?"

"And now we have," Mix Catty replies. She looks downright gleeful, bouncing on the balls of her feet. "Let's not pour out our hearts over it! They were assholes."

"They have armies!" snaps Imicanta.

Melosi the Grave looks skeptical. "Armies devoted to *them*, not the quorum."

"Which means they will be even more dangerous now that—"

"They're not even half the size of Ashway's forces, let alone all ours together!"

The voices continue bickering. Chono, who can still feel the stock of the gun in her hand, who can still see Cleric Paan beaten to death in his Pippashap room, loses her grasp on the people around her, a gray fog clouding the edges of her vision, and Esek lurking in it, and Esek smirking at her, and Esek saying, *Taught you well, didn't I?*

But she feels pressure against her knee, the back of a hand, nudging her, returning her with a snap to the room and the arguing.

"Breathe," murmurs Six.

And Chono breathes, saying in a voice that rises above the other voices, "Stop."

Surprisingly, they stop. She looks around at each of them. For once, she doesn't slip behind a mask of stoicism, but shows them instead the ferocity of her unrepentance and the full weight of her resolve. She looks at Hejar Paiye, who looks at her in a calculating way, as if seeing her for the first time.

"Are you appeased?" Chono asks.

They stare at each other. Everyone stares at them. The majority of these saan aren't even in the room, yet there is the sensation of many bodies close together, breathing in the same air, and waiting. Hejar narrows her eyes.

"You think two rebels are worth my mother's life?"

Trust the First Families to value their own lives above the common saan. Chono says, "I think you are too wise to get bogged down by that sort of mathematics." Hejar's lip quirks, a bitter smile made grotesque by her injured face. She almost looks like Seti Kess. She could be even more dangerous than Seti Kess. Chono presses, "What happened on M-4 was a tragedy perpetrated by fools. They were selfish and myopic. But you are not selfish. You are no fool." She looks at Karix, who watches her shrewdly, though she is still pale from what has happened. "Neither of you are fools. You know that an alliance with us is your best chance to protect your families. Don't let grief and anger corrupt your actions."

They answer with more angry silence. Chono nearly fills it with more words, but Six touches her knee again. A signal. She keeps quiet. After some interminable amount of time, Hejar turns her head a little toward Karix, though she never stops watching Chono.

"Giran?" Hejar asks.

Karix laughs mirthlessly. "He's waited his whole life to be the family head. Now that he thinks he is, he'll be eager for a fight."

General Ashway says, "My surgeon tells me that your uncle will live. Surely you can use that to rein Giran in."

Karix scoffs. "Your dead friends created the perfect circumstances for a coup. There's no way Giran will stand down. I'd get out of this manor if I were you. He'll unleash Som the first chance he gets, and with Kess backing him, he'll go after every rebel stronghold he can find."

"Giran wants entertainment," Six says, lazily reclining in their chair. "Right now, Riiniana has offered him some. But don't you think it might entertain him more to go up against his little sibling? Plenty of bad blood, between him and Seti."

Karix narrows her eyes. "I have bad blood with Giran, too. If I bring your offer to him, he may reject it purely out of spite for me. To say nothing of how little interest he'll have in allying with commoners who attacked his family."

"Who's to say we want Giran Moonback on our side, anyway?" Vikar Wren asks. "Motherfucker is sure to betray us. Why not just give him and his kin up for lost? No offense, Sa Karix. I'm sure we can make you a very comfortable hostage."

Mix Catty says, "It's all moot, nah? If we can take the Keep, we don't need the Moonbacks. Lay waste to the Brutal Hand, and the Families will retreat."

Chono tenses. Hejar Paiye's brow furrows—then smooths with realization. "The Keep? You know the location of the Silver Keep?"

Judging by the new energy at the table, everyone would have preferred Catty to keep her mouth shut. But before the girl can even pretend to be sorry, Yantikye says, "Aye. But we can hardly take it if our enemies are shooting us in our asses. If Khen Soon and Giran Moonback and fucking Riiniana Nightfoot fight against us, we're fucked."

"We would have the Paiyes," Zemit says.

"Will you, now?" Hejar Paiye says acidly.

"You're right," Chono interjects, afraid that someone will push Hejar too far. "We can't make any assumptions. We won't. That said, if Giran and the Nightfoots side *with* Kess, but you and Revel's loyalists join us, there will be more or less even numbers. Though not if Khen Soon follows Giran. The Paiye Family has always had an important partnership with the Khens, and . . . influence over them. If you spoke to Soon, if you convinced him—"

Hejar interrupts. "My mother had influence over Khen Obair. I can make no promises about my influence over Soon. He is . . . opaque."

Yes, Chono thinks, remembering her conference with Khen.

"Teros relies on your agricultural exports," she points out.

"Ah, so you mean me to blackmail him?" Chono opens her mouth to deny it, but Hejar makes an impatient gesture with her bound hands. "I will not begin my tenure by threatening other Families. If I choose to speak to Khen, I will respect his decision either way. Gods know he has as much right to seek recompense from you people as I do."

"We *people*," says Melosi the Grave, "are about done with you spitting on our names."

Hejar sniffs. "Show me you're more than gangsters, and I'll value you higher."

Chono feels the danger in the air, the razor edge they are balancing on and the depth of the chasm beneath. She looks at Ashway. "Tell your soldiers to release Saan Karix and Hejar."

He looks back at her thoughtfully, not bristling at the order, but hesitating nonetheless. "We don't yet have an accord."

"And Karix there is to be our hostage," says Yantikye.

"Release them," Chono answers, reining in her impulse to bark orders, and damn the consequences.

She must strike the right tone, because Ashway gives her a small deferential nod. At his signal, the soldiers cautiously unbind their captives. Karix makes a soft sound of relief, massaging her wrists. Hejar shows nothing.

Chono looks back and forth between them, and gambles. "If you wish it . . . we will let you return to your families."

The room erupts in protest, but it has barely started before Six is on their feet, and they boom like a mortar going off, "Shut up, all of you!" It must be the surprise as much as anything that makes everyone do it, staring owl-eyed at Six, who, more like themself than Esek now, says in a thunder of impatience, "There is no more time!" They point across the table at Masar. "The Jeveni are on the brink of destruction and enslavement. There is *no more time!*" Each word is like the shot of a bullet. "You claim to be the representatives of your people." They gesture at Chono this time. "She is the People's Kin! *They* chose her. They have chosen her, from Riin Kala to the fishing villages on Quietus. Will you trust her or not? Will you follow her or not? Stop. Talking! And get this fucking job done."

Esek would never be this serious about something. She certainly would never have asked people to pay attention to someone other than herself. Chono is unnerved to see Six risk behaving this way, but she conceals her reaction. Let the others be stunned, and give her time to work.

Chono tells Karix and Hejar again, "If you wish it, we will help you get home."

Karix looks earnestly at Hejar, confirming what Chono already suspected: that she will defer to the new regal. As for Hejar, she has abandoned her sneering arrogance. She glares at Chono, but it is not a glare of hostility so much as contemplation.

"You're asking me to throw my family into a fight with no clear end. You say you've found the Silver Keep. That's all well and good, but they'll be well dug in, and a siege could last years. And let's not forget the Nightfoots have the sevite. Kess has the gates. Even if we killed him, some other cloak would rise up in his place. Give me a battle I can win, Cleric Chono. How else am I to know the measure of you?"

Chono grapples to find the best answer, the right answer. Masar speaks first. "You're right that the location of the Keep isn't enough. Especially for my people. But I've got a smart-ass caster on the other side of the Black who has a plan for taking out the Keep in one shot."

Hejar Paiye lifts her eyebrows, her arrogance returning, her look scornful. "The famous Sunstep, I take it? And what does that thief have to say about this?"

With the expert timing born of a long, theatrical career, Jun Ironway's hologram pops into view. She looks older than Chono remembers, sallow with worries, radiant with purpose.

"Jun," Masar greets her. "Our new allies were just asking what the godsdamn hell it is you're planning."

With the devilment of Terotonteris in her eyes, Jun says, "Well. I thought you'd never ask."

Once, when she was stationed on Quietus, the Pippashap elders gifted Chono a week of respite on a little houseboat connected to the city by a half-mile-long cable. This ensured the houseboat had privacy but would not be lost at sea. It was a place for celebrating weddings, or going on spiritual retreat. Chono, who loved the cool breeze and bright sunshine of the summer months, spent hours on the deck, sleeping under a canopy and eating fresh-caught fish and fantasizing that this was her life. She could not imagine needing anything more.

First Families have a different concept of what *vacation* means. Reveñon Manor has twenty bedrooms, and the suite given to Chono and Six is twice the size of the room in Yeyankatayan. When the Torznol soldier brought them here earlier in the day, Chono intended to protest—but never got a chance.

"Forgive me, Burning One," the soldier had said, nervous and uncertain. "But...with the war ramping up and so many of us about to die, I only wonder if...you might bless me?"

Chono remembers the sensation of Six watching; she remembers the deep resistance she felt to playing this role. But the young man, barely more than a teenager, looked so grave and hopeful. Yes, very soon he might be dead. She went to him and spoke a blessing from Makala that left him shiny-eyed with gratitude. He stammered his thanks and went off with straight shoulders and head held high, proud to have been blessed by such a cleric.

Two hours later, Chono would shoot Siltmire and Goodrite dead.

Now, standing in the room, she considers the opulence of the Moonback accommodations as compared against her little Pippashap houseboat: floor-to-ceiling tapestries; a muraled ceiling; elaborately carved furniture with gilt edges. The four-poster bed is massive, its mattress four feet off the floor with a little step stool for getting onto it.

She should be doing something. Surely there is something she should be doing. Ministering to the fighters on the estate? Reviewing Jun's blueprints? Building goodwill with the First Families? She already tried contacting Khen Soon, but he did not answer her cast, or respond to her message. Apparently the young man who was ready to shave his head for his father's crimes is not ready to talk to her. Hejar Paiye may have more luck.

As for any other preparations Chono could make, she knows their plans by heart. She has her armor at the ready. She is as prepared as one can be to walk into death.

Chono looks at the bed again. She ignores the stool and heaves herself onto the bed, falling onto her back with her boots still on. She lies there for a moment, exhaling shakily. It's the shakiness that takes her by surprise, a sharp flex of emotion in her throat, a feeling of wind rushing past. She pulls her boots off, dropping them over the side of the bed. She doesn't have the energy to wrestle off her coat. She lies flat again. The ceiling mural depicts Makala at her leisure, surrounded by greenery and on the bank of a vibrant pool. She is half-naked and smiling beatifically, stomach swollen with pregnancy, breasts full. *Six cannot have children*, Chono thinks suddenly. She would never have imagined Six desiring children, but now that it has been taken from them, even if only temporarily, she wonders...

Somewhere in the manor, Six is having their neural link repaired. For all Chono knows, its disablement bothers Six more than the sterility. She feels guilty for not having known, until now, that it was nonfunctional in the first place. Hopefully the hardware isn't broken. Having the old neural chip replaced isn't a difficult or dangerous procedure, but it would remove Six's access to Nightfoot records. And Chono doesn't want to see them with a bandage behind their ear. The thought of anyone cutting into them makes her irrationally furious.

Which is ridiculous. The idea that she could ever protect them from a single cut is ridiculous. In the morning, she and Six will lift off the surface of Ma'kess, and speed toward their next mission, and they'll be blessed through to their bones just to succeed, let alone survive. But whatever happens, one thing is certain: She won't be separated from them again.

So she studies the ceiling, full of doubt and dread.

It's a surprise when, sometime later, she blinks her eyes open to find the room much darker than before. The tall windows reveal the inky blackness of night. She must have slept for hours. Though the manor is surely alive with activity, it's quiet in this room, and the crooning wind creates a strange feeling of isolation.

But there is a light, and she turns to find a single lamp on a bedside table, lit and spilling through the room like liquid gold. Slouched in the armchair beside it is Six.

They're asleep. She hasn't seen Six sleep since childhood: the little cot in their kinschool room; their body curled in, and sometimes with Chono's curled around it during storms.

More than once, when Chono was Esek's novitiate, she discovered her mentor sprawled on unmade beds, usually with a lover nearby. She remembers the embarrassment of seeing Esek's naked back, or her toes peeking out from under a blanket. Once, Esek leapt unclothed from one such bed, and Chono had to avert her eyes in mortification. Esek did it to mock her. And probably to flaunt her own beauty. It always left Chono with a queasy feeling, too like her experiences with other First Family members, all that presumption, all that greed.

She recalls Khen Obair's body on the ground in the M-4 atrium, a bullet through his throat. His death made her feel...nothing. Or perhaps she simply doesn't know what the feeling was yet. It's been seventeen years since he hurt her. When she saw him in the meeting room, he looked old. As old as Cleric Paan, to whom she gave a much more brutal death than Obair's. She is dispassionately aware that she wanted him dead, but the fact of his death, when she saw it in the atrium, left her cold. Far more affecting was Oyun Paiye's crumpled body, and Hejar's screaming grief. How would she have reacted if she had been there to see Six kill Esek? What welter of emotion would have overcome her?

She focuses on Six again and says their name. Her voice is rough from sleep, and she thinks they won't hear her. But their eyes snap open, their head lifting from where it had listed against the back of the chair. They blink a couple of times, the only hint of grogginess.

"What are you doing?" Chono says. For a moment they look as if they don't know. They have to tilt their head back a little, because the bed is so tall. "Gods' sake. It's late. Come sleep in a bed like a civilized person."

She expects them to make some mulish objection, but they must be tired, because they rise from the chair and come around to the other side of the bed. They grumble about the bed's ridiculousness, and hoist themself up on the mattress. Then Six and Chono are lying side by side, staring up.

The silence is not strained or awkward. Their days apart, which had seemed like years, shrink to nothing. And more years shrink, and shrink, until they could be children again, lying in their kinschool room. Chono always knew if Six was asleep or not. She could hear it in their breathing, just as they could hear it in hers. She didn't understand at the time, the intimacy of this, the vulnerability of her devotion to Six. She didn't understand that with every sparring bout, every shared classroom, every attack from older students, and every night in the cots side by side, she was weaving Six into herself, making a depression in her own body where their body fit. She didn't know that Esek would separate them, and bring them together again.

"Why did Riiniana repair your ear?" Chono asks. She doesn't know why she's asking. It shouldn't feel so significant to her.

Six snorts "She wanted me to be beautiful. Pristine. She is like those ridiculous Braemish queens who capture jungle animals and keep them in cages, clean and glossy."

This is not funny, but Chono chuckles. "Are you the jungle animal in this story?"

"Well, I am certainly not tame. I was in Verdant for only a few days, and I could feel her leash on me the whole time. I wanted to bite her throat out."

Chono imagines Six as a creature with fangs, their hands transformed into claws, their back arched in sinuous preparation to strike.

"I never paid her much mind," Chono says. "She's...very ambitious, it turns out. You two have that in common."

"Ambitious?" Six says doubtfully.

"What else would you call everything you did to replace Esek?"

"Obsessive. Ill-fated. Arrogant."

Six has never spoken of what they did like this before. She looks over at them again, brow furrowing, but Six refuses to acknowledge it, so she gives up. Only then do they speak again.

"Do you ever wonder what would have happened if Esek never came to Principes?"

Chono hesitates, surprised again. She never imagined Six engaging in a sentimental exercise.

"I—suppose things would be quite different."

"Astronomically different," they say, an edge to their voice. "If Esek had not come to Principes, I would have graduated and become some cloak's novitiate. By now I would be a commandant, and probably in line for First Cloak. All my violence would be in service to the Brutal Hand. But I would never have tried to track down the Wheel and drawn attention to what they were doing. I would never have led Esek to K-5, and Ujan Redcore would never have become a Kindom stooge. The Jeveni would have been free to relocate to Capamame as they pleased, and there would be no risk of Kess finding their gate key."

Irritation crackles in Chono's body. "Are you trying to say that everything that's happened is your fault? Because even I didn't think you were that arrogant." She can feel Six scowling. "You're making a lot of assumptions. Why do you think Kess would never have spied on the Jeveni? Their jump to Capamame would have disrupted the trade regardless of how it happened. Maybe some other agent would have tortured the gate key out of some other spoke. Maybe there would never have been uprisings in the Treble, and so there would be no rebels to call on now to help save Farren Eyce."

"Are you trying to make me feel better?" They sound disdainful.

"Your feelings aren't what matter. Your guilt doesn't help anyone.

Neither does mine. What we do to save these people—that's all that matters."

"You always were annoyingly pious," they mutter, which sounds so much like Esek—sometimes they are *so much* like Esek. But they say, "I know you, Chono. You must wish that we had never met her."

Chono considers it. Esek was a poison. Esek was an accelerant.

"She saved me from my kinschool master." Six's body tenses. Chono has a flashing memory of herself in the beds of rich patrons, just as tense, terrified, confused. She remembers Khen Obair, who brought a particular cruelty to the encounter. She remembers feeling sick over what to do. What if she did it wrong, and her kinschool master was angry? What if she did it right, and Khen or some other patron wanted her again? "I wouldn't have survived," she whispers. "If it had gone on much longer, I... wouldn't have survived."

She has never admitted this to anyone. She has barely admitted it to herself, and she can feel despair rolling off Six. She wants to tell them to stop. That it was long ago and she's past it now, and no one will ever do that to her again. She wants to say that she is not broken, and that when she looked into Khen Obair's eyes she was not afraid but contemptuous. She wants—

Six says, "I would not have let that happen. I would have found a way to protect you."

Chono smiles bitterly. "Then it would have just been someone else." Six has no answer for this. Chono, unable to hold it back anymore, whispers, "You said you would be right behind me. In Nikapraev. You swore you would set the bombs and follow us. You lied."

She hears their swallow. "I am sorry."

She shuts her eyes, willing herself to be calm. "When I cast out to you, you were already lost. I could hear it in your voice. And I couldn't come after you. You're so obsessed with protecting me. Does it ever occur to you that I want to protect you, too? Or what it does to me, when I can't?"

"Chono—"

"I don't know what would have happened if Esek never came to

Principes. I don't know who we'd be. But maybe in that other life we'd be safer than we are now. Maybe we wouldn't have to worry all the time about the other one dying and...leaving us alone." She clears her throat to keep her voice from cracking. "It's no use wondering. It's no use wishing. She did come. These are our lives. Forgive yourself."

Six lies there for so long without speaking that she has a sudden image of them falling asleep, and falling asleep with them, and both of them curled up in the respite of their closeness. But Six whispers, "She haunts me."

Chono feels a combination of fear and recognition. She wants not to say it, but she has to say it. "She haunts me, too."

"Like a voice?" Six asks, sounding relieved that she believes them.

"I...don't know," Chono says.

Six exhales. "She haunts me like a voice. Or like a living person I can see, but never see completely. She swore she would do it. As she was dying. She said that she would haunt me to my grave. I thought that I could shake her off. That if I made amends, protected you, protected the Jeveni, she would lose her grip and fade away."

Chono imagines a ghost Esek tracking Six's steps, and shivers. Then she thinks about what Six said, and she feels lost. "I can't be your absolution."

"You are not. You are the dam that holds her back. I feel her, in my head, trying to consume me, to become me, so that there is no border between us. But you..."

Another shiver. A tightening in her chest. "I can't be your savior, either."

They make an exasperated sound. "You are not listening. A savior is what you are to these saan who want you to deliver them from the Kindom. A savior is unreachable, untouchable. For so many years, you were unreachable to me. When you became Esek's novitiate, I thought I cared nothing for you anymore. But you haunted me, too. And now you are not a haunting, you are real, and I—I—"

She grabs their hand. It is an instinct. She thinks for some reason that they'll pull away from her, but instead they grab her back, desperate pressure in their grip. Their hand with its calluses and its shift of bone makes her heart beat fast, and she turns her head to look at them.

"What are you asking me?" she asks, because they are asking something. They want something, some assurance, and she doesn't dare guess.

Their throat moves. They look over at her and she sees a flash of terror, as if it takes them all their nerve to meet her eyes. "When she came to Principes, she put a curse on me. I feel that the curse extended to you... like an oil spill, spreading out. This person that you are, who kills from necessity but does not want it—I feel that it would never have happened, if not for Esek's curse. And I am sorry. I am so sorry, Chono. I have loved you since we were children, and I would give back every plot and every trophy to spare you what has happened. But I cannot. I cannot give you anything. I cannot protect you or save you. What good am I to you? Why do you need me if not for—"

She turns, covering their mouth with her palm. The action has rolled her toward them, putting them face-to-face, and she is breathing hard.

"Don't," she pleads. "Don't."

They look stricken; ashamed. She can feel the heat in their face. She stammers, "I—don't you know? After all this time, you *must* know why I need you. Why do you think I saved your letters, if I don't need you?"

The shame fades, replaced by ferocity. She pulls her hand away. They are breathing hard, too. She is so frightened, her fingers are numb. She feels like a child. She feels like a coward. They lean toward her, and she feels like a god.

The kiss is cautious and awkward. Then the kiss is gentle and firm, a gasp passed between their open mouths, a shudder in one body rolling into the other. Then the kiss is deep and hungry and generous. She feels her hands tangling in the collar of their shirt, pulling them closer, until somehow they are looming over her. She has never liked the pressure of a body on top of hers, not since her kinschool sparring days, but in this moment that weight sends heat unspooling in her belly. Fingertips skim her jaw, slip to grasp the back of her neck, holding her against them. She trembles on an exhale and their tongue darts tentatively into her mouth. A full-body shiver. A feeling of coming apart, of terrifying, joyful rightness—

But when the kiss ends and Chono's eyes flutter open, Six flinches back from her.

"No," they gasp. "Do not look."

She's startled, confused. What did she do? She must have done something, ruined something. Six reaches away from her, and Chono, alarmed, thinks that they're getting off the bed. She grabs their wrist to stop them.

"No. Please, don't. Why...?"

She realizes that they are reaching down toward the bedside table, toward the lamp. They keep their head turned away from her. Their body is hard as marble. "Do not look at her."

Realization hits like an icy wave. She watches them for a few helpless moments, lost before the image of their pain. Their body on top of hers is still warm, and somehow familiar. Tentatively, she lifts her hand. They flinch again, but she cups their face. She doesn't force them to look at her, simply holds them there for long seconds, until at last, slowly, they meet her eyes again. They're trembling. She looks up into their eyes, their beloved, familiar eyes.

"I'm not," she whispers, willing them to believe. "I'm not looking at her."

Their throat bobs. They exhale shakily. Esek's haunting, she realizes. Not just a voice or a figure out the corner of their eye, but a face in the mirror and a disguise so perfectly practiced as to trouble the line between reality and performance. A *lived* haunting.

"Six," she says. She lifts up and whispers it against their ear, over and over. "Six Six Six..."

When she pulls back to look at them again, the fear in the umber eyes has transformed to wonder, the sharp jawline relaxes, and their full mouth opens. She tangles her fingers in thick black braids, and she looks a question at them. Slowly, slowly, they breathe an answer, and she nearly sobs with relief, kissing them again.

Desperation makes them clumsy. Her coat is hard to get off, and Six has an unusual amount of buttons. Chono has had desperate sex before: a scramble for contact, no need to get undressed. But this— there is no question of getting undressed, of undressing each other, piece by piece. It's not as embarrassing as she expects, the nakedness. Six's body is all lean muscle and hot skin against her, making her own skin electric. They drop their mouth to her chest, kissing the bullet scar from *The Risen Wave*, tongue a hot drag over her skin. She gulps and whimpers, hand moving almost unconsciously toward the warmth between their thighs. They grow tense, and her hand stops at once.

"Do you...?" she asks.

Their mouth is swollen from kissing. They blink slowly, almost drunkenly. They admit, "I have not...often...wanted to."

"All right," she whispers. "I won't—"

"But," they interrupt, and reach for her hand. "But, I think, with you..."

The offer thrills her. She has never felt this kind of excitement, this kind of want, putting her hand against them, touching Six there, for the first time. They make a throaty, strangled sound. They are impatient, and put their hand between her thighs, too. The first tentative strokes make her eyes roll back. It will be quick. She's embarrassed by how quick it will be, and she can tell by their sharp, ragged breathing that it will be quick for them, too. It doesn't matter. They'll go again. They'll gorge themselves on this, finally, finally—

"Chono," Six groans, into her mouth, into her lungs, their breath in her body, becoming her blood. "Chono."

"Six," she groans back. "Six Six Six..."

CHAPTER TWENTY-TWO

1665

YEAR OF THE HARVEST

Farren Eyce
The Planet Capamame

I don't like this."

Even to his own ears, Bene sounds like a sullen teenager. It's childish to stand there on the flight deck of *The Gunner*, arms crossed and glowering at Jun as if glowering could change a thing. He reminds himself a bit of Tej right now, only Tej has ceased all sulking. Tej has become quiet and internal, and he sits in the apartment and plays his mandola and tells them whatever they want to know about Ujan. But his change of heart doesn't seem to have woken any love in him, for any of his cousins. When he looks at them, his eyes are lifeless.

Bene is not like Tej. Bene loves Jun, and now she's going to get herself killed.

He says it again. "I don't like this."

From the cockpit, Liis says, "Nobody likes this."

Jun is seated on the couch on the flight deck, legs crossed and lap desk set upon them as she hunches over Liis's prosthetic arm. She has a little soldering gun and she's welding something inside of the elbow. Apparently before coming to Farren Eyce, Liis's arm was an even split between synthetic biomaterials and metallic alloys, but that arm was destroyed in the battle on *The Risen Wave*. The new arm that the Jeveni gave her is all metal and silicone cased in realistic skin. This makes it both stronger and easier to repair. More than once, Bene has watched Jun delightedly peel it open to expose maintenance issues, her dexterous fingers tackling it like it was any circuit board. Even now, she hums a little to herself, as if the task of caring for Liis's arm gives her great pleasure—which is both morbid and weirdly sweet.

Bene gestures at Liis in the cockpit. "See? Even Liis disagrees with this!"

"I didn't say that," answers Liis.

"And even if she had," says Jun absently, "we make a sport out of disagreement."

Liis chuckles, her back turned to them and her remaining arm and hand busy over the controls as she runs a systems check. Outside the cockpit window, the flatlands of Capamame glitter beneath a setting sun, great swaths of red and orange light blanketing the horizon and spilling forward onto the ice, and onto Liis herself, turning her edges to gold. Suddenly she stands, coming onto the deck. She's not even wearing a cloth cap on her stump, the narrow, fleshy taper mid-bicep looking simultaneously fierce and vulnerable.

"May I have my arm back?" she asks, sounding dry and a little annoyed.

"Almost done," Jun singsongs, "you impatient woman."

"You tinkering show-off," Liis retorts.

They seem so relaxed, as if the prospect of heading into danger puts them at ease rather than frightening them. Perhaps because it's such familiar ground? He watches their interaction and feels, not for the first time, like an outsider. There's so much about their lives before Capamame that he doesn't know, both because Liis isn't one to share, and because Jun has clearly tried to protect him from the worst things. They are an impenetrable unit of shared experience and loyalty, and Bene finds himself wondering if his own unit is that solid. In many ways, Masar and Effegen are like Jun and Liis. They have spent their lives committed to a cause that has only become Bene's in the past year. When he betrayed them, perhaps it was not as terrible a blow as it would have been if Effegen or Masar was the traitor. Because in retaining each other, they would have retained what mattered most. Common heritage and history.

Bene asks, "Why can't you do it from here?"

She sighs. "Because it wouldn't work."

He already knew this, but that doesn't make him happy about it. "There are other casters in Ma'kess System who could go. Six themself is an expert caster."

"Six will be busy," says Jun, drawing back her soldering gun and examining the results. She sprays something from a bottle into the joint and begins to rub it down with a cloth. She looks up and winks at Liis. "Wouldn't want you to squeak, right, baby?"

Liis looks reluctantly amused. Bene huffs, and Jun's expression softens apologetically.

"Bene, if there was a better way, I promise I would—"

"How are we supposed to defend the colony without you? Either of you? Do you really think the colonists are up to this? What about your casters? Can they do this without you?"

"Yes," Jun says, with a certainly he's not expecting. "My casters are ready. As ready as anyone in this colony could be. But we are outmatched and outgunned, and the place where I can do the most good isn't in my casting lab anymore. Do you think I'll do anything less than *everything* possible to protect you? To protect Farren Eyce? I've failed enough times at that."

Confused, he frowns at her. "You never failed."

She snorts, returning to the arm. With her thumb, she presses closed the seam of dark skin that she had opened to reveal the crook of the elbow. The seam disappears as the biomaterial adheres to itself. Liis takes a sleeve cap out of her pocket and pulls it over the stump, accepting the arm next. It fixes into place with a suctioning sound, then Liis is flexing the elbow and rotating the arm. Jun watches this process with a critical eye, staunchly ignoring Bene's stare.

He repeats, "You didn't fail. Ujan wasn't your fault. None of this was your fault."

"It was neither of your faults," says Liis, bending her wrist and touching each finger to her thumb. She spreads her fingers wide, the muscle and bone tensing with the stretch. Apparently satisfied, she nods at Jun. "Feels good."

Jun nods back. "Okay. Try not to get it blown off this time." She looks at Bene again, giving him a thoughtful once-over. "What weapons did Liis give you? She won't tell me."

"I swear to the gods you look for trouble," mutters Liis, turning back to the cockpit and lowering herself into the command chair. She pulls up a starscape of Ma'kess System.

Jun tilts her head at Bene. "Well?"

He clears his throat. "A Teron blast rifle. It's a good size for me."

"Where does Liis have you stationed?"

Bene hesitates, wondering how she turned the tables on him so quickly. He glances toward a silent Liis in the cockpit and finally admits, "Level 7." Jun's face darkens. Level 7 is better than being on the surface or stationed with the frontliners on Level 8, but it's still not great. "It's where Effegen will be. Liis tried to put me on Five, but I refused."

"And what other weapons will you have?"

"Umm..." He hesitates, but it's no use keeping it from her, the grimmer side of what they may be facing. "There was a pickax in the armory. The same sort of tool I used in the mines. I'll do much better with it than I would with a knife or something. If things get close up, like that. And remember—I've been in a lot of fights in my life. I'm not helpless."

Her lips press together unhappily. She hasn't argued, he realizes. She hasn't said a word against the danger he's putting himself in. He doesn't think she's avoiding the hypocrisy of it. She's trying to explain to him why she has to go through that gate, why she has to risk her life, and who she's doing it for.

Suddenly she begins to unbuckle the gun belt she's been wearing for the past couple of days, where the Som's Edge pistol that Great Gra gave her sits neatly holstered. When it's off, she holds it all out to him. He widens his eyes at her.

"It won't be any good to me," she explains. "And I don't want to lose it."

Cautiously, he reaches out. Even after spending a few hours last night getting used to the blast rifle, the handgun and its kit feel heavy.

"You have to practice with it. The trigger is heavy."

In Najic, one of the town guardsaan once took him out with a handgun and taught him how to shoot pieces of crockery off a retaining wall behind the village. Hitting crockery at five yards is no great accomplishment, and it won't be anything like trying to shoot armored cloaksaan on the move. That's assuming he lives to exhaust the blast rifle's five thousand rounds.

Jun steps up to him, helping him put on the belt. When it's done she puts her hands on his shoulders and gives them a squeeze. She play-slaps his cheek, affectionate. Her eyes are shiny, her smile forced, but her composure doesn't break.

"I don't want you to go," he whispers, feeling small, feeling like he's back on K-5 station when his Grandmi Keena hurried him into a different shuttle from the one taking Luja and Tenje. "I'm afraid if you go, I'll never see you again."

"Ah." Jun holds up a finger. "But you and me, Bene. We traveled across the Black Ocean to find each other again. We survived Esek

Nightfoot herself. I think, if Great Gra was here, he would be proud of us. He'd be proud of you."

Bene's eyes burn, the thought of his great-grandfather gripping his heart with a fist of grief. They were all so young when it happened. There are children even younger in Farren Eyce, hiding in the lower levels, not understanding what is going on but knowing, as Bene did in the family shop that day, that it's bad bad bad...

"So, this is our pact," Jun says, gripping his shoulders again. "I'll trust you to survive, and you trust me to do the same. I know it's not always...easy to trust me, but..."

She trails off. That word again. "Easy?" he repeats. "Jun...I trust you with my whole heart."

To his confusion, her eyes widen. She blinks rapidly. This time there is no mistaking the sheen of tears, some combination of surprise and relief that he never would have expected. How can she not know? She is his big cousin. He's admired her for as long as he has memories, and in all the years they were apart, nothing has ever damaged his trust.

Suddenly, the hatch door slides up. Jun rubs her eyes and steps around him to see the newcomers: Effegen followed by a surgeon.

Without giving anyone a chance to speak, the surgeon grumbles, "I don't like this."

Bene almost laughs, but he's afraid of what it would sound like. Effegen catches his eye, and he sees understanding there, and compassion.

"There's no point in me going down to the hospital and coming back up when I can recover in the Black. What's the difference being unconscious down there versus up here? Three hours should be long enough for me to get my feet under me again."

The surgeon scowls, shifting his bag from one hand to another. "Three hours if everything goes all right. And it's not as if I have any experience with this kind of—"

"Doctor," Effegen interrupts. "We appreciate your concerns. But there is no more time."

This at least stops him arguing. Bene and Effegen step back as the activity begins, Jun returning to her perch on the couch and Liis coming back from the cockpit as the surgeon lays out his tools on a small table. As Bene watches, Liis drops into a crouch before Jun, fit into the space between her knees. They smile tightly at each other. Bene swallows, feeling the soft pressure of Effegen's fingertips against his. He grabs on to them.

The doctor brandishes a pneumatic injector. Jun tilts her head to one side. There's already a smooth patch where she shaved, and Liis reaches up with an alcohol wipe to clean the area, just as Jun cleaned her arm minutes ago.

"Are you ready?" the surgeon demands.

Jun grimaces. Liis, hands gripping Jun's knees, says lowly, "Just pretend I'm biting you."

Jun rolls her eyes. "Not the time, dear." She looks over at Bene. He watches the needle bite into her, sees her flinch. She whispers, "See you after."

Bene swallows hard. "See you after."

CHAPTER TWENTY-THREE

1665

YEAR OF THE HARVEST

The Wren's Jaw
Teros System

After days of waiting, planning, *seething* for this, Masar's war begins very quickly.

"Three Kindom warfalcons incoming. Eighteen minutes, tops. They're scrambling their fighter crows."

He stands on the bridge of *The Wren's Jaw* watching the massive view screen light up with the distant figures of Cloaksaan falcons. He privately accesses a cast view on the airfields of Capamame, the camera staring straight up at the jump gate, which glows in orbit. Today is the

Feast of Sajeven's Dear Friend. The day that Yorus Inye will return. Already two warwhales have drawn close to the Kator gate, obviously preparing to jump to Capamame. Or they had been, until Regal Hejar Paiye's fleet plowed into them. Masar is not in Kator System. He is not with Hejar Paiye, not preparing to attack the ships that threaten Farren Eyce. He prays to Sajeven that the Teron offensive will make it through the gate to Capamame and he'll have a chance to protect his people. Surely Sajeven, ceaseless kind, will not abandon them now?

Captain Vikar Wren, focused on his own measure of troublemaking, says, "Excellent. How's the present we left them?"

"We got 'em good," his crewsaan boasts. "Zemit's forces have set the shipyards on fire. Mix Catty and her kittens have taken birds from Lo-Meek, Khenphasi, and Aniso. Graisa the Honor just bombed the shit out of the Kindom headquarters on Bei continent. Probably took out a thousand of them, mostly guardsaan."

Yantikye blurts a laugh. "That's my girl. What a way to begin!"

What a way to begin, Masar thinks, his stomach tight with anxiety. Layez, Qlios, and Siel are among Zemit's fighters. They'll be in the thick of combat. He focuses on the view of Teros space, the Kindom warbirds sweeping closer. *Yes*, he thinks, full of hatred. *Come closer. Show me your throat.* Captain Wren crosses his arms over his broad chest. His hair is freshly braided and clipped with red bells; the tattoos on his face and arms are oiled to a shine. He is the very picture of a pirate king. And though pirate kings don't generally go up against whole Kindom fleets, he looks hungry and eager. A year ago, he and his crew were among the Braems who sacked Verdant, and Masar suspects he wants that glory again.

"What's the report on our other friends?" he asks.

Different crewsaan answer one after another.

"Hejar Paiye is fully engaged with the Kindom fleet. Warcrows and kites are all over her. The warwhales haven't jumped yet, but Paiye says it could happen any moment."

Another pirate says, "Melosi the Grave has invaded Nikata Leen while Oninye provides air support. They're on the charge toward

Praetima. No one saw them coming, but those city gates are gonna be murder. Still looks like most of the Secretaries are under guard in Nikapraev. They might welcome us, if we get through their captors."

"What about the civilians in Praetima?" Masar asks.

"If they took advice, they're hunkering down," Yantikye says.

Captain Wren reclaims control of the conversation. "And where's Ashway?"

"Decimating Kriistura continent ground troops," a pirate says. "The Moonbacks haven't engaged yet—Giran and Karix are still fighting it out somewhere."

Wren scoffs. "So, Revel hasn't woken up yet? Som's ass, how long does it take to come out of a coma? The surgeon said he'd live!"

"It doesn't matter," Masar says. "Giran won't stand down. Whatever Karix is doing, the longer she can keep him distracted, the better."

Wren gives a sharp nod. "What's happening in Teveet and Riin Kala?"

The second of pause before they get an answer seems interminable. The Ma'kessn forces born out of Riin Kala and Teveet are the largest on the ground. But many of them followed Goodrite and Siltmire, and didn't take well to the execution of their leaders. They're as likely to turn on the quorum as play their part in the attack.

The fifth pirate says, "They've engaged with the Cloaksaan head-quarters in both cities." More than one saan on the bridge exhales, though Masar thinks this is probably just a temporary détente, and if any of them survive the day, Goodrite's and Siltmire's fighters will have more to say about what happened. "The battle is on to reach Riin Cosas. Heavy fortifications around the temple, but we think they're outmatched."

Wren looks satisfied, turning his bright blue eyes on Masar. His gaze flits toward the Braemish tattoos still decorating Masar's face, a remnant of his days undercover with the pirates. A little smile curves Wren's mouth, not contemptuous but pleased.

"And what about your saan, kid?"

Masar sends out a cast and gets the equivalent of a rude gesture cast back at him. "Jun is ready to jump. But we need as much Kindom attention diverted from Jeve as possible."

Someone on navigation pipes up, "We're twelve minutes out from engagement. Catty is still blowing shit up on the surface."

Wren makes an exasperated noise, casting out with a sweep of his arm. Mix Catty appears on cast, glowing with pleasure.

"Cap, this ship is a dream!" She lovingly runs her hands over the helm of her brand-new Kindom warkite. She has thirty more ships in her wake, all battle-fit. "I'm gonna rename her. What do you think of this? *The Cat's Flint*. Sounds good, right? Gonna light up the Black with this thing!"

"Stop fucking around in the atmosphere and fall into position. We've got a fleet of pissed-off cloaks incoming."

"Already on my way. Damn, this is gonna be fun."

Fun, Masar thinks, watching the Kindom falcons get closer.

One of the crew calls out, "Paiye reports six new falcons have launched from Kator. They're on her starboard side and they're cutting off any retreat."

Wren growls, "Cast her."

Within moments, Hejar Paiye appears. The view rocks hard, officers behind her straining to stay on their feet as Hejar's ship, *The Bright Many*, takes fire. Yet she looks remarkably calm, as tall and majestic as her mother.

"We can stand these extra falcons," she says by way of greeting.

"My tech says they've got over a hundred warkites between the six of them," says Wren.

"They mean to drive us away from the gate," she answers.

"No shit," Yantikye says.

"We can still take at least one of the warwhales," says Hejar confidently, as the view rocks again. She grabs the helm and manages to seem cool about it. Someone on her bridge calls out a warning about hull damage. The Regal Paiye doesn't flinch, telling her officers, "All ships, target the kites surrounding the first whale. It's nearer the gate."

On the bridge of *The Wren's Jaw*, a pirate announces, "Nine minutes till contact. Catty is four minutes out."

One of Paiye's officers shouts, "They're flanking us!"

Paiye's gaze flicks aside for a moment. Her ship takes another hit, and this time her body rolls with the impact, though she doesn't lose her grip.

"Regal Paiye, we can't afford for you to get blown up," Masar warns.

She sniffs. "My ancillaries are moving into position. They'll shield me from further attack. Be advised, I've lost three ships. The sooner you can take the Teros gate, the better."

Masar feels a ghost sensation of his prosthetic eye glitching, but there is no prosthetic eye anymore. Just the complex web of the quorum's multipronged attack, temporarily overwhelming him. Stop the warwhales from jumping to Farren Eyce. Draw Kess's forces away from Jeve by decimating Kindom targets across the Black. Seize control of Nikapraev and the remaining Secretaries. Seize control of Riin Cosas and the high-ranking clerics. Take the Teros gate and jump reinforcements to Farren Eyce, to Paiye and Ashway. Clear Jun's way to the Silver Keep. And get their secret weapon onto the moon.

Too many variables. Too many ways for things to go wrong. The pirate on navigation says, "Seven minutes out."

Hejar Paiye makes a sound that's half grunt, half chuckle. She announces, "Kess is demanding an audience with Ashway and me. Would you care to join us?"

Wren laughs. "Kata's tit, would I!"

Masar says, "I want Effegen ten Crost on as well."

Hejar nods approvingly. "Do it."

In just a few moments the view splits into panels. Masar feasts on the sight of Effegen, her back straight and chin tipped up. She is not wearing her ceremonial robes, but a close-fitting tunic, and her luxurious hair has been wound into a knot on the back of her head, blue ribbons woven through the locks. Her eyes are the green of moss and new life, and from the outer corner of each there are streaks of blue powder. The ribbon and the cosmetics are a marker of this particular Feast Day, of Capamame, the dear friend. She looks like a warrior queen.

When Seti Kess appears, he seems momentarily stymied. His sharp gaze cuts through each of them. After a moment he proffers a wooden smile.

"Regal Paiye. General Ashway. Sa Crost. And—is it Masar Hawks? What an auspicious gathering. And who are *you*, Sa?"

This is contemptuously directed at Vikar Wren, who grins back with the cockiness of all pirates in their element.

"I'm the saan who's about to fuck up your cloaks."

Kess curls back his scarred lip. Masar notices a figure behind him, small and rigid. It's Riiniana Nightfoot. The pale girl looks like a servant at the elbow of her master, all humility.

Hejar must notice her, too, for she says, "Hello, Riiniana. I was pleased to learn that you are safe."

Riiniana answers demurely, "I wish *you* were safe, Regal. I assume that the rebels who murdered your mother have taken your ship and are forcing you to act against your best interests."

Hejar, who Masar sees well enough is not a humorous person, nonetheless gives a little smile of amusement. "I don't think I'm the hostage here, Riin Matri."

The use of the title, the conferring on Riiniana of the Nightfoot matriarchy, makes the girl flinch. Or maybe it's the assertion of her hostage status. Either way, her expression runs a brief gamut of shame, anger, pride—and defiance. She is younger than anyone in this game of tiles, but she is as smart and calculating as the best of them.

"Then it's true," says Seti Kess to Hejar. "You are barely regal for a day and you're on your knees for a consortium of disorganized, ungodly rebels?"

"Let's you and I not speak of godliness," says Hejar dryly.

"And you, Sa Crost"—Kess looks at Effegen—"I had thought that we were dealing with each other peaceably. Yorus Inye has described you as so very coolheaded."

"My people have considered your offer. Twelve percent wish to accept."

The number had been 17 percent a couple of days ago, but some new spirit of defiance has seized thousands more of them, dropping the number of colonists who escaped to *The Brute Crane* with Fonu and Gaeda. Fear and pride gather in Masar's chest.

Kess narrows his eyes. "That is … insufficient."

"Nevertheless, I will not require any citizen of Farren Eyce to labor in the sevite trade against their will."

A notification pings in Masar's ocular, and he sees by the shift of the bodies around him and on cast that they are receiving the same notification: The Cloaksaan headquarters of Riin Kala has been flattened by a missile assist from Ashway's forces. Kess bares his teeth in a grimacing grin.

General Ashway declares, "We won't play games with you, Sa. Resign your position as First Cloak. My allies and I will undertake to rebuild the Kindom with new First Hands, and we will revitalize the sevite trade without kidnapping and enslaving the Jeveni of Capamame."

Kess barks a hard, mechanical laugh. He turns toward Riiniana, mutters something, and with a swallow she darts away.

Hejar says, "We equal you in numbers. If you don't stand down, we will be merciless."

Kess laughs again. Then the laugh cuts off. He stares at them for so long that Masar begins to feel unnerved. There is something in his expression—the shadow of Som, but Som without purpose, without measure. The devouring, tireless hunger, without temperance.

"Where is Cleric Chono?" Kess asks.

No one answers him. He doesn't seem to care.

"And Jun Ironway." He addresses Masar. "You are her old friend, aren't you, Sa? Where is Jun Ironway?"

Masar wants to spit at him.

"Give them this message from me, wherever they are. I am sending my warbirds to Pippashap, which loves Chono so much. I'm sending my warbirds to K-5, where Jun Ironway was born. As for you, Sa Crost … I am sending my warbirds to the sevite labor camp, where your five thousand Jeveni sit helpless." Masar's jaw tenses harder and harder, molars compressing on one another. Kess goes on, cool and menacing. "How many saan are there, on Pippashap and K-5 combined? A hundred thousand? More? Certainly more than the population of Farren Eyce. And unlike Farren Eyce, they have nothing I want, nothing worth saving. As for the five thousand, I don't need them, either, as I'll soon have all you Jeveni in my factories. So tell Chono and Jun Ironway that I am going to destroy Pippashap and K-5. There will be no survivors. I will kill every Quietan in that city, and every saan on that station. I will kill every Jeveni I can find. And when all this is done, and I have Chono and Ironway and Esek Nightfoot, I'm going to strap their bodies to the mast of my ship. And all your bodies, too."

No one responds to the speech, though Masar sees from the corner of his eye that Yantikye has moved away, speaking rapidly to someone on his private cast. Kess gives them an unsettling, inhuman smile, and disappears.

Hejar orders her officers, "Notify *The Many Shadows*. Tell Oninye to break off and move to defend K-5."

Yantikye comes back, looking more serious than Masar has ever seen him. "I've contacted Pippashap. Their leaders will order any ships that can to disengage and dive."

"They better move fast," Vikar Wren says.

"Do you have *anyone* defending Quietus?" Effegen asks.

"The Endless Sea has always been our best defense," Yantikye retorts.

A Katish officer tells Hejar, "Sa, *The Many Shadows* was meant to join us after securing Melosi's route into Praetima. We can't take the Kator gate without Oninye's reinforcements."

Hejar says, "I won't abandon thousands of stationers. Oninye is closest to K-5. Tell her to go!"

"Kindom fighters are three minutes out," another pirate warns.

Vikar Wren exclaims, "We can't defend every homestead in the Treble! This is the bargain you make when you go to war!"

Effegen interjects sharply. "And my people on Ma'kess?"

Everyone hesitates. Everyone knows that the five thousand Jeveni are imprisoned in Nightfoot territory. Ashway says to someone off-screen, "Get me Karix Moonback. She has a fleet of warbirds, and they can reach the camp sooner than the cloaksaan."

Though not sooner than Riiniana's forces, if Kess orders her to slaughter the prisoners. And not if Karix, battling Giran, refuses to thin her forces for the Jeveni.

Suddenly, two dozen warships zip past them, rushing to the front of the line: Mix Catty and her captured fleet. Masar doesn't even have a chance to be glad when Hejar Paiye says, "One of the warwhales is jumping. We can't get there in time."

"I must see to my people," Effegen says. Her eyes flash toward Masar. This may be the last moment. This may be the last time—

"May all your gods protect you," she says, and disappears.

Masar casts out to Jun, shouting the words, "Jump! Jump *now!*"

CHAPTER TWENTY-FOUR

1665

YEAR OF THE HARVEST

Farren Eyce
The Planet Capamame

The warwhale comes through the gate like a grotesque birth, mammoth and monstrous as it tips toward the atmosphere of Capamame. Within moments its many bay doors open, disgorging the black darting shapes of the warcrows backlit by the waning light of the moons. Effegen stands beneath the holo dome on the surface of Capamame, aware of the colonists around her, and those who have taken position outside the dome, operating the missile launchers that Drae sen Briit bought for them so many decades ago.

But in this moment, Effegen's attention is locked on the people off world.

Listening in on comm, she hears *The Brute Crane* transmit its immediate surrender. As a phalanx of warcrows moves toward it, she holds her breath in terror and prayer. Twelve percent of the colonists are on that ship, far fewer than the forty percent Kess wants, and she saw the promise of revenge in his face just minutes ago. Will he revenge himself on *The Brute Crane* as he intends to revenge himself on the five thousand in the sevite labor camp?

"Sajeven," she whispers, "beloved, come here to us and create a path for our hope. Dissolve our weariness and shine a light to live by, we entreat you."

Nearby, one of the recently promoted collectors shouts across the frigid landing field. "Don't lose your nerve! Watch your instruments. They're well out of range."

Effegen hears the rasp in her own voice. "Sajeven, beloved, come here to us and create a path for our hope."

"Keep the route of retreat clear!" another collector hollers. "Remember, we're just bloodying noses."

Her eyes burn from not blinking. *The Brute Crane* transmits its surrender again, the crows zipping closer, each one like the flash of a bloodletter.

"Dissolve our weariness and shine a light to live by, we entreat you. Sajeven, beloved, come here to us and create a path for our hope."

Dozens more warbirds bank toward the surface of the planet, and her heart squeezes.

Someone comes alongside her. "My Star, you should go below ground now. We're set to engage in the next ten minutes."

Effegen feels the icy wind in her clothes, needles pricking her neck and the base of her skull. She feels the weight of the handgun at her hip—ridiculous, unnecessary, but how can she ask any of them to wield weapons if she will not?

"My Star, I insist."

Suddenly Yorus Inye's voice fills the bridge of *The Brute Crane*.

"Do not make any movements or alter your position. At our earliest opportunity, we will escort you through the gate to Ma'kess System. If we see any sign that you're arming your defense system, you will be fired on."

Effegen's heart thunders. Her hands at her sides are trembling, so she clasps them to control the movement, prays none of her people can see it, or see the bloodless relief on her face. Now, for the first time, she turns to look at the collector to her right. She startles, even though she knew it would be him.

"Dom..."

Dom ben Dane, recently imprisoned for collaborating with the avatar, for killing his kin collectors, for betraying the Jeveni in the worst way, looks at her solemnly. Blue powder streaks from the corners of his eyes.

"We are ready here, my Star. Go below. The forces on Level 7 are waiting for you."

Effegen keeps looking at him. There were some who did not want him released. They said he didn't belong with them. He was a traitor. But his treason was on behalf of his wife, whom he loved. And Kereth is dead now. He has no treason left in him, only the burning rage of grief and regret. He is the most senior collector in the colony. And Masar and Liis are not here.

Dom looks back at her with the expression of one who expects to be distrusted, to be scorned, but who will do his duty anyway. When she raises her hand, he actually flinches, but she presses her palm against his chest.

"By Sajeven's own mercy," she whispers, "I bless you." She feels his heart pounding under her hand; his throat bobs with a startled swallow. "I bless you, by every god in the stars. Do not fail me, Dom. Swear it."

His voice comes out cracked and fierce. "I swear it."

She nods once, and turns away, heading back toward the atrium that leads into Farren Eyce. On either side of her, the Jeveni have created a battleground of armaments and barriers. If the Cloaksaan get through the holo shield (and they will certainly get through the holo shield) there will be a payload of violence awaiting them.

In the atrium, four sentries are waiting for her. She whispers their names to herself. They flank her as she approaches the elevator bay, as she steps inside, as she sinks past Level 10, and 9, and 8. She engages a grid of views on her ocular, multiple cameras on the upper levels with perfect shots of the staircase and the elevator. Blinking fast, she acclimates to the difficult task of watching the world around her and watching the grid views at the same time. She thinks of Masar, his prosthetic eye gone, his advantages diminished, and he is so far away from her.

The elevator doors open. Tomesk and Hyre are waiting for her.

"Effegen," Hyre says. "Everyone is in position. The lower levels are locked down."

Tomesk mutters, "They'll be buried alive if the Kindom carpet-bombs us again."

"If you have faith in nothing else, my Tree," Effegen murmurs, "have faith that the Kindom will always act in the best interests of its greed."

He snorts with dark humor. She looks around herself and takes a few moments to reassess the geography of their strange battleground. Level 7 is residential, but like every level it has an enormous commons. At the center of the commons is an open-air circle, like a well dug through the middle of the colony, down which spirals the central staircase of Farren Eyce. Effegen exits the elevator car, moving toward the staircase. She looks over the high barrier, straight down to the lower levels, and up toward the surface. The Cloaksaan will be at a disadvantage, with so few entry and exit points. But Farren Eyce is at a disadvantage, too. There is nowhere to run.

"Will you finally tell us whether Seti Kess knows the layout of our colony?" Effegen recalls herself asking, just last night, when it was already too late.

Ujan had given up her bravado at some point in the last few days. Her face was thinner than ever, almost corpse-like. The wrist she had broken trying to attack her brother was set with splints and wrapped in regenerative bandages. Her eyes were red-rimmed, not with tears but with hatred and sleeplessness. Effegen, seeing that she would not answer, exhaled. In some other room, through some other view, Jun and Bene watched.

"We have to move you. The upper levels won't be safe."

"Leave me here," Ujan said, her voice an animal rasp, like the sound of claws dragging over concrete in the dark. "Seti will find me in the prison."

"We can't leave you here. You can go willingly, or we'll sedate you."

"You've taken my cast access. You've gouged my eyes out. I'd rather die than accept your pathetic version of protection."

"And yet, you will not die. Not without me trying to save you."

"I'll hate you till I die. I'll hate you afterward. My ghost will come after you."

Effegen, who had thought herself beyond the petty behavior of this diminished girl, cringed at the words, as if they were not a threat or an insult, but a curse cast upon her. When the sentries came in, Ujan fought. It took three of them to hold her down, and a fourth to inject her with the sedative. As she moved past Effegen on a float stretcher, Effegen felt an evil fury in herself. She imagined telling her sentries to throw Ujan's body over the side of the great staircase—just as Dom ben Dane had thrown the collector Uskel over. A helpless death.

Transported forward in time, Effegen hears Hyre speaking. "My Star, we must go."

Rallying herself, Effegen nods. She surveys the commons again. The colonists have created fortifications using construction equipment and furniture. From behind these shields, they'll mount their assault on the invading cloaks, and seek cover in turn. Levels 6 and 5 are similarly transformed, with the Market District having the particular advantage of its shop fronts and construction zones.

All around her, saan stand in position. Streaks of blue powder decorate the faces near and far.

"Perhaps you'd like to say something to them," Hyre whispers.

Effegen swallows. She looks out at the crowd. How she wishes Liis was here, or Masar, or Nikkelo. Gods, Nikkelo! Her old friend, dead these many months. A sudden debilitating terror flows over her, a weight of doubt that begins to crush her, punching the air out of her lungs, compressing her heart till she fears she will crumple.

In her memory, Nikkelo says, "Look, the Cloaksaan are actually pretty simple. They're trained to be assassins first, and an assassin is a solitary creature. They have no family. They slip in and out of sight with only their own glory to consider. It's that self-interest that makes them weak. But we—our glory is in each other. That's why the Jeveni will always survive. That's why our office, yours and mine, is holy."

She recalls the white crest in Nikkelo's dark hair, and the startling blueness of his eyes. The crinkles when he smiled. Even at the end of his life, he was not afraid. He was full of glory.

From the surface of Capamame, Dom ben Dane sends her a comm. "The crows are fanning out. We engage in two minutes."

Another memory comes to Effegen. Liis Konye, just this morning, looking at her with that stern but confident gravity.

"You're the former cloak, Liis," Effegen had whispered. "Can we beat them?"

"No," Liis said, with her typical simplicity, and it put a knife through Effegen's heart. "But you can slow them down." And she leaned a little closer, like a child telling a secret. "Shock them. Disorganize them. Kill as many as you can. Help will come."

Effegen looks out over her people, every one of them a bulwark against the Brutal Hand.

"Am I not your sword and shield?" Masar asked her, and they both knew the answer.

She casts her voice out over the colony, and despite everything, it does not break.

"To all the people of Farren Eyce. If you have come to fight, I bless you. If you are sheltering from harm, I bless you. If you are afraid, I bless you. If you are Jeveni, I bless you, and if you are not Jeveni, nor are you a stranger, and I bless you. Across the Treble, brave saan are risking their lives to topple a tyrant. We are among mighty company, and we are the ones who have survived everything, who will survive anything, even this. I swear to you, whatever happens, I will not leave you. I will stand by you. You are my kin."

In her aural link, she hears Dom again. "Warcrows engaging. Missiles locked on targets. Firing in five...four..."

She swallows, and her mouth is dry. She is afraid.

"Three...two..."

She is the Star.

"Fire!"

I doubt you'll be able to easily infiltrate the casting network. Find Jun Ironway as quickly as possible and use her to disarm them entirely. As far as I'm concerned, she's a more significant target now than even Effegen ten Crost. Do not lose her.

message from First Cloak Seti Kess to Yorus Inye.
Dated 1665, Year of the Harvest.

CHAPTER TWENTY-FIVE

1665

YEAR OF THE HARVEST

The Gunner
Orbiting Jeve

Jun gets one last glimpse of Capamame. One last glimpse of *The Brute Crane* waiting in orbit without defenses, and a final scan of the surface, where Farren Eyce's dome glows with life. And one last thought for her beloved, broken cousins. Then she is soaring through the gate (clenched teeth, stomach heaving toward her throat, bones rattling, and vision temporarily going dim) and, less than two minutes later, bursting into Jeve's orbit like a stone flung from a slingshot. The shock of the jump leaves her gulping for breath. She drops her head back against her seat, exhilaration and terror mixing a bright cocktail in her chest. The spot behind her ear throbs.

"Haven't done that in a while," she chokes out.

Liis at the helm smiles dryly. "Just like old times."

Jun rolls her eyes and brings up an aerial view of Jeve and a wider view of its orbit. The moon is a dark, shadowed curve beneath them. There are no visible Kindom ships, no sign of life on the surface, but Jun knows better. She hurls down her cast like a claw raking through the soil. Like buried treasure, it glints into view: an invisible holo shield of stunning strength, thick as a mountain and just as hard. Beneath the crust of the moon, there appears a structure matching Ujan's blueprints.

She casts out again, this time reaching through the Black and through the gates toward a blazing island on Teros. Curling white flames reach back, and as the Ar'tec casters sync to her, she feels the hot piercing burn of them like a power surge. She could not find Ujan's secrets alone. She cannot rebuild the gate key alone. She cannot take the Silver Keep alone—and so she will not be alone.

The Minkat appears on view, its odd face somehow conveying pleasure.

"Excellently done, oh, what a Sunstep you are! It's quite pretty, nah?"

Jun asks, "How long do you think it would take you to destroy it entirely?"

The Minkat *hmms*. "Oh, a thing like that? And all of us together drilling like miners? Days, maybe."

Jun nods, for she estimated the same. But they don't have days.

Jun reaches for the blueprints again. She spreads them out in her mind, mapping the images to the geography beneath, relying now on Ujan's intelligence. Ujan's accuracy. But there is a structure that isn't on Ujan's blueprints. A structure Jun must find. She casts out again, scouring the moon. When she finds it, her heart skips. There—still under the cover of the holo shield, but outside the boundaries of the Keep. A shaft driven down into the rock. Something more important now than any cast program Jun could wield.

This time when the Minkat speaks, its voice is eager, like the cat prowling in the jungle. "Get us in. My, but we are hungry!"

Half-distracted by her casts, Jun mutters, "Where the fuck are they?"

She would have sworn there'd be Kindom birds all over them by now. Maybe they still want to maintain their illusion that the moon is empty?

Liis, apparently as impatient for action as Jun is, says, "Hold on." She begins to transmit a flashing red emergency signal, the same as hollering into the Black, wailing for help.

The Minkat says, "Excellent," and disappears, but Jun can feel those Ar'tec casters. Prowling.

She's prowling, too. Prowling and searching for the exact right spot.

With a snap, five Kindom warcrows appear from nowhere. Though the time it took them to arrive was irritating enough, the manner of their appearance makes Jun's nostrils flare. Hooded. The assholes were Hooded, probably watching *The Gunner* the whole time to see what it would do. She's going to *kill* Six when she sees them next.

A comm fills *The Gunner*'s cockpit.

"You have entered a restricted zone. Identify yourselves and your origins immediately."

"Make it sound good, sweetheart," Liis says.

"Please!" Jun bleats. "Hold your fire! I'm from Capamame! I'm surrendering to the Kindom. I'll work the sevite factories!"

After several moments, the voice on comm demands, "Why are you in Jeve's orbit?"

"It was a bad jump!" Jun cries with mock panic. "I've never done this before!"

Liis looks like she's about to laugh, which would be very inappropriate.

"Transfer the names and number of your passengers," the voice says.

The warcrows have circled them now, drawing steadily closer, tightening the noose. Jun affectionately pats the control panel in front of her, remarking off comm, "Been awhile since she was in the Black. How's our girl handling?"

Liis smirks, her hands light on the controls. "Just like I remember."

The cloak's voice returns, icier now. "We have identified your ship as one associated with the former cloaksaan Liis Konye and the criminal caster Jun Ironway."

"That's a mistake!" Jun insists. "I'm a factory worker! It's the only ship I could find."

"Transfer your identifications!"

"Ready when you are," Liis says.

Jun holds off long enough to feel satisfied by the drama of it, then, still aping helplessness, she says, "Sorry! Sorry. Just one crew! The name is sen Briit. Drae sen Briit."

A few moments pass, followed by a skeptical reply. "Repeat, *Gunner?*"

Liis's body shifts forward.

"Yeah," Jun says. "Sorry, bad comms. That's Drae sen Go Fuck Yourself. Go fuck yourself, please. Thanks." And then, to Liis, "Punch it."

Liis does. And they're a stone in a slingshot again, *The Gunner*'s thrust propelling them through a gap in the warcrows. Slammed back in their seats, Jun and Liis exchange a quick look.

"We better be right about this," Jun says as they hurtle toward the surface.

"We are," Liis grits out, something flaming in her eyes, like purpose, like revenge. "I've waited long enough."

The warcrows come about with the agility of dancers spinning on the tips of their toes. The lead cloaksaan shouts warnings, commanding them to desist, threatening to shoot them out of the Black. Jun engages the Hood, but only for about five seconds, returning to visibility and repeating the pattern two, three times, like a power fluctuation. Teasing the Brutal Hands with the proof of who she is, with the possibility of their prize.

"Jun Ironway. Your Hood is obviously malfunctioning. Stand down and submit to be boarded."

The Gunner blasts through the moon's thin exosphere, hurtling toward the surface and the ruins of Farren Ki, a rocky outcrop of collapsed buildings and craters, the one-time capital of the Jeveni reduced to rubble—but domed by the Brutal Hand's powerful, impenetrable shield. If they try to fly into it, their ship will crumple and break apart. Good thing they're not trying to fly into it.

The warcrows zip after them but don't fire, and Jun feels cockily pleased by her own renown. Kess won't want her blasted out of the Black if instead he can take her prisoner. And he'll think her helpless, if he can't find Liis.

"You know where you're going when we land?" Jun asks, feeling the first anxiety at the prospect of their separation.

"They'll interrogate you," Liis says. "Just work fast, before they can move on to torture."

"Believe me, I have no desire to be tortured. Don't you get tortured, either."

Jun watches the surface of the moon draw closer. Their landing-approach coordinates will be obvious now. As soon as *The Gunner* touches down, cloaksaan will emerge from underground like snakes from their burrows. She'll be captured. And if the Godfire is just, marched straight into the Silver Keep.

1665

YEAR OF THE HARVEST

Farren Eyce
The Planet Capamame

It takes the Cloaksaan ten minutes to decimate the forces on the surface of Capamame.

Effegen watches the many screens across her ocular as it happens, sees with pride how her fighters pick a dozen warbirds out of the atmosphere, wielding Drae sen Briit's arsenal—but it is not enough. The Kindom ships take out the rocket and mortar launchers on the surface with sniper precision. Jeveni shuttles hit them back with a barrage of scythe missiles, but return missiles turn the landing field into craters.

Farren Eyce feels it, a low vibration through the colony's structure. Effegen watches the shuttles and launch pads exploding in deafening cracks, the black smoke flooding the sky. Her eyes cut toward the warwhale, which has glided past the abandoned *Drae's Hope* to enter Capamame's orbit. Liis said that a single warwhale could transport two hundred warcrows. If more warwhales come—

"Now," Tomesk says, startling her from her reverie. "We have to do it now."

Effegen sends the command. Suddenly the remaining Jeveni shuttles lift off the ground, sprinting up into the swarm of warbirds. The Kindom don't immediately round on them, holding their fire as if confused and contemptuous of this frontal assault from such woefully outmatched vessels. Seconds later there are figures in the air, Jeveni pilots bailing out as their ships become autopilot missiles, hurtling into the warbirds, an explosion of midair collisions.

"My Star." A voice in her aural link grabs her attention away from the fight. It's the caster that Jun left in charge of the labs, a woman called Maiye. She's a sixty-year-old Katishsaan who used to run the cast system for a hotel conglomerate. Now she's tasked with holding back the warwhale casters trying to hack their systems and disable their protective dome. What a change of pace. "They're making ground on the dome," Maiye says. "We can hold them off for about five more minutes, I think."

"Good work," Effegen says, hoping praise will do more good than questions.

The Jeveni pilots who escaped their shuttles are reaching the surface now, buoyed by their emergency chutes. But they aren't the only ones. At least thirty cloaksaan abandoned their own crows, and they fall like black rain alongside the debris. The surface missile launchers are all gone. Eighty percent of the Jeveni shuttles are gone. Warbirds coast onto the surface, landing gear sinking into the ice like talons. Within moments their ranks pour out onto the snow-packed surface already turned black from blast burns. Inside the dome, hundreds of ground troops hold position behind their barricades.

But the Jeveni pilots are not so lucky. Effegen watches in despair as the Cloaksaan pick them off one by one, these brave, brave saan who knew what fighting outside the dome would mean for them.

Standing beside her, Hyre and Tomesk look pale and livid by turns, while the faces of the many saan behind them run the gamut from terror to fury to determination. Effegen feels how insufficient she is, to encourage them. If Liis Konye was here, they would take heart from her. Effegen is no warrior. Effegen is just—

Maiye's voice suddenly pierces her ears. "My Star, we can't hold them! They have it! They're—"

The dome above Farren Eyce vanishes like vapor.

On the surface, Dom ben Dane bellows, "Hold your ground! Hold your ground!"

There are 162 fighters left on the surface, Effegen's ocular informs her. Eighty remaining warcrows. That's hundreds of cloaks. Her eyes burn as she tries to see everything, to bear witness. Even the best marksaan among the Jeveni, even the most well-trained collectors, are no match for the approaching wave. Yet how ferociously they try! Mortar fire splits the air. Mines explode amid the invading cloaks. The sounds, the cacophony of gunfire and explosions, of screaming and shouting, deafens Effegen. She realizes that panic is reaching for her, terrible and immobilizing, her fingers going numb, her skin frosting with ice as she watches the Jeveni dwindle, driven back from their shelters, hunted into retreat by helmeted inhuman Quiet Ones.

Remember, Liis Konye says in her thoughts. *We don't want to hold them back. Not forever. We need to draw them in, my Star.*

Her head clears. With a sharp intake of breath, she shouts over cast, "Retreat! Fall back to lower levels, *now!*"

"Retreat!" thunders Dom, the other command saan echoing him. "Retreat!"

They cover one another in waves, laying down fire as they fall back ten at a time into the atrium. The elevator cars are immobilized at the bottom of the colony. The retreating Jeveni take the stairs, sprinting down into the lower levels. Dozens upon dozens of them, bypassing

Levels 10 and 9, the abandoned farms, the cleared-out animal pens, before finally they enter the ghost town of the government district on Eight.

Aboveground, the cloaksaan advance, picking off the sentries who provide cover to their kin. As Effegen watches, Dom hustles the last of these behind him, hefts a rocket rifle, and stands in the atrium doorway, unloading blast after blast upon the encroaching cloaks. They scatter before the barrage. The last of the ground troops reach Level 8. In the wake of their retreat, razor wire springs into place, tangled coils creating a lethal snare on the stairs. Dom holds position, unleashing his revenge, as terrible as Som, as righteous as the Godfire—

A sniper bullet drops him where he stands. The suddenness of it staggers Effegen, as if she too has been shot. Dom is standing, and then Dom is dead. Moments later, cloaksaan breach the doors, stepping over and trampling his body as they enter the atrium.

Hyre whispers, "May the barren flourish."

"May the barren flourish," Effegen echoes, and casts out to Masar.

Despite everything, seeing him on view lifts her spirits. His body is like a mountain that no force could breach, and he is brave and beautiful and hers—

"My Star," he says.

"The cloaksaan have breached the surface atrium," she says.

His lips thin. "Remember. Patience."

She nods curtly. Levels above them, cloaks are circling the elevator pit and the stairway, examining their entry points.

"What's your report?" Effegen asks.

"The Katish forces have divided to protect Quietus and K-5 station. Hejar Paiye is continuing the battle for the gate. She's outnumbered, but her ships are holding their own. No word yet on if Karix will help the five thousand."

Effegen swallows bile, demands, "What about Jun?"

"*The Gunner* landed. We lost contact straight afterward."

"How long ago was that?"

"Twenty minutes."

"And the Ar'tec Collective? Have they made contact. Are they in?"

Masar presses his lips together. "They aren't answering our casts. Either they have no good news or they're too busy getting it done to bother with us."

"Let's hope that it's the latter." She follows her confident words by licking dry lips, and this time she thinks he sees the fear in her eyes. "What about you?"

Even as she asks, the bridge jolts around him. She hears cries from somewhere, and Vikar Wren shouting orders. Masar grabs at something and manages to keep his feet.

"We've stolen enough ships from Teros to make a menace of ourselves. Two of the Kindom warfalcons are disabled. But their warcrows are pummeling us, and the third falcon has fallen back to defend the gate. We're in a good position, but we can't get through."

The bridge rocks again. It twists his body such that for the first time she sees a long weeping scrape down his neck.

"What about the Khens?" Effegen asks.

He shakes his head grimly. "No sign of them."

So Hejar Paiye could not persuade Khen Vorkhen Soon to act. It may be all right. The Teron fighters are well situated, and with so many pirate families coming to their aid—

Through Masar's cast, she hears a new outcry. "Nightfoot ships! Nightfoot ships!"

She sees shock wash across Masar's face. They knew the Nightfoots had sided with Kess, but they hoped Riiniana's forces would remain in Ma'kess System, battling it out against Ashway. That they have come to Teros could overwhelm Wren's fleet.

"How many?" Effegen asks.

Masar says, "Dozens. Ten falcons among them." He looks at her again, and though he does not look afraid, his expression spears her with terror. "Tell Bene... tell him I love you both. I love you more than life."

The blood drains from her body. He would not say that, he would not look at her like that, unless it was goodbye.

Fury supplants her fear with a jolt. "*Do not* love us more than life. Love us more than death!"

He looks at her gravely. The ship shakes again. Someone shouts, "They've punctured our hull!"

"My Star." Hyre is suddenly beside her, grabbing her elbow and dragging her attention to him. His face is damp with sweat and his eyes are wide. "Effegen. They are coming."

She refocuses on the atrium, watching as cloaksaan take the stairs. Some are mangled by the razor wire, but their compatriots use bladed batons to slice through it. Dozens more cloaks rappel down the elevator shaft. Soon they swing themselves onto Level 9, taking position with their rifles cocked against their shoulders. The farm, green and lustrous and fully lit under the artificial sun lamps, is silent as the grave she plans to make of it.

Patience, Masar told her.

Draw them in, Liis Konye said.

They come like an infestation, whole battalions of them.

Effegen looks at Masar, whispering, "They're here."

His eye alights with murder. "Do it."

Effegen sends the order through her cast, and all across Level 9, the bombs go off.

CHAPTER TWENTY-SEVEN

1665

YEAR OF THE HARVEST

A Shuttle
Orbiting Jeve

A re you praying right now?"
Six's voice is incredulous, and slightly amused. It is not Esek's
voice, though of course Esek would have asked the same question, her
face lit up with delighted mockery. Chono rolls her eyes and realizes
that the last time she did that was probably when she and Six were
schoolkin and Six was getting her into trouble.

"Of course I'm praying," she mutters, hands on the helm and guiding it slowly, cautiously, through the flight path projected before her.

The shuttle may be under a Hood, but it remains a physical object, and if someone sees them with their eyes, they'll be fucked. The three-hour flight from Ma'kessn orbit to the moon has been blessedly uneventful for them, but full of peril for everyone else, and Chono isn't taking chances.

"To whom?" Six asks.

She flicks them a glance. Like her, they are dressed in cloaksaan armor, spacewalk ready. They've piled up their hair, and at this angle she gets a clear view of the small dark bruise behind their ear. Flushing with embarrassment, she clears her throat.

"To the Godfire, of course. And to all of them."

"The beatitudes?"

Chono snorts. "Among other things."

"I never had much use for the Six Gods or the Godfire. That is what I should have said to Esek, you know. Fuck the gods, I do not need any of them."

Chono never thought she'd grin at the memory of Esek descending on their kinschool and asking Six the age-old riddle *Who is the Sixth God?* But the thought of Six responding in that way brings a strange combination of amusement with them, and amusement with her old mentor.

"She probably would have taken you for a novitiate then and there. She loved irreverence."

"What a missed opportunity," Six ponders.

Chono guides the ship, her hand as light as if she were coaxing a skittish animal. They've already passed through the exosphere and are taking a circuitous route toward the east side of the ruins. On view, she can see the blinking light that signifies *The Gunner*, which landed twenty minutes ago. Comm access to Jun and Liis went out almost immediately.

Six asks, "So, what are you praying for?"

She chances another glance at them. They sit with about half a dozen small holographic views around their head, each one projecting tactical information about the various quorum attacks. The fighting is fierce, and the rebels are outnumbered. There is no sign of Khen Soon.

"The prayer for war's end," Chono says, and tips the nose of the shuttle down, into a steeper descent.

The ruins of Farren Ki are surrounded by the scars of the moon-wide bombing, craters and trenches scored through the surface. But there is a decent scrap of flatland not far from their target and just outside the deadly arc of the Silver Keep's holo shield.

"Do you think something like that is possible?" Six asks. "War's end, I mean."

"When in your life have you been this chatty? Are you sure Esek didn't switch bodies with you, this time?"

"Gods, what a twist that would be."

"Six—"

"It is a relevant question. If you live—"

"If *we* live."

"—you will have to answer that question."

Chono watches the surface rise toward them, dark and barren. "One thing at a time..."

Just a few minutes later, they touch down, clouds of charcoal-colored dust rising under them. Neither Six nor Chono moves for several seconds. In the distance, Farren Ki is a grotesque skyline of broken teeth. Though the original bombing flattened much of it, a few buildings have stood the test of time. One in their direct sight line has collapsed on one side, yet stands as many as ten stories tall on the other. It's like a jagged sword lifted into the Black.

Six rises first, climbing back into the cabin. Chono follows. A four-foot drill is buckled to the wall. Six holds Chono's helmet out to her. She takes it, and they look at each other. *One night.* She had one night with them. One night to be free, to be safe, to be loved—and to love in turn. Whatever shyness they have felt toward each other since, it evaporates in this moment.

"I had a dream," Chono whispers. "I've had it more than once."

Six tilts their head a little. "Tell me."

"In the dream, you're standing on an edge. You say you've been chasing me your whole life. Except now I think maybe I was the one saying that to you. Then, in the dream, you jump off the edge." Six's expression cloisters. Chono's throat aches. "I know that from here on out, you'll want to protect me, even at the cost of yourself. I know I can't change that, but Six, please"—she swallows—"please...don't jump without me."

She sees something in their face that she never saw in Esek's—a softening. A deep, yearning love. Six nods. "All right."

Her chest loosens. She actually smiles, relieved, and at the sight of it, Six's lips twitch and they shake their head a little, as if chiding her, but she can see that they're pleased.

Together, they don their helmets. Six grabs the drill and hefts it onto their shoulder with barely a grunt. The hatch door opens, and they step out onto the surface of Jeve. Though the city of Farren Ki, like all Jeveni colonies, once lay under a dome equipped with artificial gravity, here the atmosphere is buoyant, and she must immediately adjust to the urge to jump and fly. Chono's combat rifle feels too light in her hands, and she struggles to accommodate the change as she walks through the thick blackish dust on the moon's surface.

Six's dry remark reaches her over comms. "What a homecoming..."

Only then does it occur to her that Six is the first Jeveni to set foot on Jeve in over seventy-five years. Homecoming indeed.

She sends out a cast to Ar'tec Island.

We're on the surface. Three hundred meters from our location. Any word from Jun?

A few seconds tick past them, and the Minkat answers.

Stand by.

Chono and Six glance at each other. Six asks:

Are we making progress?

When a couple more seconds pass, they cast again:

Ar'tec, please respond—

Such wretched impatience! Working very hard, hard as can be, sweating buckets, and you! Bothersome!

We are standing here with our asses hanging out.

So walk! Trot! Skip! Go!

The "fuck off" is implied. Chono and Six set off, knowing that the longer it takes to get that shield down, the more vulnerable they will be. The terrain dips beneath them, their path growing rougher as they coast the border of a crater about twice the size of their shuttle. They use gravity to their advantage, quickening their strides while trying to stay cautious of the unreliable surface. They are very close now, and Chono's heart pounds from more than exertion. She feels as if she is running toward the maw of an ancient evil. Hunting for the belly of a beast from which she will not escape. The incline steepens before them. Six loses their footing and falls to one knee, the drill toppling off their shoulder.

"Are you all right?" Chono asks, her voice in her helmet uncommonly loud, echoing.

Six stands up again. "Fine," they say. But they're staring down at their hand, motionless.

"What is it?"

They show it to her. It's a rock. No, not just a rock. It is a piece of bright black stone, with sharp facets and bright red veins. They stare at it together. Chono realizes that without any oxygen in the air, the piece of jevite has not aged into gray and pink. It has been here for decades, like a skeleton. A chip of wealth that is also death. The maw she imagined before opens wider. She doesn't see what Six does with the jevite, for already they are hefting the drill again, nodding her forward with a single word:

"Faster."

Somehow, they go faster. They grapple their way up the rubble. They reach the crest at last, and stand upon the tip of it with the wide breadth of Jeve spilling before them. The path drops out beneath them again, a steep decline.

There at the bottom prowls a clutch of Brutal Hands. They see one another at the same moment. Chono's rifle comes up, and she fires.

CHAPTER TWENTY-EIGHT

1665

YEAR OF THE HARVEST

The Wren's Jaw
Teros System

Masar stands against the tide of the shuddering, creaking *Wren's Jaw* and watches Vikar Wren. The captain looks furious, excited, and maniacal at the same time, all savage grin and glittering eyes. He's diverted life support to his bridge and engine room. One-third of the ship is gone, and they are marooned in the Black, with a new phalanx of Nightfoot warbirds incoming.

"Captain," one of his crewsaan says, "we have two evacuation pods left and the war shuttle hanging on in the bay. We've gotta go."

Four Nightfoot warcrows bank toward them, clearly intent on finishing the job.

A nearby cruiser casts out, "We've got you, Wren," and charges into the gap, scattering the warbirds with a flurry of strikes.

"Just in time," Yantikye remarks.

Borrowed time. Time they don't have. Where is the Ar'tec Collective? Where is Jun? Out in the Black of Teros System, the Nightfoots have reinforced the depleted Cloaksaan fleet, forming an impenetrable blockade in front of the Teron gate. Without that gate, they can't reach any other system. They can't reach Capamame.

Wren barks the names of four of the saan on the bridge. "Get my siblings out of the engine room and bail out. That's an order."

The crew is mutinous, but Wren curses them with such poison that they actually look afraid, and they run from the bridge. Now it is just Wren and his second-in-command, and Yantikye and Masar. Wren tells his second, "Get me Ashway."

Within moments, the general appears on cast. "Captain Wren."

"The Khens aren't coming and those Ar'tec bastards have done fuck all! I need you to attack Nightfoot targets. Every fucking place they care about. The factories, the kinschools, Verdant. We have to lure this fleet out of Teros System."

"My ground troops are at their limit keeping control of Riin Cosas, and the Moonbacks have finally made a move."

Masar asks eagerly, "Karix?"

"Giran's fleet has started bombing civilian targets in Nightfoot territory. He's taking aim at your Jeveni prisoners, too. Karix has divided her forces between holding the northern continents and cutting Giran off, but she's stretched thin."

"You have to send us something," Yantikye says.

"I can't help you. Even if I could reach a gate, I'm better off reinforcing Paiye."

"Favoring Kator over Teros again!" Wren accuses.

"Her surviving ships are more powerful than yours," Ashway says neutrally.

"Gods-fucking-damnit, can't you see I'm trying to save those Je fuckers?!"

Out in the Black, there is a sudden explosion of light, instantly winked out by the vacuum as the pirate cruiser that came to their defense cracks down its center, its pieces scattering, its crewsaan doubtless having no chance to abandon ship.

Ashway says, "Fall back. Retreat."

Masar shouts, "We can't retreat! We have to give Jun time!"

"You've lost half your number."

"There's still enough of us to take out the warwhale in Capamame System."

The general is stolid. "You can't get through the gate. And Jun Ironway may be dead. Retreat is your best option."

Wren goes silent. He's considering it, considering telling the pirates and the other Teron forces to run. Masar burns with helplessness. He has a sudden irrational impulse to kill Wren and Wren's second, to seize control of the fleet, to *make them* keep going.

The Wren's Jaw groans and creaks. There is a whining sound as the escape pods break off, their slender shapes propelled toward the nearest port on the Silt moon. One of them narrowly avoids collision with a piece of the destroyed cruiser. The other darts right into the range of Nightfoot warbirds. Masar looks sharply at Wren, sees him watching on view, his fingers moving as he counts his dead, just before the pod explodes. Wren doesn't even flinch, but the tattoos on his face are livid against white skin. He and Ashway look at each other again, two warriors who understand the score.

"Good luck, Captain," Ashway says, and vanishes.

The second-in-command tells Wren, "If we suit up we can still get through the debris to reach what's left of the bay. The war shuttle is operational."

Wren scoffs. "I'm going down with my ship."

"The fuck you are!" his second hisses, and lunges at him.

Yantikye exhales disparagingly and Masar watches, almost bemused, as the Braems lock together in the ridiculous wrestle of schoolkin. To his surprise, it ends quickly, with the second getting Wren in a head-lock and stomping his ankle till he collapses onto one knee.

"Yield, damn you! Yield!"

The ship lurches. It makes a great tearing sound and transmits a warning:

LIFE SUPPORT CRITICAL. LIFE SUPPORT CRITICAL.
EVACUATE! EVACUATE!

They run. All of them.

Masar loses time, one-half of his brain acutely focused on the task before him: Pull the emergency space suits out of the bridge lockers. Put on the space suit. Steady hands. Don't forget the shotgun. Climb through the debris of shattered flooring and doors blown open. Spider-walk across exposed walls on broken frames. Get inside the shuttle bay with its gaping hull and the Black and the battlefield spread before them in darting ships and drifting wreckage—

LIFE SUPPORT CRITICAL. LIFE SUPPORT CRITICAL.
EVACUATE! EVACUATE!

Fight the vacuum and grab on to the battle shuttle. Wrestle himself and the others into the battle shuttle. Settle into one of the cannon operator pods while Wren's second takes the other, while Wren and Yantikye take the cockpit, while they thrash and force their way out of *The Wren's Jaw*. Do all of this, and don't die—

But the other side of his brain is on Capamame. It is with Farren Eyce. He imagines the traps set loose upon the Kindom invaders. Specially calibrated bombs powerful enough to kill cloaks without destroying the structure of Farren Eyce. A dangerous game, a disaster if it goes wrong and the levels buckle and bury his people alive. He pictures the cloaks on Nine trying to retreat toward Ten or descend toward Eight and getting pummeled from all sides. More bombs up top. Armored saan covering the elevator shaft, firing on the scattered cloaks. Smoke and extinguisher mist, and creatures emerging from the cloud, for cloaks are difficult to kill.

The battle shuttle, *Wren's Tooth*, darts onto the field. Masar takes hold of the cannon controls, looking for targets through the sight. Useless to go after something big in this thing, but a warcrow is fair game. He pictures Bene wielding a sharp-edged pick, and Effegen in battle gear and blue powder. Bombs are finite. Grenades only go off once. These traps will decimate the first wave of Cloaksaan, but it'll be up to the fighters on Eight to hold back the next wave, to stop the cloaks from swarming down onto Seven—

"*The Swimming Fox*!" Wren hollers from the cockpit. "Ten o'clock."

Startled by the ship's name, Masar finds it on cast, caught in the sights of half a dozen Nightfoot warbirds. Last he heard, the Foxer crew were all imprisoned, their ship confined in a Kindom shipyard. He smiles in spite of himself. One of Mix Catty's liberations, no doubt. Wren flies them into the fray, and Masar locks on one of the crows and fires. Not as reliable as a shotgun, but the controls on this thing are expert, delivering his first shot right on target. The crow spins out, body divided from its wings.

Wren twists them, banks, and dives toward another ship. This time his second unleashes the cannon missile just an instant after Masar. The second makes his shot. Masar misses and fires again. Another splintering of steel. This is so much better than being stuck on the bridge of *The Wren's Jaw*. That is, until the warbirds clock them.

"Aft!" Yamikye shouts. "Aft, damn you!"

They nearly roll over from the speed of the turn. Masar's shoulder slams into the side of the cannon pod. He grunts, regrips the guns, and sprays firepower, clipping a couple of the Nightfoot ships but nothing better than that.

The Swimming Fox casts out to them, "*Wren's Tooth*, we're coming around. Fall back and we'll cover your retreat to the Silt moon."

"Fuck that!" Wren says. "Catty? Where are you? Catty!"

Within moments Mix Catty answers merrily, "Here, Captain! This is damned wild! A story for my grandkittens!"

"Get in formation," Wren tells her, opening a comm up to the entire fleet. "Everybody who can, get in formation. I'm done with this fucking scattershot game and waiting for casters to rescue us. Are we Braems or not?! There's a warfalcon on my eight. We're going to cut it down and get whatever's behind it and we're not fucking stopping until one of us gets through that gate, hear me? We are officially a battering ram."

"Hey-oh-hey!" shouts Catty. Masar hears her crew echo the call. "Let's fucking do it!"

Half the rebel fleet is dead in the water, but the rest abandon their dogfights to join up with Wren. He barely waits for them. Masar knows that they are catapulting themselves right into a death trap. Even if they get past the falcon, and the one after that, and the one after that, the Nightfoots and Cloaksaan birds will pick them off one by one, smear them across the Black, till their battering ram is whittled down to a toothpick and there is no one left to cross over and protect Capamame.

"Sajeven," he whispers, though he rarely prays. "Sajeven, beloved . . ."

It is in that moment, as the falcon rounds on them and Mix Catty's team of war shuttles sprints to meet it, that a cast notification suddenly pings in his ocular.

It's from Fonu sen Fhaan.

Masar can't sort through his competing emotions of surprise, bafflement, and anger. He accepts the comm, saying sharply, "My River, what are you doing? If the Kindom finds out *The Brute Crane* is contacting us they'll fire on—"

Fonu cuts him off. "I am not on *The Brute Crane*, Masar."

The statement is absurd, and Masar blinks rapidly, sweat stinging his eye. Did Fonu not relocate to *The Crane* with Gaeda? He asks, "Where are you?"

"I am aboard *Drae's Hope*."

Fonu's voice is brusque and calm, but their words make no sense. Torn from his concentration, Masar reminds himself to look out over the erupting firefight. He wrenches himself out of the pod, yelling, "Yantikye! Take over the cannon!"

Yantikye looks downright delighted as he swings into the pod's chair. Masar forgoes the cockpit to stand in the cabin, grabbing a handhold as the *Wren's Tooth* dips and dives.

"What the fuck are you talking about?!" he hisses.

"I believe my words were perfectly clear," says Fonu.

"What are you—is Gaeda with you?"

Another comm reaches him, this one from Gaeda ben Kist. Her voice is as stern as ever. "I certainly am not. But Fonu couldn't be reasoned with. Now *focus*, Masar!"

"My Stone—"

"I damn well am your Stone, so listen to me. The people on *The Brute Crane* are safe. For now. But it's been almost an hour since Jun Ironway jumped to Jeve's orbit. We can't depend on her success any longer."

"You can't—" Masar tries.

Fonu interrupts. "I have a lock on the coordinates of a warwhale called *The Katanye Ten*, which is directly blocking you from the Teron gate. I need you to confirm those coordinates. Now—"

"What are you doing on *Drae's Hope*?"

"I led a small crew here several hours ago."

Masar is too stunned to answer. Like a fist pounding on a barred door, Effegen's cast signature appears. Masar pictures her small body on the other side of the door, a bomb about to go off.

"Moon arise," mutters Fonu.

"Let her in," Masar retorts.

No sooner have they done it than the Star exclaims, "What in the name of Sajeven are you doing? Why is *Drae's Hope* powering up? The warwhale is sending ships to surround you!"

Fonu says, "The warwhale went too deep into Capamame's atmosphere. Its ships are at least ten minutes away from us, and the gate is undefended. We are well within our margin."

"Margin of *what*?!" Effegen cries. "Are you trying to get yourselves and *The Brute Crane* destroyed?! We are barely holding back the cloaks from reaching Level 7!"

The ground heaves beneath Masar, the shuttle suddenly banking right and nearly flinging him off his feet. He looks toward the cockpit and sees Mix Catty's ship and two others soar into the breach.

Over comms, Vikar Wren warns Catty, "Not so eager, you hooligan!"

"Follow in my wake!" she shouts back.

Like a hand snatching him from one room into another, Fonu says, "Confirm the coordinates of *The Katanye Ten*, Masar."

Numbers fly across Masar's ocular, but they may as well be a foreign language. On his casting view, he sees that *Drae's Hope* is lining up with the mouth of the jump gate. *The Brute Crane* and its warbird entourage are nearly as far away as the warwhale.

"We made an agreement!" Effegen hisses. "Your job is to protect *The Brute Crane*! To lead our survivors if Farren Eyce falls."

"Sa Gaeda will keep that agreement," says Fonu.

"You cannot just—"

"Sajeven spare me all this recalcitrance!" Gaeda cries, "Do you think I didn't try to persuade him already? There's no more use arguing!"

Fonu breaks in, "There will be no survivors if Masar and the Terons cannot get through that gate."

"And what, by the gods, do you mean to do about it?!" Effegen shouts. "Join the fight in Teros System? *Drae's Hope* is no match for the falcons on the other side. You'll be—"

"Am I not your River?!" Fonu interrupts, yelling now, their voice more powerful than Masar has ever heard. "Am I not charged with the defense of Farren Eyce? Not Liis Konye, not Masar Hawks, but *me*!" Their words silence Effegen. Masar can't think what to say. "Every saan on this ship is Draeviin-bred and sworn to the safety of Capamame. We know what we are for. It is an ancient oath. We will see it through, but you must let us do it. Confirm the coordinates! Now!"

Somehow, amid the rocking of the shuttle, and the violent weaving of other ships out in the Black, and the sight of Mix Catty tunneling her way through Nightfoot warbirds to clear a path for them—somehow, in all of this, Masar experiences a moment of infinite stillness. Later he will think it is like the moment when a lockpick feels the final pin drop, that tiny click of sensation, opening a door. Later he will realize that things did not happen slowly, a half dozen events stretched over minutes. It all happened within a few seconds: him understanding at last what Fonu means, what Fonu means to do with... with the rest of their life, with the body that Ujan Redcore ravaged and tried to kill. And Effegen's short, choked sound, as she realizes it, too. And Yantikye butting into their comm out of nowhere, like a bad joke, like a god's fist, to provide the coordinates that Fonu has demanded.

"Gods keep you well, my River," the Quietan says.

Effegen exclaims, sharp and horrified, "No—no! Do not do this. I *forbid* you to do this! Gaeda! Tell them!"

"You foolish girl," says Gaeda ben Kist, and yet there is gentleness in it. "They go with all my prayers of blessing. They go on behalf of us all. Isn't that enough, for a spoke? Did you learn nothing from Nikkelo?"

Masar's stomach heaves with dread, with memory. Nikkelo, standing on that gangplank, as elegant and perfect as a god. Nikkelo's voice: *May the barren flourish.*

Drae's Hope vanishes through the gate.

In Teros System, Wren shouts, "Mix, falcon missiles at your five! Pull up. Pull up!"

Effegen calls out in irrational fury, "No! Do not! No!"

Gaeda's prayer lifts above her plea.

Vikar Wren booms, "Cover her, cover her!"

Masar looks out the cockpit to see Mix Catty and her arrow of ships sprinting into a viper's nest of Cloaksaan warbirds.

The pirate girl shouts, "Hey-oh-he—"

But the missiles cut her off, their slim bodies striking without sound, the flash of bright light piercing Masar's eyes. Shards of debris splinter in every direction, forcing back the Cloaksaan ships and creating a gap in the field where the girl used to be. He has no chance to feel it, to even know what he would feel, if in this moment he were not being overpowered by a blow of premonition. *You survive again*, Nikkelo told him.

Not this time, Masar thinks, just before the *Wren's Tooth* takes fire. The impact throws him off his feet. He hits the ground on one side, a lightning bolt of pain going through his arm, bone breaking into pieces like the pieces of Mix Catty's ship that stream past them.

"Masar!" Effegen shouts in his ear. "Help them! You have to help them!"

But though Wren and his whittled-down fleet are still driving toward the gate, it is too far, and Masar barely gets onto his feet again as the shuttle takes another hit. This time there is a terrible rushing sensation, an awareness of hull breach, as if Som's mouth has opened to suck them down into death. Masar reattaches the helmet of his space suit, knowing it will be little protection against the Black. Only now does he realize that the right-side command pod, and Wren's second-in-command, are gone, the empty space already sealing itself behind an emergency door.

Wren screams, "Fuck! Fuck!"

But after he screams it, he says nothing else, voice cut off either by grief or rage or by the awareness of his own impending death. Masar can't tell if Effegen is still on cast. He hopes not. He hopes she won't be there for this.

Ahead, the Teron gate churns with the activity of an approaching jump. Like a gyre it twists and twists. It hypnotizes Masar. He can't look anywhere else.

"Masar," Effegen gasps.

A moment later, *Drae's Hope* surges through the gate—and hits *The Katanye Ten* with the power of an exploding star.

CHAPTER TWENTY-NINE

1665

YEAR OF THE HARVEST

Farren Eyce
The Planet Capamame

B ene is terrified.

He hoped, when the time came, that he wouldn't be terrified. He wants to be stoic like Liis, and brave like Jun, and determined like Effegen. He wants to be a warrior worthy of Masar. But his grip on the rifle is slick and sweaty, and he's trembling, because the cloaksaan have breached Level 8, and they are swarming like roaches onto Seven.

All around Bene, the colonists of Farren Eyce open fire. The sound startles him so much that he grabs the trigger of his own rifle, stunned to find that he is shooting as well. The thousands of rounds create not just sound but vibration, reminding him of cave-ins in the Najic mines, a rumble and roar of destruction.

The first wave of cloaksaan take the brunt of it, dozens falling under the assault. Bene thinks, *Maybe this will be easy. We have cover. They're in the open. And the upper levels took out a lot of them. Maybe—*

Near to him, someone gives a sharp cry and hits the ground. Bene looks and sees a Draeviin colonist crumpled onto his side with red blooming on his chest. That isn't the only body. The Farren Eyce offensive circling the staircase forces the cloaksaan to take fire from all directions, but the cloaksaan are equal to it, breaking into wings and picking off everyone they can. A half dozen fighters within shouting distance of Bene go down, one of them the saan who was standing right next to him. Her jaw has been shot off. Her eyes stare sightlessly.

A fog comes over Bene, remembering his Uncle Coz after Esek shot him, and remembering the bodies of his father, Misek, and of Great Gra. So many staring eyes. *I wanted to be brave*, he thinks helplessly. But his vision is tunneling. His pulse is so fast he thinks his heart may be about to explode. He hasn't felt this kind of horror and fear since Ujan held them hostage in the shuttle, and he wasn't ready for it, wasn't strong enough—

Hands grab him, yanking him down into a squat behind the barricade. In disorientation he tries to focus on the face in front of him. It's Pejun.

"Fall back for the second wave!" Pejun shouts.

Only then does Bene remember that the Jeveni offensive is divided into four waves. He was part of the first. As he and Pejun crawl back to the second layer of barricades, their rifles hugged to their chests, the second wave pours forward to replace them. Next to him, someone is trying to drag an injured man to safety. Bene reaches to help them, and together they pull the man behind an overturned metal table. The man has taken a bullet through the elbow. His forearm hangs off the joint by threads of tendon and flesh, and he's hyperventilating, eyes wild. Somehow it cracks through Bene's panic. Hands shaking, he reaches into his coat for the med kit Liis gave him. He pushes a morpho syrette at the person who helped drag the man to safety.

"In his collarbone," Bene gasps. "Quick."

The saan, a Jeveni with blue powder streaking from their eyes, quickly obeys as Bene clumsily pulls a regenerative bandage out of his kit. The morpho makes the man pass out, and Bene and the Jeveni wrap the forearm and elbow in the bandages, which will not save the arm but will hopefully control the bleeding.

Gunfire sprays directly over their heads and they both duck lower. The Jeveni looks at Bene with wide, frightened eyes. "What do we do?"

Bene doesn't know where the words come from, but he answers, "Liis said to drag the injured as far back behind the line as you can. Here!" He shoves the rest of the med kit into their hands. "If you find anyone else who's hurt, use this."

The Jeveni nods, looking relieved to have instructions. They pocket the kit and grab the man by his shoulders, dragging him.

Explosions go off somewhere. Grenades, Bene realizes—though from which direction he's not sure. Will the cloaksaan lob crowd-killers on them? The Jeveni haven't got any crowd-killers.

Pejun is there again, shoving Bene's rifle back into his hands. Bene hadn't even realized he put it down.

"Hold on to this," Pejun warns him. "We're taking the worst of it on this side. The cloaksaan may breach our line."

Bene feels like throwing up. "Where is Effegen?"

"Safe behind the fourth wave."

Safe. What an absurd thing to say. She's not safe. None of them are safe.

"She needs to get down to the lower levels!"

"You can't think about that right now. Focus. We have to—fuck!"

Bene spins to see what he's looking at: a cloaksaan seems to have appeared out of nowhere in a crowd of second-wave fighters. A bloodletter in one hand and a longer blade in the other, they carve and stab in every direction, creating wide arcs of blood. Pejun races toward them, leaving Bene with his rifle and his fear and helplessness. He sits there frozen for what feels like hours before a burst of adrenaline snaps him back like a rubber band. Around him, the third wave of fighters pours forward as the second falls back. At some point, the cloaksaan Pejun went to fight has fallen. Spurred to action, Bene runs toward them anyway. Gunfire strikes the ground near his feet. More goes off above him. He staggers forward, finding several Jeveni collapsed around the dead cloak, a terrible kill field. Some are screaming and gripping at their wounds—bellies and arms and thighs. One of them lies on her back with a hand clapped over her neck, blood streaming through her fingers. Bene kneels beside her. She stares at him with white-rimmed eyes.

"Help," she gurgles, coughing up a bright bubble of blood. "Help."

Bene is suddenly furious at himself for giving his med kit away. He searches the woman's body. The hospital didn't have enough supplies to give everyone a full kit, but thank the gods, she has a small packet in her pocket. He tears the regenerative patch out and looks into her eyes. They're streaming with tears, muddying the blue powder.

"Let me see," he orders. "Let me see."

He has to pry her hand away, revealing a thick gash that spurts blood. He slaps the patch down over it, watching the edges adhere to her skin. The gash might be too deep. And her kit doesn't have any morpho. *Fuck.*

"It's okay," he tells her, looking around at the other bodies. One man has torn off his own shirt and is wrapping his calf with the fabric, teeth set. Someone else has stopped moving since the last time Bene looked at them. "It's okay," he repeats.

A message from Effegen appears in his ocular.

Where are you? Are you safe?

He thinks he can hear the terror in the voiceless words. What can he say to her?

I'm safe. Where are you?

Behind the fourth line of barricades. Bene, pull back. There's still no word from Jun. Please, pull back.

He almost weeps at the desperation in her message, knowing that he can't obey her. That however much a coward he may be, however unprepared and untrained for this moment, he cannot and will not fall back.

But she must. He casts back.

Go down into the lower levels. I'll meet you there.

A grenade goes off nearby. He throws his body over the wounded woman as sharp bits of debris strike his back.

Bene, they're decimating Level 7. Please.

I'll follow you. Go down to Level 1.

He knows she doesn't believe him. He hates for the last thing he says to her to be a lie.

I'm sorry. I love you.

She takes far too long to answer. When she does, he senses acceptance in the grief.

I love you, too.

There's no time for more words. He sits up again, conscious of stinging cuts in his back. The woman under him is still alive. But when he looks around, his stomach drops. The Cloaksaan front have breached the first barricade and are already coming over the second. All over Level 7 the structured waves of colonists are collapsing into a free fall of hand-to-hand combat. He sees some Jeveni he knows from the construction crews hefting axes and mallets against the assault. He sees a woman as old as Hosek raising a shotgun and firing into the line. He sees a group of teenagers throw themselves in a pile onto one of the cloaksaan, who disappears beneath their weight like a black beetle overwhelmed by fire ants. And he sees dozens of colonists fall, cut down by gunfire and blades, by the relentless onslaught of the Brutal Hand.

He sees one of those Hands see him.

Bene swings up his rifle to fire. The gun jams.

For several crucial seconds, he freezes, his body numb, his throat closed. He's a mouse in an open field, a fish trapped in the shallows. The cloak levels a handgun at him. Without thinking, he crawls away from the injured woman, wondering if he'll be shot in the head or the back. Will he die instantly? Will he feel it? Are gods even real? But he isn't shot anywhere. He rolls over to see that Pejun has leapt onto the cloak's back.

It's as if there is a whole new person in Bene's body. The sounds of gunfire and shouting propel him onto his feet. He grabs the pickax out of the belt around his waist and runs at Pejun and the cloak. They are grappling like wrestlers, but Pejun loses his grip and a bloodletter slices through his side. He yelps, staggering back.

Bene pretends that the cloaksaan is a slab of rock with copper ore gleaming inside it. The pick won't go through armor, but it will go through a gap, and Bene always was a precise miner. He drives the pick as hard as he can into a vulnerable slot between the shoulder pauldron and the backplate. The cloak screams, whirling around and striking Bene across the head. Bene hits the ground, vision going black for a moment. When it clears, he sees the pick sticking out of the cloak's shoulder, sees the cloak reach around themself and grab it by the handle and yank it out, as if it were no worse than a thorn.

Pejun barrels into them. They hit the ground together. Pejun has a knife, too. He tries to drive it down into the cloak's throat, but the cloak swings around with the pick and Pejun barely blocks it with his arm. The cloak hooks a leg behind Pejun's and does something that makes Pejun scream, falling sideways. The cloak gets on top of him, striking him. They wield the bloodletter again.

In a moment of complete absurdity, not knowing what else to do, Bene pulls off one of his heavy work boots and hurls it at the cloak. It hits them in the back of the head, startling them enough to halt the trajectory of the bloodletter. The cloak looks up at Bene. Bene thinks he can see the scorn behind the cloak's helmet. *What little runt is this?* the cloak must be thinking. *What poor excuse for fighters these Jeveni are.*

The cloak stands up, leaving an unconscious Pejun and stalking toward Bene, the bloodletter spinning in their hand until they hold it in a chambered grip. Bene's chest heaves, his eyes wide. His hand fumbles numbly at his side, but he's too slow, he'll always be too slow—

But then Effegen's voice is in his ear. To his surprise, it is full of awe, and hope. "Bene," she gasps. "Bene, stay alive! It's Jun. She's done it."

The Brutal Hand runs at him. Bene draws the Som's Edge pistol from its holster and fires.

CHAPTER THIRTY

1665

YEAR OF THE HARVEST

The Silver Keep
The Moon Jeve

Seti Kess comes through the doors already shouting, his body a blazing furnace. Standing in the atrium outside the brig, his cloaks, ordinarily as composed as stone monuments, shift backward from him. One of them, the brig master, falls short of concealing their unease.

"What the *fuck* happened?" Kess snarls.

The brig master coughs, buying time, and Kess fantasizes about cutting through him with a sword.

"She had—that is, she appears to have a...second neural link."

The silence in the room is as thick as tar. The last time Seti heard of anyone being foolish enough to do that, it was that shit-stain girl Redcore, and she was a pathological liar.

"Why didn't your scans find it?!"

"We had no reason to look for—"

Kess grabs them by the pauldron of their cloak and throws them against the wall. He storms into the brig, a row of holo cells spread before him and empty but for the nearest one. Inside stands a metal, tall-backed chair with thick armrests. Jun Ironway is bound to the chair. His cloaks have stripped her down to her underwear, and there is blood leaking from her mouth and nose, bruises already purpling across her body. Electric shock manacles bind her throat and wrists and ankles to the chair. Her eyes are closed, her body drenched in sweat, tight as a bow. Even Kess has a moment of surprise to realize how quickly his cloaks escalated to torture. They must be feeling very vulnerable, with Sunstep among them. Well, they should be more afraid of him than her.

He lurches toward the cage, but one of the cloaks exclaims, "Sa, the shield is charged! For your safety, please don't approach."

He jerks to a halt, realizing that when the cast reached him saying that Ironway had seized control of her prison, this is obviously what it meant. He glowers at the person who spoke, recognizing her as a captain. "What about the chair?" he says, imagining amping the electric charge so high that it burns right through to the bone, garroting Jun Ironway into decapitation.

"She has the entire cellblock under her control," the captain says, her calm tone belied by a shimmer of sweat on her jawline. "She's cut off our access to the shock mechanism, but those manacles won't budge. She can't free herself from the chair, but we can't reach her and we can't shock her."

Kess growls deep in his chest. When the door into the brig hallway opens behind him, he recognizes the steps without looking. Riiniana Nightfoot, come to observe.

"I don't care if we have to kill power to the entire brig," Kess says. "Get me inside."

"The casting lab is hard at it, Sa. But many of our casters are also engaged in coordinating the battles across the Treble. It has stretched us thin."

"Get control of this brig, *now!*"

To his surprise, Riiniana speaks before the captain can. "Does she have access to anything outside this brig?"

The captain looks to Kess uncertainly. For a moment Kess thinks to deny Riiniana just for spite, but since he needs the report anyway, he gives a curt jerk of his head.

The captain explains, "Not at the moment. But she's shielded herself from the blocks we've tried to place on her. We can only assume she's trying to expand her reach."

"I see," Riiniana says, the inane brat. "And you've been torturing her."

Her thoughtful tone makes Kess face her at last. In complete defiance of the war going on, she is dressed in an elegant blue chemise, a hoodless silk cloak draping down her back, white, as if to mock a cloaksaan cloak. She looks unaffected by the bloody woman in the cell, and turns her gaze on Kess. His stomach curdles with dislike for her, for her fine clothes, for how spoiled she is. He needs this upstart and her armies, but she is worthless otherwise. In time he'll have a child from her, an heir to the new house he will build, a house to rule the Treble for millennia, but already he is making plans to get rid of her afterward.

Riiniana asks, "What were you trying to accomplish, by torturing her?"

A ridiculous question.

The captain says, "She and her allies discovered the location of the Silver Keep. We need to determine their intentions immediately. So far, she's attacking alone, but we can only assume there will be others. She's not trained to withstand physical torture. This is the fastest way to get what we need."

In the cage, Jun Ironway's eyes are still closed, lips still moving, body heaving with exhausted breaths. She looks as focused and unreachable as a religious fanatic in a trance.

"You captured her easily," Riiniana observes.

"Her Hood program malfunctioned. We tracked her to the surface and surrounded her."

"Where are her crewsaan?"

"She was alone."

Riiniana gives the captain an open look of surprise. Kess was surprised as well, but the thorough scans and search of Ironway's ship proved it. Even Liis Konye cannot make herself invisible, however much he'd enjoy that reunion.

To Kess's surprise, Riiniana chuckles. It is not the chuckle of a girl, but of a tiny, seasoned general. Furious, he demands, "*What?*"

Riiniana looks placid but speaks with derision. "She came alone, and her Hood broke down. Really? Do you honestly believe her own tech would fail her *now*, and in that way? Perhaps if you weren't so excited by the prospect of capturing Sunstep, you would have taken the time to consider the risks of opening your doors to a thief."

Kess senses his cloaks glancing between him and Riiniana. The captain says, "That's why we disabled her neural link, Sa."

Riiniana clicks her tongue. "And look how well that turned out."

Kess's hand darts out. She is such a small thing, even the relatively restrained slap staggers her. She manages not to fall, however, and when she raises her head again to look at him, there's cold vindication in her face, and blood on her lip.

"You think you're some military strategist?" he snarls at her. "Or maybe you only want me to teach you respect. Believe me, I will."

He whirls back toward the cage, stepping within a foot of the glittering shield. "All right, Ironway. You've proved your mettle. But if you don't stop this now, you'll see what torture looks like."

For a moment there is no response. Then, slowly, Ironway opens her eyes. They are red-rimmed, blazing, ferocious enough to give him pause. She seems somehow completely absent and present at the same time. When she speaks, her voice strains with exertion.

"Sa Nightfoot is right. You should never have let a thief inside."

"You think the Silver Keep is susceptible to something as unin-spired as a cast attack? You may have seized hold of the brig, but if you're under some delusion that you can sit there all alone in that cell and single-handedly dismantle our defenses, I—"

She blurts a sound he doesn't recognize at first. It's—a *cackle*. He's stunned.

"I didn't think you'd torture me right off. But, hey, whatever keeps your attention."

"My attention—"

"I always was a lone wolf," she says, and grins with bloodied teeth. "I guess you assumed I couldn't learn new tricks."

Bravado, Kess thinks. *Delusion.*

Suddenly the captain is at his elbow again, standing too close, her voice irritatingly strained. "Sa, there's been a development with the Jeveni. One of their ships has . . . It went through the gate and exited in Teros System. It appears to have—rammed *The Katanye Ten*."

For the first time, Kess is too shocked to respond. He stands, dis-believing, for what could be moments or an entire minute. Unable to help himself, he blurts an incredulous laugh. It breaks off as soon as it starts. Laughter always feels counterfeit in his own mouth.

"Damages?"

"Sa, it was a direct hit. *The Katanye Ten* is gone, and the debris has destroyed many of the surrounding ships. Our defense of the gate is entirely compromised."

Kess's flare of humor dies. Rage returns, almost strangling him.

"Get that Je *bitch* on cast!"

Within seconds Effegen ten Crost appears. The woman (no, the girl, the fucking upstart *girl*) looks grim as a corpse, her jevite jewelry glit-tering like droplets of blood against skin gone gray. Her eyes are red, the blue war paint smeared. She's a child out of her depth, a pretender. Kess stuffs down his emotion, looking at her coolly.

"Who knew you had such a trick up your sleeve, Sa Crost."

He expects her voice to tremble, but instead she sounds as hard and steady as an anvil. "I've just destroyed your main warwhale in Teros System. The explosion took out three of the surrounding warfalcons and five kites. The rebel forces in Teros will soon jump to Capamame System. Yorus Inye's fleet will be outnumbered and your ground forces cut off from retreat."

Kess says with forced blandness, "I'm going to skewer you and cook you alive."

Her lips quirk. He can hear battle happening near her. The little brat is probably hiding as his cloaksaan destroy her colony. Inye reports that hundreds of cloaks have entered Farren Eyce. The Jeveni have no chance.

"I wonder if you people are even worth the trouble of enslavement. Do you know when we blew up your moon, the Jeveni deaths were mere collateral? You want to see a real genocide? Watch as I slaughter every last one of you. Starting with the saan on *The Brute Crane*. And then your entire colony. And if any of you survive? I'll find you. I'll stamp out any record of Sajeven or her people, and I'll rename that moon after *myself*. You'll *vanish* from history."

Effegen ten Crost flares her nostrils, and for a moment he thinks it's fear. But—

"Your cloaks are trapped in a funnel. They will soon have no path of retreat. And you'll find us very difficult to kill when you lose control of your Keep."

He gapes at her, shocked and furious, and more so when, without any leave, she vanishes. Just *vanishes*. He's going to find her. If his offensive doesn't kill her, he'll have her dragged naked through the streets of every city he conquers, till there is less left of her than the bones of Esek Nightfoot.

The lights flicker.

He shames himself by startling. He stomps the feeling of alarm down and whirls on Jun Ironway to find her eyes rolling back in her head.

"What the fuck?"

Like a javelin in his aural link, the commandant who leads the Silver Keep's casting lab suddenly casts out to him—

"Sa, we have a breach."

Kess turns his back on Ironway, determined she will not see.

"What are you *talking* about?"

"Someone has opened a channel, made a gap in our firewalls—"

A shrieking sound eclipses the commandant's voice. Kess flinches back from it, grateful when it finally stops. When the commandant comes back, he sounds almost wondering. "Casters. Some sort of— a corps or—they're coming through the gap—they're tunneling through the gap!"

Nonsense. Utter nonsense. There's no way an exterior force could break through their shields so suddenly. There's no way—

A voice says, "All they needed was for someone to open the door from the inside."

Seti Kess turns slowly toward the voice, toward the girl in the cage. Jun Ironway's expression is…mocking. A thief in the house. An animal.

Coldly he asks his captain, "What's the status on K-5?"

"Paiye diverted forces to protect the station."

"Send three more warfalcons," Kess orders.

"Sa, that will severely threaten the battle against Paiye. We don't know if more ships—"

Kess looks at her murderously, and she cuts off, nodding once. He wheels on Ironway again, satisfied to find that for all her arrogance, she's struggling to breathe. That first round of interrogation probably broke her ribs. He's going to cut her lungs out of her body.

"My cloaks have orders to destroy K-5. That's over forty thousand saan."

Ironway's eyelashes flutter, and he can see the impact of his words, the flash of emotion.

"That's right. All those station rats. All those families just like yours. I hear Esek Nightfoot shot your uncle in the head. It'll be worse this time. Half the saan will be burned alive in the first assault. Thousands will get sucked into the vacuum. Within the hour, there'll be nothing but floating debris and bodies. Maybe some will survive in little pockets of wreckage. They'll die slow deaths with no one to save them. Is that what you want?"

Ironway doesn't answer. The captain approaches again, her face drawn. "We've dispatched the ships to K-5."

"And Pippashap? What about the Jeveni in the labor camps?"

"Karix Moonback's forces are defending the camp. But we have struck a fatal blow to Pippashap. The city is destroyed."

Little comfort, Kess thinks bitterly. He asks the casting commandant, "What are you doing to contain the breach?"

"Sa, with every moment the entry point gets bigger. If they reach our remote operations system, they may be able to take control of some of our fleet."

"I asked what you are doing to stop it!"

"They're powerful, but they don't have as much power as we do. We can wrest control back with time."

"How long?"

"Fifteen minutes. But longer if they get our operations system."

Kess scoffs. "You have ten minutes."

He rears toward Ironway, ready to gloat—and somehow, she startles him again. One of her hands is free from her bindings. She cradles it to her chest for a moment, and he realizes that she has broken some of her fingers to slip the hand from its shackle. As he watches, she pulls something out of her neural port—a—what is it?

"What is that?" he cries.

It's Riiniana who says, "What kind of thief doesn't carry a lock-pick?"

In instant confirmation, Ironway gouges the tool into a mechanical port on the left wrist manacle. It releases. A few moves more, and the bands at her throat, her ankles, all snick open, revealing rings of scorched flesh. She collapses out of the chair onto her knees, before raising her face again. Her eyes glitter with triumph.

For a moment no one moves. One of the cloaks says, "Our...The neural link port must have camouflaged—"

Kess grabs him before he can react and hurls his body against the holo shield. There is a piercing *crack* and the body drops, twitching and smoking on the ground. Hopefully Ironway sees her own fate in this. She is trembling hard, but she stands. It won't last. She'll faint.

She doesn't.

Riiniana has the temerity to ask, "Is this the part where you suggest terms, Sa Ironway?"

How dare she. How dare—

Ironway rasps, "No terms."

Riiniana raises her eyebrows. "You anticipate a decisive victory."

The answering smile is tiny and malevolent. "I anticipate that we are all well past terms."

"*That* is certainly true," Kess says. "In ten minutes I'll have everything back!"

"And in an hour you'll have nothing."

He laughs—but an icy rush goes through him. She's looking at him now with a dreadful, feral intelligence, the broken hand cradled against her chest again, the blood and burns making her look like a creature out of nightmare. *A bluff*, he thinks. *A bluff.*

He is debating how to respond, how to squash her confidence, when another cast reaches him. His commandant of patrols. And what this commandant tells Seti Kess makes all the rage and uncertainty of the past few minutes dissolve into such joy as he has rarely felt. Even when he discovered Esek Nightfoot was dead, he didn't feel joy like this. For he didn't have the privilege of killing that woman. But *this* time—

"Bring her here," he says excitedly. "*Now.*" He faces Ironway again, gleeful. He can't imagine a better triumph than this. "You sneaky little bitch. But not sneaky enough."

The caster's throat moves as if with subvocal muttering, the fingers of her good hand still twitching, her body caught in the baffling and inhuman work of her casts. But he sees it nonetheless. She looks afraid.

Less than a minute later, he has the pleasure of watching that fear turn to horror, as a clutch of cloaksaan push Liis Konye into the room.

They put her on her knees immediately, hands shackled before her and rifles aimed at the back of her skull. The commandant makes excuses about not finding her on the ship in the first place. He says they tracked her down in some insignificant hallway near one of the ground shuttle bays. Kess will deal with him later. For now he is more interested in Konye's bloodied eye, and the bruises swelling the side of her face. She ignores him to sweep her gaze over Ironway, taking in all the injuries, all the destruction. Kess hopes the sight of her like this is excruciating.

"Hello, Konye," he says.

Finally, she looks at him. Her expression is as still and cool as an undisturbed lake. But she is no cloaksaan, not in her soul. She is a disgrace to the Brutal Hand, to the order that gave her life meaning—a blade's edge that reduced herself to some caster punk's bodyguard. Kess will have her in pieces soon.

"Do you know, Medisogo wanted to hunt you down after you defected? I should have let him. I'll consider your capture a gift to his memory."

She looks at him, but she does not answer.

"You were a great disappointment to me personally," he says. "Such a talent for slaughter. So unemotional and efficient. Sometimes I thought you rivaled Medisogo. I probably would have made the two of you kill each other for top position. But you had no stomach in the end, did you? Just a curse of conscience."

Her eyes are cold. Her silence goads him.

"Have you told yourself you've made up for it all with a righteous life? We know better, don't we?"

Still nothing. Just that stare. Kess sniffs in irritation. Traitor she may be, but she always was the best representative of the Cloaksaan words, going unnoticed even among her kin. So what if she's stoic and unafraid now? It won't last. And there's no stoicism in Ironway. Though delivered from her bonds, the caster is more vulnerable than ever, half-naked and small. She stares at Konye, and Kess could gag at her inability to conceal her feelings, her fear, her *love*. Always the most useful leverage at times like this.

"Now. Let's talk terms," Kess says.

Ironway warns in a voice too strained to worry him, "My allies are minutes away from seizing your operations system. We'll cut off communication in your fleet. Your birds will be marooned."

Kess shrugs. "Maybe. But your lover will be dead. What do you think? Should I shoot off her good arm before executing her?"

He jerks a head at one of the cloaks, who immediately shifts the muzzle of their rifle to set it against the wing of Konye's right shoulder.

"A certain symmetry, don't you think? Maybe I'll cut off both her ears while I'm at it. Gouge out both of her eyes."

"I'm going to kill you," Ironway says, rageful but impotent. "I'm going to kill all of you."

He laughs outright, picturing the little runt trying to fight even the smallest of his cloaks.

Konye speaks for the first time. "Focus, Jun."

"Fuck you. This was a terrible idea!" Ironway retorts.

"Focus," Konye breathes. There is something very like pain in her expression now. Perhaps it is even fear, that weakness he trains out of all his cloaksaan. Not her, apparently, not if those eyes are to be believed. Well, she should be afraid. She's about to die—and her lover next.

Kess says, "Stop your attack on my Keep. Surrender control of this brig and tell us where your caster allies are. Do it all quickly and maybe I'll let the two of you rot your lives out together in a work colony. Make me wait and I'll pick her apart."

For a moment Ironway's eyes fuzz out. Something ticks in her expression, and Kess snarls, "A count of five, do you hear me?! Then I tell my saan to put a bullet through her shoulder!"

Ironway's attention comes back with a snap. She looks desperate now. Terrified and weak. "I can't."

Konye swallows. Is this her breaking point? But though her voice is rough, her words are steady. "You can. You can do anything. You can do everything."

"The new warfalcons are arriving at K-5, Sa," the nearby captain reports.

"Ha!" Kess crows. "There we have it. Double the incentive. I'm counting now."

"Liis," Ironway sobs. "I can't. I *can't!*"

"Five," Kess says. "Four...three."

Before he can count further, Jun Ironway makes a sound so animal it startles him. Not of pain but inchoate fury, and as she does it, her bloodied hands clench and her entire body flexes. Someone in Kess's aural link says, "Wait—it—wait!"

Before he can demand an explanation, pain erupts in Kess's eye, in his ear, in his whole head. He shouts, grabbing at the side of his head, trying to claw out the threat. It tears. It burns. Fire scorching from the inside. Through shock and confusion he hears the cloaks around him crying out, startled yelps at first that transform to screams. *Tech attack*, Kess thinks through the burgeoning agony. *Tech torture.* He's used versions of it himself, and never seen anyone last long. Blood streams wet from his eye and his ear. His vision tunnels; he sways, nearly passing out and reaching out a hand for the wall. There is a crackling sound and a burning smell as someone falls against the cage of Ironway's cell. Lucky he didn't do the same. Lucky he can still see, still hear. Braced against the wall, he tries to remember the one antidote to this agony. It ratchets higher, like a spear driven from his brain stem down his spine. Choking, he remembers the escape route. He shuts off his tech like someone throwing a breaker—every bit of it, every link to his Keep and the net and the world beyond this cell.

The pain does not go away, still throbbing through him. But it fades enough for him to breathe again. He's shocked to realize that he has fallen to his knees. The clutch who had guns on Konye has collapsed, some unconscious and some raking at their heads and faces. He's never heard cloaksaan panic before. Their bodies twist and writhe, as if their very brains are liquefying under the assault. Perhaps they are.

"Turn off your tech!" he shouts at them. But it's not a shout. It's a croak. Disoriented and faint, he faces Ironway again. She stares at him with such demonic threat in her eyes that he feels that rare, incomprehensible experience: fear.

"I will kill them," Jun Ironway says, and it's as if a monster that was inside her has cracked her chest open and crawled out. His eyes widen. "I will kill every fucking one of them." She enunciates each word, her teeth bared, her body straining with a tension that she surely can't maintain, surely not, surely—

"Sa Kess!"

The sound of Riiniana's voice, when he barely remembered that Riiniana was here, baffles him. He's too stunned by the damage around him to do more than look at her. She seems not to have suffered from whatever assault struck him and his cloaks, but her eyes are wide.

"Bargain!" she cries. "Make terms!"

Her entreaty brings his rage surging back. He stumbles to his feet. He draws his sidearm, only to feel a hard jab in his side, and a blow across the arm that sends the gun skittering. He buckles sideways, but not before taking in the sight of Liis Konye on her feet, her shackles looking like little more impediment than strings, her eyes full of murder. All his memories of Liis Konye are of someone dark-willed and solemn and unnoticed. Never this creature whose face seems to open up with the devouring hunger of Som.

"The shields!" she snarls, her words aimed at Ironway, though her eyes never leave Kess.

He hears Ironway panting, hears her sudden cry, "Nearly there, nearly there!"

Kess recovers his stance, remembers who he is, and draws his bloodletter with a swell of confidence and hatred and intention.

"Come on," he tells Konye. "You've never met your match before, have you?"

Liis Konye, still fettered, bares her teeth at him.

Jun Ironway says, "Are you there? Are you there?!"

Kess barely gives attention to the words or who they're intended for. He leaps at Konye, swiping the bloodletter with enough power to cleave her head from her shoulders.

Jun Ironway suddenly gasps, "About fucking time!"

And all the lights go out.

I understand that some members of the Righteous and Clever Hands were troubled to learn that the Jeveni refugees have elected a new Wheel. I assure you that the Jeveni are too scattered now for it to make a difference. If it troubles you so much, we can find legal measures to dissolve them. But these spokes have next to nothing in the way of real power. Consider the so-called River. Historically Rivers were trusted with the defense of the dome cities. Little good that did them! They are no threat to us.

excerpt, letter from First Cloak Von Sivon Trepen to First Cleric Indes Runforth. Dated 1590, Year of the Grave.

CHAPTER THIRTY-ONE

1589

YEAR OF THE STEELTRAP

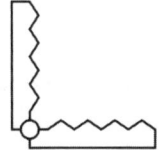

Farren Ki
The Moon Jeve

She went down, into the dark.

The hall was lit by faint emergency lights, a glow barely strong enough to see by, but Drae knew this path by heart. She spread out both her hands, barely skimming her fingers against the walls on either side of her. She thought she heard a soft skittering hiss of nails on jevite, but there was no jevite in the walls, just ordinary moonstone, worthless. This was not a jevite seam. The seams were all west of Farren Ki, but this long passage was to the east, outside the boundaries of the city. An elevator shaft within the city walls had carried her to a depth equal to the Blood Seam and delivered her to this passage. There was a narrow ground shuttle that could have zipped her the two-mile distance from the elevator shaft to this point outside the city, but instead, Drae had walked.

Though she knew that the passage was level, she had a sensation of descent, as if she were on an incline. Deeper, into the underground. Always deeper. Jeve the beast. The monster that whispered and coaxed in its melodic tones, *That's right…Keep going. Come closer.* A seduction that, Drae hoped, would wound her enemies for once, rather than her people. Gus's crews had taken their last bounty from the seams and left them for the vultures. Most of the Farren Ki residents had relocated to the other dome cities, and the last were moving quickly now, a fight against time. At least Lucos proved useful in the end: He sent the warning five hours ago that a fleet of unmarked ships was en route to Jeve from Ma'kess.

Lucos, of course, was not on Jeve. Drae sending Kati and the baby away had been too much even for his naive and myopic love. That, and Alisiana Nightfoot had called him back to Verdant. Probably to provide a final report before the Nightfoots set out to rebirth their mining operation. For of course the anonymous fleet must belong to the Nightfoots. The matriarch herself would be aboard, a promise she had made during negotiations, a gesture of goodwill, to come and meet them personally. The Secretarial Court would accompany her, Alisiana Nightfoot had said. And who knew? Perhaps the First Cleric Runforth and the First Cloak Trepen would come, too, eager for their piece. Perhaps whole branches of the Nightfoot tree would want a stake in this auspicious new beginning. One could hope.

Drae thought about the very polite and entirely bullshit leasing negotiations. Not a single Ma'kessn ingot had reached the Wheel in the two weeks since the Nightfoots signed the contract. No doubt they planned to hem and haw, to string the Jeveni along, and ultimately give them nothing while taking everything.

Drae would pay them for their arrogance. She would receive them as they deserved. Now at last she understood her dream. The figure in the red coat was not just a doppelgänger. It was *her*. The coat she wore in the dream was red with the blood of her enemies. It was she who would tear down the mines.

A cast pinged in her ocular. Dimon.

Where are you?

Not even the crush of heartbreak stopped her smiling at that, though the smile was part of her heartbreak, as Dimon was part of her heartbreak. She replied:

You were ordered to leave Farren Ki an hour ago. Go on to Farren Aul without me. I will follow.

A few moments later he answered:

I will not do that.

She chuckled this time. It caught in her throat. It was absurd to cry about this, as if all they stood to gain did not outweigh what there was to lose. She sent him a series of messages.

I am underground. I have a retreat in mind.

Do not stay in the city. You will not find me there.

Get the last stragglers out of Farren Ki. Now.

He tried to reach her via voice cast, but she ignored it. She had reached the end of the passage, come upon a jagged wall of rock, as if someone had been building a mine and simply given up.

He cast her again.

I am your sword and shield. It is my vow to protect you. I will not let you sacrifice yourself for the sake of grief.

*I do not intend to sacrifice myself. As I said, I will notify you when
I am out.*

He sent another message, but she silenced his pings altogether. She
disabled his access to the elevator shaft, because of course he would
know at once where she had gone. How betrayed he would feel. And if
in the end she *did* sacrifice herself, he would carry the weight forever.
She had no special attachment to the idea of living or dying now. But
for his sake, she hoped a little that she would live. In any case, if she
died, it would not be because of grief. Drae knew herself. She was selfish. She was, in many ways, indifferent to the wishes of others. But she
was also proud, and efficient. A death for no purpose was anathema to
her. If this venture should kill her, she was content at least that there
would be a purpose in it.

She cast out and grasped a view of the atmosphere over Jeve. Her
scans indicated that the fleet, comprised of ten ships, was just under
fourteen minutes away from Jeve's orbit.

Drae reached out a hand, feeling across the wall in front of her for
the smooth part that, to an uninformed observer, would simply look like
another idiosyncrasy of the rock. But the smooth spot was the width of a
hand, and when she pressed her palm against it, the internal sensor read
her print. There was a pause, and what had appeared to be a seamless wall
of rock bifurcated, opening upon a room that glowed with blue light.

Keep going, the moon whispered. *Come closer.*

She went inside, and the door shut behind her. The room was a
clean-cut square, paneled in cast-blocking software. On one side of the
room, there was a compartment with a pod inside it. The pod attached
to a glass chute that went to the surface, well outside the city limits. An
escape route.

The other side of the room displayed massive casting views. Drae called
up a view of the final ships and ground shuttles headed to Farren Aul, and
another view of the Black. Alisiana's fleet was less than ten minutes away
now. Moved by idle curiosity, she activated her tracker on Lucos. He was
in Riin Kala. She considered casting him. But there was no point.

Finally, she looked at the center of the room.

The opaque box was only slightly smaller than the passage that had brought it here. As she approached, the box unfolded, collapsing down into a table to reveal the gate core inside. It stood upon a plinth, as weird and unsettling as the first time she had seen it. It was large and stippled with scales, glowing from within with blue light. Most striking of all was its sentry, a floating holographic eye, slender and dark gold, that looked right at her.

"Why did you give it an eye?" Drae had asked in her last conversation with the Kai Sheep.

She recalled the Kai Sheep blinking at her, almost sleepily, but there was cunning behind it, and appreciation at being caught. Still, it teased, "Whatever, silly, do you mean?"

Of course the Collective would not admit that they had built the gate core, given it this bizarre character, this unnerving eye. "Why build it?" she asked. "Why pretend it wasn't yours yet lead us to buy it? Why help us at all? Do not say it is for money. You could make more by betraying us to the Kindom. What do you gain by aiding our mission?"

The Kai Sheep had held her in suspense. Drae wanted to ask, *Are you the Jeveni boy who fled from us? Who are you? Who are you, really?*

"What do you gain?" Drae repeated.

The Kai Sheep had smiled, leaned closer in its frame, and whispered, *"Change."* Even now, Drae shivered at the memory. She felt unnerved by the word and the Kai Sheep's intensity. It had said, "Do this thing, and what happens, nah? The Treble—it changes. We must have change. Hungry for it, in our bones.

What happens, if there is no change? The thing becomes stagnant. Becomes a parody of itself. And the only good parody is satire." Drae didn't know what this meant, but the Kai Sheep continued. "Satire, see, it demands change. And we must have change. You are our instruments of change. So we help you along. Is it strange? No."

Now, standing in the chamber deep under the surface of Jeve, Drae scowled. She did not like the implication that she was anyone else's tool. She felt more than ever that the eye of the gate core was there to watch her, to watch the Jeveni. Lot 11 had been so spare and lovely, like a dancer. Lot 12 was uncanny and monstrous. Its glittery scales reflected her face back at her. Though it was not alive, she felt the life in it, a heartbeat. A hunger. It was magnetic and it was hypnotizing, and it coaxed Drae toward an act of unspeakable blasphemy.

There was a cast pad embedded in the table's surface. Only she had the code to this one.

"Sajeven, beloved," she said, though she never prayed. "We are the despised and the forgotten. We are barren in these systems, marked for disposal. You said the barren would flourish, but how have we flourished? Is mere survival a flourishing?" She paused to consider the confession she had kept to herself for all her life. Now she finally spoke it aloud. "I have never believed. You are real to me only as a metaphor is real. I have tried, for my people's sake, to believe. But I cannot believe what they believe. I cannot believe that this place is our birthright or our blessing. If you are ceaseless kind, you could not do such a thing to us. What kind of friendship is that? What kind of love?"

Upon its plinth, Lot 12 glowed and glowed. The fleet was eight minutes out.

Drae said, "I refuse to believe that we belong to this place. If we are bound to Jeve, it must be so that we may destroy it. We must be like your maker, the Godfire, and burn evil to dust. How else am I to survive all that I have lost, unless I believe this?"

Sajeven did not answer. The gods never answered. It was just as well, for if Sajeven tried to speak to her now, to make explanations, Drae would explode with the force of a star, and the conflagration would turn her into a god, and she would hunt down all the gods and kill them. For why should the gods get to live when her child on *The Hope* no longer lived? The younger of the twins, who had gendered herself female. Five years old. Drae had learned of it just a few days ago and told no one, not even Haishik. An accident. The girl fell down the hard metal stairs between one level of the ship and another. Silly, clumsy child feet. A death with no purpose.

On *The Glitch*, Haishik had made the other twin, the older one, as good as their own son, and he thrived.

On Teros, drovers were raising her youngest, the baby not yet two, not yet gendered, and they thrived.

On Kator, Kati was almost eight years old, folded into the arms of a farming family. And he thrived.

But her daughter on *The Hope* was dead, and so a portion of Drae's hope was dead, and she felt the rest of it leaking out of her, as if from a wound that could not close. She glanced over at the escape pod, which could shoot her through a mile of rock and into the Black in a fraction of the time it would take to go up that elevator again. She had told Dimon that she had no intention of dying. After all her lies, what harm would it be to lie one more time?

She reached out and held her hand a hairsbreadth from the glowing sphere. She felt the delicious seductive nearness of her death. The eye appeared in the air again. Without a mouth, it nevertheless spoke, placid, emotionless:

"Command ready."

Unexpectedly, those words filled her with triumph, which did not come from Sajeven or her people, but from her own seething, frothing, murderous self.

In the throes of her own hunger, she received a ping.

It was not Dimon, or the Wheel, or Lucos. It was... She frowned in confusion. It was the Kai Sheep, whom she had not spoken to in many months. It sent her a simple message.

Alisiana is not with the fleet.

Drae stared a long time. Her initial feeling was confusion, then the irritation of someone receiving false information.

What?

It answered after a few moments.

There are no valuable targets with the fleet. In case that is what you were hoping. The fleet is comprised of cloaksaan.

Drae was still confused. Something she couldn't quite name began to crawl up her throat, like a worm too thick and long to swallow. Her eyes shot toward the view of the Black. She could see the armada approaching now. It bore no identifying marks. The Kai Sheep said:

We advise your people to evacuate.

She blinked. She didn't understand.

We have already left Farren Ki.

It answered:

We advise your people to evacuate Jeve.

Her bewilderment turned to sickening comprehension. Her heart was all spasming muscle, her blood too thin.
The Kai Sheep said:

Run.

It was like someone kicking an engine to make it start. Drae jerked, hurled into motion. She sent out the signal to the Wheel and to all the ships on Jeve and into every corridor and building of every dome city on the moon, and in her head she was screaming, *Evacuate! Evacuate Jeve! Run! Run now!*
Missiles pierced the exosphere.
At the first explosions, she staggered back, as if she could feel the vibration of it all this way underground. The missiles came not like a single spear, but like a wave the width of Jeve itself. Drae widened her cast field, and realized that they were attacking not just Farren Ki,

but the other dome cities as well, and the entire known breadth of the mines. They were bombing the power hubs that controlled the holo domes. As she watched, the hubs vanished into craters, and the domes came down. It was like peeling back the skin to expose muscle and bones and nerves, the beating pulse of her people, flayed alive.

Drae went silent and still.

In a vague and disoriented way, she sensed that what was happening could not be articulated. That it was something beyond language, and immeasurable to the human mind, like the ocean she had seen that time on Braemin. There were two million Jeveni on Jeve. Two million was just a number. What did two million look like? It looked like the cities exploding, like the buildings collapsing, like the little ships with their cargo of saan that had understood the evacuation order. And it looked like abandoned homes and forgotten dolls and people running without shoes and the sucking vacuum and the aborted cries. It was what the moon always longed for, when it whispered its welcome to the greedy mouths across the Treble: *Keep going. Come closer.*

She looked dully over at the gate core. Lot 12 was nothing but a useless lump now. It was defanged. For years she had held it in reserve, a bomb she could detonate if the Kindom ever landed on her moon. It had within it the power to fling warwhales from one solar system to another. Its activation, if confined underground, would trigger an explosion to dwarf all known missiles in all known history. The damage would not reach as far as the other dome cities, it would not threaten her people, but the moon would cave in below it, and the surface would collapse above it, and any Kindom Hand or First Family monster who stood in Farren Ki would be swallowed down into a darkness nearly twenty miles wide and deep. Blame it on sinkholes and crust collapse. Hadn't that been what Lucos said he was here to study, back when he pretended he was a scholar? And so the core would trigger a sinkhole as big as a sea, and Alisiana Nightfoot would die.

But Alisiana was not coming. And the moon would be destroyed anyway.

Drae knew that she should be moving, running for the elevator and her threatened city above, or even fleeing via the escape pod. She couldn't move. Pointlessly, she sent out the evacuation call again. The Wheel answered:

"Drae?" said the Star in her ear. "What is happening?"

"Get off the moon. Get everyone off the moon."

She saw on cast that there were more Jeveni ships lifting off, but—

"They're bombing the airfields," the Star told her, and though his voice was strained, he was not panicking. "Drae, where are you? It must be some Nightfoot enemy doing this. There is no other explanation."

"They wish to destroy the mines," she said with cold certainty. "They wish to destroy all knowledge of the mines."

Then no one would come looking for those mines, and no war would break out over the jevite seams, and it would spare the Kindom and the Nightfoots far more in costs than they stood to gain from restarting the trade. It was the...economical decision. She understood this because it was the same logic she had used herself throughout her life.

The Star sounded baffled. "But Drae, why would they—"

Her calm snapped long enough to shout at him. "Get off the moon!"

"We are moving now. We are nearly to the—"

His voice cut off so abruptly she felt it like a knife severing a cable. She tried to raise him again, but there was nothing, just blankness. She knew what that meant.

She turned and looked at the core again. Perhaps it wasn't useless. Perhaps the Nightfoots still meant to mine the moon, they just wanted to eliminate its denizens first. So there was still a way to enact some revenge.

She stepped toward Lot 12, full of purpose, but at that moment the door into the room opened. Two figures stepped inside. Gus ben Roq and Dimon. They were as pale gray as ash.

"What—" she began.

She had locked down the elevator shaft. Gus looked at her with defiant eyes. "You think you have more control over that elevator than I do, my River? I am the one who built it!"

He and Dimon were clean, uninjured. She realized they had been in the elevator shaft when the bombing started. Coming to find her had saved them. For the moment.

Dimon said, "There is a ship waiting. We must go."

"Tell them to leave," Drae ordered. "We will not get there in time."

"I will not tell them to leave. Come now, or I will force you."

She blinked, surprised. She saw the determination in his face. Despite being the River, she had never trained as a warrior. She could not fight.

My dream, she thought. *My revenge.*

Keep going. Come closer.

Outside the room, the small ground shuttle was waiting. Gus and Dimon had not walked the passage as she had, had not wasted time as she had. The shuttle bolted them from the gate core compartment all the way back to the elevator shaft within the city walls. Even though she knew that Dimon and Gus had just come down the elevator, she expected it to jam. Instead, the car shot upward immediately. The glide was smooth, inexplicably easy, and no one spoke. Her disorientation came back. Even as her cast reports returned footage of unrelenting destruction, even as she watched a few spare ships escape while tens of hundreds of thousands died trapped in their homes, even through all of that, the elevator ride was quiet. She was outside of time and reality. She had died, perhaps, and this was her penance. To spend eternity in the moving car, and watch her failures unspool in the endless explosions on the surface of Jeve.

But the elevator came to a halt. They went through the hallway and up some stairs into a tiny enclosure that was another short flight of stairs from the surface. She shook herself out of the stupor, and would have run for the stairs if Dimon had not stopped her, indicating the emergency cupboard in the wall with its folded space suits. Cupboards like these existed all over Farren Ki, all over the dome cities. A safety measure in the event of atmospheric decompression or dome failure.

Drae thought, *Maybe the people in the cities will put on the suits and some of them will live.*

She and Gus and Dimon helped one another into their suits. Gus's hands trembled. Dimon's did not. The ground suddenly heaved under them and shook and shook. Drae barely stopped Gus from falling over. She knew the Black would swallow up all sounds, all the crashing crunching detonating furor of the missiles, but even if she couldn't hear it, Drae could feel it in the rock beneath her as she pulled the helmet over her head and clipped the final closures.

They sprinted the stairs and burst through the doors at the top, into a building that had no roof and no southern wall. This building had been three stories high, once. The second story had included a nursery for the children of miners. Thank Sajeven there were no more children in Farren Ki. Then Drae remembered the nurseries in the other cities, and her stomach heaved. Dimon grabbed her and yanked her in the opposite direction. They raced out another door and into the open air of the moon. With the dome gone, the Black should have been clear, unobscured, but there was a thick atmosphere of smoke and dust. The building next to theirs had a massive hole in it. She imagined the impact of the missile and any hint of flame immediately extinguished by the atmosphere. But the destruction was enough without fire.

"Come," said Dimon in her aural link. "Hurry."

They ran through devasted streets. The ground sprung up beneath them and they hurtled forward. Drae didn't understand how there could be a ship waiting for them, how it could possibly have survived so far, but Dimon told her they were only a quarter mile away and the ship was secure. She realized after a couple of minutes that there seemed to be a lull in the attack on Farren Ki. Had the Nightfoots realized that it was abandoned?

Through her aural link, she heard Gus muttering prayers. He was gasping for breath. She wanted to scream at him to stop praying. Perhaps she would have, except in the distance she saw the tallest building in Farren Ki, a dormitory tower, suddenly list sideways and begin to collapse. The building was square and functional and without ornament, and now one side broke off from the other, as if a blade had sliced it into two pieces. With the dome disabled, gravity had gone light. For a moment the bigger side of the building seemed to float on the air, suspended in time. The eeriness of the sight almost made Drae stop, but time restarted, and the tower hit the surface. A great cloud rose up and rushed outward with a speed and power that suggested sentience. She realized it was closer than she had thought, far too close, for the cloud was coming at them, and the force of the collapse was striking surrounding buildings, and the buildings were coming down—

Dust rolled in and over her, not thin like fog but thick and full of grit. The ground shook. Drae fell. Everything around her was vibrating and rocking. After what seemed like a long time she managed to stand up again. She looked around herself, into the impenetrable miasma of the dust, and couldn't see anything. She was lost, and there was a sharp pain in her hip and a soreness in her shoulder from where she had fallen. When she tried to move that arm, pain cut through her and she yelped. The arm was dislocated. Just about to cast out to Dimon and Gus, she was startled almost to screaming when a hand grabbed her uninjured arm.

"Hurry," Dimon said, his voice ragged. "This way." He led her.

They had probably been running for a while when she remembered fuzzily—"Gus! Where is Gus?"

Dimon didn't answer. She flung a cast at Gus's aural link, but it was just like when the Star's voice cut off. There was nothing left on the other side. Dazedly she wondered how Dimon could see well enough to get them anywhere. Running with her dislocated shoulder was like being stabbed over and over. She thought she would vomit. She had to slow down. She opened her mouth to tell Dimon so—

Something lifted her off her feet. One moment she was running, and the next she was spinning through the air. She felt the missile's kill field hit her body as if she'd been thrown into a wall, and perhaps she was thrown into a wall, for she lost consciousness.

How long did it last? It seemed to her that she was coming in and out of it for a while. Someone was shouting, but she couldn't answer. She couldn't even feel the dislocated shoulder now. She couldn't feel anything, at first, except that something bad had happened. Through it all came a sudden, incongruous surge of relief. *My children are not here*, she thought. *They will not die in the explosions. They will not suffocate for lack of proper suiting. They will not feel the terror of this. I have done one good thing. My children are not here.*

The shouting in her ear clarified. It was one of Dimon's sentries.

"My River!" they shouted. They were standing over her and she could just barely see their eyes through their helmet. Their eyes were a color like river moss, but this was not enough to recognize them. They had her by the shoulders of her suit. "My River, can you walk?"

Where was Dimon? She couldn't answer the sentry. She couldn't move. There was a strange tightness in her abdomen. She saw the sentry look down at her body and suddenly they were behind her and dragging her by her shoulders. They dragged her through the wreckage of the moon. She passed out and woke and did it over again, and at some point the movement stopped. She realized that her helmet was gone. She wasn't lying on the ground, but on something like a cot. There were people standing over her. Someone with a knife was cutting her suit open.

"You are all right, my River," the person with the knife said. They had a pale, pinched expression, but they moved efficiently.

Her suit split apart like skin. Delirious, she looked down her body. A very thick piece of something metal was sticking out of her abdomen. There was so much blood it covered her torso up to her breasts and down to her thighs.

She said, "I cannot feel anything."

The sentry medic said, "It is all right. Just breathe."

But breathing hurt. Someone nearby was weeping. She felt the jolt and lift of a ship rising from the surface. Dimon had gotten her to the ship. The ship had survived long enough for him to reach it. This was absurd. It was something past luck. It was not a blessing.

A face suddenly swam over her, and she recognized the river-moss eyes. She remembered that this was the person who had dragged her

eyes. She remembered that this was the person who had dragged her to the ship.

"Where is Dimon?" she rasped.

The person had taken off the space suit helmet. They were a woman, unhurt. She said to Drae, "We are stabilizing you as best we can. We will get you to a surgeon."

"Where is Dimon?" she asked again.

"Do not worry, my River. He is on a different shuttle."

Drae knew at once that the sentry was lying to her. Dimon was dead. She couldn't even think to be angry about the lie. She couldn't even think to grieve, for Dimon or for Gus. Perhaps the grief would come later. She looked down at her body and thought, *Maybe not.* Either she was paralyzed or they had given her medicine to numb the pain. She felt the wrongness in her body. As the shuttle rose, as it left Jeve behind, a chasm opened inside her that was like the chasm forged by the missiles striking the moon. How much of a thing could be destroyed before it stopped being that thing? Was she still herself, when the inside of her body was destroyed?

She suddenly remembered that she had given Haishik the cypher that would allow them to arm the gate core. Why had she done that, again? Oh, yes, so that if she died, someone else could do it, someone else could finish the job. A contingency. An instinct for survival and success. The same instinct that had driven her to take Lucos as her lover. To send her children away. To purchase Lot 12 and put it underground and send the code to Haishik like an assassin handing over a poisoned blade. Suddenly she was confused and wondered if it had been instinctual after all. If it had even been her own idea. In her memory, it suddenly seemed as if a hand had moved her hand, as if a voice had spoken in her ear. Not her body's ear, not her aural link, but some other hearing thing inside her, that had reached out and been found.

She glimpsed a corner of window and realized they were in the Black. Would the Cloaksaan ships shoot them down? For the sake of all these sentries, and anyone else who had survived, she hoped not.

For her own sake, she hoped nothing, except that she could stay awake a little longer. To help, she thought of Haishik, those eyes warm and crinkled with laugh lines at the corners. She thought of Kati, and hoped he was playing somewhere and stretching his fast, fantastic mind to its limits. She thought of her twins as they were born, one after the other, wrinkled wet screaming things, their bodies placed together on her breast where she lay sweat-soaked and bloodied, laughing and sobbing. She thought of her youngest. The last one.

"Oh," she whispered, picturing them. "Oh..."

There were voices around her, urgent. There were people leaning in and she saw the flash of panicked faces. She closed her eyes. *By Sajeven's own mercy*, she thought, *I bless you. May your life have joy. May your death have purpose. More than mine, more than mine.*

A voice that was not a voice in the ship said, *All death is a return.*

And Drae's eyes flew open. The voice was true. The voice was answering! She filled with wonder to have heard it, at last, after all this time. She could have laughed. She could have sung. She called out to her children, and her children's children, and all the children in the dark. *Listen*, she said. *Listen.*

And she was sure they heard it, too.

CHAPTER THIRTY-TWO

1665

YEAR OF THE HARVEST

The Moon Jeve

When the Silver Keep's holo dome comes down, a crack and snap of power and a feeling like a pulse through Six's body, five of the cloaksaan are already dead. But not without cost.

You're doing rather poorly, Esek whispers in their ear, so close they almost feel her lips, a wet drag, but no—it's just the sweat dripping down the side of their face. They wipe at it without thinking, forgetting they can't reach it with their helmet on, and pain shoots through their side, radiating all the way to their fingertips. The clutch had the disadvantage of approaching from lower ground. Six and Chono were able to pick off four before the other five reached them, and the fight was ferocious but quick—thanks to Jun Ironway.

Esek chuckles, or is that the sound of one of the figures gurgling on the ground? No, the three surviving cloaks were screaming quite a lot before, but now they are unconscious. This is the first time Six has seen the effects of Ujan Redcore's revised tech virus. Jun modified it to target the vagus nerve. Hence, agony plus unconsciousness. What a clever little monster Jun turned out to be. Six thinks of the proud child they met in a safe house years ago, who turned out to be as hard to kill as Six themself.

"You okay?" Chono asks.

Six doesn't answer at first. The impulse to lie is instant, but it's harder to ignore her wishes than it used to be.

"My side," they admit.

Even with her helmet on, they see the flash of concern in her eyes. She comes to them, and they let her look. There's nothing to see. The spacewalker suit has already sealed up over the wound to prevent them being frozen to death by the atmosphere. But Six senses some deep injury under their ribs, near their liver.

"How bad?" Chono demands.

"I do not know."

Chono growls, "Go back to the ship."

What a ridiculous thing for her to say.

"I will not."

"Six—"

"I am as likely to die getting back as going forward. We must continue. You know this."

She doesn't answer. She has put one of her hands on their shoulder, the other on their hip. It would be like the grasp of a lover, but she is only doing it to hold them still so she can keep staring uselessly at the space where the wound is. Six breathes hard. With angry, helpless movements, Chono goes to the drill that they abandoned during the fight with the cloaksaan. She puts it on her shoulder.

You wouldn't even be able to lift that right now, Esek mocks them.

"Come on," Chono says. Her voice is strained. But it does not break.

They make their careful way down the slope, Six grimacing through it, annoyed that Chono is watching them closely. She needs to pay attention to her surroundings. There could be other clutches, saan somehow unaffected by the tech virus. If this injury ends up getting Chono killed, they will never—

A message pings across their ocular.

Getting there, we hope?

It's the Minkat. Six grunts, their side vibrating with angry nerves and torn muscles.

Two minutes out from coordinates.

Faster faster, please go faster! We have a grasp, but not forever!

Six ignores this, and one minute and forty-two seconds later they come upon an innocuous-looking smoothness of moon rock within feet of a missile crater. Their oculars project a large red circle onto the rock, though there is no evidence of an opening, or even a footprint to suggest any cloaksaan has trodden on the surface. Putting the drill down, Chono drops to her knees and begins to wipe her palms over the ground. Under what must be three inches of dust, a pale gray metal appears.

Chono looks up at Six. Six nods, and Chono stands, hefting the drill again. They help her bolt the drill's frame to the edges of the projected circle, the bit (as thick as Six's arm) pointing into its center.

"Power up," Six says, trying not to sway as they stand upright again.

The drill bit starts to spin, a massive spearpoint too fast for the eye to see. It is almost anticlimactic when the hatch cracks open within moments. The drill bit, not done with its fancy tricks, makes a *thhk* sound, prongs protracting under the surface to hook into the underside, its grip extending as far as the perimeter of the hatch. With

Chono's and Six's guidance, the drill engine pulls, straining at first and then jumping as a large plate of metal springs free. Some wrangling later, they get the bit and the plate out of the way, and find beneath it the dark throat of a clear round chute.

"Fuck," Chono murmurs.

Fuck indeed, says Esek.

According to Drae sen Briit's journal, there should be an escape pod at the bottom of the chute. Some distance away, there may also be an elevator beneath the ruins of the city, one that leads to the room and the thing that Drae referred to as Lot 12. If the Cloaksaan found that elevator when they built their Keep, they may be guarding Lot 12. Or have removed it altogether. If they *didn't* find it—

Chono messages the Minkat:

The escape shaft is here. We're heading down now.

The Minkat answers instantly.

Excellent. Very sorry. Very breathless, at this moment, and busy, for the cloaks are trying to take their kingdom back. We will need such a rest after this! But everything goes beautifully!

"That is optimistic," Six mutters, wincing against a hot throb in their side.

Chono affixes the rappelling gear to the edge of the chute, which is made of thick smooth glass. Six grimaces again, Esek's gleeful chuckle in their ear. It will be murder to go down this way, but it can't be helped. Chono comes to them with the harness and ignores their attempts to stop her helping them. When she has it fixed around their hips and across their chest and shoulders, she pauses to look at them.

"I'll go first. You need to not lose consciousness on the way down. Can you do that?"

They are relieved that she speaks to them like a soldier instead of a lover. They nod once, unsure if it's a lie. Chono's eyes through the face shield of her helmet are pained, but she doesn't question them. She lowers herself into the chute, and then she is zipping down into the dark. Six follows.

The descent is not easy. Chono has affixed the harness so that they carry their weight in their hips and legs, but the compression in their torso is excruciating, and the glass is more slippery than they expect, making it harder to control their movements. More than once, they almost pass out. Six focuses on Chono's heavy but controlled breathing, and they marshal every strategy they ever taught themself for working through pain. They're not dead yet. It can't have hit any major arteries or organs.

If you say so, Esek says.

Chono calls back to them, "How are you doing?"

Her voice is tight. Six imagines that they must sound on the verge of hyperventilation in her aural link. They feel wet under their armor.

"Fine," they say.

"Six, are you—"

A new message pings across their ocular, and, grateful for the distraction, Six anticipates the Minkat again. But it is not the Minkat.

Hello, Esek. We need to talk.

Six is so surprised that they don't answer at first. Yet somehow the message is like a shot of adrenaline, bringing clarity to their muddied thoughts. They share the cast connection with Chono, and answer:

Bright Daughter. What a surprise.

Riiniana's response is immediate.

Maybe you hoped Ironway's attack would incapacitate me?

If she means the tech virus, then Riiniana Nightfoot is in the Silver Keep. Of course she is. Kess would have wanted to keep her close, an insurance against her Nightfoot fleet disobeying him. Six answers:

It was written to attack cloaksaan. You are fortunate, Riiniana, to be spared. It appears to be quite agonizing.

Some of the cloaks shut off their tech before it could incapacitate them. There is a fight happening in the brig. You must get me out of here.

Even struggling with the rappelling kit, even nauseated with pain, Six is amused.

So eager to abandon your fiancé?

Riiniana doesn't acknowledge that question. She says,

I have hidden myself in one of the brig cells. If Liis Konye prevails, you must tell her to take me with her.

Chono breathes in sharply, which Six knows is relief. Konye is alive. Surely Jun is, too. Six recalls the battle on *The Risen Wave*, when Liis leapt off a train into a crowd of cloaks and Chono was so moved by it she nearly got herself killed trying to save her. But Six and Chono can do nothing to help Liis Konye now.

Riiniana casts out again.

If you promise to help me, I will order the Nightfoot forces to turn on Kess. He is vulnerable in both Ma'kess and Teros Systems. We can defeat him.

Gods and fire, what a negotiator! Esek says. *I'm rather proud. She must have more of me in her than I thought.*

"Tell her yes," Chono says through comms. "Tell her to send the order and we'll make sure Liis gets her out."

"*If* Liis can get her out," Six grumbles. "And that's assuming she deserves to get out."

Riiniana Nightfoot held them prisoner. She *threatened Chono.*

"Damnit, Six, enough revenge! If we can have another Family head on our side, it's worth saving her!"

Six feels that rarest of emotions: shame. Only Chono could do this to them.

Pathetic, Esek says. *Bewitched.*

Yes, Six thinks. *I am bewitched by her. But better her than you.*

They cast out to Riiniana.

Turn your dogs on Kess. Stay close to Jun Ironway. If she and Konye survive, and if you show them what you have done, Konye will take you to safety.

Swear it.

I am busy. Liis Konye is all honor. Do this thing, and she will save you.

Riiniana doesn't respond. But it doesn't matter if she responds. Beneath Six there is a light, and a change in air pressure. And then, like explorers discovering a new world, Chono and Six reach the bottom of the escape shaft. There is no more time for Riiniana.

The escape pod takes up the bottom of the shaft, but there's space between it and the ceiling of the room. A controlled glass breaker shatters them enough space to get inside. Six watches Chono detach her kit and go through the gap into the room beyond. Unclipping their own kit sends a lance of pain through Six so intense that they have to choke off a whimper. Only when they can breathe again do they swing in after her and land on their feet.

Everything around them is a surprise. If nothing else, they expected the room to be damaged, to be dark, to be perilous. They never imagined this pristine chamber, untouched by time. There is a door on the other side of the room that leads back toward the ruins of Farren Ki. The walls are without blemish, covered in cast views that look as if they've been dark for a long time. Pale blue light fills the room, emanating from a central plinth. The plinth reminds Six of something, though they can't say what, can't tell if the memory is their own, or some deep epigenetic reference point. Upon the plinth stands the large square shape of Lot 12.

"By the gods," Chono whispers.

She stands a few feet away from it, and there is a holographic eye staring back at her. It is as big as Chono's head, a terrible, unnerving, intelligent observer. When Six shifts closer, the eye shifts, too, taking them in. Six senses that it is scanning beneath the surface of them, seeing them not like a machine does but like a god. Then suddenly they imagine that it is Drae sen Briit looking at them. Their great-great-grandmi, who they can never know, whose every descendant may be dead, except for Six. They feel suddenly the magnificent burden of that. They feel like a rich artery of blood, flowing hot, DNA passed down through to them from Drae in the form of a thirty-character alphanumeric code that they and Chono have memorized in the hours since Jun gave it to them. The code to Lot 12. A branding. A mission. They step closer to the giant box on its plinth.

The eye vanishes and the box collapses, creating a table to better display its banquet. Six's breath hitches. They've never seen a gate core, not in all their travels through the Black. It is almost too bright to look at, covered in tiny facets like the scales of a monster. It calls to them. They reach out a hand toward it. They feel as if they could press their hand through it, into an untamable power. And with that power, they could tear down the walls.

The large eye flashes back into being, golden and slender. Six's hand freezes in the air. The code sings in their blood.

A voice speaks to them:

"Command ready."

CHAPTER THIRTY-THREE

1665

YEAR OF THE HARVEST

The Silver Keep
The Moon Jeve

In the first year after Jun fled the Riin Kala Academy of Archivists, fled Esek Nightfoot, and fled the terror of being forced into hiding with the rest of her family, she fell in with a group of casters who were as delighted to experiment with euphorics as with casting itself. Jun, fifteen years old and needing a place to sleep during the wet, freezing winters on Dunta continent, let them slot a euphorics coin into her neural port.

Afterward, she determined never to use euphorics again. It was too intense, too freeing, too much the sort of thing that would make her forget her commitment to save her family. She contented herself that the surging cool ecstasy of the drug sliding right into her brain was less satisfying than the world she created in her casts. For her casts have always been another kind of high, a way of touching the divine, a perfect harmony between her soul and dreams and body.

Right now, standing in the brig of the Silver Keep, tapped into the Cloaksaan casting net that has yielded to her like soil for a trowel, she feels something akin to that euphorics hit. Jun has never touched a power source like this before. Not when she was at school, not when she used her Hood program to connect the entire Jeveni fleet, not when she took over the Farren Eyce casting corps. This is almost too much for her brain to endure.

In her mindscape, she is standing at the center of the universe, and everything around her churns with stars dying and stars being born. It's not simply a matter of having tapped into a securities system or a database of almost limitless information. The Silver Keep reaches out with more arms than Terotonteris, each one ending in a claw that has its talons hooked in the Cloaksaan fleet. Every warwhale, every kite and falcon and warcrow. In the gyre of the universe around her, she sees the bright flares of thousands of other casters, and though most are the black hole shimmer of cloaksaan, there are, dotted among them, over a hundred silver shapes: the archivists of the Ar'tec Collective. They are tunneling through the Silver Keep's infrastructure. They are seizing the Cloaksaan casters like hornets seizing bees, stabbing with their stingers and mandibles, devouring with wide jaws the startled, unsuspecting cloaks. Fat with feed and left to conquer the nest, the caster hornets disable the Kindom communication system, cutting the cloak casters and ships off from one another. Yorus Inye's warwhale in Capamame System loses access to its warcrows and to the cloaksaan in Farren Eyce. It may be enough to cause chaos. It may give the Jeveni that inch of advantage they need—

Suddenly the Capamame gate bursts open, and a fleet of pirate ships jumps through.

Masar, she thinks dreamily, half-drunk on the energy swirling through her. *Fuck, if he ever finds out how high I am right now—*

She manages to shake herself into some level of coherence. She blinks rapidly and focuses on the hornet attacks. Given time, her allies could devour and destroy every bee in the hive. But she can sense how many cloaks managed to escape her tech virus. She had always known that she and the Ar'tec Collective would not be able to hold this advantage indefinitely. She predicts another thirty minutes, tops, before the Kindom casters reclaim the Keep and raise the shields again. When they do, *they* will be the hornets. Only one thing can truly decimate them. And that thing is deep underground, pulsing like the heart of a god.

When hands grab her, she thinks it is happening in the cast at first, ropes of electricity reaching to bind and suffocate. A moment later she realizes that it is actually human hands—and not Liis's hands, but smaller ones, delicate, seizing her wrist and biting in with sharp nails. The pain is so acute that Jun snaps into awareness of the room around her. A girl is standing in front of her, pale and furious-looking. The girl grabs both her arms and yanks her, until Jun finds herself pulled down behind the chair where Kess's cloaks bound and tortured her. Now she knows why it hurts so much, the girl's grip. Jun's wrists are burned almost to the bone. So are her ankles and her throat. She is half-naked and covered in blood.

"Get down!" the girl hisses. "You've almost been shot twice!"

With a hit of terror, Jun suddenly remembers—

"Liis? Where is Liis—"

Panicked, she tries to get up. The girl yanks her down again.

"Wait, damn you! There are only two left."

Jun isn't sure what that means. She suddenly realizes that the girl is Riiniana Nightfoot. Seti Kess's ally. The one who sent her Nightfoots out to attack the rebels. Why the fuck is Riiniana Nightfoot here? And why is she draping something cool and soft over Jun's shoulders?

The room goes quiet. The sounds Jun heard before, which she realizes now were the gasps and grunts of hand-to-hand combat, have ceased. There's a tread of approaching footsteps and Riiniana's grip on her arms tightens excruciatingly—

Liis drops into a crouch beside them. Broken shackles hang from her wrists, the chains clinking. One of her eyes is bloodied and swollen and she is wet with sweat, but her gaze is clear. She puts her hands on Jun's face, very carefully.

"Are you all right?" Her voice is stern, but with a crack under the surface that betrays her fear. "Are you with me?"

Jun knows, quite definitively, that she is not all right. The blast of the Silver Keep's power that hit her minutes ago temporarily numbed some of the pain, but she can feel it all again, and she realizes that she may well go into shock if Liis lets her.

"Yes," she says, her teeth chattering. "I—yes."

Liis nods, helping her up, adjusting whatever it was Riiniana draped over her—a silk cloak. Too fancy for this, already staining with Jun's blood and sweat. She blinks at the bodies of cloaks on the ground, most probably unconscious from the effects of the tech virus, but there are about five that bear the bloody aftereffects of Liis's violence. Seti Kess isn't among them.

Jun chokes out, "We have to get out of the Keep before they manage to raise their shields again. We'll be trapped."

Liis nods. "I know the route to the bay. *The Gunner* is there." She looks at Riiniana, frowning.

"I ordered the Nightfoots to turn on Kess!" Riiniana blurts. Her eyes are wide, but there is also a stubborn arrogance in them. "Esek—I mean Six—they said you would take me with you."

Liis looks at Jun, a question, and Jun dips back into the roiling universe of the cast. She reaches toward the battlegrounds in the Treble. A dozen visuals hit her at once: The Teros System dogfight has collapsed now that the pirates are in Capamame System; Zemit's forces on Teros itself are barely holding off the Kindom battalions; Nikapraev and Riin Cosas are secured, though there is no word from Melosi the Grave; Hejar Paiye's fleet is picking apart a disabled warwhale, but half her ships are in pieces; Karix's and Giran's armies are locked in battle across the southern continents of Ma'kess, many cities and factories and the Jeveni labor camp pluming with black smoke; Pippashap is gone, warcrows floating corpse-like on the Endless Sea; K-5 is surrounded and heavily damaged, but half the Cloaksaan offensive seem to have lost power, and Imicanta Oninye and her depleted Katish forces are taking them out one by one.

And then there are the Nightfoots—hundreds of warships, thousands of ground troops, every one of them throwing their might against the Kindom.

Jun looks at Liis and nods.

"All right," Liis says. "Let's go."

Walking is excruciating. Jun's ankles feel brittle as dried-out twigs. She doesn't tell Liis. She doesn't tell her that she thinks one of her ribs might be broken and stabbing into her lung, making it hard to breathe, making the feeling of the Silver Keep's power around her shift from overwhelming to frightening. Liis walks ahead of them. She has a gun in each hand and others strapped to the holsters on her cloaksaan uniform. Where did she get that? The uniform has a long slice down the back, blood glittering in the gap. Riiniana hurries along beside Jun.

Jun whispers to her, "I need you to help me walk."

It's a little startling, how quickly the slim arm loops around her waist and a hand pulls Jun's arm over her shoulder. For some reason she thought Riiniana would be too squeamish for it, but the girl matches step to Jun at once, providing just enough support to make their hurried pace bearable.

That's when Jun remembers. She casts out through the Keep.

What's happening?

Part of her is afraid she'll get no answer. But Chono's cast pings back at her.

We're in.

Jun nearly chokes on relief and excitement and the pain in her body. She does a quick calculation of the Ar'tec Collective's assault on the Cloaksaan, and the Cloaksaan's rallying counterassault. She recalculates how long it will take for the Cloaksaan to reclaim control of the Keep and their forces across the Black. She assesses the distance to the bay where *The Gunner* should be waiting, and then casts back at Chono:

> *You need to get out of there in the next twenty-four minutes. When the Silver Keep's shield goes up again, there'll be no way for you to escape.*

To her surprise, this time Chono answers with her voice.

"We're having a problem with the escape pod."

Jun opens her mouth and closes it. Ahead of her, emergency lights flicker, the hallway dark and abandoned. They had all focused on the possibility that the escape chute itself would be impassable, or that Kess would know about Lot 12 and have it under guard. Jun had assumed that if Six and Chono could get down into the Lot 12 chamber without incident, the escape pod would be able to get them back up again.

"Are the tracks damaged?" she asks.

"No, it simply won't power on."

"Can you climb up the chute?"

"Six is injured."

Suddenly Six shoulders their voice into the conversation. "I can do it."

"Fucking sit down!" Chono snaps. "You're pale as death."

Jun, too, feels pale as death. If Chono thinks Six is too weak to climb up the chute, Six is too weak to climb up the chute.

"Let me look," Jun says.

In her cast, she wades through the chaos of battling casters. She works her way slowly underground, feeling like an earthworm biting through dirt, too slow, too slow. She searches for Lot 12, for whatever power source is controlling it, for whatever cast access she can get to the escape chute and the pod. But though she can pin its location, she can't get inside it. She curses, stumbling. Somehow Riiniana keeps her upright. Liis looks back, and stops at once, coming to her.

"Let me carry you."

"You can't," Jun grits out. "You have to guard us."

"I have her," Riiniana says.

Liis looks as close to helpless as Jun has ever seen.

Jun whispers, "Six and Chono can't get out of the escape chute. I can't reach the controls. They're trapped."

Liis presses her lips together. "Guide them," she says at last.

Jun feels sluggish. "What?"

"Guide them. If there's a way to cast in and repair the escape pod from where they are, walk them through it."

"It might be mechanical."

"May as well try." Liis faces forward again, leading them onward. Surely the bay is close?

"Chono," Jun says, "is there a control panel? Can you find a cast connection?"

Chono doesn't speak for a few seconds, and in the delay, Liis signals Jun and Riiniana to a halt in front of a doorway.

"Keep back," she says, and the door irises open.

Three cloaksaan are waiting for her.

Half-collapsed against Riiniana, Jun can only watch the fight in helpless anxiety. She, who never learned to fight like that, no matter how many moves Liis taught her, feels the raw pride in what Liis can do, the economy of her movements as she inflicts more damage than saan twice her size. But Jun's admiration never outweighs her fear.

For the first time, she thinks to ask Riiniana, "Where is Kess?"

Riiniana says grimly, "Your virus hurt him. He ran while Konye was holding off the other cloaks."

Which means he's nearby. And others, probably.

"Jun," Chono cuts in. "I can't find any cast connection to the pod. There's an electrical panel, but it keeps throwing an error."

Jun blinks confusedly, struggling to focus as one of the cloaksaan swings at Liis with their fist. Gulping, Jun asks, "What does it look like?"

Liis slips and parries the attack, her leg snapping outward to collide solidly with another cloak's chest. Chono is explaining the panel, and Jun can barely pay enough attention to give a few quick instructions. Her injuries are throbbing. When Chono describes the pod's makeup, its shape, the base it's resting on, and what Jun thinks must be thrusters on its sides, her first thought is that it would be wonderful to lie down. Then Chono tells her the really important part: The pod's doors won't open.

"Where is Six?" Jun croaks.

The third cloak tries to get behind Liis and take her in a choke hold, just as the second cloak lands a punch in her side. Yet Liis slips under the choke hold, shoves up with one hand, and snaps the third cloak's arm at the elbow.

Jun is having trouble standing up. Riiniana is having trouble holding her. They both half collapse against the wall.

"Sunstep," murmurs Six. Their voice is rough, exhausted, somehow worse for the touch of humor in the name they've used. That's not good.

"Did you ever study ship mechanics?" Jun demands.

"You do not sound so good," Six says.

"Yeah, cuz I'm about to pass out. Fucking pay attention! You taught yourself how to do everything. Did you ever teach yourself *ship mechanics*?"

There is a pause before Six answers. "Yantikye taught me . . . a little."

One of the cloaks makes a screaming sound almost instantly cut off when Liis breaks their neck. Jun is a little surprised to see that all three of the cloaks are on the ground, and Liis is spitting a fat globule of blood, her bared teeth red as she faces them again. She takes in Jun's state with a glower. She storms forward and shoves a gun into Riiniana's hand.

"You can shoot, yes?" There's no doubt in Liis's voice. Riiniana nods. "Shoot anything you see."

Liis faces Jun again, her expression full of pain and fear for her. "Not far," she promises.

All Jun can do for her is try to look like she's in less pain than she is. They move forward again, as fast as Jun can make her body go. Forcing strength into her voice, she asks Chono, "Do you have a knife? Of course you fucking do. I need you to slip it underneath the control panel. When you pop the cover off, there are going to be wires and circuitry behind it. Six may understand what's there better than you will. You need to tell me exactly what you see, and I will tell you exactly what to do. We're down to nineteen minutes before the shields come up."

Six says in a ragged voice, "Chono can make it up the chute if she goes now—"

"Shut up!" Chono snarls. "Jun. The panel is off."

Liis leads them around a corridor. No cloaks in sight.

Chono tells Jun what she sees, the color and positioning and material of each piece, each wire and circuit. As Six provides mumbling contributions, Jun transposes the descriptions into her own mindscape, building a simulation of the panel in her cast. Many of her schoolkin at the archivist's academy were very good at the casting side of the discipline, good at making the narrative and slipping down into the amorphous world of casting. Not all of them had the same gift for the mechanics. That was something Ricari taught her. How to hold the tech in her hands. How to build. She builds the control panel in her mind, her whole body trembling. She shares the image with Chono and Six, who finally agree that it looks accurate. Jun tells Chono exactly what to do next.

Six rasps, "Thirteen minutes. Chono, please—"

"Sit down!" Chono snaps at them. "Before you faint."

Liis says, "We're here."

A new set of doors irises open, delivering them into a bay full of warbirds, and dozens of incapacitated cloaks lying on the ground. Not twenty feet away, Seti Kess is marching toward a warcrow, flanked by four cloaksaan. Either he doesn't know that his casters will soon have the shield back, or he doesn't trust it, because Jun would bet her eye-teeth he's abandoning the Keep.

To Jun's utter amazement, Riiniana lifts her gun and fires.

The cloak nearest to Kess drops. The rest of them spin around, rifles up.

Jun throws herself in front of Riiniana, bearing them both to the ground as gunfire spears the air. Liis has already taken out one of the other cloaks, while a third—good gods! They run! It's as if they see Liis Konye storming forward, Som incarnate, and all the bloodlust and courage of the Cloaksaan abandon them. They run away from her.

But not Kess, and not his fourth cloak.

In moments, all three of them take cover amid the machinery and detritus of the bay, reminding Jun of when Six fought Medisogo on *The Risen Wave*. She suddenly remembers that she saved Chono's life during that battle, got her out of the flight bay before the Cloaksaan could kill her. Jun's got to do it again. But there is a slinky, hypnotizing fluidity to the way that cloaksaan move, and Liis is only one person—

"What's next?" Chono shouts.

Kess and his fourth cloak diverge, taking shelter behind separate obstacles. Liis holds her ground in the cover of a mechanic's desk.

Jun says, "Disconnect A5 and A3. Switch ports."

"Done."

The fourth cloaksaan darts into view, providing cover as Kess runs for the shelter of a boxcar, succeeding, but not before Liis takes out his last compatriot as easily as plucking a flower. Then it is just Liis and Kess weaving closer to each other. Jun is suddenly aware that it is harder than ever to breathe. That damned rib. It's punctured her lung for sure.

Liis's gun jams and she throws it aside at the same moment that she throws herself behind the cover of a crate. She has her back against it and she looks across the bay at Jun. Those eyes like oil slicks. Those eyes that she loves.

Kess steps out from his own cover, stalking forward, scanning the bay. He shouts, "You're dead, Konye! You and your fucking leash holder!"

Liis draws another gun from an ankle holster, checks the chamber, and seems displeased.

"We both know how bad her injuries are," Kess goads, slinking closer. "She'll probably lose a hand. Or a foot. Maybe she can get a fancy prosthetic like you. Will that turn you on, you fucking traitor?!"

Jun says, "Chono, flip circuit 2."

A pause, and—

"Nothing."

"Fuck. Pump the manual override and flip circuit 3."

"Nothing."

"Switch A5 to C2 and pump the override again."

Liis draws a baton from her hip, triggers it to project a long blade. In a crouch, she begins to creep toward the edge of her covered position, and around it, till she's out of sight. Kess draws closer, zeroing in on her location. Jun can see him better now, rusty blood streaking from his eye and ear.

"He'll kill us," Riiniana Nightfoot whispers, voice trembling. "He'll kill us."

Jun grinds her teeth. She reaches out her awareness into the Black, into the battles happening so far away and yes, right here at the same time. Farren Eyce near to overrun. A fresh wave of warcrows launching to meet Vikar Wren's pirate horde. The shield will be up in seven minutes.

Chono says, "It's open! The pod door opened!"

"You better get off this moon, Jun Ironway," Six rasps.

"You better get in that pod," Jun retorts.

"Are you afraid to face me?" Seti Kess yells. "Is this your style, Konye? Slinking away like a coward? I should have known it! I should have known—"

Liis is on him. They're on each other. Kess's gun flies away and his arm comes up to block Liis's strike. Next moment he has a bloodletter in hand and they are grappling, a dance of thrusts and parries. Kess is taller than Liis, has more muscle than her. Jun has always believed that Liis was the greatest hand-to-hand fighter in the history of the

Cloaksaan. Yet one does not rise to the level of First Cloak without being able to—

Kess rams his knee into Liis's thigh and she jerks sideways with a grunt, striking out with the baton as if it were a whip. It slices straight across Kess's chest armor. He yelps, staggering backward. Something red gleams through the cut front of his body armor, and he looks as shocked as if Liis had slapped him. Liis gives no quarter, and suddenly they are trading blows almost too fast to follow.

Kess, Jun realizes in dread, is just as fast as Liis.

He gets under her right arm, punching toward her side with a strength that will break ribs if he connects. Liis twists to avoid the worst of it, only for his right hand to come around with the blood-letter and stab inward. This time when she dodges right, he moves with her, left fist hitting her right in the center of her chest. Strong as she is, powerful and invincible as she is, Liis is too much smaller than Kess to withstand the direct blow. She hits the ground on her back and Kess goes after her, bringing his foot down in a stomp that would crush her skull if she didn't roll away just in time.

She comes onto her knees. Kess is already there. Her baton flashes, blocking the plunge of his bloodletter. But he has another knife in his left hand now, and brings it down toward her collarbone, toward the vulnerable gap between bones and the beating heart beneath. She strikes him away at the left forearm, blocks his right with the hilt of her baton. The barrage of strikes and blocks reminds Jun incongruously of two pickpockets robbing each other blind. Liis, still on her knees, misses a parry, and Kess knocks her right arm away. Her prosthetic arm swings up, taking the knife straight through the elbow, the joints that Jun so carefully repaired before they left Capamame.

It sometimes helps, that Liis can turn off the pain receptors in that arm.

Her right arm comes around next, the flash of the bladed baton scything through the air. Kess flings himself back—but too late. The blade slits his throat. Flesh opens like a split piece of fruit. His eyes go wide, his scarred mouth gaping as he wraps both hands around his neck. Bright blood pours between his fingers as he collapses onto his knees, all of it ending so quickly for him. How disbelieving he must be, as he stares up at the woman standing over him, as his life fades out, as all his plans come to nothing. There is no crowing victory in Liis's face. There is not even the vindication of some long-dreamed-for revenge. Kess crumples onto his side in a puddle of blood and black cloak, and Liis's expression is very calm. Like a laborer who has been taking down a stone wall, and has reached the last brick, and can finally rest.

CHAPTER THIRTY-FOUR

1665

YEAR OF THE HARVEST

The Moon Jeve

Chono slaps them.

It's obviously to keep them awake, but still—

"Do not fucking do this to me again," she orders, her strong body maneuvering theirs, putting them in the pod's second seat. They feel bloodless. Their side doesn't even hurt anymore. "Do you hear me, Six? Do not jump without me."

She swings herself into the seat in front of theirs. She yanks the door to the pod down and there's a suctioning gasp of it sealing into place. Six recalls when they leapt into the escape pod under Soye's Reach.

That was an unpleasant experience. Chono is doing something in front of them, grappling with the controls. She's cursing.

All Six can think to mumble is "The core...We armed it?"

Chono says, "Yes. You armed it, with Drae's code. We have five minutes."

"Good," Six says, feeling calm.

How many of those minutes pass with Chono trying to make the pod's engines start, Six doesn't know. They find themself thinking about Drae sen Briit again. Pondering her, not as some unknowable engine of Six's fate, but as a woman who bought a gate core and decided to use it as a bomb. Six has always wondered if Esek created the ruthlessness that drove them to become what they are. To kill so many, even Alisiana Nightfoot, even Esek herself. Six has wondered if, without Esek, they would be some smaller, more peaceful creature. A drover, maybe, like Da had been.

Apparently the bloodlust is hereditary, says Esek, the ghost, the haunter.

"For you, too," Six rasps, remembering how Alisiana ordered Lucos Alanye to murder the family of the acrobat who tried to kill her. Just one of many murders Alisiana approved. The Nightfoots have created whole constellations of murder. "But she died in the end."

Hmm, yes. You killed her. Not sure you had the last word, though. What was it she said again? You'd die underground. You'd kill the one you love. Esek sounds nasty now, accusing. *Would Chono even be down here if not for you? Would any of this have happened if not for you?*

She sounds as if she thinks that she could have done a better job keeping Chono alive. As if Six has failed her somehow, in not protecting the only person Esek may have actually cared about. Six, considering that Esek is both a figment and fragment of their own consciousness, almost giggles.

"We are so fucking arrogant..." they mumble.

"Six," Chono says. "Stay awake, all right?"

Jun Ironway's voice fills the pod. "Is it working?"

As if it were just waiting for some cocky caster genius to come along, the engine starts to rumble. Chono makes a sound of helpless relief. "Engines powering up. Navigation is operational. Where are you?"

"Boarding a warcrow. Get out, Chono. Get out now!"

The cast cuts off. No use any of them talking to one another anymore. This last part, they have to do by themselves. Six hopes that Jun Ironway will live. And the indomitable Liis Konye. Even Riiniana, they suppose.

The engine roars. It seems too loud for a machine this size. Perhaps it's about to explode?

"Hold on!" Chono grunts.

The pod launches.

Six slams back in their seat, jumping from zero to—whatever speed this thing is going—so abruptly it almost chokes the breath out of them. The pod has a glass porthole, and through it they can see the streaming of sparks. It rattles dangerously, fired through a chamber too unstable to sustain it. They are going to explode. They are going to die underground.

"Hold on!" Chono shouts again.

Six wishes they could see her face. It would be wonderful, at the end, to see her face.

With a shriek and whoosh, the pod shoots through the surface of Jeve, catapulting into the atmosphere. It keeps going. Is it literally as fast as a bullet? Or maybe as fast as Six trained themself to throw a knife. Like the knife they threw at Esek, in Alisiana's sublevel apartment. That knife went straight and true, striking Esek's chest as if her heart were a magnet drawing it in. How stunned she looked. Six can taste her blood in their mouth. Or is that their own blood?

Don't close your eyes now, little fish. Look. Look.

They look. The pod has broken the atmosphere, is soaring into the Black, but Six can see Jeve beneath them still, and the ruins of Farren Ki. They see something shiver—the holo shield reengaging to cover the Silver Keep. Did Jun get out?

"How much longer?" Six mumbles.

Drae sen Briit says, *Look. Look.*

There is no sudden explosion. No breaking of the sound barrier. Instead, a depression spreads across the surface. A circle of cave-in, far bigger than the bombed-out colony, or the Silver Keep, or perhaps any of the ruins of mines underground. There is no mushroom cloud of fire, or the toxic smell of conflagration. Instead, the buckling of the surface suddenly accelerates. The center of the circle plummets, like the center of a massive tidal pool. The shock wave spreads out, moonstone crumbling for miles and miles and miles—

"Gods and fire," Chono says, her voice wavering through the comm.

In their youth, Six sometimes thought that if they ever did kill Esek Nightfoot, she would explode like a star, too grandiose in her person to do anything less. Instead, she fell like a mountain, a crumpling heap of broken bones and muscle. She collapsed in on herself, just as now the surface of Jeve collapses in on itself. Is Six imagining a face onto the moonscape, full of rage at its descent? Will the force of the core's explosion suck Six and Chono down into the widening crater, like the monster gnashing its teeth in one last death throe? For Jeve is dying, as surely as Esek died. Six wants to watch. They gave Esek the respect of watching. Right up until the moment she bit their ear off, they watched her.

But they cannot watch this time. Their eyes have slipped closed. Something bright and immutable flows through them.

"Six!" Chono shouts.

They think of her hands in their hair. The way she leans her forehead into theirs, like they are two stones holding each other up. And finally, mercifully, everything drifts away.

I shall be remembered as a shadow,
And an arrow of fire.
How I dread the coming of Som
And the revenge of my ghosts.
I fear some portal to glory is closing,
But my tearing brutal hunger never fades.

found written on the wall of a Cloaksaan barracks.

Anonymous. 1589, Year of the Steeltrap

CHAPTER THIRTY-FIVE

1665

YEAR OF THE HARVEST

Verdant
Sevres Continent
The Planet Ma'kess

Being alive feels stranger than Masar expected. When he's half asleep, it's harder to tell if he's alive at all. Some kind of cozy, restful afterlife seems more likely, especially given how bad it was when *The Wren's Jaw* crash-landed on Silt three days ago. There was a lot of crunching and tearing and smoke. Death had seemed inevitable since the battle began, but more so with the shuttle rolling over and over across the craggy flatland of Teros's moon. *The Wren's Jaw* never made it to the battle in Capamame System. Missing out on that fight had seemed worse than death to Masar when he learned of it from a hospital aide, although he was concussed and high on morpho at the time. Prone to melodrama. He doesn't mind being alive now, even if his broken arm is still healing, even if he's still in the Treble, because he's dozing on a soft divan, and sunlight comes through the window to bathe him in warmth, and he has not felt this kind of peace in weeks.

So, of course, Jun Ironway shows up and kicks him.

He yelps, barely catching himself from falling off the divan. His arm in its sling gives a throb. Jun stands over him with her hands on her hips.

"You snore like a sea elk," she says.

Masar rubs his face and glowers at her, sitting up.

"You didn't have to kick me, you fucking runt."

"Well, I could have let you sleep. But how would you know your sweetheart is here?"

The last fog of sleepiness evaporates. "Effegen?"

"Just arrived. I thought you'd like to go meet her."

He leaps up, but Jun blocks him with her body. "Gods' sake, hold on!" To his complete bafflement, she starts straightening his clothes. She goes up on her tiptoes, smells his breath, and winces. She holds out a mint reed to him. "There. Chew that. You don't want her to pass out when she kisses you."

Masar accepts it, shoving it in his mouth. "Where'd you get a mint reed?"

"Qlios gave me some."

She reaches up, smoothing his hair.

Masar recoils. "Ugh, stop grooming me! You've got Liis for that!"

She gives him a critical once-over. He can't help assessing her in turn, though guiltily he knows he looks better than she does. The regenerative bandages growing new skin around her ankles, wrists, and throat are like reddish-brown shackles, sure to leave scars behind. Her broken-fingered hand is splinted and swathed in more bandages. She looks exhausted and somehow skinnier than before. For all her typical bravado, there's a look in her eyes that didn't used to be there. But of course she'd hit him if he made any mention of it, and so he does her the kindness of saying nothing.

Finally, she announces him presentable. He spits the mint reed at her and runs out of the room to the sound of her curses.

Masar was furious when he didn't get to jump directly from the Silt moon to Capamame, but his current location on Ma'kess offers some amusement. The Verdant estate is a monument to its own opulence, the great rooms and private apartments all overdecorated and zealously maintained to accentuate the wealth that created them. So it's been very pleasant the past couple of days to see it overrun with the victors of the Feast Day battle. It must chafe Riiniana Nightfoot, but the girl has kept pretty secluded since Chono announced that they would make the estate their temporary headquarters. She owes her life to Jun and Liis, and must know how precarious her position is. She has better sense than to throw a fit over commoners in her ancestral home. But like so many high-ranking saan in the Treble right now, it's too soon to trust her.

Masar hurries down a marble staircase into the main atrium at the center of the estate, a massive room with a fountain in its center, and held up by thick filigreed columns. Glittering, opaque crystal doors lead out onto the grounds. The doors swing open, and Effegen strides purposefully into the room.

Flanked by Jeveni sentries, she looks as majestic as he's ever seen her. Head held high, chin tipped up. Masar wants to run to her, to wrap his arms around her and lift her off the floor and breathe in the scent of her safe, living body. When she spies him across the atrium, her composure does not fluctuate, but he thinks he sees the same desire in her eyes. Unfortunately, they are surrounded by other saan, including Vikar Wren and Karix Moonback. Right now it's important that she be seen as a leader, not a sweetheart.

So he goes to her, and bows low over his open palms (well, palm—the other arm is in a sling). He wishes he could make his body lower than hers, signal his smallness in comparison to how great she is.

"My Star," he says.

When he raises his eyes, hers are dancing with joy. It makes him joyful, too, and he can't restrain a tiny smile for her.

"My shield," she whispers.

All over, Masar can hear curious murmuring as the roomful of soldiers, pirates, and rebel fighters observe the newcomer. Wren and Karix approach, but any introductions they intended to make are cut short by another voice ringing across the atrium.

"Sa Effegen," Chono says.

Masar watches her stately approach, taking in the straight back and broad shoulders, the look of solemn purpose. She certainly plays the part. When she reaches Effegen, Chono bows to her as deeply as Masar has done—a signal that no one will mistake: Cleric Chono—the People's Kin, the destroyer of the Brutal Hand, and the woman whom saan across the Treble are already crediting with the Feast Day victory—has humbled herself before the leader of the Jeveni Wheel.

"Welcome to Verdant," Chono says.

Effegen bows. "Cleric Chono. To think I distrusted you when we met, and now you are a hero to my people."

"Come now, Sa," Chono answers. "You and I were never interested in heroism." She takes in the room around them, noting the many curious faces. She beckons Wren and Karix forward, as well as some of Ashway's lieutenants, introducing them to Effegen with formality but also brevity. Masar thinks Karix might be annoyed, but she doesn't say so, and Chono concludes, "The meeting of the quorum is this afternoon. We've prepared a room where you can rest in the interim."

Effegen nods graciously. "That sounds wonderful."

Masar is also pleased. Effegen took a great risk in coming here, and whatever they can do to keep her out of the way and protected is essential. Chono leads them into the west wing, toward a long hallway of guest rooms. At first the walk is peacefully silent, but after a few moments Effegen turns serious eyes toward the cleric.

"Sa Chono," she says gently. "Please accept my condolences. I know how dear Six was to you."

Chono looks straight ahead, but Masar sees the way her shoulders tighten, imagines her already controlled expression flattening even more, like doors locking shut.

She sounds both grateful and toneless. "Thank you, my Star."

"I'm told you buried them. Was there a service?"

After several steps of silence, Chono says, "A private one. On the grounds."

Effegen must see that she doesn't want to discuss it, because she leaves off on further questions. Questions Masar has, himself. After Chono escaped Jeve with Six's body, she went directly to Verdant. She burned them and buried their ashes in the Nightfoot grave-yard, among the other matriarchs. Though Masar had no love for Six, it bothers him that even in death, Six was forced to keep up the illusion of being Esek. Whatever private service Chono held, he hopes it did better justice to the person who helped destroy the Silver Keep.

Chono leads them through a door, asking, "Will this do?"

Masar watches Effegen look around herself. The "room" is a suite twice the size of her apartment in Farren Eyce, with elegant furniture and a terrace overlooking the lush grounds. The table is laid with food and drink that some Verdant chef must have prepared. No cafeteria slop for the Star of the Wheel.

Effegen smiles drolly. "I'll endure it."

Chono also smiles, but distractedly. "Good. I'll send someone to collect you ahead of the meeting."

With a short bow, she leaves the room. Masar turns his attention on the Jeveni sentries who followed their Star. He orders two of them to guard the hallway and puts the other three on the terrace. He shuts the doors after them.

Effegen asks at once, "How is she? Chono?"

Masar pulls closed the curtains on the terrace doors, turning back to her with an uncertain shrug. "Quiet."

Effegen looks sad and worried. "It's hit her hard."

"She and I were never close. I'm not sure if she's close with anyone, to be honest. She certainly hasn't talked about it to me."

Effegen nods, lifting her eyes to the ceiling in an expression of grief. "We lost so many people," she whispers.

Masar swallows, his fingers unconsciously moving in the impulse to count his dead, like Braems do: Six. Dom ben Dane. Melosi the Grave—killed in the last minutes of the fighting in Praetima. Mix Catty, theatrical to the last. Thousands of Jeveni and non-Jeveni colonists alike. And Fonu…

"Yet we saved so many," Masar reminds her. "The five thousand in the labor camp survived. And all our people in the lower levels of Farren Eyce survived."

Her head tips down again with an exhale. She meets his eyes, accepting what he says. Then, longing floods her expression. When he crosses the few feet to her, she reaches for him, careful of his slinged arm—more careful than he intends to be. He bends to bury his face in her throat, in the familiar scent of her, that he thought he would never have again.

"Bene?" he asks, for his absence is like a gap in both their hearts.

"He's all right," she promises. "Jealous he can't be here."

"I'm coming back with you," Masar declares.

This had already been decided, but it soothes them both to hear him say it. When she draws back, her hands are on his face. He's surprised by the seriousness there.

"My sword and shield," she whispers. She rises up, kissing the patch over his eye. "My love … my love."

He kisses her. She kisses him back, just as hungrily. "Why are you always injured when we do this?" she mutters.

"Maybe you can't handle me at my best."

She grins against his mouth. "I think I've handled you just fine till now. Gods—oh—B-Bene's going to be so jealous."

"Call him on cast. That worked last time, as I recall."

A peal of laughter escapes her, elated and victorious. She is already sending the cast as he wraps his good arm around her, drawing her toward the bed.

A few hours later, the long table in Verdant's luxurious west wing dining hall hosts an array of saan that would have made Alisiana Nightfoot swoon from fury. As a gesture of goodwill, the major leaders and lieutenants of the Feast Day quorum have agreed to come together in person under a banner of friendship. Each group has brought its own military forces, who patrol the grounds and the skies, wary of enemies who might take advantage of all these giants gathered together. And it would be naive to assume that those forces aren't watching one another just as closely as they watch for outside threats.

Masar looks around at the familiar faces. Imicanta Oninye's hand and forearm are wrapped in regenerative bandages. Karix Moonback stands in her uncle's stead. Regal Hejar Paiye has healed from the deep cut near her mouth, though there is a thin line of scar tissue. Zemit is here—he lost half his people in the battle on Teros and wears it grimly, his head shaved smooth. A battered Yantikye stands next to Graisa, and Vikar Wren stands next to her. There are many others, from General Ashway and his top lieutenants to, surprisingly, a representative of the Khen household, some clerk purporting to speak for Khen Soon.

And Riiniana Nightfoot is here, watching everything.

At Chono's suggestion, Ashway takes one end of the table, while Effegen sits at the other. Chono, predictably, chooses an insignificant position toward the middle of the group. Masar is quick to join Liis and Jun near Effegen. As everyone else settles into their seats, silence falls.

Until, that is, the strangest of the Verdant guests pipes up.

"Very excellently gathered we are. Most attractive in our persons. Heroic, even!"

The Minkat has come to them in animatronic form, a robot with absurd wire tangles approximating fur, and slitted metal eyes. Too small to have its own chair, it perches right on the table between an amused Yantikye and a pinch-faced Karix Moonback. Its head swivels, taking in the guests.

"Thus appointed, shall we talk now, nah?"

"Yes," General Ashway says. "We should talk. The Silver Keep and the Cloaksaan warwhales are destroyed, as well as most of their bigger birds. Thousands of Kindom guardsaan have gone to ground, and at least five hundred cloaks among them. They remain a threat."

"So does Giran." Karix Moonback speaks up. "My cousin has insisted to the whole family that my uncle failed them at M-4 station. He has declared himself the new family head. He's withdrawn his forces to Moonback territory, but Revel will have to challenge him and win back supporters with more expensive loyalty than mine. I don't know what will happen."

Yantikye hums. "Well, sorry to say, but as bad as that is for you, it could do us all good. If you Moonbacks are focused on a civil war, Giran won't have much energy to get in our way."

Karix's lips compress with anger.

"War among the Moonbacks threatens Nightfoot territory," says Riiniana Nightfoot, quiet but confident. "That, in turn, threatens all of Ma'kess."

"That's your problem," Vikar Wren says. "You fought against us right up to the end. You only changed sides when you realized you were going to lose. Why should we try to protect you from the Moonbacks?"

Riiniana's nostrils flare, but it's Ashway who says, "More than Moonbacks and Nightfoots stand to be hurt. My armies certainly deserve a break from constant bloodshed, and Riin Cosas must be protected. Also, the sevite factories are on Ma'kess. The fate of the Treble is tied up with their fate."

Wren sniffs, taking the point, but unhappily.

"Well put!" says the Minkat. "And more—'tis a very risky time. You, little Riiniana Sa, gave the Kindom control of the trade. So, who rules the trade now the Kindom is broken? Esek Nightfoot? Gods bless her vicious soul, but she is dead." Masar isn't the only one to send a searching look Chono's way, but the cleric is like a stone facade. "So who rules the sevite trade? Family line says you, Riiniana. Esek's will says the Wheel. A tricksy thing, is it not?"

The eyes around the table shift from Riiniana to Effegen, and Riiniana and Effegen look at each other. Masar tries not to show his unease. Riiniana is among the few in this room who know that Six was not Esek. Does the contract that Ilius Redquill wrote stand, if Riiniana reveals that fact? Surely it benefits her to inherit the trade?

But to his surprise, the girl says nothing.

General Ashway interjects. "Wills and lines of succession are meaningless in the aftermath of war. We're the victors. The sevite trade is ours now."

Many in the room sound their agreement, but Hejar Paiye shakes her head. "Seize everything for yourselves, and our Families will demand that we go to war with you. We joined your alliance in good faith. We've already conceded that we will no longer receive fifteen percent share in the trade. Stripping us of any financial stake, even just that which we had before, is unacceptable."

Imicanta says coolly, "Perhaps the Families should think less about their financial stakes and more about our collective well-being."

Hejar makes a disdainful noise. "It is in our *collective well-being* not to destroy the existing economy and the Families who make it run."

For a few seconds no one speaks, hostility crackling between them.

It's Chono who offers détente. "There's another option. Sa Effegen, would you mind telling everyone the proposal that you brought to Sa Nightfoot and me?"

No one appears to have expected this, and there are flashes of irritation from those who don't like the idea of negotiations happening behind their backs. But Effegen ignores the looks of suspicion, her voice composed:

"We all agree that the structure of power should change in the Treble."

Karix immediately cuts in. "You *left* the Treble."

"But the Treble did not leave us," Effegen says. "Our original wishes for Capamame are irrelevant. There are those among my people who want to return. There are those who may want to come back and forth. We may choose not to live under Treble authority, but peace in the Treble benefits us. And the fact is, Sa Nightfoot gave us a gift. When she first offered us the sevite trade, we refused it. We didn't want to replace its masters and become masters ourselves. That feeling hasn't changed. However, I believe Esek gave us the trade because she thought we would use it more wisely than our predecessors."

Vikar Wren waves a hand. "That's more credit than Esek deserves."

Chono snaps, "Shut your mouth."

Her words startle them all. Wren blinks like a dog that's had his nose swatted, clearly remembering who "Esek" was to Chono. At last he makes a cautious, appeasing motion. Chono folds back into herself.

After a few more tense moments, Effegen says, "I do not want the trade to exist at the cost of all reason and morality. I want it to have ethical labor practices, high standards of quality control, and responsible distribution. Workers who receive fair pay and pensions. There will be no more of the labor shortages that have threatened the Treble over the past year if this becomes an industry that saan want to work in."

Karix demands, "And the profits?"

Effegen looks at her coolly. "Its success will be its profit."

Karix scoffs. She gives Riiniana an incredulous look. "You *agree* with this?"

Riiniana glowers without answering.

"It's exactly what the people have been demanding. What *you* have demanded," Chono says. "Fair access to sevite means improved trade and freedom of movement. It means *community*, and partnership, and the good of the Treble over the profits of a few."

Hejar Paiye sniffs. "Noble words. But in practical terms—"

"My people took Trin-Ma because they want a better world," Zemit interrupts. "Not because they thought it would be easy."

"This is an entirely different undertaking," Imicanta Oninye warns.

The Minkat makes a whirring noise of excitement, body wriggling. "Oh, but to undertake! A new Treble. A transformation! Yes, yes. We must do this. This difficult thing. We must have change. Hungry for it, in our bones!"

The creature's enthusiasm pauses everyone for a moment, until one of Ashway's lieutenants asks, "Who would even manage the logistics?"

"A board of governors," Effegen says.

Karix throws up her hands. "A *board* of *governors?*"

"Yes," Chono says.

"The board will include some of the people in this room," Effegen continues. "Members of the First Families, Riiniana among them, *and* quorum leaders. You'll share the management of the trade. But half the governors will be outsiders. That will help this quorum avoid the temptation of making themselves into new kings."

Nobody seems to like the implied accusation, but they don't argue. There are several moments of silence before Ashway says pensively, "Bad actors will try to undermine it. Armies may rise up to take control of the factories. Giran Moonback will certainly try."

"Which is why we agree to protect them," Chono replies. "All of us. We commit members of our forces to create a military arm whose sole responsibility is to protect the integrity of the sevite trade and its workers."

"A military arm?" Vikar Wren says. "You mean a new Brutal Hand."

Jun rolls her eyes exaggeratedly. "The Cloaksaan were assassins who used guardsaan as their front line. Their job was to control the Treble and squash uprisings."

"Every idealist thinks its military will be noble," Wren says. "And it always becomes the same thing over and over. Petty saan waving guns at the weak."

Masar barely contains his laughter. "That's rich coming from you. Or maybe you think the pirates should be in charge?"

"At least we're honest about who we are."

General Ashway says, "Thousands of Trini-son soldiers turned with me against Kess because it was the righteous thing to do. I reject the implication that all soldiers are criminals. We can weed out those who are and instill a value for the new order in any new forces we raise. In other words, an ethical, righteous military."

"Delusion," Karix says.

Masar is inclined to agree.

Chono says, "It would be difficult, yes. But what did we all do this for if we don't believe we can build something better?"

The Minkat animatron exclaims, "We must have change! Change change change!"

The room quiets as everyone ponders their own position. These people rebelled with similar and disparate goals. The Jeveni, on the other hand, never entertained trying to fight the Kindom. They never dreamed of supplanting its power. They chose, instead, to leave. But these saan can't leave. So what will they do with what they've won?

"A board is a good idea," Hejar Paiye says at last, clearly surprising a number of them. She addresses Effegen. "If you are the creator of this board, then I must ask—will you take advice from all of us on its members?"

Effegen nods. "Yes."

"Not Khen," says Zemit, his face a thundercloud as he looks over at the heretofore silent clerk. Khen's representative seems unnerved. Zemit hisses, "Not anyone who didn't fight on the right side!"

The clerk says cautiously, "Sa Khen never fought for First Cloak Seti—"

"He may as well have!" Zemit snaps back. "He's a fucking coward. He didn't even come here himself—he sent *you*."

"Zemit," Chono says quietly. "Khen Soon *will* have a say."

Her declaration meets with amazement; even the clerk blinks. For the first time, Zemit looks at her in anger, shooting back, "You *and* Sa Paiye asked Khen Soon to help us. He did not come! He risked nothing and now you want him to share in the reward?!"

"Each Family must have a say," Chono answers, her voice calm, uncombative. She looks at Zemit in a way that validates his anger while refusing his demand. "If we cut one of them out, it becomes another threat. Like Giran."

Masar feels for Zemit. Though he can understand Chono's logic, and suspects that Zemit does, too, what a blow this must be to the young man, after all he's lost. And yet Zemit subsides, his face stony. The clerk is wise enough not to speak, though he does scribble something on his cast tablet. Masar catches Jun's eye, and she gives a little nod, understanding him. By the time the next person at the table starts speaking, she'll have cast her way into that tablet and cloned the contents. Better not to assume that the Khens are well-intentioned now.

Paiye is the first to break the silence. "This board will share responsibility for the trade—its successes *and* failures. I don't like to fail. And I don't like people who make me fail." She glares right at the clerk. "If Khen Soon can't show his value to the board, or if his passivity threatens it, I will check him. Which I'm sure he will not like." The clerk keeps scribbling. Hejar barks, "Make sure to put those words in front of him, since apparently he doesn't always get my messages."

Her spite makes Yantikye whistle in amusement.

Hejar ignores him, addressing the table at large. "But if I'm going to commit my family's resources, a board of governors isn't enough. There's far more to ruling the Treble than protecting the trade. We've effectively disbanded the Brutal Hand. But we have a wealth of knowledge and experience in the surviving Secretaries. And the Righteous Hand is the centerpiece of Treblen religious practice. Some systems are too deeply entrenched to just replace. The Kindom is one of those."

Predictably, the restlessness in the room climbs again. Masar notices Riiniana Nightfoot coiling up like a spring, her eyes sharp.

"There's no Secretarial Court," Hejar continues. "There's no First Cleric. We should fill those roles with saan we can trust and give them a mandate to reform the Hands."

Yantikye chuckles. "Shocking. Regal Paiye wants to protect an institution that has always served the interests of her family."

"Were you under some illusion that I've become a philanthropist?" Hejar retorts. "And the Families aren't the only ones who benefit from a stable Kindom."

Graisa the Honor speaks for the first time. "She's right. My allies go to temple and love the gods. So do I. We need the Righteous Hand."

Yantikye sighs gustily, but gets no reaction from her. Masar suspects that their difference in methods and philosophy won't change anytime soon, and father and daughter will remain at odds.

Imicanta Oninye says, "We need the Clever Hand as well, but only if it changes. Sixty percent of the students at the University of Hestos are studying law and economics. Their career prospects have always been limited because of the supremacy of the Secretaries. We could change the admission practices for the kinschools. Make it possible for common students to ascend in Kindom government."

Graisa nods. "And there are many religious community leaders who have as much to give to the Righteous Hand as anyone in the Kindom."

"That's all very well," Hejar says, sounding disinterested. "But of course, we know the real key to stabilizing the clerics and securing the people's faith in the Kindom."

There's little chance of anyone misunderstanding her. When they all look at Chono this time, Chono is looking at the tabletop, her hands folded before her and her expression unreadable.

"There's a reason my mother agreed to introduce Chono to the other Family heads," Hejar continues. "There's a reason why all of you wanted her to join your fight. Fair or not, her legend is only growing. In the history texts, they'll say that *she* won the Battle of Feast Day, and we were merely her ancillaries. She's the People's Kin."

"So, you want to prop her up as a figurehead," Jun drawls. "A public relations move."

Hejar smiles grimly. "For once, I'm not that cynical. Chono is the only one qualified to fill this role."

General Ashway says, "I'm not one for bullshit. Even those of us who haven't admitted it to ourselves have known something like this would have to happen."

"It's what the people want," Zemit says, his ire seeming to have faded with a return of hope. "We have an obligation to respect their beliefs."

"She'll be more than the First Cleric," Yantikye observes. "Renown like that? She'll be the de facto head of the Kindom itself." He looks over at Chono. "You've got some big shoulders there. Are they big enough?"

Chono raises her eyes from the table. Masar can almost see the resistance coming off her like steam, as if she is suddenly facing down a death sentence that she thought she might escape. Finally, she opens her mouth, but—

"The Kindom is and always has been corrupt," Riiniana Nightfoot says heatedly. "It can't be redeemed. It needs to come down altogether!"

Her vitriol takes the room off guard. Her voice rises: "I've known clerics all my life. I don't care how moral Chono appears. There's nothing worse than someone who thinks they carry the power of the gods. Give her a few years and that shiny ethical exterior will come off like scales. She'll be just another corrupt bureaucrat. And you're all *fools* if you think otherwise."

Surprise makes everyone silent, but Masar can see them considering her words. For her part, Chono watches Riiniana thoughtfully, looking unoffended. Riiniana looks back at her with a hatred that seems too deep to have anything to do with Chono herself.

"She's right," Chono says. There are drawn breaths. Bodies shifting in discomfort. "I'm as corruptible as anyone. I'm already corrupted. None of you should idolize me. We certainly shouldn't encourage the Treble to do so."

"Very noble," says Yantikye, looking bored. "But if we make anyone else First Cleric, the people will riot."

"I won't give a single guardsaan to the protection of the Kindom," hisses Riiniana.

"Good," Karix answers. "I, for one, don't want your armies lurking about. I don't trust someone who's been pretending to be a lamb when she's really a wolf."

Riiniana narrows her eyes. "I could tell you things about *pretending*, believe me."

"Let's not lose focus," says Effegen, watching Riiniana with unmistakable warning.

Riiniana looks furious, but she holds her tongue.

Vikar Wren scowls. "I hate to say it, but I agree with the girl. The Kindom will never grow out of its roots, no matter who we put at the helm."

"So, you don't even want to *try*?" Zemit exclaims. "We can change! We can be better."

"We can build something new," Imicanta agrees.

"And if you *can't*?" Wren retorts.

"No one can," Liis Konye says.

In the welter of intensifying emotion and animosity, her voice brings stillness to the room. She doesn't look at anyone in particular, just taps her thumb slowly on the tabletop, as if she were counting out the beats of a poem.

"There is no such thing as an incorruptible government. There is no such thing as an incorruptible military, or an incorruptible person. We should all be realistic about what we're saying today." She looks around at them. Her manner is a little haughty, like an adult fed up with children. Masar feels rather delighted by her sternness. All these saan could use being taken down a peg. Liis says, "The board of governors is a good idea. Military protection for the trade is a good idea. Such a military should also commit itself to *protecting* the Treble rather than policing it. But someday, if not immediately, corrupt actors will occupy those forces, and others will become corrupt through their proximity to power. The Treble is full of uncertainty. There is much to rebuild, from literal cities to the will and hope of the people. Uprisings, coups, assassination attempts—these are inevitable. Maybe they happen soon. Maybe in a year, or ten years. That is the way of the worlds. But it doesn't mean you do nothing. You build communities that take care of each other. You work to instill values that will outlive you. You hope that the long arc of history will see more good than bad come from what you do. It's the only route forward."

She pauses, taking in the intensity of all the saan watching her. Her lip quirks.

"But gods forbid you take the word of a cloaksaan."

Next to her, Jun smothers a smile behind her hand. The little

Minkat animatron makes purring mechanical noises, but its opinion or desires are invisible to Masar. He is a collector, an observer of saan. Now he takes in not just the people around him, but what exists between them. Who looks at who, and with what emotion, and to what response? Hostility between this pair. Open friendship among some others. Hesitance. Assessment. Over a dozen egos and many more motives, some aligned, some at cross-purposes. Yes, he realizes. The fight has just begun.

"Cleric Chono," Hejar says at last. "Your great humility aside, you don't strike me as one to ignore the needs of your people. As Sa Konye says, this is the only route forward. This is what the Treble needs. Will you accept the Godfire ring or not?"

They all wait with bated breath. Maybe some of them, like Zemit, want this very much, while others, like Riiniana, are simply adding it to a secret calculus by which she'll plot her next move. Chono, to her credit, doesn't keep anyone in suspense.

But her soft voice is tinged with grief:

"I am the servant of the Godfire."

CHAPTER THIRTY-SIX

1665

YEAR OF THE HARVEST

Riin Cosas
Sevres Continent
The Planet Ma'kess

Standing on the tarmac of the Riin Kala airfields, Jun watches the shuttle come to a soft landing some hundred or so feet away. Though the injuries she sustained in the Silver Keep have long since healed, she's developed a habit of flexing her wrists, like she can still feel the bands binding her to the chair in the interrogation room, the flashes of fire as they shocked her. Some days are better than others. Today is a bad day. Her neck and the base of her spine feel stiff; the joints in her wrists twitch. She stuffs her hands in her pockets. The first time Liis commented on it, Jun promised her that it's only bad when she's under stress. To which Liis responded with a look that asked, *And when are you not stressed?*

The shuttle hatch opens with a whoosh, and Bene comes down first. Jun's chest expands, some of the stiffness in her neck dissipating. She's seen him on cast in the past few weeks, but as he spots her across the tarmac, his face lights up, and she realizes how desperate she's been to see him in the flesh. Safe. It feels almost selfish, to be so happy. So many died in the battle of Farren Eyce, so many families cracked apart. And Jun, who saw her own family splintered and crushed by the impact of a single, cruel Hand, knows better than anyone how deep the pain will go for those who lost their loved ones. But here is Bene. And he is alive. Joy sings in her heart.

It's almost enough to stop her tensing again as another figure comes down the gangplank. Ujan looks smaller than Jun remembers. The sentries who lead her in Jun's direction, even Bene walking alongside her, seem to tower over her stooped figure. She glares around her with all the malice Jun expects, but she looks exhausted, diminished, with a shadow of defeat in her dark, spiteful eyes. Her hands are bound in front of her. Jun watches Bene lean in, saying something that makes her roll her eyes. He breaks away from her, jogging ahead. When he gets close enough, Jun hauls him into her arms.

They stand like that for several moments, gripping tight. The bright Ma'kessn sun washes them in warmth, and she feels a rich swell of hope.

By the time they break apart, Ujan and the sentries have reached them. Ujan watches Jun coldly, though to Jun's surprise, she makes no snide remarks. Jun tries to think what to say to this girl she never really knew.

"Hello, Ujan," she says.

Ujan doesn't answer. Her broken wrist is fully healed now, but she holds that arm a little awkwardly, as if her body can't forget the injury. Jun relates. Dismissing Ujan for the moment, she looks at Bene again, smiling and squeezing his shoulders in a last burst of affection before she gestures them toward the ground shuttle waiting nearby. In the distance, the city of Riin Kala is a profile of spires, backdropped by a purple mountain range that looks majestic under the rich blue sky. Once they're all in the shuttle, Ujan between two of the sentries, the driver coasts them onto a main road, and they zip toward the temple Riin Cosas.

No one speaks in the shuttle. Bene looks out the window with a marveling expression. He's never been to Ma'kess, she realizes; never been to any of the Treble planets except Braemin, where he lived his childhood and adolescence in a single mining town. His life has always been constrained. Bound to a single station; bound to a single town; bound to Farren Eyce. Yet he's never indicated any of the claustrophobia that Jun fears she would experience in his place. When this errand is done, he'll go back to Capamame and be happy. That is his constitution. To be happy. Jun loves him for it, even if it baffles her.

When he speaks, his voice is soft, his eyes still on the window. "Tej stayed."

Quiet as he is, Ujan still hears him, if her sudden tensing is any indication.

Jun hesitates, then asks uneasily, "For good?"

"I'm not sure. I think he's still...figuring out what he wants. Effegen put him on a farm crew."

Jun thinks of her surly, immature, frightened little cousin. He worked a farm station for most of his life. For all his carousing and laziness in the past year, he may take some relief from returning to that work under more equitable circumstances. She nods, as if the nod were a blanket acceptance.

"Well...better that than the prison cell," Jun says.

Behind them, Ujan snorts derisively. But there's no heart in it.

It doesn't take long to reach the temple. Laid in a sprawling green valley, it glints like a multifaceted diamond, its domed roof reflecting back the bright sunlight. Though Jun has little need of gods or temples, even she has to acknowledge that Riin Cosas is magnificent.

But living here for the past month has been weird. She'll be happy to leave soon.

The ground shuttle rolls to a stop, and they all disembark. Jun leads them toward the temple doors. Liis is there, as well as two novitiates in their simple brown uniforms. When Bene sees Liis, he breaks into a grin again, and they embrace. Liis is smiling.

"You did well," she says.

Bene's face turns more serious, a flicker of dark memories in his eyes. Jun knows the battle was hard on him, and he hasn't yet found the heart to tell her about it. But she thinks he will someday. She thinks he'll trust her with that.

"You did pretty well yourselves," he murmurs, and Jun squeezes his shoulder.

One of the novitiates steps closer, looking nervous but eager to please. "Welcome. The First Cleric is happy to receive you in her offices. Do you require refreshment? Rest?"

"We're ready now," Bene says, and looks at Ujan. "Right?"

Ujan's nostrils flare. She speaks for the first time. "Might as well get this joke over with."

Nobody dignifies that with a response. Inside, the temple gardens are vibrant with color. Little birds chirp amid the flowers and other plant life, while polished statues of the Six Gods hold court over the temple's bounty. There are a couple dozen clerics in the courtyard today, some of them gardening, their coats cast off and their hands moving in the dirt. Others mill under the awnings that limn the square. An eerie hush falls over them as the novitiates lead Jun's party inside, many eyes taking in the newcomers with apprehension. Jun wonders how long it will take the Righteous Hand to recover from the terror and humiliation of their standing under Seti Kess. What's worse for them—the way the First Cloak kept them under guard both here and across their stations in the Treble? Or the fact that they are now under new authority with new ideas about their role? Well, the First Cleric is far from interested in pampering their vanity.

"Gods and fire," breathes Bene. "It's beautiful."

Jun sniffs. "The gardens are full of insects and frogs. It gets fucking noisy at night."

"How would you know?" Liis asks. "You pass out as soon as your head hits the pillow."

"I am a very busy, very important person. I need my rest."

Bene laughs. Ujan scowls.

They take a walkway to the eastern corner of the courtyard and step inside one of the temple's main rooms. It's a high-ceilinged, opulent space that suits everything else about Riin Cosas. Nearby are the double doors leading into the clerics' private gathering space, an adage blazoned above them: TO BURN LIKE STARS. Jun doesn't take her cousins that way. Instead, they follow the novitiate down a short hallway to the First Cleric's office. A quick knock on the door, and a voice from inside calls, "Enter."

They all walk in.

Seated at the large desk, illuminated from the sunshine coming through the ceiling, Chono scribbles something onto a cast tablet. Since Six's death, she has continued shaving her head in the symbol of Teron mourning. Perhaps she'll keep it like this forever, just another mark of her austerity. Indeed, though she looks regal in her red coat with its gold threading, her hand adorned by a ring of fat Godfire stone, there is nothing flashy about her or her office. No signals of wealth. No ostentatious decorations. Indeed, the only thing that stands out is sitting on a shelf behind her: a lockbox, small enough to fit in a travel pack. Nothing stylized or remarkable about it, and yet it has a pull on Jun, the pull of curiosity, which has led her to so many things in her life. She wishes she had the nerve to ask Chono what it is. But Chono is so damned mysterious...

The First Cleric of the Kindom looks up, taking them all in with her serious gray eyes. After a moment, her lip twitches.

"This is a very nice office. But I fear we're a bit cramped as is. Sentries, you can wait outside." At their hesitation, the little smile on Chono's lips turns droll. "With Liis Konye in attendance, you can hardly worry for my safety."

This convinces them, and they begin to file out, but—

"Before you go, please unbind Sa Redcore's wrists. There's no need for such treatment."

Reluctantly one of them comes forward and unbuckles the metal locks. Ujan's hands drop to her sides. As the sentries depart, Chono gestures at the chairs on the other side of her desk.

"Please. Sit."

Of course, Liis remains on her feet, but the rest of them accept the invitation, Ujan moving warily into the center chair. Instead of addressing her, Chono smiles at Bene.

"How are you, Bene?"

He beams at her, his dark memories from before clearly overwhelmed by his excitement. "I'm well, First Cleric. I'm honored to be here."

Jun expects Chono to brush this aside, but she doesn't.

"I hear the repairs in Farren Eyce are going well?"

"Slow but steady."

"Good. Sa Effegen tells me you are back on the construction crew."

He looks momentarily shy, clearing his throat. "Yes. I, um...I seem to have earned back some goodwill."

She nods approvingly. "I'm glad. I know what it's like to be distrusted by the people around me. For years, my kin clerics looked at me as if I were a threat. And I suppose they had reason. I have a lot of work ahead of me, to build their trust and respect. As for you, you have the trust of wise and admirable people. I think you'll do all right for yourself."

Bene looks pleased, relieved, as if she has conferred a blessing. Maybe she has.

Chono's eyes shift to Ujan Redcore. She doesn't grow cold, or suspicious. She looks at the girl long and thoughtfully. From what Jun remembers, Chono never spent any time with Ujan in those months between *The Risen Wave*'s jump to Capamame and Chono's return with Six to the Treble. When she lived in Farren Eyce, Chono helped with the logistics of relocating so many Jeveni to the colony. She assisted with the assignment of apartments, credits, and employment, proving herself a pretty savvy bureaucrat. When she wasn't doing that, she worked with Six in the farms or on various construction and renovation projects. What she never did was hang around the casting labs, where Ujan began her apprenticeship as Luja Ironway—back when Jun thought her cousin knew next to nothing about casting.

It's likely Chono had no opinion of the girl Luja. And having never met Ujan Redcore, either, she holds this moment lightly, without any apparent preconceived notions. Or maybe that's just her infernal stoicism.

"So," Chono says, "I understand that you wish to return to the Treble."

Ujan's lip curls back, but her voice is a little hoarse. "I understand that you're my judge and jury. And my executioner, probably."

Chono smiles faintly. "Quite a number of Seti Kess's pawns in Farren Eyce have made the same petition. I've already spoken to some of them. I intend to speak to every petitioner. There are a great many Kess loyalists in the Treble. It's important that I understand what these petitioners want, in coming back here. Though from what I can see, none of them knew they were working for Kess. They thought they were working for Ilius Redquill."

"Which only shows how pathetic they are," Ujan retorts. "Since Redquill was pathetic."

Chono considers this. "He was like a lot of people. He had beliefs that he wanted to protect above anything. The possibility that he could be wrong was so painful to him that he was willing to destroy everything around him to uphold his vision of the worlds."

Ujan snorts. "And I guess you think I'm the same?"

Chono spreads her hands apart. The Godfire ring glitters. "I don't know you, Ujan Redcore. I can only guess at your motivations." Ujan glares at her, mutinous. "How long have you been without cast access?"

The girl's eyes widen, as if a stranger has pointed out her nakedness. Before she can control it, shame and misery flash across her face.

"Over two months."

"That's a long time, for a caster. If I let you return to the Treble, and you get your cast access back, what will you do?"

Ujan doesn't answer. She's not blinking, and her eyes look red with exhaustion. More than once, Jun has experienced the unique violation of being cut off from the casting net, but those experiences were always brief. The thought of living like that for weeks is enough to light an ember of compassion in her.

Chono, seeming unperturbed by the girl's silence, continues. "Let me tell you what I think you'll do. As soon as you think it's safe, you'll begin seeking out the remnants of the Cloaksaan. You'll ally yourself to Kess's loyalists, and do whatever you can to undermine the board of governors. You'll seek ways to hurt Farren Eyce. And though you and I don't know each other and mean nothing to each other, you'll try to hurt me, too. You'll take it as your mission to eliminate Kess's enemies. Maybe you'll do it for revenge. Maybe you'll do it for glory. But the fact is you admired him. He saved you, in a way, and in him you saw a model that you wanted to emulate. I'm hardly in a position to judge you for that."

Ujan's eyes burn. "Is this your game? Appeal to our *similarity*? Both our mentors are dead, so now we have something in common? Your *lover* is dead, so you know what it's like to hate now?"

If Ujan is looking for a sign of pain, for any hint of how lost Chono must feel without Six by her side, she doesn't get it. Just as Jun hasn't gotten it, in all this time. Chono is as contained and quiet as she ever was. Even catapulted to a level of authority that she has taken firmly in both hands, she is still the same humble, venerable cleric. If she grieves, she's doing it alone.

"We're not the same, Sa Redcore. I don't need to have something in common with a person to try to understand them."

"I don't fucking need your understanding. You think I don't know what's happening here? You think I don't know what you're going to do? The Je are too fucking cowardly to build a real prison, so they've handed me over to you. What'll it be? The prison in Praetima? Or some work colony? Better not send me to Ar'tec Island." She laughs nastily. "That won't work out well for you."

It takes all Jun's self-control not to laugh at her. What does she think? That if she goes to Ar'tec she'll be welcomed in and handed some honored place among the echelons of caster geniuses and archivist masterminds? The Collective would eat her alive. Jun fights the impulse to bring her down a notch. She flexes her wrists. Feels the phantom burn of the electrified bindings.

"Ujan…" Bene's voice is gentle. Could anything, any injury or disappointment, defeat that core of gentleness in him? "You said you wanted to come back to the Treble. Don't you think you should listen to Cleric Chono?"

Ujan declares, "I don't need to listen to Cleric Chono. She's a walking expiration date. Kess's people are all over the Black, gunning for her. And that's just the most obvious threat. These allies of yours, *Burning One*? You think they're just going to live happily ever after? You think the rebel armies will be content to maintain peace with the Families? And what about the Families? The Moonbacks are in the middle of civil war. The Paiyes are going to milk this new arrangement for all the power they can get. And the Nightfoots?!" She laughs shrilly. "You took the trade from them! You got their matriarch killed, as far as they know. Now some fifteen-year-old is trying to corral them. Soon the infighting will explode, and don't think whoever comes out on top will be your friend. You're a fucking pacifist surrounded by wolves. They'll tear you apart!"

After a pause, Chono's eyebrows lift in surprise, and she looks— *amused*?

"Pacifist," she repeats, as if testing out the word, tasting it for familiarity. She actually chuckles. "How interesting. Do you suppose many people think so of me?"

Ujan's brow furrows at the reaction.

Chono makes a gesture, brushing the question away. "All right," she says. "If there's no point talking to me, what do you propose I do?"

"Put me in a prison."

"Ujan," Bene sighs.

"What, you think I can't handle it? I did fine on the farming station, and that was just a different kind of prison. I'll bide my time until whoever is next takes power from Chono, and I'll try my luck with them."

Jun wants to strangle her. But Chono replies with a slow, sage nod. What the fuck is she doing, pampering this behavior, nodding like that, as if Ujan was making very wise points? Why are clerics so fucking *weird*?

"I assume you're making all these threats so that I will conclude that the only solution is to have you executed," Chono remarks.

Jun darts a startled look at Bene, watching the color drain out of his face.

Ujan shifts in her chair, sneering brazenly. "Not that you have the guts to do it."

"And what about *being* executed? Does that take guts?"

"You think I'm afraid?"

Chono shrugs. "I think you didn't get the life you want. You wouldn't be the first person to look for an out. You've lost your brother and your parents. You've rejected your other family. Kess is gone and you can't imagine anyone else worth following. And you're young."

"Don't fucking patronize me."

"You're young, and foolish, and arrogant. And you have no neural link. Which I imagine feels like being stuck in the bottom of a well."

Ujan looks at her murderously, but her eyes are wet.

Chono sighs. "One of your lieutenants in Farren Eyce was a Quietan named Aris the Beauty, yes?" Ujan doesn't answer. "She also asked to come back to the Treble. I've remanded her to the custody of another Quietan and...while he's hardly a paragon of virtue, he's agreed to help her adjust to a new reality. She'll work for him until he and I decide that she can at least be trusted not to sabotage us. It may not take long. I have the impression that Aris simply wants to go about her slightly unsavory business, and that she's not much for revenge after everything that's happened. Who knows? She may stay with Yantikye by choice. I'm told he can be charismatic."

Chono grimaces, a rare glimpse at her true feelings.

"I'll arrange similar paroles for the other Farren Eyce spies. If Tej ever decides to return to the Treble, I'll arrange that for him as well. But then there's you. I can't give you a neural link. You're too dangerous. And I'm not sure there's anyone in the Treble I trust quite enough to make them your handler. So, you see, we have to do it a different way."

"And how's that?" Ujan says acidly.

"I will be your handler."

Though Jun imagined this conversation going in many different directions, she absolutely did not expect *that*.

She isn't alone. Bene makes a startled sound, looking at Ujan and then at Jun, then back at Chono with wide eyes. Ujan, for her part, doesn't move a muscle, holding Chono's stare as if it were a standoff. Jun wishes Liis didn't have this annoying habit of lurking in the background. She'd like to see her lover's reaction, muted though it would probably be.

"My *handler*?" Ujan rasps.

"Yes. You'll live here and contribute to the care and keep of the temple. You'll attend me during meetings and prayer services."

"You've got to be *fucking* kidding me."

"When I travel, you'll travel with me and I'll find ways to keep you active. You'll be answerable to me for your actions, and if you try to run away or betray me or get your hands on a neural link, I'll know it, and we'll discuss ramifications together."

"You can't be serious."

"Ujan," Bene says pleadingly.

"What is this?" Ujan cries, shifting in her chair. "You think I'm gonna be one of your godsdamned novitiates? Follow you around and bow at your feet?"

Chono makes a sound of dismissal. "Novitiates train in the kin-school first. You're past that."

"I'm not going to be your fucking servant."

"Contributing to your home is not servitude. And nothing I'll ask of you is something I wouldn't do myself. You're not required to worship, and while you'll report to me, you won't be my assistant. You'll have the opportunity to attend important meetings of important people."

"Uh," Jun interjects, wrists itching. "I don't know that that's such a good idea, Chono. You know, letting her listen in on—"

"You won't have access to classified information," Chono interrupts, still speaking to Ujan. "But you'll learn what the service of a Hand to their people is meant to look like. You'll gain insight into the economies and cultures of the communities I visit. You'll watch firsthand as my allies and I introduce new policies in the Treble. You'll see my successes, and my failures. And I'll see yours."

Bene, leaning into Ujan, murmurs, "It could be a good thing. A way to start over."

Ujan makes a disgusted sound, leaning away from him, realizing she's closer to Jun now, and sitting up straight.

"I never knew Kess to be likable," Chono remarks. "Perhaps you only loved him because it meant proximity to power. In this new position, you'll have that proximity, though power may not be what you're expecting."

Past her mask of defiance, Ujan seems more panicked than anything. With false bravado, she demands, "And if I say no?"

Chono looks at her sternly. "This isn't an offer. It's a pronouncement."

"A *sentence*, you mean!"

"Yes. Isn't that why you came back to the Treble? To be sentenced?"

Jun watches as Ujan's fear and anger amp toward an outburst that, when it comes, carries all the viciousness of a teenager lashing out.

"I guess with the whole Treble pretending to worship you, you must want someone around who isn't a sycophant. Six is dead, so they can't do it. Or any of the other things they did for you. If you think I'm going to be your bed warmer—"

"You will not say such things," Chono interrupts. Her voice isn't low and stoic this time. It's like a slap, startling Ujan into silence. Chono's expression has become something quiet and terrible, and dangerous as the clean edge of a bloodletter. "You won't accuse me of such abuses, or make light of those abuses when they happen to others. If you believe anything of me, Sa Redcore, believe that I will be merciless with anyone who uses their power to terrorize those who are weaker than them."

The intensity of her eyes unnerves Jun. It seems to unnerve Ujan, as well, and for a few moments the room feels like an overheating gate core. At last, Chono's expression relaxes, her feelings fading behind the old mask of composure.

"Well. Do you have any questions?"

Ujan's rebelliousness comes back impressively quickly. "Yeah, I've got a question. You said yourself I'm dangerous. Aren't you afraid I'll cut your throat?"

From behind, Jun hears Liis make her first sound. A brief, soft chuckle.

Chono gives the girl an almost pitying look. "Sa Redcore. Look into my eyes. Do you think that I am afraid of you? I have kept company with monsters. I've served the will of tyrants and genociders, and whatever guilt you're pretending you don't feel for what you've done, I have contended with much worse. You will inevitably test my patience and my compassion. When those moments come, I promise that you'll be more afraid than I am."

Well, Jun thinks, fighting down a nervous impulse to laugh, *this is going to be interesting.*

Abruptly, Chono stands. "Let me show you your room."

A few minutes later, Bene and Jun and Liis stand out in the courtyard walkway. Chono and a couple of novitiates have led Ujan's small, hunched form into the guest quarters. Out on the walkway, the sounds of the gardens are bright, all trilling birds and buzzing insects, and the *thhk* sound of trowels sinking into soil.

"It could be good for her," Bene says, toe scuffing the ground as he scratches the back of his head. He needs a haircut.

"Are you kidding?" Jun says. "Chono must have a death wish."

"Chono will be fine," Liis says.

"What is she thinking?" Jun argues anyway. "Why would she do this for Ujan? Why not let her cool her heels in a prison for a while before sending her to some rehabilitation community? Why do this for her? What does she owe her?"

Saying the words is like opening a door, or breaking an enchantment. Jun's heart thumps as she remembers. Her eyes flick to Bene, who looks back at her. She sees it there, the haunting of K-5 station. The legacy of Esek Nightfoot.

"But she wasn't there," Jun objects. "She wasn't in the workshop. She never hurt us."

"She was Esek's novitiate," Liis replies.

Jun doesn't answer, but she feels suddenly, vaguely embarrassed, and hot on the back of her neck where the metal burned almost through to the bone. She rotates her neck reflexively, starts twisting her wrists in sharp circles, until Liis's hand slips against her own, fingertips pressing on her pulse point until Jun stops.

The door into the wing opens, and Chono steps out again. She's so damned tall, and without Masar there to match her, Jun feels like she and Liis and Bene are a trio of children looking up at her. Which is ridiculous and also kind of funny and Jun feels out of her depth.

"She's resting," Chono says, which seems about as likely as Ujan swearing herself to the Righteous Hand. Before any of them can ask questions, Chono looks at Bene. "You've been traveling for hours. You must want to rest, eat?"

But he shakes his head. "No. I slept on ship. And I'm a bit…anxious to get back."

Jun nearly rolls her eyes. Ever since Masar returned to Farren Eyce, Bene has been very fussy about being apart from him and Effegen for more than two seconds. But he suffered through it to accompany Ujan here.

Nevertheless, he says, "I'll stay a few hours, though. Once Ujan's cooled off, I'd like to talk to her a little more."

Grimacing with how little she wants to do the same, Jun tries to think how to change the subject, but stops short at the soft, sympathetic smile on Chono's face.

"Bene...Ujan asked that I send you away without letting you speak to her again."

The words shouldn't surprise Jun, yet they go in like a knife. She sets her teeth, the sudden hurt in Bene's eyes making her stiffen with anger. Of course Ujan would do this. Of course she would find one last, cruel way to show him that he doesn't matter to her.

"Oh," he says.

Chono continues to give him that gentle smile. "A lot has happened. She may change her mind someday. But if she doesn't, it's not your fault. Sometimes...there are parts of us we can't look at anymore. We have to let them go for good."

Blinking rapidly, Bene nods, though he averts his eyes from all of them. Jun feels sick. Why couldn't she stop this? What could she have done differently, that would have stopped all of this? It's unbearable, to feel this much regret, to feel time move you relentlessly forward and away from the moment when you could have changed everything.

Liis says, "*The Gunner* is packed and fueled, and it'll wait. Let's have a meal. Bene, I promise you the food here is better than it is on that ship."

Bene smiles weakly, and Jun smiles, too. When Bene looks at her, she thinks she can feel his weariness in her own body, can feel the deep cut that went through them all those many years ago, like a javelin that could reach all the way from K-5 to the Academy of Archivists. A shared impalement, all the bodies of the Ironways locked together by that mortal thrust. And now there are just the remnants of them, carrying their scars. Jun has the thought that maybe Effegen will have a baby. But she won't be like Drae sen Brilt, who scattered her children across the Black, or like Six, who scattered the Ironways across the Treble. It'll be different this time. A new start.

Jun has a feeling that that isn't really how it works, that children are never really a new start, but the same start, trying again. But she can hope.

Eight hours later, *The Gunner* drifts in the orbit of the Ma'kess gate, queued up behind another four ships waiting to jump to various locales in the Treble. Activity at the gates has increased since the fall of the Kindom (or the old Kindom, as one might call it), but with the sevite industry reorganizing, there are still limits on jump travel and fuel purchases. The new governors have their work cut out for them.

A ship ahead of theirs drifts into the gravitational pull of the gate, and winks out, like a fish caught and dragged into a current. For the first time Jun lets herself consider the magnitude of their return to Farren Eyce.

"I sort of thought we'd die," she admits.

Liis *hmms*, hands gently guiding the controls.

"Should we really settle down? I dunno, like...have a kid or something?"

"Do you *want* a kid?"

"No."

"Well, then, we probably shouldn't do that."

Jun picks at the frayed upholstery on her seat. In the back of the tiny bridge, Bene sleeps on the sofa, sprawled like a child but strapped in with a safety belt for when the jump starts. She remembers Masar trying to relax on that sofa. He was too big for it. He'll make a good River, she thinks. If the dead know anything about the living, Nikkelo sen Rieve will be proud. Maybe he'll be proud of Jun, too. He was the one who brought her in, after all—who gave her the casting labs, who asked her to be one of them. Maybe it's turned out how he hoped, and somewhere in Som's realm, he's content to have died, horrible as it was, because his death kept Jun and Masar alive, and saved his people, and set a course worth following.

But—

"We'll be bored to death in Farren Eyce," Jun says glumly.

"Gods grant we have an opportunity find out."

"We could go to *The Glitch*! Track down Drae's descendants!"

Liis makes a noncommittal sound and guides *The Gunner* forward as another ship disappears into the gate. Jun lets the idea slide. Even if Drae knew that someone other than Haishik Deck would uncover her gate core cypher and her hidden child, it's not for Jun and Liis to follow that thread of mystery.

Liis suggests after a moment, "We could become mercenaries. Hunt the renegade cloaks."

Jun swells with excitement—but it deflates. "You're getting old." Liis blurts a laugh. "It's true! How long before someone young comes along who's just as good as you, someone like Six?"

"I could have wiped the floor with Six."

Such a turn-on, that confidence.

"Maybe we shouldn't make a decision like this right now," Liis says. "We're going back to Farren Eyce. There's a lot to do. I don't think either of us is in danger of getting bored soon. But if, someday, we do get bored, we'll do something else."

They're two ships from the gate now, and on the couch Bene snores and shuffles around. Great Gra used to sleep on a sofa in the family workshop. His mouth would hang open and the seesaw sound of the snoring would get so loud that Grandmi Hosek and the other adults would burst into childish giggles. That is Jun's earliest memory of realizing that the adults were children once. It had stunned her. It still stuns her.

"Do you think Tej will want to move back into the apartment?" she asks.

"I think Bene will probably live with Masar or Effegen after this. Maybe both of them. Tej won't want to come back to the apartment if it's just the two of us. We should probably offer to move someplace smaller."

Jun doesn't know whether to be sad, or relieved. In a place like Farren Eyce, big as it is, it would be possible for her and Tej to never see each other. Him up on the farm levels, her down in the labs. They could go the rest of their lives and never cross paths.

Her hand drifts almost unconsciously to the necklace of scar tissue around her throat. But Liis will notice, and worry, so she puts her hands into the pockets of her jacket. And feels something hard against her hand.

She takes it out, instantly baffled by the sight of it. It's a marble, smooth as glass and perfectly spherical, black with red striations—

Jun thinks, *It can't be.*

"Liis," she says.

Liis looks over. Jun is holding up the little sphere between thumb and forefinger so she can see it clearly. Liis's brows furrow and then lift. She scoffs. "Did you *steal* that?"

Jun scoffs back, offended. "I didn't! It was in my pocket."

"Since when?"

"Since now! *I* didn't put it there."

Liis frowns, still gently guiding *The Gunner* forward. Jun rolls the sphere between her fingers. It feels good. So smooth and cool against her skin. The red veins are telling. Exposure to oxygen slowly leaches jevite of its brightness. Only fresh jevite has this vibrancy. The Jeveni who fled during the genocide found a way to preserve the bits of jevite they brought with them, to arrest the fading process. That's why Effegen's jewelry glints bloodred on black. That must be why this little marble looks as it does. Some preserved piece of jevite, from the days of Drae sen Briit.

But who would give it to her? And why? And *when*, for that fucking matter? She doesn't remember anyone getting close enough at the temple to slip it into her pocket. But she was also distracted...

"A gift from Chono?" she suggests to Liis.

Liis says, "She doesn't strike me as the type to give secretive gifts."

Jun nods, conceding the point. She holds it up to the light, watching it glitter. The ship ahead of them disappears through the gate. Jun says, "You know what it reminds me of?"

Liis nods. "The jevite sphere that Caskori gave to Alisiana."

"Yeah. Just... smaller. Kind of fitting, isn't it?"

"Fitting?" Liis asks.

"You know. Like... we've come full circle."

"But not to the same beginning," Liis observes, looking over at her. The black twists of her hair peek out from under her cap, adorable renegades. A smile twitches on her lips. Her oil-brown eyes flash with humor and adventure, and she's as beautiful as a sunlit day. "Or do you think this is the end?" Liis asks.

Jun grins, squeezing her hand around the tiny sphere, feeling its power in her palm.

"Never," she says.

The gate opens up before them, flashing like the eye of the Godfire. The old flood of terror and eagerness comes over her. She licks her lips, staring down the path into darkness. Her fingers itch for the sweep and glide of a cast, as if with just the right program, she could gather the gate up, form it into a ball, and hide it in her own chest.

"Brace yourself," says Liis, and they burst through the stars.

CHAPTER THIRTY-SEVEN

1665

YEAR OF THE HARVEST

Principes
Loez Continent
The Planet Ma'kess

Her ship alights on the tarmac with a purr, hot air billowing out from beneath the thrusters. She unbuckles from her flight seat and goes to the hatch door, which opens with a hiss. There is the usual unpleasant smell of the gate that so recently spit her into Ma'kess's orbit, but there's also the smell of Principes: stone, soil, sable plains, and the nearness of the ocean and the humidity in the air. When she steps onto the tarmac, she stands for a moment to take it all in. The school looms before her. Statues of the Six Gods gaze down at her from the second-floor parapet. She flashes back to her memories of childhood, when she first stood in this outer courtyard. She had looked up at the gods and felt frightened by their stone faces, their watchfulness. But even as a child, she was devoted to the Godfire, and she thought to herself, *If the gods dislike me, the Godfire will protect me.*

What a strange thought to have had, as a child.

She looks over her shoulder to see a scowling Ujan Redcore standing at the mouth of the hatch, looking around with the sharp attentiveness of someone memorizing useful information.

In the three months since Ujan came to Riin Cosas, she has done better than Chono expected. She has tried to escape four times. She has gotten into three physical altercations with novitiates. She has tried to foment one rebellion among the clerics at the temple. If such things continue, Chono will have to confront her and determine some new course of action, but for now she lets her fail, and says nothing about it. This actually seems to frustrate the girl more than if she'd been hauled into Chono's office for punishment.

"This is the kinschool where I had my training," Chono remarks.

Ujan scoffs. "You think I don't know that?"

"It's an interesting thing, coming home," Chono muses.

Ujan mutters, "I wouldn't know. Thanks to *you.*"

Chono smiles dryly. Twenty-one years old, and Ujan is as sulky and disagreeable as a teenager. Perhaps she didn't have the luxury of sulkiness during her adolescence on the farming station. Perhaps her bosses would have beaten her for sass. Chono's smile fades. She can appreciate that. Once, a kinschool master boxed her ears for mispronouncing a Katish passage in the Godtexts.

At that moment, a figure emerges from within the school grounds. Imicanta Oninye is a big-bodied woman with a tower of hair and the bearing of a ship's prow. She strides forward, proud and refined in her scholar's uniform, and smiling warmly. Chono meets her halfway, both of them standing under the gaze of the Six Gods. Imicanta bows low over her hands. She wears no finger bracelets.

"First Cleric. Welcome to Principes."

"Gods keep you well," Chono replies, stopping herself from bowing in return, and gives a quick blessing instead. Things are different now. She must respect the hierarchies. She indicates Ujan. "This is my ward, Ujan Redcore."

Imicanta smiles tightly at the girl. She already knows who she is, and like most of the saan in power now, she disapproves of Chono keeping Ujan on. Too much risk to their First Cleric. Too much instability.

Nevertheless, Imicanta politely says, "Hello, Ujan."

Ujan sneers.

Imicanta gladly redirects her attention to Chono. "The students are at lunch. If you'd like, I can introduce you in the cafeteria."

Chono immediately shakes her head. "No, I don't want to disturb their meal. I'd rather speak to each year in private. We'll start with the tenth-years."

Imicanta pauses. "Tough crowd," she warns.

"Yes, I'm sure. How many tenth-years are there?"

"Twelve."

Chono nods. In her day, there were only six students in each age grouping. Principes was one of the smaller and more competitive schools, with never more than forty-eight students altogether. Usually fewer, because students often failed out. Other kinschools had as many as a hundred students, and with ten schools across the Treble, they might turn out fifty new Hands a year, all told. The Hands were always a fraction of the population of the Treble, and yet they held such power.

"How many of the tenth-years are new?" Chono asks.

"Seven. Their skills and education vary. Most are in remedial classes. Two of them are on par with the tenth-years who made it to this level under the previous regime."

Previous regime. Yes, they're still trying to decide what to call the powers that answered to Aver Paiye, Seti Kess, and the Secretarial Court. With all those saan dead, new figures have risen to power. The Secretarial Court is now comprised of three old regime secretaries and three of the governors. Many lawyers and economists who never had a chance at a kinschool have joined the ranks of the Clever Hand.

The Brutal Hand, now stripped of its name and its cloaks (so many black birds biding their time in the shadows), has become a military arm under Ashway, ranks swollen with the fighters who battled on Feast Day, and top lieutenants recruited from every corner of the Treble. What Kindom guardsaan did not flee have either left service or sworn oaths to Ashway, but they are under close guard, and Ashway, unlike Chono, has not let any enemies into his inner circle.

Then there are the clerics who never loved Chono. Who distrusted and despised her when she was a common Hand. Trained up like a cloaksaan. Beloved of that reprobate Esek Nightfoot. Not beautiful. Not loquacious. And now, she is their leader. They have mostly acclimated to the change. They are wary of her, unfriendly, but not disrespectful. They resent the other spiritual leaders who have joined their ranks, but they only say so in private. Perhaps Chono's storied past has frightened them into obeisance. Murderer of Hands that she is.

But in many ways, the true battlefield is the kinschools, full of children who have trained for years to enter the old regime. They have labored under excruciating circumstances so that they might become burning clerics, prudent secretaries, quiet cloaks. And now instead they will enter a system in flux, a restructuring of power that they never expected.

Principes is the true test. At Principes, Chono has installed new students, children from across the Black who have done nothing to prove themselves in the eyes of the other schoolkin. Chono can appreciate the sting for tenth-year students suddenly sharing space with newcomers who have suffered none of their hardships. Many are scions of the First Families, who expected to rise to leadership in the Kindom, but instead find themselves competing with strangers. It will be a hard road.

In time, Chono will send new students to the other kinschools. But first she will watch Principes, to see what happens. With Imicanta Oninye at the helm, she has some hope.

Chono asks, "How long until the tenth-years are ready for me?"

"The lunch hour just started, Sa. If you'd like, you can wait in my office."

"Actually, I thought I might do a little wandering. Reminisce."

Imicanta looks surprised. "Of course. Would you like an escort? I can certainly—"

"Oh, no," Chono says. "I'd prefer some solitude. I wonder, could you take Ujan to the cafeteria? She hasn't eaten since breakfast."

Imicanta looks askance at Ujan. Chono turns back toward the shuttle, gesturing. Two sentries who had been standing by the shuttle join them. Dressed smartly, one would hardly guess that a few months ago, these saan were among Zemit's scrappy rebels in Trin-Ma.

"My people will accompany her," Chono explains. She looks into Ujan's mulish face. "You'll be all right, I assume? There's a casting lab in one corner of the estate. It doesn't have outside access to the Treble-wide net, but you could entertain yourself, I'm sure."

Ujan's eyes widen, her pique forgotten in shock at Chono's offer. Chono doesn't make the offer carelessly. Without a neural link, Ujan won't be able to cause any damage, but she'll get a taste of the world she's been missing. Perhaps it will even remind her of what she stands to gain, if she can learn to move past her anger.

The girl shutters her expression, glowering again. "Fine."

"After lunch, then," Chono says.

They walk into the central courtyard. A few moments later, Imicanta leads Ujan and the sentries into the east wing. Chono can sense how it discomfits Imicanta, to let her wander without bodyguards. The governors are all very anxious about Chono's well-being. Perhaps Imicanta fears that some resentful student will find her in dark hallways and take revenge?

Chono smiles sadly, and walks through a door into the west wing.

She visited the school with Esek once, toward the end of her novitiancy, but that was many years ago. Still, she doesn't look upon the place with child eyes anymore, or at least, not only with child eyes. The narrow hallways of stonework. The walls decorated with portraiture.

The doorways leading into classrooms, and other hallways, and staircases that go up and down through the labyrinth levels of the school. In the beginning she got lost a dozen times. In the end, she could have traversed the space in complete darkness.

Once or twice she comes across another teacher. They quickly bow and make the hastiest of retreats. Chono has commanded the kinschool masters to remove any particularly tyrannical teachers, and to hire new ones, but those she encounters in the hallways must be old. She sees the flash of terror in their eyes. One of them, a woman quite advanced in years, looks vaguely familiar. Perhaps she taught Chono once. Perhaps she remembers what happened to her.

It's strange, how people treat Chono now. Deference. Obedience. Reverence sometimes. Or fear. Those who belonged to the Kindom before see her as a usurper and threat, and those who fought to install her see her as a to-be-determined quantity, and the average saan of the Treble hope and pray that power will not corrupt her. Or else they think that power is her right, conferred on her by the Godfire.

Chono was never popular, in the Kindom. She made no allies among Esek's other novitiates, nor among the clerics when she earned her coat. Friendship, for her, existed in strange pockets. She was friends with Six, in their childhood. Later on, she became friends with Ilius Redquill, and briefly his lover. When she toured the Treble with Aver Paiye, he showed her friendship, but the difference in power between them, and her own leeriness of powerful Hands, always made their intimacy a brittle thing.

On Pippashap she had a friend. It's only now that she realizes it. That was her longest post, that year on the Quietan boat city. There was a saan whose fishing skiff was docked near the little temple to Capamame, but he never came for prayers. Nonetheless whenever he saw her at the end of the day, he would have a fat fresh fish for her, and sometimes she even convinced him to sit down to tea. She never preached. He never sought counsel. They spoke very little, but watched the sun set over the Endless Sea, and it was friendship.

And now? Who are her friends now? The Jeveni, in a way. Jun

Ironway, perhaps. Some of her compatriots from the Feast Day battle look at her with warmth, viewing her as more than her office. But there are strict lines of separation. There must be. She understands that, and feels oddly unbothered by it. She will commit her life to justice and peace, and if she stands at a remove from other people, so be it. She was marked out for loneliness long ago.

Her path through the west wing takes her up a flight of stairs. While she has been wandering without purpose, now a specific location draws her in. She hasn't visited this place since childhood, but she knows the steps.

The door creaks open just as she remembers, a squeak on the upper hinge when the door reaches forty degrees. A whine as she pushes it farther, and then quiet. She steps inside. The room has ten single beds arranged in a grid. This is four more than when Chono lived here, and the room is a little cramped. Any more occupants and they'll have to install bunk beds. Each bed has a large chest sitting at its foot, for clothes and personal belongings. Each bed is pristinely made, not a wrinkle in sight. Did the old students teach the new ones how to do this? Or were they left to figure it out on their own?

Chono lived in this dormitory for nine years. She recognizes her bed. Is it a new mattress? The old mattress had a bloodstain on it from her menarche. Oh, she was badly whipped for that one. Six put a laxative in the offending teacher's tea, to hilarious results.

"Memories," drawls a voice on the other side of the room, where the door into the shower room stands open. "And look at us now."

Chono looks at them, and her heart gives a little lurch, just as it has done every time in the past few months that they have found a way to see her. This time, the lurch is not just happiness and relief, but startlement.

"Six..." she whispers.

They give her a wry grin. She's seen the results of their last two surgeries already. Minor surgeries, but with strikingly effective results. Around the eyes. Around the nose. But this latest round takes her breath away. Their skin tone has changed. It's no longer the bright umber of Esek's skin, but a cooler, darker tone, like soil in the gardens of Riin Cosas. They have dyed their hair a dark auburn, cut close, and particularly striking is their new gendermark: a Katish mark, slightly pale and the same one they wore in their youth. That paleness, designed to make the mark harder to read at a distance, is somewhat taboo. Yet it makes Chono's chest warm to see them gender themself as they wish.

She approaches them slowly. Even now, they must approach each other slowly. She watches them watch her, and it is almost like a sparring match. When she stands right in front of them, she lifts a hand. They don't flinch as she drifts her fingers down the side of their face.

"By the gods," she murmurs.

Six's eyes glitter with self-satisfaction. They've removed the Esek implants, so now their eyes are deep and dark. "It does the trick, does it not?" they ask.

She doesn't care about that. She cares that—

"This is what it looked like before." Her voice, to her embarrassment, tremors. "I remember. This…you…"

Six's expression shifts, bravado transforming to uncertainty. They go guarded and quiet, and when she realizes why, she gives them a chastising look.

"You could have any face in the Treble, and I would know you."

It's worth it to see their flash of surprise and shyness. In the few times they have found to be alone together since the events on Jeve, Chono has put aside her usual stoicism, and let Six see the full measure of her devotion. She thinks Six hasn't yet acclimated to that, nor even realized how much devotion they return her, in the merest glance or briefest touch. Like an annoyed cat, they push their forehead into hers for a moment. Their kiss, when it comes, is slow and singular. Chono has discovered that she has an open well inside her body, and no matter how much tenderness and love Six pours into it, she wants more. And she wants to pour the same into them, till the two of them are as full as oceans.

After a moment, Six slips out of her grasp. She watches them step away from her so they can take in the room. The lean cut of Esek's body has not changed, but right now they're wearing the unremarkable clothes of a kinschool servant, perhaps some denizen of the town of Principes, come to clean toilets. It's enough to make Chono smirk. Esek would hate those clothes.

Six says, "I cannot believe you brought the girl with you."

A never-ending argument. Six was frankly incensed by Chono's decision to take on Ujan. Chono says, "In another life, this could have been her room. It's a marvel that the Ironways never attracted kin-school masters to their door."

Six snorts. "Jun would have made a very bad Hand."

"So did we," Chono observes.

"Yes," Six muses, eyes fixing on what was once their bed, next to Chono's. "So did we."

They face her again. It's remarkable how little the new face matters to her.

"It has been more than three months," they say.

Her body tightens. So does theirs. They regard each other across a space of five or six feet. Chono is sure Six sees the conflict in her expression, whereas she sees the entreaty in theirs.

"I am changed," they say.

A part of her heart cracks, her own longing a powerful force, but she shakes her head. "Not enough. And I won't have you torture your body through more serious surgeries. Not a second time."

Their nostrils flare. "We cannot continue like this. Your sentries are perfectly acceptable"—they say it as though "acceptable" is one small step above "atrocious"—"but you need more than sentries. You need a sounding board. You need a partner."

"I take advice from the board of governors. And you don't have to live at Riin Cosas to be my partner."

Six scowls.

Chono softens her voice. "It's not safe."

"Nothing is safe. Leaving you there alone is not safe. You are too wise not to know it, Chono. You know the vulnerability of your circumstances. The clerics will take any chance to remove you from office. Giran Moonback will *definitely* send assassins. The fucking Red-core girl could find a way to sabotage your cast access. And that is just the people who you know want to take you down. The Treble is in a moment of calm, but it will not last. There will be new wars for power, and all these saan you have allied to? Hejar, Ashway, Imicanta—they could turn on you."

"And you will what?" she asks. "Hold back all threats like a dam?"

"Yes."

She laughs, half-believing, half-exasperated. "We made this decision together. If you come back, and if people realize who you are—and they *will* realize who you are—it will upend everything we've built. People will say the Jeveni had no authority to create the board of governors. Not if Esek is alive. It will open up investigations even you can't thwart. They'll realize that you were never Esek—"

"There are dozens of people who know I am not Esek!" Six interrupts hotly. "Ujan herself has told the clerics so."

"They don't believe her. It's mere rumor, with no evidence. You returning would provide the evidence. It would threaten all confidence in the will. We need time to rebuild what is broken and establish stability. You are many things, my love, but stability was never your gift."

Six glares at her. They look just as mulish as Ujan. It would make Chono smile, but her own words devastate her, too.

"I am an excellent actor," Six whispers. "Hire me as a grounds-keeper. Raise me slowly to your side. I can fool them. I can fool everyone."

"And if you fail?"

Their dark eyes narrow. Stubborn and defiant as they may be, they committed to the new order just as she did, and they're no fool. They know she's right.

"What would you have me do instead?" they ask, voice lower, almost rasping.

She sighs. "I'm not your keeper, Six. I can give you advice, not orders."

"Advice, then," they snap.

"Stop organizing your entire life around another person."

They balk, maybe at the words, or maybe at the fact that she answers so readily. She wishes the words were medical bots that she could pour into their chest—a violent but necessary repair.

"For decades Esek drove your every move. And this past year, my survival has driven your every move. You want to continue in that way, but I can't let you." Stabbing her own heart to do it, she whispers, "You have to walk away from me."

Their dark skin drains of color. For a moment they split apart in prisms, but she blinks the tears away.

Fury shivers under the flatness of their voice. "You said you wanted absolution. We came back here so that we could make amends. And we did. We dethroned tyrants. We saved the five thousand. And now you are building a just Treble. You have a mission. But you want to deny me the same?"

"No," she says. "But you've said it yourself—*absolution* was my mission. And your mission became *me*. It can't be like that anymore, Six. You have to do something else. You have to make a different kind of amends. You won't do that if you stay with me."

"This is ridiculous."

"I had a dream." She steps toward them. They freeze, looking at her, something haunted in their eyes. "I dreamed there was a saan in a hallway gleaming with jevite, and they tore down the walls with their fingers. But it wasn't destruction they left behind. It was an open field. Kai sheep feeding on the grass. A drover and his child."

Chono sees something she has never seen before: tears, in Six's eyes. Tears, and realization. But Six's pallor disappears in a sudden flush of resistance.

"How can you ask me for this? How can you send me away? Just... leave you here, surrounded by vultures?"

She gives them an impatient look. "I am no one's carrion, Six."

"Vipers, then! Jaw spiders! People who will take the first chance to bring you down!"

"Am I not quiet and terrible?"

"You will be alone! *I* will be alone!"

"No." She steps closer, full of supplication. "No. Never. You'll come back. Or I'll find you. We'll always come back to each other. Haven't we proved that already? We are like...like seasons. We'll always come back. But sometimes we have to go, too. You have to *go*, Six."

Her friend has turned to prisms again. She dashes the tears away, but they are running down her face, and Six's face.

"Where would you have me go?" they whisper.

She waits a moment, and answers, "Where can you imagine going?"

They open their mouth, probably to say they don't want to go anywhere, but they shut it again. They look startled, and even amazed, as if the answer has struck like a hammer on an anvil. They don't tell her what they're thinking, but they look at her with a grief past bearing.

"I have loved you all my life," they whisper.

She goes to them. This time Six is the one to cradle her face in their hands. She grips the shoulders of their tunic, exhaling roughly.

"And I you. Always. My dear, dear friend..."

Chono spends the rest of the afternoon with Imicanta Oninye, who escorts her through the different classrooms. Ujan is in the casting lab with her sentry escorts. Doubtless the girl will do everything she can to cause trouble. Chono suspects that even failure won't poison the joy of the experience. Not that Ujan will show an inch of that joy when they are reunited again.

As Chono visits the different classrooms, she is glad for her lauded impassiveness. The welter of emotion inside her needs a heavy shield to guard it from view. The restless run of her thoughts is not so overpowering that she can't listen to reports on the students, note the resentment of some, the hope and reverence of others. As she suspected, the older years are the worst. One of the eighth-years proclaims with the oratorical skill of a cleric in training that the kinschools won't bend for Chono—that the old Hands will rise again. Imicanta is angry and embarrassed, but Chono takes the pronouncement in stride. The student reminds her of Esek's chief novitiate, Rekiav. Pricked with curiosity, she searches on private cast for Rekiav's whereabouts. Unknown. Killed in action? Or disappeared into the shadows?

Chono leaves the eighth-year to marinate in defiance. More classrooms to see. More students to observe. In time, Imicanta leads her down a narrow flight of steps that turns onto the landing of a wider staircase. The staircase is made from deep blue marble, reflective and pristine. She goes to the banister and looks down at the room below.

"Fourth-years?" she whispers.

Imicanta confirms it. The scholar cannot possibly know what a coincidence this is, how unsettling to Chono, who gazes upon the sparring court and is transported through time. Only, in her memory, she is not standing on the landing. She is part of a strict line of students holding foam staves. She is a pillar of discipline, but even so she senses the arrival of the Righteous Hand, the powerful cleric who radiates something rich and dark and seductive.

Chono walks down the stairs. The students, ten of them, look at her cautiously. They all have gendermarks, which is interesting. Some of the old guard students have refused to take advantage of the new policies. They have maintained their "it" pronouns, rejected any name but a number. These fourth-years, though, hint that the shift away from dehumanization of children may be possible.

They aren't holding foam staves, but they have affected a soldierly posture. They look straight ahead, but watch her from the corners of their eyes as she slowly walks up and down their line, taking note of each one. When she reaches the fifth child, she stops. This one is a girl, tall and slender, her bare arms and legs slimly muscular, like a foal. There upon her face is the tattoo of the Jeveni wheel.

What Chono feels in this moment is hard to categorize. It's pride. It's humor. But most of all, it's sorrow. Is this the better world? One where the marginalized rise by infiltrating realms of power, rather than tearing the realms down? In this child, she sees herself. She sees her own resistance and rebellion. She doesn't want to be First Cleric. She hates the weight of Aver's Godfire ring on her finger. The Kindom is a mountain. How is she to change a mountain? How is she to carve some new, just structure into all that stone?

More likely, the mountain will crush her. Or she will become just another boulder in its mammoth shape. *I will be corrupted*, she thinks, her heart racing with terror. This is the great corrupter. It lures its victims in with promises of righteous change, of something new, of something *different*. But it is always the same mountain. Inexorable.

"Hello," Chono murmurs to the girl.

The girl blinks, surprised, and meets her eyes. She says cautiously, "Hello…"

"Do you know who I am?" Chono asks.

"Yes, Burning One. You are First Cleric Chono."

Chono smiles gently, hoping to reassure her. "Please forgive me, but I was wondering if you would answer a riddle for me. Who is the Sixth God?"

The girl hesitates. Her little brow furrows. Surely she will say Sajeven, the goddess of her people, the one to whom she's sworn by history and heritage.

The girl says, "I'm sorry, Sa. I…don't know."

Around them, the other children shift, restless with surprise and probably anxiety. Chono has to fight very hard not to show her own surprise, since it might terrify the girl.

"No?" Chono asks.

The girl's eyes dart away. "I'm…I haven't…I don't know that riddle."

Why does Chono react as she does, with such an explosion of feeling? Not externally—no, she remains as placid as ever. But in her breast, wings take flight. She feels something akin to terror, but also, rhapsody. She nearly laughs. Only the girl's reddening cheeks and a hint of humiliated tears stop her.

Quickly Chono says, "That's all right." Her voice is gentle. The girl watches her uncertainly. Chono smiles, imagining that she is on Pippashap comforting some little dockside child, as barefoot and brilliant with life as this student in her kinschool. "It's all right," she says again.

"It's a silly riddle. Honestly, it doesn't mean anything. Aren't words funny?"

At last the girl gives a hopeful nod and smile of her own.

For the first time since she took the mantle of the First Cleric, Chono feels pure, unadulterated hope for the Treble, for its people—for herself. Hope enough to make a woman sing. But she doesn't sing. That would be a bit ostentatious for her tastes. Instead, she continues down the line, introducing herself to each child. She will know all their names. She will bless them under the Godfire's burning light.

And you, child, who have lived in the dark. Someday you will grow old. Someday your life will tempt you to forget. All tyrants were children once. Do not be like your forebears, who abandoned you, who scratched your name from the ledgers, who made your bodies into kindling. Burn brighter than kindling. Burn brighter even than the Godfire. Burn justice and mercy into the worlds, and there will be no god greater than you.

The Beatitudes, 1:10. Godtexts, pre-Treble

CHAPTER THIRTY-EIGHT

1665

YEAR OF THE HARVEST

The Luster Wings
Lo-Meek
Bei Continent
The Planet Teros

You got any experience on long hauls?" the captain asks. She looks skeptical, assessing them like they're just another piece of cargo, a potential burden on her flight time. "People don't usually sign on for things like this at the last minute."

"It was a last-minute decision."

The captain narrows her eyes. "Because . . . ?"

Six gives her a flat look. They could make up a lie. But even after all these years, they can never shake their core of recalcitrance. "Is that your concern?" they ask.

"Yeah, actually. People get into trouble. They get it into their heads that the best place to run to is the frontier. But all they do is bring their trouble with them. And I don't want somebody tracking my ship because you've got an unpaid debt."

"I am not in trouble," says Six, though as for unpaid debts...

The captain looks dubious.

"Your fare is due up front. I don't give anybody a ride until I know they can pay. And it's one way. Once I get you there, it's your own business how you get back. Or if you get back."

"I understand."

"This is a trade hauler. My crew are hard workers. They'll resent you if you don't contribute. What I'm saying is, if you think you're about to go on a yearlong vacation, you've got another thing coming. Nothing on *The Luster Wings* is fancy. Small cabins, plain food, nothing to do but work and play tiles. And if you cause trouble, I stick you in the brig."

Six says, "I am happy to contribute during the voyage. I do not need a large cabin or decadent food. Or do I look like some kind of First Family brat to you?"

For the first time, the captain cracks a smile, and looks them over with new consideration. She says cautiously, "Well...I suppose you're built right for labor. But I'm shutting the hatch in two hours. You haven't got much time to get yourself in order. What luggage are you bringing?" Six nods to the single duffel bag at their feet. The captain raises her eyebrows. "Travel light, huh? Any weapons?"

"Naturally."

"They'll have to go in the armory for the duration of the voyage. I don't let guns out unless we're attacked."

"Very well."

After another hard moment of eye contact, the captain gestures acquiescence. Six transfers her the fare. They unholster their two handguns and lay them on the captain's desk. Reluctantly, they unbuckle the bloodletter and its sheath from their belt and set it next to the guns. When the captain sees the bloodletter, her mouth drops open. She looks at Six with renewed suspicion.

"Are you a fucking cloaksaan?"

It's not a wild conclusion. All across the Treble, cloaks have gone into hiding. Some will regroup and go to war against Chono. Others will fade into new lives. Some will doubtless strike out for a frontier station.

Six shakes their head. "No."

"So, how the fuck did you get a bloodletter?"

I killed Esek Nightfoot, they want to say. *Then someone stole it. Then I stole it back.*

"I won it," they say instead. "In the war."

The captain's expression shifts from alarm to slow understanding. "You fought for the rebels?" she asks.

"Yes."

She grunts, which could mean approval or indifference. "I stayed out of it, myself."

"Of course."

She narrows her eyes, obviously wondering if this is an insult, but a search of their face seems to appease her. "I suppose you're tired of it. Want to get out before the next wave starts? I don't blame you. That business on Jeve will hardly be the end of it. I heard that now Esek Nightfoot is dead, Riiniana is the new matriarch. You can believe her handlers will use her to go after the trade again. This board of governors thing. It won't last."

Six thinks how chatty the captain is, and wonders if her crew are the same, and whether that might be the worst part of the journey. The captain tilts her head and gives Six another of those appraising once-overs.

"You look like her, you know. Just a little bit."

"Who? Riiniana?"

"Nah. Esek. Hard to describe. Just something about your face."

"How strange."

"You know, I met her once."

That gives Six pause. They don't even have to feign their curiosity. "Did you?"

"Yeah. About ten years ago. I was carting sevite between Ma'kess and the Locali mining stations. There was some official tour of the cargo ships, and she was there. She asked me how I liked hauling sevite around, and I said the pay could be better. I was a reckless kid, you know? Could have got myself killed. She just gave me this look like she thought it was hilarious. A week later, I hear from the bosses that we're getting a three percent pay bump."

It's almost enough to make Six laugh. Esek and her caprices. Her random acts of patronage balanced against her flashes of spite; her mercies and her cruelties following an indifferent logic.

The captain says, "You know, they say a lot about the shit she pulled while she was alive, but she did all right by me. And I guess, in the end, she did all right by the Treble."

This time there is no impulse to laugh. The words pierce Six like an arrow. The captain doesn't seem to notice, switching subjects flawlessly. She casts them the lock key to their private cabin, as well as to some of the other places on ship (the mess, the commodes, the rec room). She calls over one of her crew, a grizzled old Teron in a blue flat cap.

"This is Sa Briit," the captain tells him. "Show them to their cabin."

The Teron crewsaan is friendly, gesturing Six to follow him. As they walk, Six hears the captain's words running a loop in their head. *In the end, she did all right by the Treble... In the end, she did all right by the Treble...*

Would this be Esek's legacy? A rebel hero? A martyr to the cause of Treble freedom? Not the tool of her tyrannical family, but the architect of its diminishment?

In Six's mind, Esek huffs. *I can't decide if I'm more annoyed or amused.*

Six's Teron crewsaan is chatting to them about the layout of *The*

Luster Wings. Its rules of conduct, its schedule. Six, who has researched the ship thoroughly and knows these things already, ignores him. Their emotions are oscillating as much as Esek's. Though the poles are more extreme. On one end, they feel a deep-down burn of molten fury, and on the other end, apathy. But they're not without a sense of humor. They can recognize when something is hilarious.

"Here's you," says the Teron, showing them a door in a hallway of doors.

Six casts their code at the lock pad, and the door slips into its pocket in the wall. The room inside is no worse than a hundred other rooms where they stayed during their years of stalking Esek. A simple bed, a desk and chair, a sink with a mirror and shelves underneath. Six predicts that most passengers stack their belongings in the one empty corner.

"I'll let you get settled in," the crewsaan says. "But Captain wants everyone on Deck 3 for the pre-jump. She gives a little speech and we all strap in together." He grins at them, readjusting his blue cap. "It's not so long a trip. At least we're not hiding underground like fucking Jes, right?"

The crewsaan is obviously waiting for Six to laugh. Six stares at him. Eventually he looks uncomfortable and leaves. The door shuts. Standing in their small room, Six looks around. Fresh linens are folded on top of the bed, so they unfold the linens and make the bed, taking care to do it properly, as the kinschool taught them. They put their duffel bag on the bed and unzip it. The contents are meager. Some changes of clothes. An extra pair of shoes. A casting tablet.

They take the tablet out first, the repository of their most recent research project. They extract the files and toss them into the air, creating a carousel overhead. All things considered, it was easier than they expected to track down the official records of Haishik Deck. Born in 1536 on Crisper Node, *The Glitch*. Never married. Died in 1603—a long life for a Glitcher. Recorded a child in the station census in 1586. That child would one day gender themself with the Jeveni pronoun for female masculine. She eventually became an engineer, like Haishik.

She married. She had three children, but only one reached adulthood and had two children of her own. According to the data in the air, one of those children has her own child, a young man about ten years Six's junior. A professor, of all things, at *The Glitch*'s emergent university. Because of that profession, there's more data on him than the others. He's written a dozen research papers on the history and theory of asteroid mining. He's given public talks. There's a biography of him, on the university casting net. School records and work records. No medical catastrophes. No run-ins with *The Glitch*'s version of law enforcement. He is not a pampered saan (no one on *The Glitch* is pampered), but nor has he seen his life cleaved apart by violence and tragedy. This young man, this Professor Deck of *The Glitch*, has lived a life full of purpose, family, and friendship.

Six takes in the image of him.

What can Six possibly have in common with this person? What can they hope to accomplish? Isn't it enough to know that Drae's frontier child lived? To hope that somewhere in some afterlife she knows it, and is content?

They draw the cast data out of the air and back into the tablet, and realize for the first time that their hands and forearms are filthy. Putting the tablet down, they go to the sink and wash. The cold water is bracing. Red Teron dust sloughs off their face and neck and arms. Almost without meaning to, they raise their eyes to the mirror. Water drips off their chin. They study themself. It's been a long time since they were able to look at their reflection without a nauseating surge of self-hatred. They tilt their head this way and that, scowling. Yantikye's surgeon did enough, but Esek is still there, a ghost in their face. They run a hand through the short cut of their cloudy auburn hair and decide that when it's long enough, they'll put it in twists like Liis Konye does. A rejection of Esek's crown of braids.

Do you really think it's that easy? her voice murmurs. They blink, almost, *almost* seeing her reflection in the glass. She goads them. *Take off my mask. Run away into the stars. You think I can't follow you?*

A shiver travels from the base of Six's spine to the top of their head.

And now what? she asks, her breath a phantom on their repaired ear. *You're going to look up the fancy Professor Deck and his kin? A family reunion, is that it? Don't you remember how the last one turned out?*

Six breathes in shakily and lets it out with a tremor, recalling their Braemish relatives. The descendants of Kati sen Briit. They were innocent saan who welcomed Six among them, and for their trouble, Six led Esek right to their door. It was a slaughter.

Six grabs the edges of the sink, locking their elbows to stop the sudden shaking.

You are a walking death rite, Esek's liquid voice continues. *What can you do but bring more death to the professor? Think of your life. You carry a train of bodies as long as my own. Sa Enye the weapons merchant. Your little cousins. Ricari Ironway and his grandsons. Jeveni collectors. Alisiana...*

"Alisiana," Six says, some of their strength coming back. "And *you*. You fucking disease on the worlds. I would kill you a thousand times."

A disease? she purrs. *Yes, I like that. A disease. I promised you, didn't I? Even when you're dead, my ghost will come after you. I'll haunt you into the ground...*

A ping in Six's neural link startles them so badly that they jerk away from the sink. They pull up the message, a text calling all saan to Deck 3 for the pre-jump. Six squints in confusion. How long were they rereading the records on the tablet? How long were they staring into the mirror?

The ping comes again, insistent as a grumpy parent. Six dries off their body and dons a hooded jacket, slouching their way out the door and down the hallway. All around them, saan come together like driftwood drawn from a dozen tributaries into the current of a single river. Deck 3 is big and full of collapsible jump seats, but no one sits down yet. Six assesses the growing crowd. About 70 percent crew (this is a trade ship, after all) and 30 percent passengers. Maybe seventy-five saan altogether? A diverse crowd of Ma'kessn and Teron, of Katish-saan and Braems, and even a trio of Quietans, their hair in beautifully oiled locs. Six can't help it. They look for threats. They seek out an opportunity for suspicion. They wonder—are there cloaksaan on *The Luster Wings*? Runaway monsters looking to be chased?

The captain spends about fifteen minutes giving detailed instructions and, as the Teron crewsaan predicted, a little speech about the great adventure and responsibility of their journey to *The Glitch*. Once it's over, they all take their jump seats. Six ends up sitting next to a Katishsaan with copper finger bracelets and a friendly smile.

"First time to the frontier?" she asks.

Six, inwardly grimacing at the thought that they must now make *small talk*, smiles tightly back. "Yes."

"Third for me!" she chirps. "I've got family out there. It's a big production, but what's life for if you can't go exploring every once in a while?"

Six nods politely.

"What takes you out there?" she presses.

"Uh."

When has Six ever said, "Uh"?

"I—family. I am looking for some family I have never met."

In disbelief Six realizes that they have just volunteered the truth to a stranger, and done it without ulterior motive. The woman nods sagely.

"Thinking you'll settle there for good?"

Through them blazes the image of Chono, a fire in their heart, a magnet that will never stop drawing on them.

"No. I have a good reason to come back."

"Me, too," she agrees, still smiling. "Hurts to leave the ones you love. But that's how life is, sometimes. You go, you come back, you go again."

How asinine, mutters Esek.

Six, to their embarrassment, finds the words shockingly profound. But their conversation is cut off as *The Luster Wings* breaks away from its dock in a roar of machinery. The bolt toward orbit draws whoops of delight and excited clapping from among the saan on Deck 3. As they coast into the Black, a massive view screen against the farthest wall reveals the architectural wonder of the jump gate, distant now, but closer every moment.

Six supposes that they could leap from their seat. Make a run for the bays and commandeer a shuttle. It probably wouldn't even be that hard, to break out and fly toward Ma'kess, and the continent of Sevres where Esek was born, and the temple Riin Cosas, where Chono faces off with a challenge that few could bear.

As if she can hear these thoughts, the Katishsaan laughs, elbowing them. "No turning back now!"

With a racing heart, Six realizes it's true. No road but the road ahead. No escape from the past or the future.

Haunt you, Esek snarls in their ear, her ire rising, her hunger insatiable.

Haunt you haunt you haunt you . . .

You'll never escape, Alisiana vowed, in her death throes.

Maybe not, Six thinks.

But to go. To come back. To *live*. Oh, to live! To have their own face as they walk through the worlds. To carry the ghosts of Verdant, and one day to die. Esek will be there, at the long table of their life, and she will be as horrific as she ever was, as magnetic and devouring and seductive as she ever was. But across from her will sit Chono. And Chono's voice—that resonant, warm, beloved voice—will have more power than Esek's ever did.

They will talk, the three of them. A long, fearless talk, about the kinschool sparring court where they met, and about the many winding hunting trails that glitter in the Black.

AUTHOR'S NOTE

When I began writing the Kindom Trilogy in 2018, it was far less common to hear the general public talk about genocide. Though schools still teach the Holocaust, many of the college students I taught in the 2010s didn't understand that there were other genocides in human history. This was particularly true of my white students. Most didn't understand that the Holocaust represents a threat that remains for Jewish people. Certainly they weren't widely aware of genocides in Bosnia, or Rwanda, or of the eradication of the Rohingya of Myanmar or the Uyghurs of China.

A week before *These Burning Stars* was published, Hamas's attack on Israel killed 1,195 people. Hours later, Israel invaded Gaza in a campaign that has since killed tens of thousands and destroyed the lives of many, many more. During that time, the discourse around genocide has erupted. I never imagined it would be so controversial to assert that *genocide* is a term that applies both to the murderous project of antisemitism and to the ongoing carnage in Palestine. There is so much quibbling about what *genocide* means that I think we miss the crucial point: that the oppression, displacement, and killing of people groups is a curse that humanity keeps inflicting on itself.

I think a lot about genocide, from the transatlantic slave trade to the Trail of Tears to Indian boarding schools to attempts by radical feminists and the radical right to erase trans people. I conceive of the term as a wide tent with terrible precedents. While writing these books, I've continually returned to Sven Lindqvist's *Exterminate All the Brutes*, a feverish, insightful study on how the West has codified mass extermination, built its identity on terror and control, and often couched that campaign in religious rhetoric. Just like the Kindom.

The Kindom Trilogy is fundamentally about genocide, both its survivors and those who don't survive, and its perpetrators and those who are complicit in its perpetration. It's a dark thing to know you are complicit. I think that's why a lot of people relate to Chono's struggle to accept guilt and seek justice, which is a battle that never ends. Most of my characters are actually very well-intentioned people who keep making mistakes and keep fighting for a better world. Esek, so diabolical and charismatic, has no good intentions, and she's able to have no good intentions because she feels no guilt. Is that what it takes to live a cheerful life devoid of anxiety and depression? No guilt? Is that why Esek will always haunt Six and Chono? Because, however terrible to acknowledge, there remains something seductive about looking away, turning off empathy? Pretending there's nothing to be ashamed of?

The best genre writers (Ursula K. Le Guin, N. K. Jemisin, Octavia Butler, Ann Leckie) don't pretend that there are simple resolutions. I've tried to follow their example. If you've made it to the end of this series, you know that for these characters, the legacy of genocide remains the threat of its reemergence. Revolution doesn't solve hate and self-interest. I also hope you've seen that joy is still possible. Love is still alive. Hope itself is worthy to be sought.

As I write this on March 25, 2025, the ceasefire between Israel and Palestine has ended, and the bombs are dropping. I struggle to have hope. I struggle to do good. I don't even know if this note is worth writing, if it's simply self-serving, if it will alienate or, as Loretta Ross says, call people in. I simply felt I had to write it. So, let's keep looking. Let's suffer the grief and anxiety that comes from choosing empathy. I don't know if you noticed, but Esek is an utter failure. It's Bene, my cinnamon-roll optimist, who knows best of any of them how to live.

ACKNOWLEDGMENTS

I'll keep it quick this time, but you better believe my feelings are as big and bright as the Black. Thank you to the Orbit publishing team, from my editor Tiana Coven to my copyeditor Will Tyler to my artists Alexia Pereira, Thom Tenery, and Tim Paul. Thank you to Bridget Smith, my agent. Thank you, Waffle Wednesday friends, and Buffalo friends, and writer friends. Thank you to the very good dogs on the City of Buffalo Animal Shelter Instagram account. Thank you to the sapphic romance writers who I read last year because I just needed some rest. Thank you, bed. Thank you, sugar. Thank you, gym! Thank you, Finnick. Thank you to my family—the past few years have been so hard, but I love you to the end of time. Thank you, Mary. You could have any face in the world, and I would know you.

MEET THE AUTHOR

Mary Ganster

BETHANY JACOBS is a former college instructor of writing and science fiction. In 2019, she left academia for the ed tech sector so that she would have more time to write. When not working on her novels, she is an introvert of predictable habits. She likes reading, cooking, writing fanfiction, and snuggling in bed with an audiobook. She lives in Buffalo, New York, with her wife and her dog. She is the winner of the 2024 Philip K. Dick Award, as well as a finalist for awards from Worldcon, BSFS, Dragon Con, and Locus.

Find out more about Bethany Jacobs and other Orbit authors by registering for the free monthly newsletter at orbitbooks.net.

RAISING READERS
Books Build Bright Futures

Thank you for reading this book and for being a reader of books in general. We are so grateful to share being part of a community of readers with you, and we hope you will join us in passing our love of books on to the next generation of readers.

Did you know that reading for enjoyment is the single biggest predictor of a child's future happiness and success?

More than family circumstances, parents' educational background, or income, reading impacts a child's future academic performance, emotional well-being, communication skills, economic security, ambition, and happiness.

Studies show that kids reading for enjoyment in the US is in rapid decline:

- In 2012, 53% of 9-year-olds read almost every day. Just 10 years later, in 2022, the number had fallen to 39%.
- In 2012, 27% of 13-year-olds read for fun daily. By 2023, that number was just 14%.

Together, we can commit to **Raising Readers** and change this trend. How?

- Read to children in your life daily.
- Model reading as a fun activity.
- Reduce screen time.
- Start a family, school, or community book club.
- Visit bookstores and libraries regularly.
- Listen to audiobooks.
- Read the book before you see the movie.
- Encourage your child to read aloud to a pet or stuffed animal.
- Give books as gifts.
- Donate books to families and communities in need.

BOB1217

Books build bright futures, and **Raising Readers** is our shared responsibility.

For more information, visit **JoinRaisingReaders.com**

Sources: National Endowment for the Arts, National Assessment of Educational Progress, WorldBookDay.org, Nielsen BookData's 2023 "Understanding the Children's Book Consumer"

orbit

Follow us:

f **/orbitbooksUS**

X **/orbitbooks**

▶ **/orbitbooks**

Join our mailing list
to receive alerts on our
latest releases and deals.

orbitbooks.net

Enter our monthly
giveaway for the chance
to win some epic prizes.

orbitloot.com